Praise

"The heroine's dialogue and inner thoughts had me chuckling from the first page. Beverley Kendall's *Token* is a smart, sexy rom-com with wry social commentary and a satisfying HEA. I loved it."

— **BRENDA JACKSON**, *New York Times* and *USA TODAY* bestselling author of *The House on Blueberry Lane*

"This romance has it all—flirty banter, deep emotion, and a smart, sassy heroine I fell in love with."

— **JENNIFER PROBST**, *New York Times* bestselling author of the Twist of Fate series

"Both an incisive, wryly funny tale of a strong, smart Black woman carving a place of power for herself in corporate America and a sizzling second-chance love story, *Token* is the romantic comedy holy grail: full of laughs, sexy as hell, and as thoughtful about its characters' inner lives as it is our collective social one. I can't wait to see what Beverley Kendall brings us next."

— **ASHLEY WINSTEAD**, author of *Fool Me Once*

More praise for Beverley Kendall

"What drives this surprisingly deep novel are its revelations and their aftermath... Highly recommended."

— *Library Journal*, starred review, on *An Heir of Deception*

"*Sinful Surrender* is very sexy and there are many twists and turns that keep this story quite entertaining. It is an exceptional debut and one I highly recommend."

— *SmexyBooks*

"I just enjoyed the hell out of Alex, Charlotte, their lust, their love, and their battle to live happily ever after. It was such fun to read."

— *Dear Author* on *An Heir of Deception*

Also from Beverley Kendall
and Graydon House

Token

For additional books by Beverley Kendall,
visit her website, www.beverleykendall.com.

TOKEN

BEVERLEY KENDALL

GRAYDON
HOUSE

GRAYDON
HOUSE®

Recycling programs
for this product may
not exist in your area.

ISBN-13: 978-1-525-89997-3

Token

This is a work of fiction. Names, characters, places and incidents are either the product
of the author's imagination or are used fictitiously. Any resemblance to actual persons,
living or dead, businesses, companies, events or locales is entirely coincidental.

Graydon House
22 Adelaide St. West, 41st Floor
Toronto, Ontario M5H 4E3, Canada
www.GraydonHouseBooks.com
www.BookClubbish.com

Printed in U.S.A.

This one is for you, Mum, and you alone.
I will love and miss you always.

TOKEN

1

Looking for a job sucked.

Getting laid off sucked even more.

Three weeks ago, Kennedy Mitchell found herself in both unenviable positions.

While searching for a new job in her field of expertise—marketing and five solid years of it—she'd accepted a four-week receptionist position to tide her over. Hey, student loans didn't pay off themselves and they couldn't care less about your employment status. But, as grateful as she was to have money coming in, she hated the part of the job that had her slapping herself awake every five minutes.

That also sucked.

It would be one thing if the place were a bevy of human activity (she generally liked people and they tended to like her back). Nope, that wasn't even close to what she was dealing with. Per the visitor log, a grand total of six had passed through the first-floor lobby of ECO Apparel in the two weeks she'd been there. Three on one day alone. And during the hours when the employees were upstairs ensconced at their desks, the place resembled a ghost town. Seriously, she wouldn't be surprised to see tumbleweed roll past the reception desk one fine windy day. Although, for a ghost town, the lobby was sleekly modern, all sharp angles, and glass and chrome.

Glancing down at her cell phone, Kennedy released a long-suffering sigh. How was it possible that only three minutes and not an hour had passed since her last five-minute check-in? This was usually when she prayed for one of two things: the power to control time, or another job.

Since the chances of either happening within the next seventy-two hours were zero to none, she grudgingly resigned herself to her fate and tapped the keyboard, bringing the sleeping monitor back to life, and the email from an interested recruiter back into view. Seven hours to go, and the jury was still out on whether she would make it until noon—much less to the end of the day.

The ding of the elevator broke the lonely silence and was soon followed by the click of heels on the faux marble floors. Twisting in her seat, Kennedy spotted Nadine from Administrative Services striding purposely toward her, folder and purse in hand. She hastily closed out of her email and treated the brunette to a bright smile.

"Hey, Nadine, is it break time already?" The pretty admin assistant usually came to relieve her for a midmorning break at ten. Currently, it was an hour shy of that, and taking a break right now would upset the monotony of her day. How would she cope with the upheaval?

"Mr. Mullins wants to see you in his office, and I'll be filling in for you for the rest of the day," her coworker announced abruptly.

Kennedy stiffened and her eyebrows rose at the hint of annoyance and resentment threading Nadine's tone.

Well, good morning to you too.

What the hell happened to the pleasant, chatty girl of not even twenty-four hours ago? And why on earth did the director of Human Resources want to see her in his office? Especially as she, like Nadine, reported to the manager of Administrative Services.

Then Nadine's folder landed with a *splat* on the desk near the monitor. Kennedy's gaze flew to hers and she found herself on the receiving end of a very pointed *come on—get a move on, girlie. There's only one chair and you're sitting in it* look.

That was enough to galvanize Kennedy into action even as her jaw ticked and she prayed for calm. She hurriedly collected her purse from the bottom drawer before surrendering her seat to her visibly impatient coworker.

As if it's my fault she's getting stuck down here answering the phone.

Despite Kennedy's own growing annoyance, she paused and turned before leaving, her shoulders squared, and chin lifted. "Any idea why Mr. Mullins wants to see me?" Her voice was stiff but scrupulously polite.

Since her interaction with him was limited to a brief walk-by wave on her first day during a tour of the offices, she was at a loss.

Nadine gave a bored shrug. "I hear no evil and speak no evil. They tell me nothing. I just go where I'm told to go, and do the work they pay me to do, if you know what I mean."

Kennedy's heart instantly softened, and she excused Nadine's uncustomary churlishness for what appeared to be the frustration that came with being the Jane-of-all-menial-work of the company.

"Believe me, I know *exactly* what you mean." They shared a commiserative *what we women have to put up with* look before Kennedy took the elevator up to the eighth floor.

Honestly, the drawbacks of possessing a vagina were sometimes too much. Giving birth was only one of them. Or so she'd been told. Her turn in the stirrups hadn't come yet, but she assumed one day it would, and it wouldn't be pretty.

The company directory alone pointed to an obvious gender bias. Not one woman held an executive, director, or senior-level management position.

Not. One.

And it had been eight years since the previously all-male clothier had ventured into female clothing. One would think that *one woman* would have made it to the ranks of at least a senior manager position by now. What were they waiting for, a march on Washington?

But wait. If she didn't think it could get worse, it did. Kennedy had yet to see one Black face of any hue in the parade of employees who walked by her every day—that was, unless she looked in a mirror, and her hue skewed to the lighter shade of that spectrum. She wouldn't be surprised if that was one of the reasons she'd been picked to grace the reception desk.

In the twenty-first century, one would think that impossible. Especially in the city that didn't sleep, and could be touted as America's United Nations, every race, ethnicity, language, *and* sexual orientation duly represented on the postage-stamp island.

Be that as it may, Kennedy knew better than most that the city tended more toward separate individual dishes—*separate* being the operative word—rather than one big old melting pot.

Once off the elevator, she detoured to the bathroom, where she freshened her lipstick, powdered the shine off her forehead, and gave her long, thick brown curls a few twists.

With her hair and face in order, she ran a critical eye over her outfit, a purchase of pure indulgence. Although had she even the vaguest idea that she'd be unemployed a week after she bought it, she most assuredly would not have indulged.

But the cream pencil skirt and the baby blue fitted shirt ensemble had called out to her. *Buy me. I come in your size. Your body will thank you in the end.* And Kennedy, self-proclaimed clotheshorse that she was, hadn't been able to resist the Siren's call.

Okay, so maybe due to financial constraints she was more a clothes pony.

After ensuring no visible panty lines ruined the overall effect of polished professionalism and stylishness, she proceeded to Mr. Mullins's office.

She found him at his desk, the door to his office wide-open. Upon seeing her, a smile broke out across his face. "Ah, Miss Mitchell, come in."

Kennedy met him halfway, where they shook hands, and she offered a pleasant greeting. He then gestured toward the table and chairs at the other end of the room. "Please sit down. Make yourself comfortable."

Average in height and build, hair graying and thinning at the crown, the man himself was as nondescript as middle-aged white men came. If his smile—wide and genuine—was any indication, she could relax, which she did one vertebra at a time. It didn't look as if she was about to be let go early. Typically, people didn't smile like that when they were about to deliver bad news. Unless, of course, they were psychopaths. No, they tended to furrow their brow, feigning concern and sympathy.

Kennedy took a seat where instructed as Mr. Mullins swiped a sheaf of papers off his desk before joining her. She looked around for somewhere to put her purse that was not on the table or the floor and found nothing suitable. In the end, she simply plopped it on her lap.

Sliding on a pair of reading glasses, Mr. Mullins glanced down at the papers in front of him before directing his attention back to her. "So how are you settling in? Everyone treating you all right? No one bothering you, I hope."

Yeah, nope! Absolutely not. No way was she falling into that trap. This was the kind of throwaway question people asked when they didn't want or expect an honest answer.

"No, everyone has been great." She certainly wasn't going to tell him that two of the managers had asked for her number and the head of IT asked her out for dinner. As someone personally opposed to mixing business with pleasure, and that included dating coworkers—been there, regretted that—invitations like that were shot down faster than a clay pigeon at a skeet shooting competition.

"Good, good, good. Now, I've just been looking over your résumé—" he paused, glanced at it and then back at her over the rim of his glasses "—and by the looks of things—your previous experience and education—it's apparent that you're overqualified for the receptionist position. Any receptionist position, for that matter."

For the measly sum of two hundred and fifty grand—the majority of which had been covered by scholarships or else she wouldn't have been able to afford a school like Columbia—for both her undergraduate and graduate degrees, she sure hoped she was overqualified for the task of greeting visitors and forwarding calls.

"Yes, but this wasn't supposed to be permanent. The agency said it was a four-week assignment."

Mr. Mullins nodded. "That's right. I've been told Nancy should be back in a few weeks." He lowered her résumé, but still held it loosely between his fingers. "Does that mean you aren't interested in a permanent, full-time position? I might have thought you'd prefer something in Marketing."

Kennedy watched as he turned the situation over in his mind. He seemed determined to solve the mystery of the overqualified temporary receptionist. But this wasn't Agatha Christie-level stuff. No amateur sleuthing required.

"I was laid off and this just sort of fell into my lap. The right job at the moment," she stated simply.

There were layoffs and then there were layoffs. Hers had been the latter, as she'd been assured she'd keep her job after the merger. The following week, she'd walked into the offices of Kenners in the morning and was carting a box with every personal item she'd accumulated over the course of five years—including a dazzling pink slip—out the front door by the time the clock struck noon.

Just like that, five years of job—no, *financial* security—ripped out from under her. And to add insult to injury, two weeks of severance was all she had to show for years spent busting her ass putting in fifty- and sixty-hour weeks.

God, how she hated them, pink slips, which shouldn't be pink at all. They should be black like the hearts of the people who played favorites with other people's livelihoods.

"Completely understandable," he replied, nodding. "Now, getting to the reason I wanted to speak with you. I assume you've heard of Sahara, right? She's a singer. Won several Grammys. I believe she's recently gotten into acting. Really a lovely young woman."

Have I ever heard of her?

Almost everyone on planet Earth had heard of Sahara, and she wasn't just some wannabe actress. Her first role garnered her an Oscar nod. Not too shabby for a small-town girl from New Jersey, who bore such a striking resemblance to Aaliyah, some people in the music industry called her Baby Girl. Rumor had it she hated the name with the fires of a thousand suns. If true, Kennedy didn't blame her.

She's a woman. *Call her by her stage name, dammit!*

Ironically, her real name was Whitney Richardson, a name she decided not to use professionally, fearing it would invite *certain* comparisons. One Black superstar singer named Whitney was enough.

"That's a pretty sound assumption." Especially since her songs were on heavy rotation on every major radio station in almost every major city in the country. "She's very popular."

Popular was an understatement. Sahara was *huge*. As big as Beyoncé but with first-rate acting chops. And her social media game was, bar none, the best Kennedy had ever seen. Her fans called themselves the Desert Stormers and congregated at OASIS, an online community, to discuss everything Sahara. And God forbid anyone say one bad word about their *Desert Queen*, they went after them guns blazing.

"I had a feeling you would," he said with a smugness Kennedy found hard to fathom. It wasn't as if he'd discovered Jimmy Hoffa's remains or the identity of Jack the Ripper. "Well, this afternoon we are going to have the pleasure of her company. She and her representatives will be meeting with our executive team."

"That's…wonderful." She didn't know what he expected her to say. Was he looking for tips on how to interact with young Black women and assumed she was an expert on the subject? Should she tell him she hadn't yet read this month's issue of *The Secret Guide to the Black Female Mind*?

His expression became earnest as he leaned forward, bringing his face closer to hers. "The CEO of the company would like you to attend."

Her jaw dropped. A sound escaped from her suddenly dry throat.

Okay, *that* she hadn't seen coming.

She reflexively convinced herself he couldn't have meant

what she thought he did, since she was certain she'd heard him correctly.

"Do you mean attend the meeting? With Sahara?" She needed to make sure they were reading from the same hymnal.

His mouth twitched. "Yes."

Her fingers curled around her purse strap. "Why would Mr. Edwards want *me* there?" She was a temp. How did the CEO of the company know who she was? Or that she even existed? She only knew his name because it was at the top of the company directory. She couldn't say for sure she'd actually seen him in the flesh, and if she had, he certainly hadn't introduced himself.

"Well, you see, Kennedy, I believe the collective thought was that you represent exactly the type of young woman Sahara will be targeting with her clothing line, and having you in the meeting would make her...more comfortable. Put her at ease."

Ah, yes. She got it, all right. As clear as glass.

"I'm afraid I'm not sure what you mean. What type of woman is that?" she asked, all wide-eyed and guileless.

Surely, he meant intelligent, professional, ambitious, and highly educated?

Yeah, right.

The crests of his cheeks reddened, but he was stalwart in his determination to hold her gaze. "Well, you're a beautiful young woman with an obvious eye for fashion, and her line hopes to encompass all aspects of work, life, and play."

Nice save, bub. But not good enough.

"And the fact that I'm Black didn't have *anything* to do with the decision? Not even a little?" she coaxed, doubting anyone had ever taken him to task on the subject of race this directly, if at all.

His Adam's apple bobbed. "Well, yes, there is that too."

No, there was no *too*—that was the whole of it.

Suddenly, his expression turned apprehensive. "I hope that didn't offend you. With this whole #MeToo movement, I'm not sure if I just crossed the line. Am I still allowed to compliment you on your looks?"

Oh dear lord, shoot me now.

Did this man not interact with *any* women in a professional capacity? A sensitivity class or four wouldn't go awry at this company.

"No, I'm not offended." At work, she generally took such compliments in stride. As long as they weren't accompanied by a suggestive leer and a hotel room key card pressed into her palm during a handshake. True story. That had actually happened.

"Things have changed so much lately, sometimes it's best to ask, or the next thing you know... Well, who knows what will happen," he finished, flashing her an awkward smile.

"Anyway," Kennedy said, eager to get back to the subject at hand, "about the meeting. As much as it would be a thrill to meet her, I'm not sure I'd be comfortable with that. I don't know very much about the inner workings of the company. I'm probably not the right person—"

But Mr. Mullins was having none of that, bulldozing her objections with, "For your additional responsibilities, you'll receive five thousand dollars."

Kennedy had to steel herself from physically reacting. On the inside, however, it was nothing but fits of jubilation. Cartwheels and back handsprings that would make the women's Olympic gymnastics team proud.

Five thousand dollars! Found money, all of it. And to think of how happy she'd been last month when she found a twenty between the cushions of her sofa and last year when she'd discovered a ten spot in the pocket of an old pair of jeans.

Careful to calibrate her response, she began slowly, "That is—"

"No, no, my mistake," Mr. Mullins interjected again, his eyes darting from her face to the paper in front of him, which he proceeded to tap repeatedly with his finger. "I meant seventy-five hundred. An additional seventy-five hundred."

Kennedy sat there utterly gobsmacked. "Mr. Mullins—"

"Ten thousand."

Another minute and Kennedy was certain the strain in his voice would give way to full-blown panic.

Ten thousand dollars for one meeting? *Oh my god, that's wild.*

But the best kind.

With dollar signs flashing like a bright neon sign in her mind, she smiled. "What time should I be there?"

2

Some stereotypes existed for a reason and Maureen Somers turned out to be the quintessential efficient, unflappable middle-aged woman one would expect to hold the position of the executive assistant to the CEO.

In the span of sixty short minutes, she put all those qualities to effective use, setting up a space for Kennedy in the smaller of the two conference rooms on the ninth floor, supplying her with a gold executive name badge, a spare laptop, a quick overview of the company, and a thumb drive containing the PowerPoint presentation being delivered to Sahara and her representatives that afternoon.

No one expected that Kennedy would be asked any questions—that was the VP of Marketing's wheelhouse—but just in case, she was instructed to respond in generalities and make sure to emphasize her social media experience. Next, she went down to see Sally in HR, who not only took care of the housekeeping issues that allowed them to pay her the bonus directly, rather than through the temp agency, but shed total light on the seeming urgency of the situation.

It appeared yesterday Sahara had walked into a meeting with one of their competitors, looked at those in attendance, and had promptly walked out without saying a word when she didn't see one Black face in the room. Which was why ECO Apparel was willing to pay ten grand to make sure the same thing didn't happen to them.

Ten grand!

Every time Kennedy thought about it, she wanted to pinch herself. She was torn between the desire to pay down what remained on her student loan or stash the bulk of it away for a rainy day. Like if she didn't get a job right away, she'd at least be able to pay her rent for a few months without emptying her savings.

By the time lunch rolled around, Kennedy's stomach was filled with too many butterflies to accommodate actual food, so she donned a pair of sunglasses and went to the deli across the street. There, she bought a large lemonade, grabbed an empty table in the back where it was quiet enough to have a conversation, and hit the speed dial on her phone to call her best friend, Aurora.

The two met when they were seventeen, their senior year in high school, at a national debate competition and had been best friends since. She was the one who'd convinced Kennedy to apply to universities in New York. They'd both been accepted to Columbia, become roomies, and the rest, as they say, was history. Now, after nine years in the Big Apple, Kennedy couldn't imagine herself anywhere else. This was home.

Aurora picked up on the first ring and skipped preliminary greetings. "Hey, I was just thinking about you, and I have a plan. If you don't find a decent-paying job by the end of the month, I can talk to Nate."

Near-bursting with excitement over her newfound fortune, Kennedy's train of thought was immediately sidetracked. "Ror, for the last time, I'm not working for your brother," she exclaimed, rolling her eyes.

This wasn't the first or undoubtedly the last time Aurora would raise the subject. She'd said the same thing when Kennedy started looking for a job after they'd graduated, and then every time she expressed an inkling of dissatisfaction with said job.

Work for Nate, he's brilliant. Work for Nate, he's good to his employees. Work for Nate, he pays great.

While all of that might be true, Nate could be a teensy bit intimidating—okay, plenty intimidating. And coming from someone who pulled off cool and collected as if she'd been born to play the role, that said a lot.

Kennedy had dealt with her fair share of good-looking men of all strata her entire adult life. Nathaniel Robert Vaughn, however, was an entirely different species. He was *too* everything: too good-looking, too smart, too opaque, too driven, too cool and detached, and *way* too far out of her league.

And that was the rub. Something she hated admitting even to herself. Suffice it to say, the less she had to do with him, the better. A job at his company would open a door best kept closed.

Her objection wasn't *entirely* personal. At the age of thirty-two, he was the founder and CEO of Constellation, a tech company in the vein of Amazon and Apple, and *she* had no technical skills to speak of.

"Look, I know my brother can be a little…standoffish, but I promise, he likes you. He thinks you're a good influence on me. Anyway, you wouldn't be working directly for him, and you'd barely see him."

He likes you.

That was debatable.

Agitated, Kennedy began toying with her hair, winding a dark ringlet around her index finger. "It's not a matter of having to see him," she lied. "It's a tech company, which means he'd literally have to create a position just for me." Not a lie, that one.

"Actually, he's been talking about bringing Constellation's marketing in-house."

For a brief second, that piqued Kennedy's interest, before she squashed it beneath her stiletto-clad toe. "Well, until he does, this discussion is over." Softening her tone, she continued soothingly, "Don't worry. I'll find something by the end of the month. As a matter of fact—"

"And if you don't, do you promise you'll let me talk to Nate?" Aurora cut in. "You know he'd hire you in a heartbeat."

Because his baby sister would make him.

The thought brought a reluctant smile to her face. Not just her best friend in the whole world, Aurora was her fiercest defender. Her blonde ninja. And she loved her to bits because of it. "I promise."

"Cross your heart?"

"Oh, you wound me!" Kennedy exclaimed, feigning affront. "Is my word not good enough anymore?"

Aurora snickered. "Hey, I know you."

"Have faith, Ror. I'm going to get a fantastic job. Speaking of which, can we *finally* get to the reason I called?" she asked, breathless excitement back in her voice.

"Of course. What's up? You sound jazzed." The distant blare of an ambulance could be heard in the background.

"I've just been tokenized," Kennedy stated in her brightest

fake it till you make it voice. "*But* it looks like it's going to pay off for me this time."

"Wait—hold on. Let me put my earbuds in. The traffic out here is too damn loud," Aurora muttered, and after a pause said, "Okay, now back the truck up and tell me what happened and whose ass I need to kick."

Kennedy chuckled at the image that came to mind. Mama Bear Vaughn to the rescue clad in skinny jeans and a pair of Jimmy Choo heels, wielding a Gucci shoulder bag. Fierce.

"You heard me. But here's the thing—for once, being the token Black female in the *entire* company comes with benefits. At two o'clock, I'm going to meet Sahara, the Desert Queen, herself." She paused a dramatic beat to allow the news to sink in. "*And* they're paying me ten grand to do it." Had she not been out in public, she would have *squeed* with joy. This must be how people felt when they won the lottery, because let's face it—this was the closest she'd ever come.

Several seconds of "street noise" followed her announcement. She heard the occasional car horn, but apparently her friend was speechless.

"You've got to be shitting me." Aurora sounded semi-outraged and flummoxed at the same time.

"Shitting about which part? Meeting Sahara or the money I'm being paid to do it?"

"I don't know. All of it, I guess. How is being a token ever a good thing, and how the hell are you getting to meet Sahara?"

After Kennedy calmly recounted her meeting with Mr. Mullins, Aurora exclaimed, "They're paying you ten thousand dollars for that?"

"Yeah, but listen, there's more."

"How much more can there be?"

Kennedy flashed a smile at the couple taking up residence at the table next to hers, lowered her voice, and told Aurora what she'd learned from Sally in HR about Sahara walking out of the meeting yesterday.

Aurora let out a short burst of laughter. "Oh my god, I love it! You know what this means, don't you?"

"Yeah, I'm ten grand richer."

"I'm not just talking about the money."

"You haven't seen my bank balance," Kennedy remarked dryly. "Right now, money *is* my number one priority."

"No," Aurora said, a note of urgency to her tone. "Listen to me. Right now, they need you a lot more than you need them."

"Again, my bank balance begs to differ."

"Ken, if things go the way I think they will, they're going to offer you a job. And you're going to negotiate yourself a salary fifteen percent—no, twenty percent—higher than what you made at your last job."

Kennedy let out a dismissive huff. "Why on earth would they offer me a job? They're already paying me a small fortune just to attend the meeting." Although, to be fair, ten grand didn't go as far in New York as it would in North Carolina. She couldn't afford a Birkin handbag, but she could pay down her interest-compounding student loan.

"This isn't a one-and-done deal, Ken. They're going to need you, if for nothing else, for show."

"Yeah, but—"

"No buts. They're going to offer you a job and you're going to negotiate yourself the biggest raise you've ever had. And while you're at it, make sure to ask for a signing bonus, and don't take anything less than ten thousand, got it?"

In the midst of sipping lemonade, Kennedy nearly choked. "Are you serious?"

"Trust me, this is the stuff I do for a living, and these guys are currently operating in crisis mode. Without you, they're sunk."

★ ★ ★

When Maureen instructed her to go on in and make herself comfortable, Kennedy hadn't expected that when she entered, *you could hear a pin drop* silence would descend on the conference room, or seven pairs of eyes would lock in on her like heat-seeking missiles.

Seven men were seated around a long lacquered table with a projector and laptop set up at the end.

Clearly, she hadn't received the memo outlining appropriate meeting attire, as all of the men wore, if not Brooks Brothers suits, then a close stylistic relation, in varying shades of gray and dark gray. She approximated their ages ranged from late thirties to midsixties.

She was, quite literally, the one spot of color in the room, and the only woman. What, they couldn't rope in another woman to be part of the charade? Or had she filled that quota too?

Kennedy was long accustomed to being the only Black person in the room—any room. However, being the only woman added a whole other level of self-consciousness.

Suck it up. This is the world you live in.

And so, with that bit of wry encouragement, she lifted her chin. "Good afternoon, gentlemen." Her tone, friendly and polite, conveyed a confidence she could construct at will with little more than ego and pride.

Their response came in a chorus of perfectly courteous *good afternoons* and more than one speculative glance.

It was funny when she thought about it. They greeted her every day when they passed the reception desk, yet today, they would sit shoulder to shoulder with her, pretending to be her peers.

"Yes, over there will be fine." Maureen ushered two deliverymen carrying platters of food into the room and directed them to the table by the windows overlooking the congested streets of lower Manhattan.

Kennedy stepped aside, allowing the men to pass while eyeing the platter of gourmet sandwiches and chocolaty desserts, and thinking about the lunch she'd skipped and the current state of her appetite. Ferocious.

The sound of voices in the outer office caught everyone's attention. Heads turned, necks craned, and spines straightened.

The star had arrived.

Boy, she really did look like Aaliyah, was Kennedy's first thought when she finally laid eyes on the singer. She looked younger than the twenty-eight listed on her Wikipedia page. Other than that, she looked the same, from her long dark brown box braids, flawless skin, and perfectly made-up face, right down to a pair of skinny pre-ripped jeans and strappy three-inch sandals. Chic casual. And she rocked the look with enviable confidence and panache.

Mr. Donald Edwards, all smiles and bonhomie, shepherded the Grammy winner and her accompanying three-woman team into the conference room. That the team was all female and diverse—Black, Hispanic, and Asian—didn't come as a huge surprise, but it drew a marked contrast to the company's almost all-white male team.

Maureen silently indicated Kennedy's place at the table, where the spare laptop she'd been using was on and fully charged, before departing with the deliverymen.

Except for the new arrivals, who were still conversing, everyone else sat quietly, waiting. Watching.

"Okay, it looks like everyone's here," Mr. Edwards announced with a brief look around, "so why don't we get started?"

That was when Sahara turned her attention from him to the rest of the ECO team.

Kennedy, who liked to believe she could read people pretty well—with some notable exceptions—saw a *girding of the loins* wariness in the way the singer's gaze scanned the faces around the table. Which made sense, given what had happened yesterday. She was no doubt wondering if she'd be walking out on another meeting. Then Sahara's gaze met hers and pleasure mingled with relief, producing a smile that reached her big brown eyes.

The ripple effect of that relief played out in the expressions of every male executive in the room; a mental wiping of the brow followed by a gratified *initial hurdle cleared*.

When Mr. Edwards flashed Kennedy an approving smile, she berated herself for selling out for a mere ten thousand dollars. *Pittance.* She should have held out for twenty and she probably would have gotten it.

Mr. Edwards performed the introductions, and when it was Kennedy's turn—last but not least—she gracefully stood and shook hands with the beautiful singer and her team while the CEO offered a brief description of her fictitious role in the company. "Kennedy is our media relations expert in charge of all aspects of our print, TV, and digital campaigns."

Expert, huh? In the span of hours, not only had they elevated her title but her expertise level as well. The heels she had to fill were getting higher by the minute.

"And here I thought you'd brought in one of the models auditioning one of the designs," Sahara said with an audacious wink. Kennedy smiled faintly and a smatter of chuckles erupted around the table.

Look who's talking, Kennedy wanted to say, not sure if the singer was joking or not, but it made for a flattering, lighthearted icebreaker.

"Beautiful as well as talented—that's our Kennedy."

Our Kennedy? When exactly had they graduated to that level of intimacy? Dare she tell Mr. CEO that he was laying it on a tad thick? Or better yet, she should instruct him to add another zero to the amount on her bonus check—then he could *"Our Kennedy"* all he wanted.

"Can I just say that I love, *love* what you're wearing. That outfit is fire." Sahara waved red manicured fingers at Kennedy's skirt. "The bow is a fabulous touch. And the cuffs, are they Neapolitan?"

Kennedy felt safe in concluding the singer wasn't referring to the ice cream or the people of Naples.

"It's not one of our designs, but you're right about the cuffs," John Cavendish, head of Design, cut in smoothly.

"I've been studying up," Sahara admitted, grinning and showing off her adorable dimples. "And now I have more clothing design books than I know what to do with. Figured I needed to know a little more about creating a clothing line than what I like to wear."

It was at that moment Kennedy made up her mind about the singer. She was good people, as her father would say. Definitely not the stuck-up celebrity type. It would be great working with her.

Whoa! Slow your roll, Miss Thing. Are you forgetting that your part in this is all make-believe? You're an overqualified temp making twenty-two dollars an hour. The company is using you and you're being rewarded handsomely for it.

A fact she kept front of mind as the presentation commenced.

"I'd like to incorporate green, yellow, and red into a few of the summer pieces." Sahara addressed John as they approached the end of the meeting, a full two hours later. "And black and white, if it wouldn't look too busy."

"Do the colors have a certain significance?" he asked, his expression mildly indulgent.

"They're the colors of the Guyanese flag," Kennedy supplied without thinking. When everyone looked at her, brows raised, she responded to the question in their eyes. "Sahara's father is from Guyana." A fact anyone could learn from her Wikipedia page. "And so is my mother," she tagged on belatedly.

"Your mother's from Guyana!" the singer exclaimed, showcasing her impressive vocal range. "Which part?"

Kennedy pressed her lips together, containing a smile. "Georgetown."

"That's where my dad's from." Sahara's eyes danced with excitement. "Oh my god. What are the chances? Small world, right? Listen, after we're done here, can we go somewhere private to talk? Like your office?" she suggested helpfully.

Or it would have been helpful had they existed in a world where temporary worker Kennedy Mitchell had an office. And as she did not, alarm struck the heart of every man in the room. Their furtive gazes bounced between each other. *What do we do? What could she possibly have to say to her that we're not privy to? Good god, Kennedy's not even a real employee.*

If Kennedy had intended to respond, Mr. Edwards's look would have cut her off at the quick. "That's a wonderful idea. Unfortunately, with renovations going on, I'm not sure it's habitable right now."

"Oh, you don't need to worry about me—I'm easy. I don't mind a little mess. Plus, I'm curious to see where you work," she said, looking at Kennedy.

That makes two of us.

Mr. Edwards visibly swallowed, his gambit proving unsuccessful. "Then let me have a word with Maureen since she's in charge of the renovations." With that, he got up and quickly exited the room.

The meeting wrapped fifteen minutes later, and as everyone availed themselves of what remained of the sandwiches and desserts, Kennedy and Sahara proceeded down the hall to "her office."

Minutes before, a text from an unfamiliar number appeared on her phone, which she could only surmise came from Maureen.

212-555-7862: The office is the fourth door on the right when you leave the conference room.

Kennedy was about to find out what lay behind door #4. Holding her breath, she opened the door and was immediately struck by dark furniture and tall wooden bookshelves. The identity of the office's current occupant had been wiped clean. No family pictures or personal memorabilia could be seen anywhere. A large monitor, a stack of folders, and a paperweight sat on the desk, and a large drop cloth covered furniture in the corner, which fit perfectly with the renovation narrative. *Quick thinking.*

The singer didn't walk so much as she sashayed, slim hips swinging with a smooth glide to her step when she preceded Kennedy in and crooned a delighted, "Impressive."

"Thanks." It was nice but totally not her style. Too much testosterone. Lighter wood and pastel colors were more to her taste.

"Was it totally obnoxious of me to ask to see your office?" Sahara had a mischievous grin on her face as she made herself comfortable in one of the high-backed guest chairs.

"Of course not. I'm sure they see it as a good thing." When she took a seat in *her chair*, Kennedy had to bite down on her bottom lip to suppress a moan of pleasure, certain that this chair, with its soft supple leather and gorgeous wood, could spoil her ass for the rest of her life.

"Okay, first things first. Can I get your card? If everything pans out—which I think it will—I'd like you to be my personal contact. Sarah, Ellen, and Mariah can deal with everyone else."

Kennedy didn't panic easily, but she also didn't possess the natural instincts of a consummate liar.

Shit shit shit!

A business card? Even if they'd been able to magically produce one in time for the meeting, what good would it be without a working phone number and extension?

"Um, why don't I give you my cell number? That way you can get in touch with me night or day. Let me just write it down."

Kennedy's gaze made a thorough sweep of the desk. Seriously, not one pen or pencil? Lovely. She tried to open the top drawer, only to find it locked. She then tried the one below. It opened to reveal a box of condoms and a tube of K-Y Jelly. Stifling a gasp, she hastily slammed it shut.

"Wow, someone must have oiled the gears," she said, her laugh strangled. "Kind of slipped out of my grasp."

She could really use a drink right now. Pretending to be someone she wasn't was turning out to be thirsty work.

"No worries," Sahara said and began rifling through her green Hermès handbag. Pulling out a card, she leaned forward and handed it to Kennedy. "Here, why don't you take mine? You can leave your number with the message service."

The card was black and gold with an embossed silhouette of Nefertiti on the front, a desert oasis on the back, and was made from superior card stock, as one would expect from a star of her caliber.

"Works for me." Kennedy tucked it in her purse. An office, business cards—how many other bullets would she have to dodge before the end of the day?

"Hey, can I ask you a question?" Sahara studied her closely.

"Sure." Kennedy could only pray she'd be able to answer it.

"Are those contacts?"

Kennedy's laugh was part amusement, part relief. "Nope, these are my eyes. Got them from my dad." Her uncommon slate blue eyes were a frequent topic of conversation, compliments, and stares.

"So, your dad's what, white?"

"No, he's Black."

Sahara's mouth fell open. "Really. Okay. Wow."

"He was born in North Carolina. Came from a long line of slaves and slave owners."

"And your mom's Black too?"

"Yep. Born in Georgetown. Immigrated to the States when she was seventeen. Met my dad in college. Got married and had four children, and here I am, the youngest of the bunch," Kennedy concluded with a smile.

One day she might do one of those 23andMe tests to see what her complete genetic makeup looked like, but to the world she was a light-skinned Black woman who probably had some mixing going on in her bloodlines on both sides of her family tree.

"So do you have any brothers?" She waggled her eyebrows suggestively.

"Two, both older. Both single."

Sahara's gaze turned coy. "Either of them have your daddy's eyes?"

"The eldest." Kennedy got this all the time. "He lives in California."

From the Grammy Award winner and Oscar nominee who

could probably have any man she set her mind to without having to bat those thick-lashed eyes at them, more coyness. "You'll have to introduce us one day."

Kennedy snorted a laugh. "I'm sure he'd like that." Cameron would get a kick out of this, not that his already oversized ego needed to be fed any more.

Sahara's expression turned sheepish. "God, I'm so nosy, aren't I? I didn't mean to get all up in your business."

"No, you're fine," Kennedy said, dismissing her concerns with a wave of her hand. "I get it all the time. Especially the questions about my brothers. By the way, my other brother is good-looking too."

"Then make that two introductions," the singer said, her manner playful. "Anyway, the real reason I wanted to talk to you alone was because I like you, and I don't believe in holding any punches. It's this thing with me—I meet someone and either I click with them or I don't. And that's the vibe I'm getting from you—we click. You're smart, ambitious, and put together as all hell, but my one concern about working with this company is that you were the only Black person in there." She gestured in the direction of the conference room. "Please tell me the company and your team are a lot more diverse than the guys sitting in that room."

It seemed the moment of reckoning had come sooner than expected. What the hell was she supposed to say? The truth would most likely kill any hopes of Sahara partnering with ECO. But how could she lie? The company was about as diverse as the US Olympic equestrian team. More important, she *didn't* have a team, diverse or otherwise.

But you could have one, a voice in her head whispered, and with that came all sorts of possibilities. Visions of diversification and the end of college loan payments began to dance in her head.

Could she?

Should she?

You could and you definitely should. Judging by the volume and clarity of the voice in her head, it sounded very adamant about that.

Mind made up, Kennedy met Sahara's steady and somber gaze. "I can assure you, it's much more diverse."

3

An hour after Sahara and her team left the building, Kennedy had upgraded her office—as a guest—although this one was equally dark but larger, with a nicer view. She faced the CEO across his desk.

"Sahara appears quite taken with you." Mr. Edwards's scrutiny of her was intense in the most benign manner possible.

"I assure you, the feeling is mutual," Kennedy replied.

"Good. That's good." He paused. "If we're fortunate enough to partner with her, that would mean a great deal to the company's bottom line. It would also open new doors for us. A celebrity of her status would give us the kind of exposure that money can't buy."

Not only were celebrity endorsements worth their weight in gold, but when stamped by the celebrity's own particular brand—think Air Jordans—the sky was the limit when it came to earning potential.

"So, I'm sure it won't surprise you when I say I would like you to stay on with us in a marketing capacity."

And there it was, the job offer, just as Aurora had predicted. Now all she had to do was play it cool.

Kennedy treated him to a level gaze. "I feel I need to remind you that I'm currently temping at the reception desk."

Strictly speaking, I don't even work for the company and I just saved your heinie big-time.

His smile thinned. "Yes, I'm painfully aware of that. I wish we'd had you on full-time long before now."

Look how much money it would have saved us went left unsaid.

"You could have five years ago when I applied."

That caught his attention. "You applied for a position here?" he asked, his tone sharp and gaze probing.

Kennedy nodded, feeling a certain sense of karmic vindication. "Right out of college."

A shadow crossed his face. "Were you brought in for an interview?"

"No."

"What about a telephone screening?"

"Nothing. Never heard a word back."

"I see." He drew out both words.

This couldn't possibly come as a surprise to him. Had he not ventured beyond the ninth floor to mingle with the peasants on the lower floors in their cubicles? Not a single Black employee existed at the company.

She discreetly appraised his stalky build in his iron gray suit, with his salt-and-pepper hair and air of self-importance and obliviousness.

Likely not.

"I guess that was our loss." His statement came as close to self-deprecation as she imagined he could muster.

"Given the way things turned out, some would say so."

"I hope you won't hold that against us and are open to a job offer. And this has no bearing on the outcome of any partnership with Sahara."

Oh yes, he was now seeing the benefits of actually having a Black person on the payroll, come what may. Whoever said money was the greatest motivator of all was proved right time and time again.

"I do have two interviews next week." She was glad to be able to throw that out there. Nothing like a bit of competition to apply the right kind of pressure and let him know she wasn't so desperate for a job she'd be willing to accept any lowball offers.

"Both I hope you'll cancel. After you consider my offer, that is."

"I guess that will depend on the offer."

Mr. Edwards smiled then, looking entirely too pleased with himself. He handed her a sheet of paper that represented the opening bid in salary negotiations. "Why don't you look this over and tell me what you think?"

"I hope you're open to negotiations." She was certainly game. An offer printed up and presented to her in less than an hour said they wanted her bad. Needed her.

She skimmed the document until her eyes came upon a number. An eye-popping *shrimp and salmon can be added to the grocery list* number. Kennedy had to force herself not to visibly react because the annual salary listed was 25 percent higher than her previous job.

Her heart picked up its pace. Farther down on the sheet, another number caught her eye. The sight of the words *signing bonus* followed by thirty grand set fireworks off in her brain. They'd now ventured into complete student loan repayment territory.

Breathe. Breathe. You hold the cards here. Never let them know how much you want it.

Never back down from asking for what you're worth. Her father had driven that into her and her siblings' heads.

But before she presented her counteroffer, there was the not-so-little matter of the promise she'd made the singer. "Sahara mentioned the lack of diversity and wanted assurances that the company and *my* team were more diverse than the men at the meeting. I told her it was, so you're going to have to hire more people if you want to keep her happy." It wasn't a threat, simply a statement of fact.

Mr. Edwards barely batted an eyelash when he replied, "Then I guess we'll be hiring more people. You can take the lead on that and you'll receive our standard recruiting fee of twenty-five percent."

Be cool. You can jump up and down and scream when you get home.

"Sounds good to me. As for the offer, I propose ten percent more on the base salary. Six weeks of vacation and Election Day off."

His mouth quirked in reluctant admiration. "That sounds fair."

If she'd asked for 20 percent more, Kennedy was sure he would've agreed, which gave her more than a moment's pause. Worried she was rushing into this without enough thought, she slammed on the brakes and said smoothly, "Wonderful. Now, I hope you don't mind if I take the night to think it over."

"Of course, of course. Take until the end of the week, if you want," Mr. Edwards said with an understanding nod.

Kennedy intended to do just that.

"Get in here, you," Aurora cried the second she opened her front door to Kennedy and all but yanked her inside. Clad in red sweat shorts and a white crop top with her highlighted gold-blond tresses, her best friend looked like the ultimate sun-kissed California beach girl.

Kennedy had come straight there after her meeting with Mr. Edwards. In her excitement, she'd almost called Aurora before she left the office. But in the end, she decided it wasn't the kind of news she wanted to share over the phone. That kind of instant gratification couldn't compete with seeing the look on her bestie's face when she told her in person. So she'd texted that she was on her way over and turned off her phone.

"How dare you hold out on me," Aurora chided, all mock aggrieved. "We don't do cryptic. We don't make each other wait. We don't do torture. Now tell me what happened with Sahara. Did they offer you a job? Come on, spill," she commanded and tugged Kennedy by the arm into the living room.

Aurora's brownstone wasn't how the other half lived; this was the lifestyle of the one-percenters. Kennedy wasn't sure she'd ever get used to the place. A beautiful three-bedroom in swanky New York's Upper East Side was far removed from her tiny one-bedroom apartment in Brooklyn. Her best friend enjoyed high ceilings, crown molding, gorgeous built-in shelving, tall arched windows, and a kitchen to die for. Nate bought it for her the year his company went public—his junior year at Columbia—and Kennedy didn't even want to know what he'd paid for it. All she knew was that in Lenox Hill everything cost a fortune—and then some. One day she'd be able to afford something one-tenth the price and half the size. Just not in New York City.

Kennedy let her friend pull her down onto the oversized sofa in front of the fireplace. "Okay, okay," she said, laughing. "I'll tell you if you promise to make me one of your famous brown cow floats."

"You drive a hard bargain, but I think I can manage that.

And count yourself lucky that I just replenished my stock of Kahlúa. Now spill. I want all the details. Great outfit, by the way."

That was Aurora in a nutshell. A hundred thoughts and only one mouth from which to voice them.

"Okay, let's start with Sahara, who is absolutely fabulous. Really down-to-earth. She's as beautiful in person as she is in the mags and on TV. Looks younger too. Anyway, we hit it off. I mean, I really think she likes me. She asked for *my* phone number. Oh my god, the Desert Queen has my personal phone number." Hours after the fact, she was only now grasping the enormity of that. Even though Aurora's parents rubbed elbows with a lot of big stars, Aurora rarely did, and Kennedy never had. This was a big f-ing deal.

"Of course she does. Everyone *loves* you."

Kennedy snorted gleefully. "Well, I don't know about Mr. Edwards, since I'm about to take a nice bite out of ECO's payroll." She blew on her nails and buffed them against her shoulder, feeling supremely proud of herself.

Aurora let out a high-pitched squeal. "Yes! Yes! I knew it."

Kennedy couldn't help laughing along with her. "But I demanded ten percent more than they initially offered, which was already twenty-five percent more than my last salary, and the signing bonus was three times more than you told me to ask for."

Rendered momentarily speechless, Aurora gaped, her blue eyes wide. "Are you shitting me?" she asked, her voice a whisper of hushed disbelief.

"Nope. And I have a feeling I can ask for even more, and with that kind of money, I'll finally be able to pay off my student loan. Which means I'm free, Rory. Free!" Giddy, Kennedy threw her hands in the air and wriggled happily in place.

"And I'll be able to afford an apartment closer to the city." Or at the very least, in a nicer part of Brooklyn.

Boisterous celebration ensued, the women giggling as they hugged and high-fived like a bunch of giddy teenagers. When the giggling finally subsided, Aurora sat back, one slender leg tucked under the other, and regarded her soberly. "Those bastards. They're getting way more out of you than you are of them. How dare they use you like that?"

"Don't worry." Kennedy gave her friend's hand a gentle pat and squeeze. "I'm using them right back. Guess who's in charge of diversifying their staff? And each hire comes with a *very* generous recruiting fee."

Aurora stared at her for another somber beat before erupting into laughter. "Oh my god, that is a thing of beauty. This is genius-level *how to capitalize on a crisis*. You know what, screw working with them and come work with me. We'd make a formidable team."

"We would, wouldn't we," Kennedy said, a wistful note in her voice. "You know, I've been thinking about that a lot lately. Being my own boss. Working for myself."

Since she'd been laid off, it was almost all she thought about. A business of her own. Where she failed or succeeded on her own merits. Where the fate of her employment wasn't subject to the whims and desires of someone else.

But debt-ridden temporarily employed media relations specialists weren't exactly great credit risks, and banks actually expected repayment of their loans. They were funny like that. Which meant striking out on her own would have to wait. How long, she wasn't sure, but with the end of her student loan payments tantalizingly close, it could be much sooner than she dared hope.

Much sooner.

"You will. One day. We both will," Aurora assured her,

and probably herself. How could she not, considering her family? Her father was a Hollywood director, her mother a model-turned-actress-turned-executive producer, and her three brothers were all super successful in their chosen fields—although, Nate was *the* overachiever to beat all overachievers. Naturally, Aurora, the baby of the family, wanted to forge a path of her own.

Just like Kennedy.

"We should open up our own PR agency." As soon as the words were out, Kennedy slapped a hand over her mouth.

Where had that come from?

By much sooner, *I guess you meant right now,* another voice answered.

Aurora's eyes widened in surprise, then narrowed. "Are you serious?"

This morning she could barely afford to open a lemonade stand, much less her own agency, but everything *had* changed. Now she knew her worth. At least, to ECO. That knowledge changed the trajectory of her life and what was possible.

As to the question of whether she was serious or not, Kennedy didn't need to mull it over long. "Yeah. Yeah, I think I am." Her voice grew more emphatic with each word, the agency's mission and purpose taking shape in her mind.

"Look at what happened to me today. The company needed me so Sahara wouldn't take one look around the conference room and take her business elsewhere. Which tells me if that's happening at ECO, it's happening at a lot of other companies. And with the growing pressure on Hollywood, boardrooms, educational institutions, and Big Tech to diversify, I'd say the pool of potential clients could make an agency that manages issues of a *'diverse nature'*—" she air quoted the term "—very profitable, wouldn't you agree?"

"So you want to *help* those companies?" Aurora asked, look-ing understandably skeptical.

"Okay, I know what you're thinking, but hear me out. I think we can agree that most companies aren't like your brother's. He made it a priority to create an inclusive and diverse workforce. Most companies have to be dragged kicking and screaming into the twenty-first century, just like ECO Apparel. But now that I have my foot in the door, I can push for those kinds of changes, especially if I have someone like Sahara making it a condition of partnering with them."

Aurora sighed, nodding. "I can't argue with you on that. Constellation is definitely the odd company out, especially in the tech industry."

Kennedy had to give it to Nate—he'd built a company any-one would be proud of.

"And as we grow, we can expand our services by offering diversity and inclusivity, and sexual harassment classes and training." Kennedy had taken a certification course to teach both at her last job. It had been cheaper for the company than paying an outside firm.

By the gleam in her eyes, Kennedy could see Aurora's en-thusiasm for the idea growing. "And with my background in crisis management, we'll have all the bases covered."

"Exactly." It would be a full-service boutique PR agency with an emphasis on diversity and inclusivity.

"Oh my god, I love it." Aurora's eyes were fever bright. "Does that mean you're going to turn down the job and I'm going to quit mine?"

Kennedy's nod and smile were tentative. "I think so. But only if you're in."

"Oh, I'm definitely in."

A kaleidoscope of butterflies took up residence in her stomach. "Have we lost our minds?" Kennedy asked in a hushed voice, unable to believe they were actually going to do this.

Aurora grabbed her hand and squeezed hard enough to cause Kennedy to wince, barely able to contain her excitement. "We're two badass women ready to make our mark."

"Yeah, that's us, two badasses," Kennedy said, laughing.

"So what are you going to do about ECO? They're counting on you to land Sahara."

Kennedy had been giving that some thought. "I'm going to tell them the truth. I can't be their employee, but they can be our client. Our first."

"That was my thought too. And this way we'll be able to charge them a lot more than what they were offering." Aurora's expression became thoughtful. "So, what do you want to call it?"

Like a lightning strike or a tornado, the name seemed to come out of nowhere but resonated in every single part of her being. "Token. I want to call it *Token*."

She'd been one almost her entire life, but this time she was going to turn the meaning on its head and to everyone's advantage.

At the kitchen island an hour later, Kennedy sipped on a brown cow float and Aurora on a glass of red wine, their euphoria having settled into a *lady badass bosses* glow.

"Okay, I think we've got all we need right now." Aurora closed the laptop and finished her wine. Their rudimentary business plan now resided on the computer's hard drive and three cloud services, because it was better to be safe than sorry. They'd both learned that the hard way in college.

Kennedy turned and looked out the window. She grimaced when she thought about the subway ride back to Brooklyn. Maybe today she'd splurge and take an Uber. "And I should be getting home. Can't be late tomorrow."

The knock on the front door had her swinging her gaze back to her friend. "You expecting anyone?"

Aurora shot a glance at the digital clock on the wall. "Oh my goodness, it's after seven. I almost forgot about dinner," she exclaimed, sliding off the stool and rushing from the kitchen.

Still seated at the island, Kennedy puzzled over how, in the past hour, Aurora could have ordered food delivery without her being aware of it.

When her friend returned not even a half minute later, she brought company—in the brooding form of her brother Nate.

An audible gasp escaped before Kennedy could prevent it.

"Surprise! Guess who's in town and brought dinner?" Aurora chortled, triumphantly holding up two Mama Napoli paper bags, the smell of garlic and tomato sauce already permeating the air.

"You know how I hate surprises," Kennedy groused, glaring at her friend. "That took two years off my life. All I saw was a man behind you, and I thought we were about to be kidnapped or robbed." There was a millisecond of truth in that.

"Don't recognize me anymore, Kennedy?" His voice was arid dry.

As if.

To that, she put her best smile forward and played the part. "I certainly do now. Hello, Nate."

The right corner of his mouth inched up a fraction. "Hello, Kennedy. I take it Aurora didn't mention I'd be coming by?" If ever a voice matched someone's appearance, it was Nate's. Deep and broody.

It would be too clichéd to describe him as tall, dark, and handsome—his hair being dark blond and all. No, he required more nuance than that, as his features were too chiseled to classify him as a pretty boy, but those lips of his were...sin incarnate—a weakness of hers that predated their introduction. The only word she could use to describe them was *lush*, bringing favorable comparisons to the likes of Theo James. She also preferred men who possessed more lean muscle than bulk, and unfortunately, Nate fit that bill too.

The disconcerting truth was this: when it came to Nate Vaughn, she always felt like she swam a little too far from the shore, and being at best a mediocre swimmer, put herself at significant risk of drowning.

"Clearly not. The last I heard, you were wining and dining susceptible women all over France." She'd learned long ago that wit and humor were her best defenses against him.

"I *have* been accused of spreading myself too thin."

Too thin could also be applied to the current state of the barely there smile on his face. If prior experience hadn't shown her that he did in fact have a sense of humor—not much but some—she wouldn't be able to tell now.

Aurora claimed that since Nate started his company—in college, no less, because apparently Zuckerberg had set some invisible bar for all the serious techies out there—her brother suffered from an all-work-no-play syndrome. Which left him little time for girlfriends. He certainly never brought any home, which was now his mother's biggest complaint. A year ago, he'd decided it was time to expand beyond America's shores and was now setting up a European office and warehouse in France.

"I don't remember using the word *susceptible*," Aurora said innocently as she placed the bags on the island and began unpacking savory container after savory container.

Kennedy sent her friend a chiding look. *Et tu, Aurora? Can no one in your family take a joke anymore?*

Nate wandered deeper into the kitchen, hands buried in the pockets of his cargo shorts. "Speaking of wining and dining, how many hearts have *you* broken lately?"

Yep, that was her, Kennedy Mitchell, *femme fatale extraordinaire*, collecting and breaking hearts since puberty.

"Too many to count," she answered breezily. "But I'll be sure to let you know when I get the annual body count down under twenty."

The corner of his mouth might have lifted at that. It was hard to tell, the movement was so fleeting.

"You should see the guy she's dating now. She's got him wrapped—"

Kennedy cut her off with a muttered sound of outrage and gave her friend a quelling look. "Aurora, boundaries," she bit out in a sharply worded reprimand.

The status of her dating life was absolutely none of his business.

"Ooops, sorry." Aurora zipped her mouth shut and threw away the key in dramatic pantomime fashion. Only she didn't look all that sorry, a reminder to Kennedy of how close the siblings were. Aurora probably shared more with him about Kennedy than she would ever be comfortable with.

"Okay, enough small talk. Let's eat." Her friend walked over to the cupboards where she kept the plates and bowls.

Kennedy sent one longing look at the containers on the counter and inhaled the scent of everything good about Italian food. The sandwich and brownie she'd had during the meeting felt like a lifetime ago. But as much as it pained her, she couldn't stay and indulge. Not in the food or the company. Especially the company.

"Sorry, Ror, I have to get my butt in gear. I need to be getting home." She offered an apologetic smile.

Aurora's expression immediately fell. "No, you have to stay. Nate brought our favorites—stuffed manicotti with meat sauce and chicken primavera Alfredo. You can do either or both."

Damn him. He was the devil's own foot soldier.

Be strong. It's only food. There's more of that where it came from.

Shaking her head, Kennedy circled the island and gave Aurora a hug. "I've got to go. I have a big day tomorrow and I need my beauty sleep."

Nate made a sound in his throat and met her raised eyebrow with an arched brow of his own. "Beauty sleep?"

"Well, some of us don't just wake up in the morning, run a hand through our hair, and look perfectly presentable," she said airily. "Unlike you, some of us mere mortals need our beauty sleep."

Without even cracking a smile, he pulled his hands out of his pockets and glanced at his watch. "Stay and eat and I'll give you a ride home. It's probably not a good idea to be taking the subway this late at night anyway."

"It's quarter after seven, Nate."

"It'll be dark soon."

"Right, in an hour, and I should be home by then."

"Oh, for goodness' sake, just let him drive you home." Aurora sounded like she was dealing with two squabbling children.

"No, Rory, I really have to go. I've got so much stuff still to do tonight. Plus, I'm going to take an Uber anyway." She directed her next remark to Nate. "Thanks for the offer. It's very sweet of you, but I'll be fine."

For a second it looked like he was going to argue, but then he gave a brisk nod. "Okay, suit yourself."

After bidding Nate a cheerier than normal goodbye—her mouth strained under the burden of the smile—she and Aurora made their way to the front to wait for the Uber to arrive.

"Do you want to do something with us this weekend? Nate is flying back to Paris on Sunday."

Aurora? In a heartbeat. Nate? Not so much. These days, she could only handle him in small, digestible doses. Taciturn men had their places. In her company for any extended amount of time wasn't one of them.

"Sorry, Ror, I've got a million errands to run, and an apartment to clean once I'm done running myself ragged. Plus, your brother deserves to spend quality time with his favorite sister—"

"I'm his *only* sister," she interjected, rolling her eyes.

"—without me around."

"Okay, fine, you don't want to come." Aurora went full woebegone on her. "But we're going to miss you."

"Maybe *you* will, but I doubt your brother will."

Just then, the man in question appeared in her periphery. She instinctively turned in his direction.

"I take it we won't see each other before I head back?" If he'd heard her last comment, his expression didn't let on.

Hitching her purse strap higher on her shoulder, she made her tone light. "Looks that way. But I'm sure I'll see you whenever you're back in town. Take care and don't be such a stranger."

For two people who'd known each other as long as they had, a hug or a kiss on the cheek wouldn't have been amiss, but he made no move in her direction and she always wisely followed his lead.

"Right. Take care, Kennedy."

And that was the last she'd see of Nate Vaughn for a while.

4

Two years later

Men are impossible.

"Mr. Carter—"

"Please, I told you to call me Peter."

Yes, but that had been last year, when she'd had higher hopes for him and the company. He'd had an entire year and had yet to institute one change she'd painstakingly detailed in the diversification and inclusivity plan Token had created for the company. A plan for which he'd paid the agency a nice chunk of change.

Spine straight, legs decorously crossed, and clasped hands resting comfortably in her lap, Kennedy sat in her ex-client's office, a massive redwood desk between them.

Peter Carter, the president and CEO of Moves, prided himself on being able—at fifty-eight—to bench-press two and a half times his body weight. (He may have mentioned it a time or four during their last conversation.) The thick hair on top of his head was all his—he'd slipped that in too—although the same couldn't be said for the color, which she attributed to Just For Men medium brown.

In meeting with him today, Kennedy had been strategic, selecting a tailored pantsuit because the last *and* first time they'd met, he'd remarked—quite casually and with absolutely zero sense of self-awareness—that legs like hers were made for dresses and skirts. This he'd said directly to her face. She'd responded with a bland smile, and then politely asked if the company had mandatory sensitivity training for all its employees, including management. Without batting so much as an eyelash, he'd *un*ironically replied that while the company abided by the state mandate, he personally hadn't attended the sessions, and what a shocker that had been.

Not.

"All right, then, *Peter*, but I'm not sure what you want me to do for you." Just five minutes into their meeting, and the man was already wearing on her nerves. "You were supposed to start diversifying this division last year. That was the agreement."

Granted, it was verbal, but an agreement, nonetheless.

"I didn't know they were going to start grading us and putting out a fucking scorecard." He sounded defensive and resentful.

Kennedy's eyes widened a fraction. Since when had they reached a point in their acquaintance that the f-word could be thrown around so blithely and without so much as a *pardon my French* tagged on to soften the impact? And how very nice of him to admit he hadn't expected anyone to hold him accountable and therefore had had no compunction in going back on his word. Unfortunately, she dealt with too many men like him. Reluctant to do even the bare minimum, and *only* doing so when it threatened their bottom line.

"It's a scorecard, Peter, not a lawsuit."

"But that kind of publicity is bad for the company. And whatever's bad for the company is bad for business."

And that business was athletic footwear and apparel. Of course, he didn't want his customers to know that Moves would be getting a failing diversity grade. Not in this political climate. She could already see the hashtags on social media excoriating the company. There'd certainly be calls for a boycott, which would have a decent possibility of gaining traction, given the nature of the products and target audience.

"Which is why I can't help you this time." She wasn't being entirely truthful. All right, fine. She didn't *want* to help him. Not this time. He was looking for another quick fix because he had zero interest in doing the work. No doubt didn't think he had to.

"Then help me mitigate it." His tone was too demanding to be considered cajoling, but was the closest it could ever come to the spirit of the word. "I just need to get a few folks in here by the time the blasted scorecard comes out. That way, when those vultures call for a comment, I can tell them how the company is aware of the problem and is working hard to correct it."

She could understand his frustration, but calling reporters vultures for doing their jobs? Unnecessarily harsh.

"I'm sorry, but—"

He leaned forward, his clasped hands on his desk. "Antonio Jackson is coming in for a meeting tomorrow. What the hell am I going to do?"

Ah! Antonio Jackson. Just your typical equality and social justice warrior. He knelt, he marched, and most of all, he put his money where his mouth was. He was also the best forward in the NBA, with three championship titles to his name, two MVP rings, and the guy had yet to celebrate his thirtieth birthday.

Oh, and with his legion of fans, he wielded his influence with the might of Thor's hammer.

"You can't expect me to believe that you're only finding out about this now?" Kennedy asked, her eyebrow arched skeptically. There was no way he hadn't known about the meeting *well* in advance.

In silence, she watched as he straightened to his full height, which couldn't be more than two inches taller than her own five feet eight inches, and emerged from behind his desk. Agitated, he tugged on his tie and trod the length of the spacious office.

"It doesn't matter when I knew. What matters is that he just announced he's donating thirty percent of all proceeds from the sales of his *the ball's in your court* shirts and wristbands to charity—charities that support diversity in education and sports. Diversity is a big deal to him now."

"Yes, well, he has been kneeling for over a year," she pointed out.

"Right, and that didn't have any effect on his Nike contract, and I know the guys over there and they're no better than we are."

"He signed the contract with them well before his activism. Now he expects more from the companies he partners with. Plus, if you're arguing that as long as you meet their low standards, he should be okay with it, I'd work on the pitch."

"Obviously, that's not what I'm saying," he said. "But it would have been better if he'd been public about it a month ago."

"Things have changed, Peter. I was under the impression you realized that when you hired me last year." Sometimes, pointing out the obvious was the most important part of her job.

He stopped next to her chair and peered down at her. "Yes,

but it was nothing like this. Last year, one of the managers sent an inappropriate email to the wrong person, and you took care of it."

"No, Peter, it was your *vice president* of Global Sales, and as I'm sure you remember—" She didn't sugarcoat things for her clients. By the time they reached out to her, they needed brutal honesty delivered via IV drip. "—the email was racist and sexist, and it denigrated the Black and Asian communities. And we had an agreement, which you've since failed to honor."

Peter had had no choice but to fire the guy, or the scandal would have exploded onto the national stage. It had been the agency's most lucrative contract at the time, as he'd hired Kennedy to be the face of the coming change. It had been the agency's job to create a plan to make their offices in New York and New Jersey reflect the diversity of the country, which she and Aurora had spent the ensuing three months doing. In the end, she didn't know if he'd even read the summary.

He lowered himself onto the edge of his desk. "Kennedy, we're going to make the changes. I give you my word. I mean, we have to, right? Like you said, times have changed and we either keep up or we may as well drop out of the race."

Right—she'd heard this song before.

"Then my advice to you is to be up-front with him. About what's going to come out in the report and what you plan to do in the future." And let the chips fall where they may.

His laugh was entirely without humor. "Except the truth isn't our friend."

"Then I suggest you make it your friend." The problem with men like him was they operated under the assumption that everyone was like them.

"If you do as I say—and what we agreed to—I assure you, this won't happen again," she stated evenly. The best she could do was lead the horse to water, as she'd done last year. She

should have known this one would require a kick in the ass—
and for Antonio Jackson's contract with Nike to come up for
renewal—to make him drink.

"*Or* you can come to the meeting. *You* can explain things
to him. What we plan to do. Coming from you, he'll listen.
I know he will."

Kennedy began shaking her head before he could finish,
her hair swishing softly against her shoulders. "Listen to what?
I said the same thing last year. And. Nothing. Happened."

"That you're back to help implement the plan." She could
see, by the sudden spark in his eyes, a light bulb literally going
on in his mind. "Because we couldn't do it without you. Which
would be the truth," he added with a cajoling smile—if sharks
could smile.

"Peter—"

"We'll pay you double your fee." If this were an auction,
he was going for broke. "And I promise you this—by the end
of the year, no less than seven percent of our employees will
be men and women of color, and a total of fifteen percent the
following year."

Kennedy uncrossed her legs and recrossed them the other
way. A large dose of healthy skepticism was the only way he
should or could be taken.

"And I will put that in writing. Send me a contract and I'll
have it back to you signed and dated first thing in the morning. Everything will be done on *your* terms. You can screen
the hires, tell us what kind of diversity classes we need to take,
and whatever else is in your plan. You lead and we will follow."

"Peter, I don't have the bandwidth to—"

"Three times your fee. And if you need help, hire as many
people as you need. I realize you have a business to run, so you
can work from whichever base is most convenient for you."

Forget broke, he was going for bankruptcy.

Kennedy's mind went back to a similar conversation she'd had two years ago with ECO. Back then, the initial offer of five grand had taken her breath away. Today's offer put enough wind in her sails to get her from New York to the Bahamas and back. This was the kind of money no sane businesswoman could turn down.

"I'm not going to lie to him," she warned. She'd come perilously close a time or two, but that was a line she just wouldn't cross.

"I'm not asking you to," he said, raising his hands in the universal *nothing to see here* gesture. "But I'm sure when you explain what we have planned, he'll jump on board with both feet."

With this infusion of cash, the agency could expand its services and bring on Cecelia Catawnee, their part-time graphic designer, full-time.

"And my first recommendation is that you immediately begin the process of diversifying senior management."

"You must have read my mind. Don't worry—I'm already on it," he replied, sending her a wink.

"Good. Then if there's any way you can delay the meeting with Mr. Jackson three or four days—although a week would be preferable—that would give me enough time to put together a stronger and more convincing pitch." She could think of several people she wanted in place or with guaranteed start dates before the meeting, and she planned on reaching out to them ASAP.

"I'll make some calls, see if I can pull a few strings."

He looked so hopeful, she felt it imperative to remind him, "You know he may not sign with you." Win or fail, her services were going to cost him.

"Of that, I'm quite aware."

They studied each other for another moment more before she rose and extended her hand. "Good. Then we have a deal."

Being late was an inescapable fact of life. Everyone fell victim to it. Kennedy hated being late, and despite how many times she'd asked the ultimate power-that-be to gift her with the power of time control, there still remained only so many seconds in a minute and minutes in an hour, et cetera, et cetera.

She'd returned to the office after her meeting with Peter—which had run an hour longer than scheduled—apprised Aurora of the outcome, and called their contract lawyer, Julie Hwang, and requested she draw up a contract for Moves to have ready by the end of the day. Kennedy would go over it after she got home—but first, dinner with Aidan.

"Hi, my name is Cammie and I'll be your hostess for the evening. You must be Ms. Mitchell." A smiling brunette greeted Kennedy when she entered the restaurant. It was as if she'd been waiting for her to arrive.

"Don't tell me my boyfriend put you on lookout duty," Kennedy joked, checking her phone again. Okay, she was officially fifteen minutes late, but on a scale of one to ten of her shortcomings, the rare case of tardiness shouldn't even register.

Cammie, who didn't look much older than her, gave a tinkling laugh. "He told me you'd be the most beautiful woman to come in tonight, and he was right."

Yep, that sounded like Aidan. Always with the flattery. She just wished he thought as highly of her ambition as he did her looks. But no man was perfect, and she was determined not to throw in the towel prematurely—she'd been told she had a habit of doing that. Their relationship was solid. She had no *major* complaints.

"If you'll follow me. Your table is right over here." She motioned toward the area in the back near the windows. "Mr. Anderson specifically asked for somewhere quiet."

The restaurant as a whole was quiet, with the tables spaced maneuverable distances apart. Candles and fresh flowers graced white linen–covered tables, and the chairs were upholstered in a deep burgundy cloth. Aidan had never taken her here before, but based on appearances, she'd bet her next paycheck the prices weren't listed on the menus.

And it was only Wednesday. She couldn't imagine what he had in store for her this weekend.

A smile curved her mouth when she spotted him sitting alone at the table, head down and fingers tapping away on his cell phone. As if sensing her gaze, he looked up and their eyes met. He quickly pocketed his phone and pushed to his feet, pleasure lighting his eyes and a wide smile on his face.

Brown skinned, and dark hair cropped short, Aidan Anderson stood six feet three inches and sported a neatly trimmed goatee. People frequently told them they made a beautiful couple, as if it mattered that they looked good together. She knew they meant it as a compliment, but for some inexplicable reason, it rankled. On the other hand, Aidan appeared to wear it as a badge of honor, and that rankled too.

Tonight, he looked dapper in a blue pin-striped suit and had her wishing she'd first gone home and changed into something less businesslike. Power-broker pantsuits were fine for meetings with clients like Peter Carter but looked out of place here, where elegant dresses and skirts appeared to be the order of the day.

"I'll give you a couple minutes to look over the menu before I send over your waitress," Cammie chirped when they arrived at the table, before turning on her heel and departing.

"You look beautiful. As usual," Aidan said, giving her a quick kiss on the cheek. One inhalation and Kennedy could

immediately tell he'd been more liberal than usual in the application of his cologne. It was a good thing she was the one
who'd selected it.

"You look pretty good yourself." She eyed him appreciatively and then added in hushed tones, "And this place looks
très expensive."

Aidan played the gentleman to a tee, pulling out her chair
and whispering in her ear, "Only the best for my woman."

My woman. Something about that term struck a discordant
chord with her. It made her think of big wooden clubs and
women being dragged by their hair across rocky terrain. When
Aidan used the term, he was usually trying to be romantic
and she didn't have the heart to tell him that she wasn't into
cavemen, not those in the past, present, or future.

She pushed that tiny grievance aside as he resumed his seat.
"Sorry I'm late. Work was…hectic."

"Sooo…" He quirked an eyebrow. "I shouldn't ask about
your day?"

Kennedy huffed a laugh. "I just told you about it. It was
hectic."

Aidan simply smiled in response. He could be so romantic. The way he couldn't seem to keep his eyes off her. But
as the silence lengthened and he continued to watch her, his
lids drifting to half-mast and his gaze unwavering, she began
to feel self-conscious.

Did she have something on her face?

Hmm, doubtful since she determined the look was closer
to one of adoration than *you have spinach between your teeth*.

"What's that look all about?" she teased, trying for a bit of
levity. "If you're thinking about asking me for a kidney, my
sister already called dibs. And with her being family and all…"
She trailed off into a delicate shrug.

Aidan's shoulders shook in silent laughter. "You got me."

He raised his hands in mock surrender. "Your sister gets your kidney. You won't get any argument from me."

"Good. I'll be sure to tell her."

Aidan had met her older sister last year when Cheryl visited from Raleigh. They'd gotten on as well as Kennedy could hope. Her boyfriend set out to charm, and since prickly and suspicious toward all men (with the exception of her husband, brothers, and their father) was her sister's default disposition, the fact that Cheryl hadn't told her to *dump his sorry ass* spoke volumes.

"Your champagne, sir." The black-and-white-uniformed maître d' appeared out of nowhere—the restaurant was dimly lit and he had stealth and size on his side—and placed two empty flutes on the table.

Kennedy shot her boyfriend a look of surprise. He flashed her a secretive smile.

Nervous laughter bubbled in her throat. "Wha—what's going on? Are we celebrating something?"

Aidan's mouth twitched, but he remained silent.

And then with all the dramatics and flourish of a matador entering the ring, the maître d' popped the cork and filled the glasses before departing with a formal bow, because apparently it was going to be that kind of dining experience.

"Did you get a promotion? Am I sitting across from the new vice president of Business Development?" she asked, hopeful.

Aidan worked for FastTrack, a light-rail manufacturer that was developing passenger trains for future high-speed rail service around the country. His boss had retired last month and Aidan was in line for his position.

Instead of answering, he handed her one of the glasses and then picked up the other one.

She gave a confused laugh. "You're not going to tell me?"

Without removing his gaze from hers, he reached slowly

into the inner pocket of his jacket and retrieved a black velvet jewelry box. He placed it in front of her, opening it with the flick of his thumb.

"Will you marry me?"

It happened simultaneously, Kennedy clapping her eyes on the ring and the question hitting her eardrums with noise-canceling clarity.

The last time a man proposed to her had been six years ago. Eight years her senior, Malcolm had wanted to marry and settle down. She'd been twenty-three, working a full-time job as well as attending evening classes in pursuit of her master's degree. A night full of promise, and good food and music, went south faster than they could finish their wine. Sadly, she saw this one heading in the same trajectory.

Slowly, she lifted her gaze from the gorgeous square-cut diamond to the expectation in his dark brown eyes. And just like that, his expression altered.

He knew.

She didn't even have to say the words.

With the exhalation of one long ragged breath, Aidan deflated before her very eyes. "In my experience, tears of joy usually come with a smile, and you're not smiling."

Tears? Kennedy tentatively touched her face, and only then did she realize her cheek was wet, proving that guilt and sorrow were a potent mix of emotions. Her hand trembled as she placed the untouched glass of champagne back on the table. "Marriage is such a huge step, and we're just getting the agency off the ground, and—"

"We don't have to get married right away."

Ugh. She should have kept her big mouth shut instead of trying to justify what they both knew was a refusal. Instead, she'd opened the door just enough to give him room to try to slip through.

"Aid, I'm not ready. I'm not ready for any of it," she whispered, her voice choked with emotion. Abject misery. More tears fell, slow and relentless.

For what seemed like forever, but in reality was probably only seconds, he stared at her, his expression retreating behind a mask of inscrutability. Suddenly, his hand shot out, snapped the jewelry box closed, and returned it to his pocket.

Kennedy blinked at the suddenness of the action. As if he wanted to take it back. The proposal. The ring. Everything.

A crash of thunder quickly followed a flash of lightning, briefly lighting up the Manhattan skyline. Because of course, thunder and lightning were the appropriate end to the evening.

"I'm sorry." She could apologize until the cows came home, but she knew it wouldn't make a difference. Aidan would never be able to forgive her. His pride wouldn't allow it. For all intents and purposes, he was a catch. He was a good-looking, highly educated Black man making it in corporate America. He wasn't going places—he had arrived.

Kennedy started when pelting rain began to splatter the windows a foot from them. Meanwhile, Aidan continued to study her.

"Can I ask you a question?" The bass in his voice was more pronounced than usual.

No, this whole thing is hard enough. No more. "Of course."

"Are you saying you'd have said yes if not for your agency?"

How did she answer that? "It's not you, Aidan. I don't want to marry anyone right now." She'd get married when the time was right for her and not a minute before.

"Is there someone else?"

Kennedy's eyes went wide. "No. Of course not. No." She gave her head an emphatic shake. Why was it so hard for some men to accept that refusing a proposal of marriage didn't necessarily mean there was someone else? Unless this was just Aidan covering all the bases. She hoped it was the latter.

"I'm not sure where we go from here," he finally said.

She didn't either because she didn't want to break up with him. But while she was happy with their current relationship, clearly he was not.

"It would probably be a good idea if we took a break," he said when she failed to offer up a solution of her own.

Kennedy swallowed hard. "If that's what you want."

"It's not what I want, Ken, but then, it seems I'm not going to get what I want, am I?" The slight bite in his tone conveyed a great deal more than his words.

At that point it became untenable to hold his gaze. She discreetly directed hers over his right shoulder and replied softly, "You're right. Sometimes we can't get what we want. It happens to all of us."

5

Three weeks later

"We got another one," Jonathan Hanson, Token's office manager of two years, called out as Kennedy passed his office on the way to hers.

"Another what?" she asked absently, her mind preoccupied with the conversation she'd had with Aidan last night when she'd ended things once and for all. After too many sleepless, guilt-filled nights, she'd known the only way forward was a clean break. Yesterday, she'd made it official, and for all its brevity, it had been every bit as excruciating as she'd dreaded.

Aidan had tried to convince her to give things more time, but she knew she'd only be delaying the inevitable. In his heart of hearts, he knew it too. They were done. Both free to go on with their lives the way the relationship gods intended. Very much apart.

And the two women closest to her agreed she'd done the right thing. *Marriage isn't something you enter into lightly,* her happily married sister, Cheryl, had wisely advised, and Aurora agreed that she needed to be *all in or not at all* before even committing to taking the plunge.

When there wasn't so much as a pause in her stride, Jonathan sprang from his desk and followed her into her office, which was sparse in its decor with its pale gray walls and economical furniture.

"Another request for a Brit. Ideally biracial or Black." He shook his head, tsking. "They've got Regé on the brain."

Kennedy sat down at her desk, booted up her computer, and took her time putting away her handbag. "Too bad Trevor doesn't have a twin," she stated dryly.

"And was British," Jonathan added. "Or could at least fake the accent."

Last year, Token had worked with Goldberg & Johnson, a law firm with a history of defending large corporations against gender- and race-based discrimination class-action lawsuits. They'd racked up some pretty impressive wins, like the one defending the largest retailer in the country. But with the shifting tides of public opinion, they'd wanted to expand their specialization and for the makeup of their legal teams to be more representative of the country at large. With the legal profession being one of the least diverse in the country, that was no small feat.

Trevor Markham, a reputable young Black civil rights attorney, whom she'd briefly dated, had more than fit the bill. He'd been perfect. That he was also *way* too easy on the eyes was providence if one believed looks mattered to the public at large. It shouldn't but it did. Too bad there'd been no chemistry between them. She genuinely liked him.

Kennedy clicked the mouse to open the calendar app on her desktop. "Did you tell them we're not central casting and this is the United States?" In no way, shape, or form could posh British accents or good looks be considered necessary components for diversity or inclusivity.

"She said it wasn't mandatory, just nice to have."

Kennedy rolled her eyes. "Of course, it was a she, and *she* probably just binge-watched *Bridgerton*."

It didn't happen often, but when it did, it was amazing how specific a company's requests could get.

Kennedy stared at her schedule and sighed. Three conference calls in the morning and one meeting downtown. She grew exhausted just looking at it. Next, she pulled up her email and was overcome with the sheer number that remained unread. Honestly, she needed to talk to Keith, their IT guy, about employing a better spam filter.

Jonathan cleared his throat, jerking her attention up to where he stood, legs spread and arms crossed over his chest, leveling her with a knowing stare. "Okay, what happened?"

Damn. He must have been a psychic or mind reader in his former life.

"Don't give me that look," he lightly scolded. "It's obvious something's wrong. You look like you're in mourning. And since when did you start wearing burgundy and hunter green in the middle of the summer?"

At his candid critique, Kennedy's gaze immediately dropped to her houndstooth sheath dress. "But it's sleeveless and rayon."

"You know you're strictly pastels in the summer."

"I wear black sometimes," she protested.

"Pants, and only when it's that time of the month." It was criminal how much he knew about her.

"TMI, Jonathan. TMI."

He smirked. "Then you should never have told me." After a moment of silence, his expression sobered. "I repeat, what is wrong?"

Kennedy released a heavy sigh and leaned back in her chair. "Aidan and I broke up last night."

His hands dropped abruptly to his sides. "No!" It was a forceful denial filled with rightful indignation.

"It's true."

Jonathan's mouth opened and closed several times before sound finally emerged in the form of a question. "Are you telling me Aidan is single?"

A spontaneous burst of laughter sputtered from her lips as she picked up the stress ball she kept on her desk and threw it at his head.

He let out a feigned grunt of injury when it glanced his left temple and landed harmlessly on the carpeted floor behind him. "Ouch, that hurt."

Lips pressed together, she fought back a smile. "For the last time, Aidan isn't gay."

Jonathan appeared to consider her assertion before asking facetiously, "But are you sure he isn't bi? Leave me with some hope."

Married to his husband for five years, Jonathan staunchly abided by the *look but don't touch* philosophy. He would never be unfaithful to Darrell but deemed discreetly ogling her boyfriend totally permissible.

Kennedy shook her head, chuckling helplessly. "You are incorrigible."

He grinned, flashing his gorgeous smile. "Yet every day you curse the gods that you'll never be able to have me. Why might that be?" he inquired, eyebrow raised and tongue planted firmly in cheek.

"You also have an ego the size of Texas," she said with a snort.

No ands or buts, her office manager received his fair share of attention—mostly female, he claimed, because he wasn't easy to pick up on people's gaydar. Seriously, he said it as if gaydar was an actual thing.

Personally, he reminded her of a clean-shaven Odell Beckham Jr. without the two-toned hair. And while she wouldn't say he was a slave to fashion, the man did know how to dress. Business attire, like today, was pressed trousers uncompromisingly creased, a collared light-colored shirt, and a blazer in a coordinating color.

"Still didn't answer my question," he teased. A moment later, he pushed the guest chair closer to her desk and sat. "Okay, all jokes aside, what really happened? The guy is nuts about you. There's no way he wanted to break up. He sent you a dozen roses a month ago, and those puppies cost a pretty penny."

And it hadn't been her birthday or Valentine's Day. Aidan had said it was just because she was the best thing that ever happened to him. She should have known something was up then. Should have known that while she'd been content cruising at the speed limit, he'd wanted to press down on the gas.

Kennedy gave another weighty sigh. "He proposed and—"

"God Almighty, please don't tell me you turned him down," he cut in, his feelings on the matter evident in his tone. He sounded appalled and worried about her ability to reason. Or lack thereof.

She, in turn, retorted defensively, "I'm not ready to get married."

"Have I taught you nothing in the time we've known each other? Guys like Aidan Anderson don't come along every day. Or every week, month, or year. You guys are perfect together. You were the Black super couple I looked up to. Who am I supposed to look up to now?"

"Why on earth do you need anyone to look up to at all? You and Darrell have a wonderful relationship as it is. And you know how it goes—the minute *after* you're put on a pedestal is the minute someone else begins to knock you down, inch by brutal inch."

Jonathan tipped his head back and studied her with narrowed eyes. "So cynical for one so young and beautiful."

"Try realistic," she quipped.

Sadness flickered in his eyes. Or perhaps it was pity—probably a combination of both. "So that's it, it's over?"

She picked up the pen and idly tapped it on the lined notepad. "At first, we were on a break, but—"

"Breaks never work," Jonathan interjected.

"Thank you!" Kennedy exclaimed. "Which is exactly what I told Aidan last night. Once there's a proposal and no engagement, it's over. He knew it and I knew it, but I wanted to give him time to get used to the idea."

To be fair, he wasn't the only one. While she might not necessarily want to marry him—at this time in her extremely busy life—she had enjoyed dating him. She stopped fidgeting and put down the pen.

"Well, you know what they say. You can't force love," Jonathan remarked.

"I thought it was you can't hurry love, which I believe is a song."

"Force, hurry—" Jonathan shrugged "—means the same thing." After a beat, he continued lightly, "I'm going to have to start calling you Heartbreaker Kennedy. Most people won't receive two marriage proposals in a lifetime, and you've managed it in twenty-nine years, and turned them both down."

Heartbreaker. Kennedy winced inwardly. Nate had said something similar the last time she saw him.

The sound of the agency's main door opening saved her from a discussion she didn't want to have right now...or really ever.

"It's about time," Kennedy called out. "I was getting ready

to call 9-1-1 for a welfare check." Aurora was usually in an hour early and it was already half past eight now. The rest of the office staff usually trickled in right before their nine o'clock opening.

Her greeting was met with silence. Brows furrowed, Jonathan glanced at her before getting up and walking to her office doorway. The smile that blossomed over his face told her they weren't being robbed.

"Here to see Aurora?" Jonathan asked as he exited her office, posing his question to the person arriving before opening hours.

"Is she in?" a male voice responded.

Kennedy froze. A voice she immediately recognized.

Before she could fully grasp what was happening, Nathaniel Vaughn stood framed in her doorway, his hair looking like a strong wind gust had gone a few rounds with it and won. A day's worth of bristle covered his square jaw.

Unfortunately, tousled-hair, unshaven Nate looked just as good as the perfectly coiffed, clean-shaven one.

"Nate, you're here," she said, staring at him blankly.

No, he's on the moon, idiot.

"I mean, what are you doing here?" The last she'd heard, he was still in France.

Without waiting for an invitation, he stepped inside. "Here in your office or back stateside?" he asked casually, closing the door behind him.

And just like that, her office was reduced to the size of a broom closet.

"Both." Aurora always told her when Nate was in town, and she usually invited her to join them for dinner before he flew out. But she hadn't said a word about him being in town when they'd spoken last night.

"I took a red-eye in this morning."

Kennedy ran her gaze over him again. *And it shows.* As casual as the dress code was at his company, jeans, T-shirt, *and* sneakers were discouraged at headquarters. He looked as if he'd slept in his.

"Don't mind if I sit," he murmured and dropped into the chair Jonathan had recently vacated.

"Why, hello, Nate. Nice to see you too. I assume you're here to see your sister."

He shot a pointed look at her closed office door. "No, I'm here to see you."

Kennedy blinked twice at that. "Me? What for?"

"It's obvious you haven't heard."

"Heard what?"

"I'm being sued for job discrimination."

"You're being sued? You are?" If he didn't look so serious, the idea would have been comical. "On the basis of what?"

"Gender and race," he replied tersely.

Kennedy stared at him, agape. "Are you being serious right now?"

"No, which is why I caught the first flight out of Paris so I could come back here and have company lawyers advise me that twelve of my current and six of my former employees are *not* suing me—I mean, the company. So yes, Kennedy, I'm dead serious."

"Hey, ease up on the snark. You'll forgive me for being caught off guard when you show up out of nowhere and spring something like that on me. I'm still trying to wrap my brain around it."

Nate sighed wearily. "Look, I'm sorry. I must get this way when I'm dealing with class-action lawsuits."

"I don't understand. Your company is touted as one of the most diverse tech companies in the country. Last year's diver-

sity scorecard had it at a solid B+, the best in the industry."
The top three in the country.

"The lawsuit alleges women and African Americans are
being passed over for advancement within the company. Here,
read this." Leaning forward, he tossed over the newspaper
clutched in his hand.

Startled, Kennedy glanced at him warily before smoothing
open the curled edges of the paper—she was strictly a digital
girl, so it had been a while—and started reading everything
highlighted in yellow.

The invisible glass ceiling is as present as ever in the most
diverse tech company in the country.

…After digging a little deeper into the numbers, we
found that despite Constellation's boast of a diverse workforce of 19%, once you get into midlevel and upper management, the percentage drops significantly. White males
comprise 89% of all upper-management jobs, South
Asians 6%, Southeast Asians 3%, women (white) 2%.

Kennedy's gaze darted from the article to Nate. "Not one
Black person in upper management?" she asked, puzzled. "I
thought your CFO was Black."

"He was, but Jacob left last year. Took a job in San Fran-
cisco, where his wife was doing her medical residency."

"He wasn't the company's only Black executive, was he? I
remember Aurora telling me a Black woman is in charge of
Sales." An MIT grad, if she remembered correctly.

"Carol left six months before Jacob."

"Okay, so the only two Black executives quit within six
months of each other? Great timing," she stated dryly. "Did

you know your numbers with Blacks and women were this abysmal?" She gestured at the article.

Reclined in the chair, Nate groaned low in his throat and rubbed a palm over his face. "No. Yes. I mean, I was aware of the overall numbers, which I thought were pretty damn good."

"Yeah, well, sometimes numbers don't always tell the whole story."

Raising his head slightly, he eyed her. "What does that mean?"

"It means that at *least* eighteen of your employees believe there's a race- and gender-based glass ceiling at the company impeding possible advancement."

He held her gaze for a couple moments before tipping his head back and growling, "*Fuck!* I thought we were on top of this. Ahead of our time *and* the bloody competition. I thought, except for the normal butting of heads and battle of wills, my employees didn't have much to complain about."

"Hey, don't start beating yourself up about this. No company's perfect."

"Most companies also don't have a class-action discrimination lawsuit hanging over their head," he shot back wryly.

"Your company employs over fifteen thousand people. You have more diversity than your competition. You'll get through this. You just need to take things one day at a time."

"Meanwhile, they're writing shit like *the tone is set at the top*, and everyone knows what that's code for. That everyone is taking their cues from me. That I'm the one encouraging this shit."

"You've been in France for practically the last three years. Someone else has been in charge," Kennedy offered in his defense.

"Nobody is going to give a shit about that. It's my company. I'm the owner and CEO. The buck stops with me."

He was right. The newspapers and reporters wouldn't give a whit if he'd been a Tibetan monk in Timbuktu the last five years. He'd still been the person in charge, the one whose net worth climbed every time the Dow saw a gain.

Leaning forward, he propped his forearms on his spread thighs and looked her directly in the eye. "I need your help." It was more a demand than an entreaty. Typical Nate.

"I'm sure Aurora will—"

"No, not my sister. I need you. This is your area of expertise. This is where you shine."

Kennedy furrowed her brow, genuinely perplexed. "But, Nate, you already have a diverse workforce. You don't need me." At the end of the day, that was the ultimate goal of her services. The lawsuit was a hiccup.

"No, you're wrong. I do need you," he said, and for a fleeting moment, she thought he meant more than just her professional services. But of course that couldn't be it. He didn't feel that way about her. He'd made that clear enough the past several years.

"Come on, Nate. You know the rules," she lightly chided. "Representing family can be...problematic."

"But we're not family, which is why I'm asking you."

Kennedy shifted uncomfortably but managed to maintain eye contact. "But Aurora *is*, and she owns half the agency."

"And because of that, you're going to deny me your expertise?" he asked with an arched brow.

Okay, if she had to judge herself objectively, she would humbly admit that she was good, but she wasn't the only game in town and certainly not the most esteemed. "How do you know how good I am? You've been in France since we opened the agency." And they'd had a total of twenty clients, none of which his company had ever done business with. At least, not that she was aware of.

A softening around his mouth eased the grimness of his expression. "Because I know you. Not only did you graduate at the top of your class, you're good at anything you set your mind to. Why wouldn't I want you on my side?"

Kennedy slowly shook her head. "I'm really sorry, Nate, but it's an agency policy I can't break." Work with Nate? Take him on as a client? Nope, not in a million years.

Her refusal sent him into used-car-salesman mode. "C'mon, Kennedy. You're a genius at this stuff. I've seen you in action. You can charm the mustache and beard off Santa Claus. You'll have the guys who put out those hit-job pieces eating out of your hand. All I want you to do is put your talents to use for me. And to prove I'm on the up-and-up, I won't even ask for a discount. As a matter of fact, I'm willing to pay above the going rate if you can squeeze me in today."

If you can squeeze me in today. Kennedy simultaneously cleared her throat and dragged her mind out of the gutter. "I can recommend the best—"

"No. No." He held up his hand to her. "I don't want anyone else. There's no one better at this than you. And as my sister's best friend, I would think you'd want me to be represented by the best."

He looked and sounded as if he meant it. That he wasn't simply trying to flatter her.

"I'm sorry, Nate, but I can't." She intended to come across as firm and decisive, but her voice refused to cooperate. A part of her came perilously close to wavering. Thankfully, it wasn't enough to overcome her sense of self-preservation. "You need someone who is—who is less—" Damn, how did she say it without showing all her cards?

In an abrupt move, he leaned forward in his chair. "No one else is going to know me like you do."

Her heart thumped in response as she gave a short laugh. "Nate, we've barely seen each other the last two years. I would hardly say I know you that well anymore."

He sat up straight, his brows shooting up. "What? So now you don't know me?"

His words struck her ears like a challenge. Perhaps she should have phrased it differently, but it was too late to take it back. In for a pound and all that.

Stiffening her spine, she replied, "No, Nate, I don't think I do. At least, not the man you are now," she tagged on, to give more credence to her statement.

Chuckling low in his throat, he caught and held her gaze. "Kennedy, I was your first. You gave me your virginity. If that doesn't say you know me and I know you, then I don't know what does."

6

Kennedy's breath caught in her throat as she stared at him, unblinking. She couldn't believe he'd gone there. A place they'd never gone before. Not in all the years since it had happened.

An involuntary shiver delayed her response.

In the breach of silence, Nate watched her, head tipped to the side and brows lifted. "What?" he asked, a note of challenge in his dulcet tones. A bit of smugness there too. "I was only stating facts, since you appear to have forgotten just how—" he inserted a meaningful pause "—intimately we're acquainted."

Not coincidentally, the recovery of speech coincided with the collection of her wits. "Why would you say that?"

She was genuinely bewildered because between them existed an unwritten agreement to never speak about the incident. Correction, incidents plural, since it had happened more than once. Okay, more than twice. Fine, it had happened more times than she had fingers, but that wasn't the point. The point was they shouldn't be having this discussion.

But apparently, telepathic agreements weren't worth the paper they weren't written on, because he'd rebutted her claims as if he'd been quietly biding his time, waiting for just this moment to arise.

And now it was out there, sitting between them like a piece of luggage left in the middle of a hallway that could hardly contain its bulk. For years, it had sat there unencumbered yet an impediment. They had been the ones encumbered, ever careful not to disturb it as they'd sidled by, bodies pressed tightly against the wall to avoid contact.

It was clear Nate had made the decision he wasn't sidling anymore. The luggage had to go.

The hell it does. That luggage was her shield, fortified and strengthened by the time passed.

He continued to toy with her, asking, "Say what? The truth?"

"I'm saying, why would you even bring that up?"

Seriously, the gall of the man. He had come to *her* asking for her services, and this was the way he behaved? Sitting there, legs spread like he owned the place as he needled her about a past she tried hard to forget. Some days she managed it better than others.

"Did you or did you not give your virginity to me?" He posed the question as if it were a frequent topic of everyday conversation, which of course it was not. Not by a long shot. Especially when they'd only ever talked about it once after the fact.

The memory of their first time together swamped her, his words ringing in her mind with the clarity of Dolby Digital Plus. *If I didn't know better, I'd think this was your first time,* he'd half groaned once he was hilt-deep inside her.

Kennedy slammed her eyes shut, a brief respite from having to look at his face. His ridiculously gorgeous face. She willed herself not to think about it.

That he was purposely taking her on a trip down memory lane only made her angrier. Slitting her gaze to *skewer him like a shish kebab* range, she pressed her lips together, refusing to rise to the bait because that was exactly what he wanted.

"Not admitting to it won't change what happened."

Kennedy literally had to sit on her hands to stop herself from reaching across her desk and wringing the obnoxiousness out of him. "What does one thing have to do with the other?" she asked snippily.

"What does you professing not to know me have to do with me being your first, is that what you're asking?" Chuckling softly, Nate shook his head. "You can't even say it."

Cheeks on fire, Kennedy was a hairbreadth away from attempting to bodily remove him from her office. However, since he outweighed her by a good seventy pounds, he wouldn't exactly be in danger of being manhandled. A good tongue-lashing, however, she could deliver.

There will be no tongue anything.

Again with this? For the love of God, would you please get your mind out of the gutter?

"I'm saying *whoopee*, we had sex, so what?"

His gaze sharpened on her. "You gave *me* your virginity."

"And? The last I checked, that still counts as sex."

"Are you saying it meant nothing?"

Kennedy lifted her shoulder in a negligent shrug, purposely evading the question. "I had to give it to someone eventually."

An ominous stillness settled over her first-ever lover. "Yes, because I suppose at the age of nineteen you would have given your virginity to anyone who looked at you twice." Despite the already hot eighty-two degrees outside, an early winter frost lurked in the depths of his blue eyes.

"First of all, I was eighteen, and it wasn't as if we were in a relationship. What we had was a—was a—a series of—of one-night stands." Okay, she'd blown that big-time. It was impossible to achieve convincing nonchalance without a smooth delivery.

But so what if she hadn't lost her virginity earlier? Eighteen wasn't exactly ancient. And she could honestly say that in high school, she hadn't been ready, much to the frustration of two boyfriends who'd tried their best to cajole her into giving it up to them. Steadfast and true to her convictions, she'd been convinced she'd know when the time was right.

Then Nate materialized like a manna from the virginity gods, and she had known. Her body had definitely known. He'd hit every one of her buttons, and a few she hadn't known existed. From their very first meeting, her attraction to him had skirted the edges of idolatry. It had also scared the shit out of her because she'd never felt that way before about anyone.

How he'd felt about her…? To this day she still didn't know exactly. Had she been a notch on his bedpost? A *Pretty Little Thing*? A novelty? It was over before she was able to squirrel it out of him.

"A series of one-night stands over the course of four weeks?" A skeptical raised brow accompanied his question.

Kennedy bit back a growl of frustration. "Oh, for goodness' sake, what I'm trying to say is that just because you took—that you were my—that we—that we had sex, it doesn't mean that I *know* you or that you know me."

"I know *you* well enough to call you on your bullshit, which is exactly what's coming out of your mouth right now," he stated baldly.

"Is this how you are with all the women you've *ever* slept with? It's been over ten years."

Eleven years and five months, but really, who's counting?

Certainly not you, Miss "After All These Years, Nate Vaughn Is STILL the Best Sex I Ever Had" Mitchell.

Oh hush, you. Drawing comparisons helps no one.

Nate scowled. "Don't. Don't do that."

"Don't do what?"

"Don't talk as if what happened between us meant nothing."

Kennedy stared at him, unable or perhaps unwilling to believe what she was hearing. Tiptoeing up to the invisible line she'd drawn and had done her best not to cross, she asked, "Are you saying it meant something to you?"

He smoothly sidestepped her question with one of his own. "Are you saying it didn't mean *anything* to you? It was just sex?"

Nope. Not going there. That is a field littered with emotional land mines.

"Can we not talk about this now?" Or ever. "I mean, why did you even bring it up? It happened eons ago. We've both moved on."

Ancient history. She'd be celebrating her thirtieth birthday at the end of the year, and at a doddering thirty-four, wasn't it about time he started losing his hair? But looking at his mussed dark blond locks, she reluctantly concluded that his hairline wasn't going anywhere anytime soon, if at all. His father still had a full head of hair, and he was in his sixties.

Nate blew out an exasperated breath. "Jesus Christ, Kennedy, why is everything with you a battle?"

"It's not. I just don't understand why you had to bring it up." As if she needed a reminder of just how far down the Nate hole she'd gone before having to violently pull herself back to reality. She wasn't Cinderella and he wasn't her prince. "Clearly, it's not something I want to talk about." Especially with *him*.

Although, it was something she'd never be able to forget.

A woman never forgot her first.

Nate's eyes narrowed as silence gained a foothold in the room. She dreaded what he would say next. Worried about how she'd respond. If today had taught her anything, it was that as much as she'd wanted to close that chapter in her life, her feelings for him weren't anything close to resolved.

"You're right and I'm sorry. I should never have asked for your help. This isn't your problem, it's mine, and it was selfish of me to ask you to break the rules for me."

Kennedy blinked. *Wait—what just happened?*

Shoving back his chair, he came abruptly to his feet.

"I—I—" She was too disoriented by his sudden change to form a coherent sentence.

He stayed her attempted protest with a decisive shake of his head. "No, you don't have to say anything. I'm just going to get out of your hair so you can get back to work." He flashed her a wooden smile.

Kennedy stared at him, feeling utterly helpless. Despite her refusal, this wasn't how she wanted to leave things between them. And it wasn't that she didn't want to help him. She did. If only—

A perfunctory knock interrupted her thoughts. Before Kennedy could respond, her office door swung open, and Aurora, hair done up in a pretty French braid ponytail, and summery in a blue polka-dot blouse and slim ankle pants, breezed right on in.

"Good morning," she said, although her singsong salutation didn't match the warning glint in her eyes. "You can imagine my surprise when Jonathan informed me that my darling brother was *here* and not in Paris, where he was the last time I spoke to him—oh, let me see—" head tilted, she touched a contemplative finger to her chin "—the day before yesterday."

She fixed him with a pointed look, appearing every inch the aggrieved baby sister. Then her gaze turned faintly accusing when it swung in Kennedy's direction. "Then I find you two locked in here together."

Kennedy huffed at the gross exaggeration. "We weren't locked behind closed doors."

"Are you saying the door wasn't closed?" Aurora asked, gesturing at it.

"Yes, but not locked. Big difference."

"Is that the greeting I get?" Nate regarded his sister fondly, her arrival eliciting the first genuine smile Kennedy had yet to see on his face today.

Aurora would not be swayed—at least, not easily—crossing her arms over her chest. "What kind of greeting did you expect when you sneak into the country without a single word to me and then beat me to my office in the morning? Who does that?"

Grinning, Nate easily closed the distance between them and tugged her into his arms with a gruff, "Come here, brat. Give your brother a hug."

Aurora quickly abandoned the petulant-little-sister act and threw her arms around his neck, giggling as she returned his embrace. "Oh my god, it's so good to see you."

He planted a kiss on her cheek. "It's good to see you too."

The second he released her, she slapped him lightly on the arm and chided, "What are you doing home so early? I thought you said you needed a few more months before you moved back."

Kennedy blinked at her friend. Nate had planned to return to New York for good? Why hadn't Aurora said anything to her about it?

"Believe me, this wasn't part of the plan," Nate said, his expression clouding over.

Aurora stilled, her gaze volleying between Kennedy and her brother. "What? What's going on? Did something happen? You're not sick, are you?"

"Relax, Ror, your brother isn't sick," Kennedy assured her, before her friend's mind took her on a tour of the worst WebMD.com had to offer.

Aurora audibly exhaled, her shoulders slumping in relief.

"Yes, you'll be happy to know that I'm not dying. The company is just being sued for discrimination."

"So what are you going to do? Does Jack know about this?" Aurora gave her head a shake. "What am I saying? Of course Jack knows. What did he say?"

The discussion had moved from Kennedy's office to his sister's five minutes ago. Nate told her as much as he knew, and as expected, Rory ditched her sister cap and donned her crisis-management one.

His sister, The Fixer.

"He was shocked. Swears he never saw it coming. Called me yesterday as soon as Legal notified him." As exhausted as he was from over ten hours of travel, a sense of restlessness kept him on his feet, his shoulder propped against the wall by the door. He had to get back to his office and didn't intend to stay much longer.

With his request to Kennedy having been met with a re-sounding no, he regretted having asked in the first place. She'd been right to turn him down. Rules were rules. No taking on family as paying clients, and he sure as hell wouldn't ask her to take him on pro bono.

And no, he wouldn't have used it as a way to get close to her.

You sure about that? The question niggled at the back of his mind. No conclusive answer yet.

And that was probably because he couldn't deny his attraction to her hadn't gone anywhere and didn't appear to be going anywhere anytime soon. But he'd deal with it as he had in the past. Ignore it and hope it'd eventually go away.

She wasn't the only beautiful woman in New York.

But then, Kennedy was a lot more than her looks. A helluva lot more. He'd realized that the first time he'd really spoken to her. Although he'd been mesmerized by her gorgeous blue-gray eyes, her intellect and sweetness had been a huge turn-on. And the more he'd gotten to know her, the more he'd liked her. He'd liked that her sweetness came with an acerbic bite and that she'd been genuinely interested in him *and* the one thing he was most passionate about—his company.

Rory sat on the lip of her desk, her hands gripping the edge and shoulders squared. "All right, here's what I'm going to advise you to do. You need to hold a press conference. None of this statement shit, no matter what your PR team tells you. Statements aren't worth their weight in a sheet of copy paper," she said disdainfully. "No, what you need to do is hold a presser, invite the media, say what you have to say, and take a few questions. Reporters and the public will appreciate that more. They'll be more inclined to believe you when you tell them you're looking into the allegations, and you intend to get to the bottom of them. When you look them square in the eye and tell them you're going to fix it."

His sister was a pistol and a half. Yeah, she might look sweet and delicate—she especially had reporters eating out of her hands—but she was ruthlessly smart, incredibly astute, and unfailingly loyal to the people she cared about. He happened to be pretty high on that list. Some people would say at the top. Those people would be their parents and older brothers.

"I had a feeling that's what you were going to say." His sister preferred to face things head-on, no matter how difficult the circumstance, which was one of the things that made her so good at her job.

Hopping off the desk, she walked over to him. "That's a relief. Glad to know I won't have to browbeat you into it," she said with a smirk, but the worry in her eyes lingered.

"I hate talking to the press," he groused. More than anything, he hated this kind of attention. As it stood, he was currently the villain of the piece, when he was accustomed to being lauded. Success at a young age could do that, a success that had nothing to do with his parents' careers, even though it had been their seed money he'd used to start the company. Although, the Vaughn name probably opened a few doors that would otherwise have been closed to him.

His sister reached up and patted his hair-roughened cheek, reminding him he was overdue for a shave. "But they love this gorgeous face of yours," she teased.

Nate rolled his eyes.

"And you know what they say about necessary evils. This, my dear brother, is mandatory and lesson three in Crisis Management 101. On the bright side—"

"I'm glad you see a bright side to this," he muttered darkly.

"—I usually charge a pretty penny for this kind of advice, but I'm giving you the family discount. Free." She gave his cheek another affectionate tap before moving to take a seat in the chair behind her desk.

"What the hell are you smiling about?"

"Look again. What you're seeing is optimism. And I'm optimistic because I know you, and I know that not only are you and the company going to get through this with flying colors, you're both going to come out stronger on the other side. Trust me."

Aurora he trusted with his life. It was the lawyers on the other side he didn't trust. They were strictly in this for the payout. And then there were the tabloids. God all-fucking-mighty, they were going to make his life hell by digging up whatever they could about him and then they'd distort it and report it as fact.

"Oh, and could you do me a favor and be nice to Kennedy?"

Nate stiffened defensively before shouldering off the wall. "What the hell are you talking about? I'm always nice to her."

Nice was an understatement and almost laughable, given his sister knew about their past relationship. The brat had wheedled it out of him years ago.

Kennedy was the one who always got prickly with him. The only time he ever saw a real smile on her face was when she was bestowing it on someone else. He received the ones that never quite made it past her lips.

"Oh, don't get all offended. I simply mean she's going through a rough patch right now, so just…just, you know, be extra nice."

"Difficult time? Why? What happened?" he asked, his voice level and interest high.

Sighing, Aurora touched a hand to her ponytail and lowered her voice to a whisper. "You have to promise not to say a word to her…but do you remember me telling you about her boyfriend a few months ago? The one I said she'd been dating for two years and who was head over heels in love with her?"

How could he forget? A week after that conversation, he made up his mind that it was time to return home to New York for good. His team in France were more than capable of managing the business in Europe. They didn't need him there anymore.

"What about him?" he asked, bracing himself. The guy better not have hurt her.

"They broke up last month."

Nate released the breath he'd been holding. "And?"

His sister sent him a disapproving look. "You're terrible."

"No, seriously, why is she going through a rough patch? Is he the one who broke up with her?" It was hard to imagine that being the case, but why else would his sister want him to be *extra* nice to her? Was Kennedy nursing a broken heart? God, he hoped not.

"No, it's the exact opposite. He asked her to marry him and she said no, so that was that," she concluded with a sigh and a shrug.

Nate wasn't about to examine why learning she was single felt like a huge weight off his shoulders when the five-thousand-pound class-action lawsuit still remained.

No need for a whole lot of self-examination, bud. You want her back in your bed.

That was his dick talking, and he never allowed it to rule his head. Not the one on his shoulders.

"What did you think of the guy?" curiosity drove him to ask.

"Aidan? Oh, I think he's great. But to be honest, I never saw them making it in the long run. He always struck me as someone who wants a traditional wife. The kind that would stop working the second kids came along, and that's not Kennie at all."

Nope, Kennedy wanted it all. The career and the family. She'd told him so all those years ago. When they'd both felt free to talk about their dreams and plans for the future. She'd been about to start her freshman year at Columbia, and Constellation had already made him a millionaire several times over.

"I'm sure she won't be alone for long. There's probably already a line of single guys banging on her door." Some of the married ones too.

Aurora's eyebrows flattened. "They just broke up, for heaven's sake. She needs time to grieve. The end of a relationship can be like a death, you know."

"I hate to break it to you, Rory, but the only thing *like* death *is* death. It has no equivalent."

His sister rolled her eyes and muttered, "Okay, fine, whatever. Anyway, like I was saying, be extra nice to her. When she's around, try cracking a smile or two and then just *maybe* she'll agree to join us on the rare occasion I want to hang out with you."

"Very funny." He was her favorite brother. She loved hanging out with him more than she cared to admit. "And quit trying to paint me as the bad guy. I've always been perfectly nice to Kennedy." There'd been that time when he'd made her come with his tongue. He was pretty sure she'd thought he was being nice then. "The last time I offered to drive her home, she was the one who turned me down."

"Yeah, but you were kinda crabby about it. Honestly, sometimes I can't decide if you still have a thing for her, or if, for reasons I can't fathom, you truly don't like her anymore." The last part had her narrowing her eyes at him, her look downright accusatory.

"I don't have a *thing* for her," Nate said, scowling, annoyed at his sister for calling him out. "And I've got no problem with her."

Yeah, that sounded convincing. "I like her," he quickly amended.

"Then try acting like it."

Nate bit back a laugh. "Okay, from now on, I'll be the picture of sunshine whenever she's around. That work for you?" He'd have to find a middle ground between sexually disinterested and wanting to take her on the nearest surface, be it a floor, a bed, a counter, or up against a wall.

"Just don't be fake about it."

Exasperated, Nate threw up his hands, the motion flutter-

ing a small stack of papers on her desk. "First the press conference and now this. Can you cut me some slack? I'm here
to put out fires and keep my company out of court and off
the Justice Department's radar. A bit of understanding would
be appreciated."

"Oh, come on. You know you have nothing to fear from
the DOJ," Aurora scoffed. "And this lawsuit will never make
it to court. If your legal team doesn't make that clear to you,
then you need to hire another one. The biggest thing at stake
is the reputation of your company, and I, for one, will not
allow it to be tarnished by this. At least, not for long."

"Good. That makes two of us," he said with a soft grunt
of agreement.

7

Kennedy waited five minutes after Nate left—without even an au revoir, adios, or sayonara to her, not that she'd expected one—before making a beeline to her best friend's office.

Aurora stopped typing on the computer when Kennedy sat down in the chair opposite and crossed her legs with an air of studied nonchalance.

She regarded her friend expectantly. "So what's the verdict? On a scale of one to ten, how bad is it?"

Aurora made a face as she leaned forward and set her elbows on the desk. "Six. He's holding a press conference tomorrow, so hopefully that will take things down to a five."

Kennedy understood the look. There were about five thousand things Nate enjoyed more than talking to the press, like acid baths and circus clowns—Pennywise really left a mark on him.

"And of course, you're going to be there, am I right?" It was a rhetorical question. There was no way Aurora wasn't going.

Propping her chin on her interlaced fingers, her friend released a wispy sigh. "He's going to need all the support he can get. You know how they can be. You should see what they're saying on social media. They're calling Constellation a falling star." She shivered dramatically. "Those people are brutal. Won't even wait to hear what the other side has to say."

Social media also had a way of bringing out the cutting creativity in people, as "Reaching for the Stars" was Constellation's tagline.

A frisson of guilt shot through her. She could help. A friend *would* help.

"That's social media for you. Kicking a man when he's down is what it does best. But I wouldn't worry too much if I were you. You know Nate—he's a fighter. And remember, he has all those diversity programs he started and is involved with working in his favor. He's going to be fine." Better than fine. Knowing him, he'd come out of this being touted as the way CEOs should handle discrimination issues like this.

"What does your day look like tomorrow? Do you have a hole in your schedule between one and three?"

Kennedy feared she looked like a cornered mouse, a cat within pouncing distance.

Aurora read her expression correctly and took out her rarely utilized friend card. "I told you, he's going to need all the support he can get, and you're his friend, right?"

The fraught question was impossible to answer truthfully without opening a can of worms.

"All right, fine, then," Aurora continued, giving her only a beat to respond. "You're my best friend and he's my brother and you love me to pieces."

"Look, I can't promise you anything, but I'll have to check my schedule." Kennedy could have easily made up an appointment and said she was busy. So why hadn't she?

Because it's Nate. Your first.

Maybe if his sister wasn't her best friend and she hadn't had to interact with him over the years following their—for want of a better word—fling, she wouldn't still have a soft spot for him.

Aurora smiled. "You're the best. I'm going to need to re-schedule a couple appointments myself."

"I'll be there if I can," Kennedy promised.

If she ended up going, she wouldn't stay long. She'd be a support beam that faded into the background.

"In other news, what's going on with Adam Faulkner? Jon-athan mentioned he called the agency yesterday. I hope for his sake he doesn't need your services again."

Adam Faulkner was the lieutenant governor of New York and Aurora had worked with him at her old crisis-management firm when he'd been accused of accepting gifts from a wealthy donor in exchange for political favors. The corruption case against him had been dropped—the indictment had been shoddy, rushed, and politically motivated—when it came to light that the wealthy donor was Faulkner's daughter's godfather, and the gift—a car—had been purchased for said daughter.

As for the political favor? It had been a zoning permit, which was revealed to have been granted to Mr. Leeds two years before the lieutenant governor was elected. Someone had transposed a date and a clerk had been fired to cover for the mistake missed by everyone and their mother.

Fully vindicated, the embattled lieutenant governor had gone on to seek another term, handily winning it in a land-slide, because who didn't love a righteous comeback story?

"Oh, it's nothing like that," Aurora said with a negligent wave. "He called to ask if I could get my hands on a backstage pass to Sahara's charity concert in September for his daughter. Brittany's a huge fan. Like, *really* huge."

As Kennedy had predicted, her best friend and the singer got on like a house on fire right from the start, and the three had developed a strong bond, making a point to get together whenever Sahara was in town.

"What could've possibly given him the idea that you have that kind of clout?" Kennedy asked coyly.

Aurora's eyes danced mischievously. "I *may* have mentioned that I have her personal cell number on speed dial and that whenever she's in town, we all do lunch."

Kennedy gave an amused snort. Her parents were Hollywood royalty, yet it was Sahara's name she'd dropped. "Mentioned, huh? Don't you mean bragged?"

"What?" Aurora exclaimed, laughing. "I had to prove my bona fides after he told me he had the biggest Sahara fan living under his roof."

Ah, yes, his nineteen-year-old daughter. Now it made sense. Her friend usually wasn't one to drop names all willy-nilly.

"Brittany is a Desert Stormer. She's got the jacket, the sweatshirt, the baseball cap—the whole works," Aurora said, gesturing widely with her hands.

Whether Sahara liked it or not, she was more than a celebrity to girls and young women like Brittany Faulkner—she was the ultimate role model. Personally, she didn't know how Sahara dealt with the weighty responsibility that came with it.

"When was this?" His corruption scandal had been four years ago, years before Kennedy had met Sahara.

"I ran into him a few months ago at a fundraiser my mother dragged me to."

Kennedy nodded. She remembered the weekend Aurora's parents flew in from LA. The Vaughns loved a good cause and these days had thrown their considerable celebrity heft behind saving the planet, women's rights, and closing the wealth gap.

"Has he said anything about whether he plans to run for

governor?" The election was still two years away, but many of the potential opponents had already started jockeying for position in what looked to be a crowded primary. It was widely believed that the party nomination was his if he chose to run.

"Not to me he hasn't," Aurora replied.

"Well, the next time you talk to him, tell him to keep his nose clean. He can't afford another scandal, even one that isn't his fault."

Aurora let out a short, dry laugh. "Believe me, he knows."

"Damn, the press is down there in full force. I've never seen the lobby that packed," Jack Walters, the company's CTO, announced upon entering Nate's office.

Friends since high school, he and Jack had attended Columbia together, both Computer and Information Science majors. He'd been working for another tech company when Nate started Constellation and had offered his talents before Nate had a chance to ask him to join the small team it had been at the time.

"What did you expect? They're here for the show." Nate finished the rest of his lukewarm coffee and set the empty mug on his desk. It was his fourth for the day and the only thing keeping him awake.

Between the lawsuit, meetings with the legal team and senior management, and almost no sleep in the past forty-eight hours combined with a wicked case of jet lag, he was wiped out. One-thirty in the morning was when he'd stumbled into his apartment drunk with sleep deprivation. He might as well have slept at the office. At least he'd have been able to catch a couple more z's and been saved the morning commute. But then he wouldn't have been able to change clothes, and it had been nice to sleep in his own bed and shower in his own bathroom. He hadn't realized how much he missed it until he was back.

Kennedy probably has something to do with that.

He swiftly pushed the thought aside. No matter what he felt about her, Kennedy had made her feelings for him very clear. She wasn't interested in starting anything up with him again.

Jack stopped in front of his desk. "You want me to do this? I don't mind dealing with the press. I've been told I have a nice speaking voice and I won't need a microphone."

"By who, your mother?" Nate quipped, eliciting an amused smile from his friend. Mrs. Holly Walters made helicopter parents look like '70s-style hippies.

Nate glanced down at the printed statement he'd spent an hour writing up last night and now knew by heart. "Nah, I have it covered. Anyway, Aurora said it'll go over better coming from me."

"She's probably right," Jack conceded as he rocked back on his heels, hands shoved in his pant pockets.

"As I have you here, has anyone in HR been able to find Alberta Simpson's last performance review?" This was the stuff that made him lose his shit. How was it that no one could find the performance review of the person at the forefront of the lawsuit? Not only did the company keep printed copies of them, they were also digitized. The damn thing had to be sitting on one of the servers.

"Not yet, but I'm sure it'll come up. Bonnie probably filed it in the wrong place. But don't worry. I'm having IT search the backup servers." Jack sounded irritatingly unperturbed.

"You're sure she was given a paper copy?" In the lawsuit, Alberta claimed otherwise.

"Bonnie swears Alberta received one once she signed off on it. Said it was sent to her via internal mail. If Alberta didn't receive it, why didn't she say something at the time? Annual reviews were over six months ago."

Fair question, Nate silently acknowledged, but it didn't explain why the company couldn't find their copy of the damn thing.

"She probably misplaced it."

Nate slanted him a look. "I don't know. It might look like we're hiding something."

Jack let out a short laugh. "Hide what?" Pulling his hands from his pockets, he raised them in surrender. *Check me, I'm clean.* "We've got nothing to hide."

Nate couldn't afford to have his CTO's confidence, not when there was so much at stake: the company's reputation, employee morale. Not being able to attract top-notch talent would affect the company's ability to grow.

"Didn't you read the lawsuit in full? In that *missing* review, she claims Flynn promised her the position that went to Brent."

Duncan Flynn, the director of Project Management, couldn't have picked a worse time to get married. Sun, warm weather, clear blue skies, and sandy beaches… What sane man would opt for that when he could be in Manhattan, where the humidity was 500 percent? Currently, the lucky bastard was in Greece on his honeymoon and wouldn't be returning to work for another two weeks. Jack had left a message at the emergency number Flynn had provided but had yet to hear back. Undoubtedly for a good reason. He was busy screwing his new wife.

"As far as I'm aware, Duncan always had Brent in mind for the position when it opened up. It makes no sense he'd promise it to Alberta."

"Fine, but we've got to get our hands on the damn performance review. I don't care what it takes—I want it for the next meeting Legal has with their lawyers." His current and former employees were being represented by Goldberg & Johnson. If this had happened four years ago, the law firm would more likely be defending Constellation.

Funny how things change with time.

Not that he'd have wanted them representing the company. He wasn't out to crush his workers. No, his goal was to do whatever he had to do to make things right, and if that meant signing his name on a big fat check, so be it. They had more than enough money. What was most important were the results of the investigation. Did the allegations have merit, and could they be validated? If so, he wanted the problem fixed, and he'd do whatever it took to get it done. Constellation wasn't the most diverse tech company in the industry by accident. He and his team had put the process in place to make it happen. But if there was something wrong in the gears, he wanted it fixed.

Jack nodded. "Aye, aye, boss. I'll see what I can do." Before leaving, he paused at the door. "You're absolutely *sure* you don't want me to do this presser?" He quirked a brow. "Or I could stand up there behind you, you know, for moral support?"

"Nah. It'll look better if I'm standing there alone. Just me taking responsibility and willing to field questions from reporters."

"All right, then, I'll just stand in the back. See you in a few. And good luck."

After Jack's departure, Nate stared at the empty doorway.

Good luck.

He looked at his statement and prayed much wouldn't be needed.

The founders of tech giants had become a common source of news over the years; their hobbies, their passions, their philanthropy, their politics. But toss in the controversy of a law-suit alleging racial and gender discrimination and the media would break down the door with a battering ram for a story, although—to be fair—they much preferred to be invited in. Which was why Kennedy wasn't surprised by the size of the crowd gathered in the lobby of Constellation's headquarters, a portion of which had been roped off for the occasion.

An impressive bit of architecture here, with lots of glass, light wood, and geometric elements throughout. The ceiling loomed three or four stories above and contained bright recessed lighting.

A glance at her watch had her quickening her pace. The press conference should be starting soon. On her way to her destination—preferably a spot in the back—she caught a glimpse of Aurora. She was sitting in the front row, chatting with the woman next to her, her hands gesturing as if she had more than a drop of Italian blood in her. On any other day, Kennedy would have joined her, but today she aimed to be as unobtrusive as possible…which must be the reason that this morning, of all days, she'd gone to her closet and pulled out a sleeveless multicolored "look at me" floral wrap dress to wear to work. Plus, every seat in the place was taken and the *standing room only* area was already three rows deep.

She found a spot near the floor-to-ceiling windows behind a cluster of women. Thankfully, they were all shorter than her, meaning she'd have an unobstructed view of Nate when he finally took his place behind the podium set up at the front.

"Are you a member of the press?"

Kennedy gave a slight start, her head swiveling to take in the man who now occupied the spot next to her. He looked to be in his mid to late thirties and had dark hair, a prominent nose, squinty Clint Eastwood eyes, and a wiry build. In her heels, they stood around the same height, putting him just shy of six feet. Judging by his attire—blue slacks, a white shirt, and a matching blazer—she pegged him as an employee. The male reporters wore ties.

"No, I'm not."

"And you're not an employee, because I would have remembered you," he replied, but not in a way that gave her the impression he was coming on to her. Just a simple statement of fact.

"But clearly you are," Kennedy said, making sure to keep an eye on what was going on up front.

His mouth quirked. "That I am. Jack Walters, chief technology officer." His chin dipped in an informal nod of greeting. "And you are?"

"Kennedy Mitchell." If she were keeping to the example he set, she would have tagged on *small-business owner.*

"So, Kennedy Mitchell, what brings you to my neck of the woods if you're not here to give my boss a hard time?"

At that, she smiled to herself. Give Nate a hard time indeed. After vacillating all morning, she'd caved. She'd made the decision to come by, telling herself she'd be a familiar and friendly face in the midst of a sometimes aggressive and unforgiving press.

"I'm a friend of the family."

Jack Walters did a double take, his light brown eyes taking a tour of her body before stopping at her face. "Ah, yes, that Kennedy. Aurora's friend."

"Do you know Aurora?"

"Since she was a kid. Nate and I went to high school and college together."

Kennedy's eyes widened a fraction. So he wasn't just Nate's CTO but also his friend. And a good friend, by the sound of it. Funny, Aurora had never mentioned Jack to her. But then again, why should she? They'd had little reason to talk about Nate most of the time, much less his friends—even the ones who worked for him. It wasn't as if their professional and social lives had intersected over the years. Today was a first and she and Aurora weren't doing it in an official capacity.

"And now you're working together. That must be nice."

Jack chuckled and shot a glance at the podium before replying, "I don't sign his checks—he signs mine. But I try not to hold that against him."

Kennedy didn't know what to make of his remark. There was something there she couldn't quite put her finger on. Jealousy? Envy? Or a man simply ragging on a close friend? Sometimes—not often—she read too much into things where additional scrutiny wasn't warranted.

"Aurora assures me he's a wonderful boss, but she could be biased," she quipped.

Jack snorted a laugh. "You can't believe a word she says. In her eyes, he can do no wrong. Speak of the devil…" His gaze drifted from hers as his voice trailed off.

The din of the crowd increased to a swell as the man in question entered her line of vision to take his place behind the podium on the makeshift stage.

Kennedy's stomach dipped at the first sight of him looking every inch the handsome and successful CEO in a slate blue suit, the shirt unbuttoned at his throat. Nate hated ties.

He gave the crowd of reporters a cursory look as he adjusted the microphone.

"Good afternoon, everyone. My name is Nathaniel Vaughn, and I'm the founder and CEO of Constellation. I'd like to thank you all for coming. And I'm not going to take up too much of your time this afternoon," he began. "As you're all aware, Constellation is currently facing a lawsuit accusing the company of racial and gender discrimination. I would like you

and everyone to know that I take these allegations very seriously and will do everything in my power to rectify the matter for all parties involved. The diversity of the staff is one of
our greatest strengths and one of my biggest sources of pride. I
value each and every one of our employees and am committed
to making sure the path to advancement is open to everyone
equally. Glass ceilings will not be tolerated at Constellation.
That is all I have to say for now, and I'm willing to take a few
questions before I go."

Hands immediately went up, as questions were pelted at
him like tennis balls from an automatic launcher.

"Do you intend to fight the case, or would you like to settle?"

"Mr. Vaughn, do you have something against Black women?"
A man shouted the question.

Kennedy's mouth tightened and her eyes narrowed. She
recognized the reporter. He worked for one of the national
twenty-four-hour cable news stations. Not once had she ever
seen him ask a question and not be a dick about it. She called
him a provocateur because that was his sole role. Got to get
the sound bite that fueled the clicks.

"Would you say the allegations in the lawsuit constitute a
hostile work environment?" asked the woman sitting next to
Aurora.

Nate directed his attention to her, replying smoothly, "I
believe the allegations would make for an unhappy employee
and I intend to do whatever I can to change that, if at all
possible."

"Mr. Vaughn, is it true that there were allegations of both
racial and sexual harassment on the set of *Calamity John*?"

Kennedy would tell herself later that she only responded
because the reporter, who *had taken God out of her thoughts* (as
her mother would say), to pose such an outrageous question,

was standing feet from her. She was currently staring a hole in the back of her blond head.

"What on earth does what happened on his father's set twenty years ago have to do with Mr. Vaughn? If you have no relevant questions to ask, I suggest you allow the reporters who do to ask theirs." Kennedy was a combination of annoyed and infuriated and it was evident in her voice. Her loud voice.

8

Silence landed with a thud and then blanketed the entire area for long enough for its impact to be felt and heard.

The blonde turned and glared at her. It seemed everyone in attendance followed her lead, except the predominant expression on their faces was one of shock and then unabashed amusement.

Jack let out a laugh-covering cough. Seriously, she didn't know why he bothered. Miss Piggy attempting to hide behind a blade of glass was less obvious.

Ignoring the woman she'd just publicly rebuked, Kennedy returned her attention to Nate, who was staring at her as if realizing her presence for the first time. She offered him a rueful smile. *Ooops, sorry.*

But the offended reporter wasn't about to allow Kennedy's remarks to go uncontested. "Excuse me? Who do you think you are?"

"I'm someone who knows an irrelevant question when I hear one," she replied calmly.

Jack leaned over and whispered, "We need to hire you."

Nate cleared his throat in an obvious effort to direct attention back to him. It mostly worked. "Miss Mitchell is right. What happened on my father's set has nothing to do with this lawsuit. Next question?" He pointed at a female reporter seated in the back.

The reporter opened with, "I have two questions. First, since it appears your company's biggest issue is with Black women, how do you propose to address it? Second, do you believe that because senior management within the company is predominantly white and male, their lack of personal exposure to women of color negatively influences their judgment when dealing with them in a professional capacity?"

The latter was a doozy of a question. Kennedy could only imagine how much Nate hated the situation he was in.

"The company has hired an external law firm to investigate the allegations. That's the first step. We're also urging both current and former employees from historically underrepresented groups to come forward with relevant information or complaints. In the meantime, the company has implemented new diversity and inclusivity training for the senior management team and all hiring managers."

Kennedy's eyebrows rose at that. She wondered if he wouldn't mind letting her have a look at it. Not all classes were the same. And she had some ideas if he needed to have their résumé selection process redone.

Stay out of it, a voice in her head warned.

"Next question," Nate said, pointing to another reporter.

But the reporter who'd posed the two questions refused to let him move on without answering the other one. "Mr. Vaughn, do you believe that lack of personal exposure to women of color has created a discriminatory environment within your company?"

Nate wasn't close enough, but she knew him well enough to know his jaw was ticking. He had that stony, taut-jawed look on his face.

"Until the investigation is complete, I'm going to refute your assumption that the environment in the company is discriminatory. As for the *personal* lives of the senior management staff, I'm not going to presume to know the diversity of their personal relationships." He then directed his attention to the reporter he'd called on prior.

"Following up with Miss Garcia's question—"

The reporters sure picked a fine time to tag team. Where was this sense of camaraderie when the world was on fire and answers were needed to more important questions?

"—do you believe that the diversity of *your* own personal relationships have a bearing on what's happened to the company? You've surrounded yourself with men who look like you. Does that indicate something about you and the example you've set?"

Even Kennedy winced at that. No matter how bad they were making it look, they were wrong.

Jack leaned over again and muttered under his breath, "I'm surprised you have nothing to say about that."

She did. And once again, loud enough that she didn't need the amplification of a microphone. "The operative word here is *personal,* and I don't think anyone here is entitled to know the details of Mr. Vaughn's or any of his managers' personal lives unless there's proof of criminality or that it breaks the employment laws of the state."

Good lord, now she sounded like a lawyer. Or an avid watcher of *Law & Order*—all one hundred seasons. She was the one who wasn't required to attend law school or pass the New York State Bar.

Pressing his fist to his mouth, Jack muffled a laugh.

This time when the attendees turned to regard her, they appeared more speculative than amused.

"What are you, his spokesperson or something?" a male reporter called from across the room.

Kennedy glanced at Nate, who looked decidedly uncomfortable and had her wondering at the overall soundness of the intelligence she professed to have.

"Miss Mitchell is a friend," Nate announced evenly. Nothing but the facts.

A derisive snort was followed by, "An African American female friend. Very convenient."

It was the jackass provocateur at it again.

"What kind of friend?" a woman snarked.

It took only one or two to turn the whole thing into a spectacle and there were at least that many in the crowd. But she couldn't blame it all on them. If she'd kept her big mouth shut, none of this would be happening.

"Is she a reporter? Why is she here?" someone behind her asked.

Kennedy didn't bother to turn and see who was demanding Nate justify her presence.

"I believe it's still a free country, or was I in France too long?" Nate remarked dryly.

Her cell phone began vibrating. Kennedy instinctively glanced down at her handbag, placing her hand over the tan leather as if that would stop it.

She lifted her gaze to find the blonde she'd previously rebuked glaring at her and then speaking to the woman beside her in a faux whisper meant for others to hear. "I don't believe it. I think she's a plant."

Kennedy refused to dignify her accusation with a response. But what was becoming tragically clear was that she and her well-meaning self had made things worse for Nate.

The irony? It didn't escape her.

As if seeing the writing scrawled on the wall where some-one had hastily written *Kennedy fucked up*, Nate called the press conference to a blessed close. "That'll be all for now. I want to thank everyone for coming, and I will personally keep the public apprised of the results of the investigation."

Kennedy released a long breath. It was over, and not a min-ute too soon. Now she needed to haul her butt to the phar-macist and get something for the foot-in-mouth disease she'd obviously contracted.

She turned to the man who had encouraged—no, goaded—her to defend Nate, only to find the spot beside her empty, Jack nowhere in sight. When he'd slipped away, she didn't have a clue.

The sound of chairs scraping on the shiny tiled floors com-bined with the buzz of conversation as the attendees prepared to leave. Not an insignificant lot of them kept looking her way. And she knew what they were thinking.

She smiled when she saw Aurora hastening toward her.

"Wow. Can I just say wow," she said breathlessly upon reach-ing Kennedy's side. "We'll have to talk about it later because I gotta run. See you back at the office." Then she was gone, as fast as her white Jimmy Choos could take her toward the exit.

"'Bye," Kennedy called out to her retreating back.

Suddenly she felt a hand grip her elbow, firmly. Startled, she turned to find a grim-faced Nate peering down at her.

"*You*—" his voice was clipped "—are coming with me."

That's what I get for taking questions for the sake of transparency. The presser hadn't gone as planned, and Nate had the slender arm of the cause of its derailment firmly in his grasp as he led her to the covered parking lot at the rear of the building. To his surprise, she offered no resistance. Instead, she was full of apologies.

"I know. I made a mess of things. I'm sorry. But honestly, some of those questions—" She concluded her statement with a frustrated growl.

"They're reporters. That's what they do. You're not supposed to take the bait." The automatic glass doors before them slid open. He immediately slowed his pace once it became clear that she could barely keep up with his long strides.

As if only just realizing where they were, she furrowed her brow and asked, "Where are we going?"

He released her arm and placed his hand on the small of her back, steering her to where his car was parked in the first row. "For a walk in the park," he answered wryly.

"Funny. But seriously, where are you taking me? I have an appointment uptown in an hour and a half."

"Don't worry. I'll make sure you get there on time. And in comfort. Where're you headed to?" He opened the passenger door for her.

She rambled off the address and made a move to get in the car, before pausing, glancing inside and then back up at him. "Are you at least going to feed me? I skipped lunch to make your press conference."

Nate's mouth hitched at the corner. "Anything you want. Now get in before people think you're being kidnapped." They probably already thought that. As soon as he'd stepped off the stage, he'd made a beeline to her, oblivious to how it might appear to onlookers. After he'd literally spirited her away, he could only imagine the number of eyebrows it would raise and the kind of coverage it might garner. None in his favor.

"Are you serious? They think we're partners in crime, not kidnapper and kidnappee," she said with a snort.

While she buckled in, he closed the door and made his way to the driver side and slid behind the wheel. He'd driven out of the parking lot before anyone spoke again.

"I meant what I said. I'm *really* sorry." She truly sounded contrite. "And you're right. I shouldn't have taken the bait. We live in a world of sound bites and clickbait headlines. I should have kept that in mind before I opened my mouth."

"For someone who didn't want to get involved, you sure picked the highest cliff on the Eastern Seaboard to take that dive." She'd ignored her own warning. She'd said this was what would happen, and it looked like she'd been right.

"I know, right? But in my own defense, their questions were *way* over the line."

Of course, she was right. He may have initially been irritated with her when it became clear that, by the end, a good number of those in attendance believed her appearance and fervent defense of him weren't exactly on the up-and-up. But it was impossible to stay mad at her for long. His irritation had lasted the length of the walk to his car. Her heart had been in the right place, even if her sense of situational awareness needed work. Add that to the list of things he admired about her, her unyielding sense of fair play.

"But you know what they think now, don't you?" He stopped the car at the stoplight.

Kennedy huffed, indignant. "Yeah, that the whole thing was staged and I'm your Black defender."

"Yes, that or that I'm fuc—sleeping with you." He wasn't able to course correct in time.

His remark elicited a narrow side-eye, a look he found sexy as fuck. She had incredible eyes. He used to stare deep into them when he was fucking her.

Memories. Good times.

"You do realize that not everything between a man and a woman boils down to sex."

"Not everything," he agreed, because not every woman was Kennedy. "But when it comes to women as beautiful as you, that's where a lot of minds go. Especially men." He shot her a quick look before he resumed driving.

At his compliment, she simultaneously rolled her eyes and blushed, a faint stain of red on the crests of her cheeks.

"Our situation is different, though, because it isn't as if someone happened to see us together out on the town one night. The press conference was planned, and the press was explicitly invited. For those reasons, they think we wanted them to know about our 'so-called' relationship. *Nudge, nudge, wink, wink.* And there's only one reason we'd do that. To give you cover for the lawsuit. You have to know that. Honestly, right now, you'd be better off if they truly believed we were *fucking*."

A bolt of lust hit him directly in the groin. The sound of that word on her lips really did it for him. Eyes on the road, he schooled his expression to hide the moment of tumult.

"Really? How so?"

"Because it's better we convince them we're lovers *or*, at a minimum, that our relationship is real, or they're going to think you're underhanded and sneaky and willing to do just about anything for favorable coverage. And if that's what they believe—" shaking her head, she gave a mirthless laugh "—they're going to do their best to make your life hell."

There wasn't one ounce of doubt in his mind that was precisely what they'd do. The snarky remarks at the presser were only a taste of things to come, unless they were able to nip this in the bud. It was a good thing he didn't have to warm to the idea. Pretending to be her lover would be like riding a bike. All they needed to do was to work out the kinks and get their story nice and cohesive.

"How can we expect them to believe we're in a relationship when I only just came back from France yesterday, where I've been living for the last three years? And what about you? I'm sure you're dating someone. Perhaps several someones," he mused aloud, his tone guileless.

Since Aurora had made him promise not to say anything to her about the proposal and her ex-boyfriend, he thought it best to play ignorant on the matter of her dating life.

Kennedy eyed him suspiciously, wondering if he knew about Aidan. "I'm not seeing anyone now. Are you?" Her breakup was fresh, yet it felt like it had happened a lifetime ago. Nate sweeping back into her life had upended its structured orderliness. Now she didn't know what to expect from one minute to another. And he hadn't even been back forty-eight hours.

"No."

Good.

She resented the sense of peace the single word brought her. "Okay, well, I think the most important thing we need to do is prove we had a relationship in the past. And to that end, I may still have some pictures of when—" she fluttered her fingers "—when we were, you know, involved."

Briefly tearing his eyes off the road, he shot her an arch look. "Involved?"

"Okay, fine, sleeping together." Why did he have to be so annoying?

Nate's shoulders shook with laughter. "I'm gonna be honest with you, but I don't remember a whole lot of sleeping going on. Why is it so hard for you to say it? We had sex. We fucked."

"Okay, fine, when we were fucking. Happy?" she asked snippily.

He smiled to himself. "I'll let you know when I'm happy."

Kennedy didn't even want to know what he meant by that. Prolonged proximity to him was playing havoc with her lady parts.

"So tell me about these pictures. You have some of us? Together?" He sounded more than a little intrigued at the prospect.

"I don't delete *anything*, and I think there's a couple of us out there in the cloud. I'll have to check." The compunction to explain why she kept pictures of him, and worse, of them together, made her sound defensive.

There were nine pictures exactly, and they resided on her phone and laptop. Unlike print photos, which gave people the satisfaction of ripping them into little pieces in a fit of rage or sobbing heartbreak, digital photos only required the click of a button to send them into digital purgatory where they weren't actually deleted. Not close to dramatic enough.

"When did you take pictures of us? You're going to have to show me."

"I don't know. I think it was that time we went to Coney Island." Those she'd had to scan because she'd bought physical prints taken by the Pennywise-looking clown photographer. Did he even remember that?

"You mean the one taken by that creepy-looking clown of me, you, and Rory?"

She nodded. Of course, he remembered. Honestly, Stephen King had a lot to answer for.

"We hadn't slept together yet."

There was an implicit *so you had a thing for me then* in his statement. The guy had an ego on him.

"Right, but I don't have any of us in bed together, so…

the one with your arm around me at Coney Island is going to have to do," she said, the sarcasm dripping from her lips.

A smile tugged at the corner of his mouth. "Funny, funny, lady."

"Difficult, difficult, man," she retorted with equal mockery. "Anyhoo, I will take care of getting the picture to the press, and then hopefully by tomorrow or the day after, there won't be a doubt in anyone's mind that what went on at the press conference wasn't staged."

"Isn't what you're proposing against agency rules?" he asked innocently.

"You won't be a paying client, and as far as I'm concerned, this has nothing to do with the agency. This is personal. And it's the least I can do after what I did back there," she said, grimacing inwardly.

He glanced at her and then looked away, only to return his gaze to her a moment later. "Seriously, though, what do I owe you for this?"

"Your undying gratitude and your firstborn. However, I will settle for a Broadway season package and dinner at the best restaurant in the city. I'm a simple woman with simple needs," she declared airily.

Only after the words emerged sounding more provocative than flippant did she ask herself that age-old question, *What the fuck is wrong with you?*

The man sitting beside you is fire. Don't play with him.

His mouth quirked and he murmured, "Yes, I believe I have a vague recollection of some of those needs."

Nate, on the other hand, didn't hold back his punches. He just went in for the kill. No insinuation. No beating around the bush. Why should he when she'd all but lined up the pins for him so that all they required was a light tap to knock them down?

"Those aren't the needs I was talking about." Technically, that was the truth. The lie had been about her being a simple woman with simple needs. Simple she was not.

"Yes, it was. Don't lie."

Kennedy was smart enough to walk away from fights she couldn't win, this being one of them. "Honestly, Nate, you don't owe me anything."

Pausing at another stoplight, he turned, his gaze flicking from her eyes to her mouth, and then back to her eyes again. "So we're doing this." He paused a beat. "How does dinner this weekend sound?"

She huffed a laugh. "I'm not going to even consider dinner until you feed me the lunch you promised and get me to my meeting on time."

His smile didn't do a thing to put her at ease.

"Don't worry—I got you. Leave everything in my hands."

Nor did his words. Those she found more terrifying.

9

"All righty, missy, what is going on?"

Kennedy's head shot up as her best friend swept into her office.

"What the hell did I miss yesterday? It's clear I can't leave the two of you alone together," Aurora said, walking to her desk and thrusting her iPad in Kennedy's face.

Kennedy took it from her, her eyes immediately scouring the headlines.

OLD PHOTO SHOWS CONSTELLATION CEO ENJOYING THE BENEFITS OF HAVING THE RIGHT KIND OF FRIENDS.

Flicking a look at Aurora, Kennedy rolled her eyes. "Ha ha ha. Benefits with friends, get it? Honestly, these headline writers try to be too cute by half."

"Tell me about it," Aurora said, her tone equally wry.

Kennedy resumed reading.

Days after a class-action discrimination lawsuit was filed on behalf of current and former employees, and not even a day after its CEO, Nathaniel Vaughn, son of Hollywood powerhouse couple Kurt and Sylvia Vaughn, held a press conference to address the matter, an old picture has surfaced of him and beautiful Kennedy Mitchell in a clincher of an embrace. Her passionate defense of him at his press conference yesterday started intense speculation about the nature of their "so-called" friendship. Cynics concluded it wasn't a coincidence that he was being defended by Ms. Mitchell, who just happens to be African American, from a lawsuit accusing his company of racial discrimination. In this case, however, it appears the cynics were wrong. The picture proves their relationship— whatever the nature—goes back many years…

And so on and so on.

The picture of Nate with his arm around her was posted above the story. And it was hardly a *clincher of an embrace*. Anyone with eyes could see that. She couldn't even tell Aurora had been cropped out of the picture. All hail Photoshop. Cecelia was the expert, but over the years, Kennedy had gotten pretty good at it, if she said so herself.

Seriously, it was criminal how easy it was to plant stories in the papers. You just had to know the right people. In this instance, the right person had been Naomi Smith, a *Page Six* reporter she'd met through Sahara.

Kennedy beamed a smile at her friend. "Wow, that was fast. Naomi said she didn't think she'd be able to get the story out until tomorrow. Talk about service."

Signaling her impatience, Aurora tapped the tip of a pink polished nail on her watch face. "So are you going to clue me in or what?"

"Come on. Get that pouty look off your face. I was going to tell you today. This morning, in fact. Like as soon as you got in."

"Tell me what?"

"Nate and I have come to an arrangement. I'll be helping him with damage control. I mean, after what happened during the presser, it's the least I can do, right? I should have followed your lead and kept my mouth shut."

"Well, take it from this *unbiased* observer—" Aurora said, her tone flippant "—that reporter was a tool. I'd have said something myself if I hadn't been the one to advise him on the dos and don'ts."

"I have no idea what came over me. They were so obnoxious and I just kinda snapped. You know me—I'm usually pretty levelheaded. Anyway, what I realized *after the fact* was the only way for me to help repair the damage I caused—because you know nobody is going to believe the whole thing wasn't staged—was to prove we genuinely have a relationship that predates the lawsuit, with indisputable visual evidence. Voilà." Kennedy pointed at the picture.

They really did look cute together, both wearing sleeveless T-shirts and shorts, wide smiles on their faces. Pennywise had done a good job at capturing the moment.

"You're okay with people believing there's something going on between you two?" Her friend looked surprised.

"Sure. Why not?" Kennedy shrugged. "I'm not going out with Aidan anymore, and if it'll help, it's the least I can do."

Aurora smiled. "You're the best. I'll always be grateful our paths crossed that day at nationals."

"Okay now, don't go getting me all weepy," she said, handing the iPad back to her. "I would do this for any best friend of mine whose brother needed a Black female beard."

"A Black female beard?" Aurora snorted a laugh. "Is that your new name for it?"

"If the beard fits," Kennedy replied as she stroked her chin and then pantomimed tugging at an imaginary beard. Aurora giggled. "Oh, by the way, your brother is taking me out to dinner this weekend, so don't be surprised if there's something about that in the papers next week. Although, with everything else going on with our new client, I don't think our date is going to make news unless it's a *really* slow news day."

"Some best friendly advice when it comes to my brother—please be careful with him."

"Please be careful *with* him?" Kennedy repeated, utterly bemused. If Aurora had said *watch out for him*, she'd understand.

"You just got out of a relationship and…well, you know." Aurora ended with a shrug.

Kennedy was having a hard time understanding what she was getting at. "Hold on a sec—you think *I* might do something to *him*?" And not the other way around? Something like taking a meat tenderizer to her heart again?

Aurora gave her the *who do you think you're fooling?* look. "C'mon, Ken. You have to know by now that he has a thing for you. Has for a long time. Why do you think he's always been kind of standoffish with you?"

Mind blown, Kennedy sat there, eyes wide and mouth at risk of catching flies. "I don't understand," she croaked once her shock wore off. Where was this coming from? Had he told his sister about them?

"He used to ask me about you all the time. Pretended it was about our parents and that he wanted to make sure you weren't trying to use me to get to them." Aurora huffed a laugh. "It's a good thing he's good at what he does, because he can't act his way out of a paper bag."

"I—I'm sure you're wrong," Kennedy protested. Not the

part about him being attracted to her—maybe still was—but that she had the ability to hurt him. No way did she hold that much sway over him.

Aurora planted her hand on her hip, arm akimbo. "Believe me, I know my brother."

Kennedy's pulse pounded loudly in her ears. She swallowed hard before asking, "Why didn't you say anything about it before?"

"Because you were going out with Xavier at the time. And then remember I told you about the one and only time he went out with one of my friends? Jessie and I stopped speaking after they broke up. It completely destroyed our friendship, and I didn't want that to happen to us."

Of course she remembered. Which was why a year later when she and Nate got together, she hadn't said a word about it to Aurora.

"Well, I can guarantee you one thing—it isn't like that with Nate. We're cool and everything, but that's it," Kennedy assured her.

Lies. All lies.

"All right, if you say so." Aurora didn't appear entirely convinced. "Anyway, I've got to get going. I have a meeting in less than an hour. See you in a bit," she said before exiting with a breezy wave.

Moments later, Jonathan poked his head in as if he'd been waiting for her to leave. "Roger O'Brien is here. He's early, so do you want a few minutes to get your notes together, or are you ready to see him now?"

Roger O'Brien was the NHL player who'd been caught on tape uttering a racial slur. After the video surfaced, he lost two endorsement deals and his coach announced his one-month suspension. A loud and vocal minority didn't think that was good enough. That was when the assistant coach had contacted her. She'd been recommended to him by Phil Draper, one of the executives she'd worked with at ECO Apparel, who'd gone as far as to tell them she'd be able to quiet the throng demanding Mr. O'Brien be kicked out of the league.

Kennedy checked the time, then took a quick look around her office. She wouldn't call herself a neat freak, but she appreciated an organized space, which was how she strove to keep her workspace. Today it would make her neat-conscious mother proud. Tidy home, tidy mind and all that.

"Go ahead and send him in."

"Roger that," Jonathan deadpanned.

"*Very* funny."

He responded with a deep laugh. "Thought you'd enjoy that one."

After he left, Kennedy came to her feet and smoothed the flyaway curls around her face. Moments later, the starting left wing for the New York Scouts entered her office.

Good lord, he was big. Broad shoulders, big arms, thick thighs, and a jaw that resembled a bristled block of wood. He wasn't bad looking, if you liked blunt features, spiky blond hair, and a wide forehead.

"Good morning, Mr. O'Brien. It's nice to meet you."

They shook hands. His was only slightly damp, and she hoped that was the result of nerves.

"Likewise." There was a wariness in his brown eyes, conveying a level of uncertainty.

Kennedy added more teeth to her smile. "You don't need to be nervous. I've been told I'm fairly harmless."

Only then did he respond in kind, displaying a mouthful of pearly whites. Whether they were the originals, she couldn't tell. Most hockey players had to have their dentists on speed dial, an oral surgeon if things got really bad. It was the nature of the game featuring a piece of vulcanized rubber that could reach speeds up to one hundred miles per hour. She'd done her research before agreeing to take the young left winger on as a client and was now as well versed in hockey jargon as she would ever be.

Once they were both seated, Kennedy opened with, "Feel free to call me Kennedy."

He merely nodded, his unease still evident.

"Before we start, do you have any questions for me?"

"I just want you to know that I'm not a racist. You can ask any of my friends. I don't have a racist—"

"Okay, Roger, I'm going to stop you before you complete that statement." The phrase should be struck from the English language, if for no other reason than it was nonsensical. "I'm going to let you in on a little secret. Bones aren't racist and the only organ you need to worry about regarding that is your brain. Now, I know what you're thinking—that it's a saying and you didn't mean it literally?"

He gave a cautious nod as he watched her intently.

"Right, because what you're really trying to say is how much of a racist you're not, and I get that. But the truth is you're a white man born and raised in this country, which means at the very least, even if we could attribute racism to any of the 206 bones in your body, the probability is pretty high that at least one of them is a tiny bit racist. In any case, saying you don't have a racist bone in your body is always a nonstarter and something I like my clients to know from the get-go. Now, why don't you start again?"

A deep red climbed up his thick neck to his already flushed face. "I didn't call anyone the N-word. Not the way the media is portraying it. I'm not like that. My parents brought me up better than that. I'm not a racist. I don't care what color you are or your sexual orientation. If I don't like someone, it's usually because they're a fu—jerk."

"I agree. No one likes a fucking jerk."

That elicited both a laugh and a smile, bringing the tension in the room down a smidgen.

"Don't worry about the language. We're pretty informal around here, and I know how to curse in English, Spanish, and French."

"Nice," he said approvingly.

"Believe me, it comes in handy sometimes. Okay, I've spoken briefly to your coach and I listened to the audio. In your own words, I want you to tell me what happened and anything else you think I should know."

The damning audio in question was of Roger calling his friend the N-word but with what some considered the more acceptable "gga" ending, because that wasn't offensive. Cue mental eye roll. It was like some people never learned.

"Me and my buddy were playing *GTA* and talking shit the way we always do. When I called him the—you know—N-word, I didn't say it in a nasty way. It's just a name we call each other sometimes. I wasn't saying it to be racist. How could I—he's white."

That was his saving grace in the entire situation. Had he said it to a Black person, he wouldn't be sitting in front of her.

"But why that word when there's a host of other names you could choose from? My best friend is white, and I call her Ror or Rory because her name is Aurora. What's your friend's name?"

"Weston."

"Then why not West or Wes? Or maybe even *dickface*, if your aim is to be affectionately insulting?" Of course, she knew why, but her job was to get him to understand his own motivation.

"I'm sorry, but dickface? That's fucking lame," he huffed, because apparently *that* was insulting.

Seattle Public Library
Beacon Hill Branch
(206) 684-4711

03/09/23 05:13PM

Token /
0010106543498   Date Due: 03/30/23
acbk

The house of Eve /
0010106948440   Date Due: 03/30/23
acbk

TOTAL ITEMS: 2

Visit us on the Web at www.spl.org

"*Ah*, so you think calling Weston the N-word sounds cool?" He'd probably watched one too many rap videos.

A look of discomfort contorted his face. "I don't know. Maybe. I mean, that's what some of the Black guys I know call each other."

Kennedy wrinkled her nose in distaste. "I know. And I'm not a fan of that either." She really wanted to say *if they jumped off a cliff, would you?* but wisely refrained. There was a grave-yard of recalcitrant youth at the bottom of that cliff. No need to add to the ever-growing body count.

However, in the good-news category, he knew some Black guys. "All right, then. How many Black men do you know and how well do you know them?"

Two or more would be a godsend, but she'd settle for one.

He shifted in his seat and started drumming his fingers on the arm of the chair. "There're a few guys who hang out at a sports bar downtown. I usually see them there when I go out with my teammates."

Hmm. What initially sounded promising was beginning to look less so.

"Would you consider them acquaintances?"

"Not exactly," he hedged.

"Ever talk to them?" Kennedy picked up a pen and held it poised over her notepad as she continued to regard him.

"Maybe once or twice."

She bet the number was closer to a lonely one. "Could you pick them out in a lineup?" she asked dryly.

Dark brows furrowed in contemplation, he answered with the solemnity of a murder witness under oath. "I think I'd recognize them if I saw them."

He only *thought* he could pick them out of a lineup. The suspected murderer was walking for sure.

Kennedy carefully placed her pen on the lined pad. "So let

me get this straight. You don't know these men, you wouldn't consider them acquaintances, and you aren't one hundred percent sure you'd recognize them if you saw them again, but you're suggesting they influenced you enough for you to pick up their slang?"

With each incriminating point, the NHL left winger seemed to sink lower in the chair. Only four years separated them, yet his chastened expression made her feel much, much older.

"I think the word *know* is doing a lot of heavy lifting here, wouldn't you agree?"

He grimaced. "I guess I don't technically know them."

"Technically or otherwise, I'd say." Picking up the pen again, she absently jotted his name at the top of the page. "Do you have *any* Black friends?" Despite enormous skepticism, she had to make sure to cover all the bases.

Roger hesitated before reluctantly shaking his head.

She treated him to what she hoped was an encouraging smile. "Don't be embarrassed. There are no wrong answers. I'm simply trying to get a lay of the land. Get an idea of what I have to work with. Now, have you *ever* had a Black friend?"

Despite her assurances, he responded with more sheepish head shaking and red-tipped ears.

"How about *any* friends of color. Ever?" In his case, ever was twenty-five years. Maybe he'd had one in preschool she could leverage.

Sighing, he sent her a chagrined look. "There weren't many where I grew up, and in college, hockey was my life and there weren't any on my team. It isn't that much different in the national league either. Although, there's a Black guy with Tampa who seems pretty nice."

"Right. I understand." And she did, completely. What this meant, though, was she'd have to employ the *fake* Black friend card. And when that was employed, actions had to speak louder than words. Especially as the phrase *I have a Black friend* in all its varied iterations was henceforth stricken from his repertoire, as stated in the company handbook on page three in the *Show Don't Tell* section.

"Hold on a sec—I did know a couple. They were Black—I mean, African American. They lived five or six houses down from us when I was growing up. In the first year of high school, I used to mow their lawn. I wouldn't exactly call them friends and I haven't seen them in a while, but…that's something, right?"

Squee! An older Black couple whose lawn he used to mow. She'd hit the character-witness lottery. "That is more than something. They're the perfect place to start. Do you have any idea if they still live there?"

Nodding, Roger returned her smile. "I'm pretty sure they do. My mom would've told me if they'd moved. She keeps track of all that stuff. The neighbors call her their one-woman neighborhood watch."

"Perfect!" she exclaimed, relieved by how quickly things were coming together. "We're going to need to get in touch with them and hopefully get them to provide a statement on your behalf. Do you think they'd do that? I assume you were on friendly terms the last time you were in contact, correct?"

"Sure," he said with a shrug. "They were always nice to me. Mrs. Simmons sent homemade cookies when I was drafted."

She quickly jotted their name down under FRIENDS. "Next question—are you currently dating anyone?"

"Not anymore."

"Does your ex-girlfriend know all your friends?"

"Some, not all."

"Would any of your family and friends be surprised by the fact that you have a Black friend?"

"Maybe a little, but they also realize that living in the city and being on the road a lot means I'm always meeting all types of people." His tone became subdued and his eyes downcast. "You know what the fucked-up part of this whole thing is, though?"

"No, what?"

"My mom blames herself. She said if she'd made sure I had a wider circle of friends and exposed me to different cultures, this wouldn't have happened." He let out a bitter laugh. "The day before yesterday, she sent me a book called *White Fragility* and she's also trying to get everyone in her book club to read it."

Kennedy's heart squeezed. Poor woman. "Mothers, they do carry the world on their shoulders, don't they?"

"My dad told her it wasn't her fault I was a dumbass because it can't be inherited."

Kennedy couldn't help but laugh. "Fathers, they tell it like it is, while accepting only the credit for their children's successes and none of the blame for their failures."

A faint smile curved his lips. "Yeah, that sounds like my dad. He sure won't be going around bragging about me being a professional hockey player."

"Hey, all isn't lost. You're going to be back on the starting lineup this fall."

She couldn't say when exactly, as that wasn't up to her. Her job was to rehabilitate his reputation enough to tamp down calls for his job, and the key to that was keeping his name out of the news. The public had the memory of an amnesiac, and in any moment another scandal was certain to kick him off the front pages of the tabloids. A leader in the Black community had outright dismissed the idea that he should lose his career over something he believed equated to poor judgment, not racism. His was a lone voice now, but it carried a lot of weight, and she hoped more would join.

"For now, getting me back on the roster is good enough."

Kennedy agreed with him, but she liked to shoot for the stars. "I've put together a plan to do precisely that. First, I'm going to have you meet Zion. He's twenty-six, from Buffalo, and played a little hockey growing up. Best of all, he's a Scouts season ticket holder. I've made arrangements for you two to meet up sometime this week at a sports bar by the name of All Bets Are On. It's not far from Central Park. Do you know it?"

Roger nodded, then added, "A season ticket holder, huh?"

Kennedy wasn't surprised that of everything she'd said, that impressed him the most. "Yes, *huge* hockey fan."

If someone had told her a year ago that she'd need a young Black hockey-loving Scouts season ticket holder willing to contract for Token, she'd have called it mission impossible. Then about nine months ago, during a particularly boisterous office happy hour, she'd learned Jonathan's brother-in-law, Zion, lived and breathed hockey. And basketball. And football. All right, the man loved his sports. Getting him on board with the plan had been child's play, or so Jonathan claimed.

"Do you think it's going to work?"

"This one is solely for you. Like many men with your upbringing, I think there's a stereotype of Black people you carry around in your mind that's been shaped by what you see on TV and the movies or hear on the radio. It'll be good for you to get some firsthand experience, and that's what I hope making friends with Zion will do.

"Having said that," she continued, "diversity in your personal relationships can only help your predicament as long as people believe you're being authentic."

Roger did something she didn't expect. He looked at her and grinned, a chuckle not far behind.

Kennedy's smile faltered. "What's so funny?" She was always up for a good joke, as long as she wasn't the butt of it.

"Nothing. It was nothing," he said, shaking his head, his smile still in place.

"Oh, come on. Tell me," she coaxed. Now more than ever she *needed* to know. This cat wasn't dying of curiosity.

"It's crazy." He shook his head, a blush staining his cheeks. "But when you said diversity in my personal relationships, it occurred to me that I've never dated…you know…someone like you before."

Caught in a moment of déjà vu, Kennedy bit her lip to stop herself from laughing. "Someone like me?" she asked, giving him the wide-eyed innocent look she employed for these occasions.

Swallowing visibly, he nodded. "I've never gone out with a Black woman before."

"Have that on your bucket list, do you?" she asked drolly, doing her damnedest not to snicker.

"It never really occurred to me until now," he said with a bashful grin. "You're beautiful. I've never seen eyes like yours before."

Kennedy couldn't help but smile. He was so adorably inept at this. "That's very nice of you to say, but I suggest you put something else on that bucket list of yours. Believe me, you're much better off with me helping you in this capacity. I'm excellent at my job. And I'm sure a professional hockey player like yourself won't have any trouble making all the friends you want from all walks of life."

"It was just a thought. I told you it was crazy."

"I promise, you'll be in good company with Zion."

She paused before laying out the last two items on his reputation resuscitation to-do list. "You'll need to issue an apology in front of the cameras. The statement put out by the team wasn't bad, but at the agency, we find situations like this warrant the personal touch. People want to see your face when you apologize. That way they can judge your sincerity for themselves."

Roger looked as if she'd suggested he swim injured and bleeding in shark-infested waters. But like the trooper he was, he agreed.

"And the last thing I'm going to have you do is sign up as a volunteer for at-risk youths. I already have the organization picked out. It would be two to three days a week while you're on suspension. Once your suspension is lifted, it can be whenever you can fit it into your schedule, but at least twice a month."

He gave a brisk nod of agreement. "Sounds like a plan."

"Oh, and one last question before you go. Are you aware of any other videos or audios that might put you at odds with the public and the league?"

"You mean like a sex tape or something like that?" he asked, brows furrowed. "Because I've been with a lot of women." He gave her a rather chagrined *so sue me, I love women and I love sex* look.

For a grown man making millions, he was incredibly naive. A sex tape would be the least of his worries. Hell, it would probably do to hockey what Tiger Woods did to golf. Make more people watch the damn sport. He might even get an offer for a reality show out of it.

"Actually, I was thinking something more along the same lines as the one out now. Anything with you saying something that could be interpreted as...culturally offensive."

"No," he replied adamantly. "I'm not like that. And I never

thought calling Wes that name would ever be considered rac-ist."

"I believe, more than anything, you never thought what you said to your friend in the comfort of your own home would become public."

How many reputations could survive the public airing of private conversations? The number could probably be counted on one hand.

"You can say that again."

"Don't look so glum. Things are going to get better. I'm going to make sure of it." Then she offered him a bit of dat-ing advice, should the need ever arise. "And, Roger, a word to the wise. If you ever find yourself thinking about asking a Black woman out on a date—actually, this applies to any woman of color—never preface it by telling her you've never asked someone of her race out before. Got it?" she asked, fighting back a smile.

"I kind of hoped you wouldn't remember that," Roger said, blushing.

Kennedy laughed outright. "Not a chance. I remember everything."

10

Nate had to school his features, this time to hide his annoyance as he watched Kennedy emerge from the car. Instead of accepting his offer of a ride or use of the company car, the stubborn woman had hired an Uber and refused to let him pay for it.

They'd arranged to meet in front of Chelsea's Restaurant & Lounge. Kennedy reasoned it didn't make sense for him to drive to Brooklyn to pick her up, only to have to turn around and drive back to the city. He hadn't pushed as hard as he wanted—as he should have—fearing she'd balk and back out of their agreement. But this transportation deal they had going needed to be renegotiated.

He'd talk to her about it later. Right now, his gaze remained riveted on the sight of her walking toward him. She wore a fitted pale green minidress that flared at the hips. Flimsy spaghetti straps left her arms and shoulders delectably bare. She looked beautiful. But then again, she looked beautiful no matter what she wore. Sans clothes, she took his breath away.

Her short walk from the curb to where he stood near the entrance of the restaurant attracted a number of double takes and a grunt of appreciation so loud he turned and leveled a cold stare at the offending individual—a young Black guy who didn't appear to be waiting to go inside.

Unable to avoid his glare, the guy regarded him and tipped his chin at Kennedy. "She with you?"

Nate's nod was curt.

"Sorry, man."

Nate didn't acknowledge the apology, returning his attention to his date as she reached his side. She smelled good, a delicate, floral scent.

"You look lovely," he said, trying to express the right amount of admiration without coming across as too effusive.

Kennedy beamed a smile at him that traveled to his groin on the southern rapid express. "Thank you, kind sir."

He placed his hand on her lower back and kissed her lightly on the cheek. It was subtle, but he felt the slight tensing of her body and the hitch in her breath, proof she wasn't as immune to him as she would have him believe.

Bringing his mouth close to her ear, he quietly informed her, "Next time, I'm picking you up. No more of this arriving separately shit." On his drive over, it had occurred to him that ferrying her to and from their dates would be the only chance he'd get to be alone with her, an opportunity he was determined to seize.

"You do understand we're not actually dating and this is all for show, right?" There was a note of teasing in her whispered response.

"You're doing this for me. The least I can do is provide your transportation," he argued, continuing to keep his voice low as he opened the door to the restaurant and carefully guided her in.

Once inside, they joined the line for the hostess and Kennedy turned to him. "I get the feeling you're a man used to getting your way. Tell me I'm wrong."

Nate gave a low chuckle. He hadn't exactly gotten his way with her. Not the way he'd wanted. "First you demanded my firstborn. I'm giving you transportation instead. That seems like a fair trade. Anyway, it'll look better if we arrive together, right?" He said nothing about the benefits his presence would have at deterring the kind of crude remarks she unfortunately tended to evoke from men like her young admirer.

A smile, slow no doubt due to its reluctance, spread across her face, lighting those gorgeous blue-gray eyes of hers. "Fine, you win. But when this whole thing is over, if I end up so spoiled I start turning my nose up at public transportation, it'll be all *your* fault."

When this whole thing is over.

If he had his way, the lawsuit stuff would end right now. But their relationship was another matter. He didn't want it to go back to the way it used to be, especially now that he was home for good.

"You want a car for work? Because that can be arranged." He kept his tone light, but he was serious as a heart attack. All she had to do was say the word.

"Okay, now you're just playing with me."

Nate suppressed a smile. *If only.*

"Kennedy?"

The sound of her name stopped them short. Nate turned to find a tall Black man wearing round wireless glasses staring intently at her.

"Kennedy Mitchell? Hi, it's Sam Morgan."

One thing was clear—the two didn't know each other well or hadn't seen each other in a while. Maybe someone she knew from college?

Kennedy's eyes flared in recognition. "Sam. Oh my goodness, it's so good to see you. How have you been? You look great."

In Nate's impartial opinion—unhindered by his own feelings for her, of course—the guy was more Eddie Murphy in *Dr. Dolittle* than Idris Elba in *just about anything*. He reminded him of a staid college professor.

At her welcoming smile, Sam strode over. "The second you walked in, I knew it was you. You haven't changed a bit. You look great." He darted a glance at Nate.

"Nate, this is Sam. We met a few years ago." She turned to Sam and asked, "How long has it been? Two years?"

"It was right after I got tenure, which was over two years ago." He directed his next remark to Nate. "We went out on a blind date."

Bingo. He'd been right about the guy's profession.

"And we had a perfectly nice time," Kennedy said kindly.

"But not nice enough for you to go out with me again," he teased lightly.

A spark of discomfort flashed in her eyes. "Yes, well, that was a crazy time in my life. I was laid off around that time. A week or so after, I think."

Sam frowned. "Really? I'm sorry to hear that."

"Actually, it turned out to be one of the best things to happen to me," she said. "I'm working for myself now."

"That's wonderful, and congratulations." His smile tempered when confronted with Nate's tight-lipped expression. He couldn't help that forced cordiality wasn't one of his strong suits. "I should probably let you get back to your...evening. It was nice seeing you again." To Nate, he gave a brisk nod.

Not a horrible encounter, but Nate wasn't sorry to see the back of the man, and he sensed the feeling was mutual.

"'Bye, Sam," Kennedy said. As soon as he strode off, she turned to Nate, her mouth set in a pink line of disapproval.

"What?" he asked innocently, an eyebrow raised in query.

"Thanks for nothing."

Whatever crime he was being accused of, he stood blameless. "I didn't do anything."

"My point exactly. Would it have killed you to be nice?"

"What do you mean? I was being nice," he protested. He'd politely nodded hello and stood quietly by while they'd caught up.

Kennedy huffed. "You know you can be pretty intimidating. I think you made him nervous."

"Oh really? What did you want me to do, ask him to join us for dinner?"

"I would have welcomed the company," came her cheeky response.

"If I didn't think there was a good chance he would've accepted, I would have," Nate said dryly.

Once they reached the hostess, she greeted them and waved them in. They then proceeded down a short hallway that led to the main room, and it was only then Kennedy spotted the stage at the front.

Pausing, she shot Nate a look, pleasure lighting her eyes. "*Oooh*, a live band. Dinner *and* entertainment. How exciting."

"Dinner and entertainment, yes, but no live band."

Kennedy's eyes went back to the stage. "Then what's that for?"

"Karaoke."

Aurora had informed him Kennedy was a big fan. That was one of the benefits of having a knowledgeable and trusted source on the inside. But also a complication. He'd made the mistake of dating one of his sister's friends before and it hadn't ended well. Since then, he'd made sure to give not just his sister's friends but *all* clingy women a wide berth. Kennedy, however, he hadn't been able to resist, and frankly, he could have tolerated a little clingy from her.

"You like karaoke?" Her question emerged in amused disbelief.

They resumed course, passing the lounge area as they headed toward the dining area in the rear. "I don't like or dislike it, but I'm guessing you do," Nate said as he stopped at the first of the few empty tables available and pulled out a chair for his beautiful date. Kennedy gracefully sat and cast a curious look around.

The place had the feel of a Vegas nightclub, moody and dimly lit, the patronage a mix of young hipsters and white-collar happy-hour regulars.

"You took a wild guess I was a karaoke fan?" She appeared skeptical that his predictive skills were that good, watching him as if her bullshit meter was going off loudly in her head.

"Or you may have said something to me about it. I can't remember," he replied evasively as he sat down across from her.

It had been embarrassing. He'd been like a high school boy instead of the more experienced college graduate he'd been at the time. Even with a couple long-term relationships under his belt, he'd tried to find out everything he could about his sister's friend. But he'd had to be subtle in his questioning, slipping into the protective older-brother role, expressing a justified interest in the beautiful stranger his baby sister had recently befriended. As the son of celebrity parents, he'd met more than his share of women who'd tried to use him to get to them in hopes of wedging their foot or pinky toe in the exclusive door to Hollywood success.

Sandwiched between *Is she an aspiring model or actress?* and *Did she know who you were when you met?*, he'd casually dropped, *What does she like to do for fun?* Aurora had told him what he wanted to know, but in the end, she wasn't fooled. Apparently, he hadn't been as clever in hiding his real motives as he'd thought.

"Nope, it wasn't me." Kennedy regarded him with a knowing smile.

"What does it matter who told me? What's important is that you're here, and hopefully, everything will be to your satisfaction." The company above all else.

"Well, however you found out, I'm surprised you remembered." There was something coy in the way she looked at him. "Should I be flattered?"

"I don't know—you tell me. Does it flatter you to know there isn't a thing I've forgotten about you?" he asked.

Heat flooded Kennedy's face. She briefly averted her gaze.

Was it her or was Nate doing that mixed-signal thing again? Sometimes it was hard to tell if flirting with her was purely reflexive. An instinct born from his good looks and how most women responded to him. Or was his interest real? And she wasn't talking about sex. He'd been there and sampled that. It had lasted four weeks and then he'd wanted them to be "friends."

How's that a blow to the ego?

"Is that because you have an amazing memory? Aurora told me it's practically photographic."

Oh wonderful, she was playing her own game of *Jeopardy!* *Stupid questions for five hundred, Alex.*

Nate chuckled as if he were in on the game. "My memory is good, but it's nowhere near photographic. I do tend to remember things that are important to me, though."

This time Kennedy met his gaze squarely. "Are you flirting with me?" she asked baldly.

"If telling the truth is a form of flirting, I guess I am."

She narrowed her eyes. "Then don't."

"Tell the truth?"

Argh. He was being deliberately obtuse. "No, I meant don't flirt with me. I'm doing this as a friend." There was that word again. "It wouldn't be good if either of us got the wrong idea, don't you agree?" And by either of them, she meant her.

"What idea would that be?" he asked, his gaze dropping to her mouth.

Lowering her voice, she leaned forward and said, "Stop playing games. You know exactly what I mean."

Something flashed in his eyes. "You don't want to play games, fine, I won't. You can start by telling me why you refused to speak to me after we stopped sleeping together."

Where the hell did that come from? With only seconds to recover from the second full-on assault of their time together in as many days, she responded with the only arrow in her quiver. "I distinctly remember you saying we didn't do a whole lotta sleeping."

The self-satisfaction she felt at her quick-witted comeback was a thing of beauty. She couldn't pat herself on the back enough.

Nate glanced around as if to make a point, his gaze idly touring the room full of patrons, before leaning over and whispering in her ear. "I didn't think you'd appreciate me using that kind of language in public. However, if I remember correctly, you liked when I said it when I was actually fucking you."

Kennedy's face went up in flames, burning away her momentary smugness. *Okay, then.* The man did have effective tools in his arsenal to render her silent and he wasn't afraid to use them.

He continued to regard her, brows raised, his expression as guileless as a card cheat. "Well?"

Oh wow, he seriously wanted to know. As if he couldn't have guessed the answer himself a long time ago.

"I didn't stop talking to you."

Suddenly, a shadow fell over the table. Kennedy looked up to find a smiling young man, who vaguely reminded her of the latest actor to play Spider-Man, clad in the requisite black-and-white server's uniform.

"Hi, my name is Rodney and I'll be your server for the evening. Can I start you folks off with a drink?"

Smiling, he handed each a dinner and dessert menu before taking their drink orders. At her request for a virgin piña colada, Nate's mouth gave a discernible twitch. Kennedy studiously ignored him. She certainly wasn't about to explain to him, of all people, that in dealing with him, complete sobriety was a must. He ordered a whiskey neat.

When their waiter left, Nate continued as if they hadn't been interrupted. "You did when you told me not to call."

Kennedy audibly exhaled. She'd told him he didn't *have* to call. Big difference. "What was the point? I mean, what was there to talk about? You told me to go to school, live it up, and have a good time. Well, that's exactly what I was doing. Plus, it wasn't as if we'd been in a relationship."

"And here I thought we were going to be friends. That's what we agreed on."

What else was she going to say when he'd made it clear that he was going to be super busy building his company and wouldn't have time for a girlfriend? She got that, for him, their time together was all about having fun. No harm, no foul. Because of Aurora, they'd be in touch, so why not make the best of it by going on as friends?

She'd nodded in agreement and assured him that things would be good between them going forward. And she'd meant it…at the time. She hadn't realized that her sadness and hurt had hardened into anger until his first phone call—that came three weeks after classes started. Seriously, the nerve of him thinking he could call her out of the blue like that. It wasn't as if her heart had leaped to her throat every time her phone rang in all the days preceding. Or that she'd swallowed down a heartbreak of disappointment when it hadn't been him. That hadn't happened.

"Actually, the whole us-being-friends thing was your idea." If a trip down memory lane meant setting the record straight, she'd act as the stenographer.

"Are you saying you didn't want to be friends?"

"What I'm saying is after classes started it put things in perspective. What happened between us happened. But it didn't mean we had to force a friendship that wasn't there from the beginning. Before, we only ever saw or spoke to each other because of Aurora. I figured we could go back to that." What would they have to talk about, in any case? Their respective boyfriends and girlfriends? Yeah, that wasn't going to happen.

Nate's head dipped in a slow nod. "It would have been nice if you told me that's how you felt."

"I did when I said you didn't have to call me anymore." She'd given him an out and he'd pushed the door open the rest of the way and run through it so fast it made her head spin. He'd never called her again.

He laughed wryly, watching her from the corner of his eye. "Yeah, well, you made it pretty damn clear you didn't want me calling anymore."

Kennedy had to bite her tongue to stop herself from saying, *You know, for a guy with such a high IQ, you're not all that bright when it comes to women.*

Once again, their conversation was put on hold when Rodney returned with their drinks. He remained another minute while they belatedly perused the menu and ordered their entrées.

Determined to take control of the conversation—and end it once and for all—as soon as Rodney was out of earshot, Kennedy asked, "Why are you bringing this up now?"

Nate stared at her, his expression inscrutable. "Do you realize we haven't been alone together like this in over ten years?"

Come again? "What is that supposed to mean? And why do you always answer a question with a question?"

"I am answering your question," he stated calmly. "You want to know why now. The answer is because this is the first time the opportunity presented itself—and when you're not rushing off to a meeting. Don't you think it's time to clear the air?"

There he goes again.

"Clear the air about what?" Now it was her turn to play obtuse. "You're my best friend's brother. I've always been nice to you, even after…everything. If anyone started acting different, it was you, not me."

Three months after he'd skillfully (and pleasurably) relieved her of her virginity, the next time they'd seen each other was when Aurora invited her to Thanksgiving at their parents' apartment in New York. Nate, who'd been traveling a lot at the time, initially said he wouldn't be able to make it. He'd surprised everyone by arriving a half hour before they sat down to eat, claiming he'd been able to clear his schedule at the last minute. As expected, Aurora and her parents had been overjoyed at his change of plans. Kennedy, on the other hand, would've appreciated him giving a girl a heads-up so she could prepare herself for the emotional upheaval of coming face-to-face with him.

In the end, the tumult of emotion had been exclusively on her side. Nate had been unfailingly polite to her. And it had gutted her. The entire evening had gone from one form of torture to another. The catered dinner she'd been looking forward to eating, she'd barely touched. And she hadn't said more than a few words during the after-dinner chat and drinks. Nate could not have been more remote and cool to her if he'd deliberately set out to make sure she knew how little she meant to him. The only good thing to come out of the evening had been Kennedy's renewed sense of self-possession and pride, because she wouldn't allow him to take them from her. She'd made a mistake in getting involved with him, but mistakes were how people learned. No one could ever accuse her of not being a quick study.

"You said you wanted me to go back to just being your friend's brother and that's what I did," he replied, with an *I gave you what you asked for, it's not my fault you didn't like it* glibness.

"What did you expect me to say? You made it very clear you didn't have time for a girlfriend." He conveniently kept leaving that part out. "Aurora was my best friend. Of course I wanted us to get along. But clearly I didn't realize what a little shit you'd been before," she retorted.

Who did he think he was fooling? He'd wanted to have it both ways. He hadn't wanted her to be his girlfriend, but he'd been certain she'd be thrilled whenever he deigned to sprinkle some attention her way.

Yeah, she was not that girl and had never been.

Nate studied her, a myriad of emotions flitting across his face. After a long pause, he asked in a seductively quiet voice, "Ever think maybe *you* had no idea what you wanted?"

For several seconds, Kennedy forgot to breathe. When the ability returned, it came in a rush of anger. But as quickly as he sent her blood pressure soaring, she forcibly restrained herself. Allowing him to poke or prod her into losing control of her emotions would give him the upper hand, which was exactly what he wanted.

"Why don't we drop the subject before I say something I'll probably regret? Let's agree to leave the past where it is and concentrate on preserving your company's reputation."

Nate's expression didn't change in the slightest. After a beat, he said, "Fine, we'll do it your way. So who were you dating before me?"

"As topics of conversation go, my dating life is off-limits," she replied crisply.

Nate took a drink of his whiskey before remarking with a little too much smugness, "The operative word is *were*. You seem to be forgetting that, for now, I *am* your dating life."

"You're my fake dating life," she corrected.

He arched a dark blond eyebrow. "You either have a real dating life or a fake one. You can't have both. The last thing I need are stories of my girlfriend dating other men."

Kennedy absently stirred her piña colada with the straw. Did he think she was stupid? Of course she knew she couldn't date anyone else while they were supposed to be together. It was also none of his business who she'd been dating before. She gave a fleeting thought to Aidan, marveling at how little she'd thought of him since Nate had appeared on the scene.

"What about my male friends? I do have them, you know." Jonathan and Darrell were good friends and she loved hanging out with them. No need to tell Nate that she didn't have any straight male friends. She'd tried it in the past, but it never worked. Every guy who'd ever told her they were fine just being friends had been lying. Shocking.

Nate stared into her eyes and then made a head-to-toe sweep of her. She deeply resented what the look did to her insides, the way her stomach bottomed out in reaction to it. "You do, do you? Then what are we? Do you consider us friends?"

The way he was looking at her—the heat in his gaze—had her swallowing hard and her face warming to embarrassing degrees of discomfort.

"Apparently not according to your exact definition of the word," she replied with a forced laugh in an attempt to bring the conversation back to a friendlier footing.

Nate returned her smile, his easy and relaxed. "Then how about we shoot for simply getting along? I'll take that."

Kennedy held up her glass. "I'll toast to that."

11

Today was one of those days that Nate wished for a campus like Apple Park in California. The tech giant was headquartered on one hundred and seventy-five acres and had cycling and jogging trails—an impossibility in a city nicknamed the Concrete Jungle. Constellation's corporate offices were housed in two twenty-two-story buildings connected by a glass sky bridge and not located close enough to Central Park to offer a view indicating they were in anyplace except a big city no matter which floor you were on.

In renovating the buildings, he'd had to work with what he had, creating separate outdoor work and eating areas in the courtyard. The work section came equipped with tables that seated four, and electrical outlets. On warm summer days like today, when the humidity wouldn't have him sweating through his shirt, he found it preferable to work out here rather than upstairs cloistered in his office.

"I thought this was where I'd find you."

Nate shot a glance over his shoulder and watched Jack's un-hurried approach. Like him, his friend wore chinos and one of the company's short-sleeved collared shirts featuring their logo, which was a constellation, because of course.

"So that's Kennedy," Jack remarked, spinning the chair across from Nate around and casually straddling it. After drop-ping his folder on the table, he rested his forearms along the back of the chair.

"Yeah, that's Kennedy." Nate returned his attention to his laptop but could feel his friend's gaze on him, a ridiculous smirk on his face. It looked like everyone had either seen the press conference or the picture of them in the papers last week. His mother had called him that night to commend him on his skillful handling of the situation. She'd also taken the time to defend her husband against the twenty-year-old allegation the reporter had raised. *Impertinent upstart. Your father handled the situation the best he could. Saved the production, if you ask me.*

"Funny, whenever you talked about her, I don't remember you saying anything about how hot she was. You leave that part out for a reason?"

Nate ignored questions that didn't warrant an answer. His friend was being a dick.

"Where'd you disappear to after the press conference? You didn't go back to your office."

"I took Kennedy to lunch and then gave her a ride to her appointment." She'd gotten her pizza.

Jack strangled a laugh. "A ride, huh?"

Nate cast his eyes skyward and prayed for strength. "What are you, six? She's Aurora's best friend." It was amazing that someone as brilliant as his friend still possessed the sense of humor of a middle grader.

"Ah, c'mon. Don't lie and tell me there's nothing going on

between you. Besides the scene at the press conference, I saw the picture of you two in the papers."

"Since when did you start reading gossip?"

"I don't. My mom emailed it to me. I taught her how to save an image on the internet last month, and as you can see, she's putting her new skills to good use."

That didn't surprise Nate one bit. Divorced from Jack's father for five years, she lived in Long Island and had gone from devoting her life to her banker husband and two children, to devouring the latest celebrity news like it was her job and she was gunning for a promotion.

"I know she didn't send it without commentary." Sighing, Nate snapped his laptop closed and regarded his friend. "Let me guess. She said something about Kennedy being Black?"

The look of discomfort on his friend's face confirmed he'd hit the nail on the head. The woman was as predictable as she was closed-minded.

In pitiful defense, Jack said, "You know my mom. She's old-fashioned."

And by old-fashioned, he meant racist as fuck. A throwback from the 1950s even though she was born in the early '70s, she also disapproved of bikinis and miniskirts, and constantly complained that professional women tried too hard to be like men by committing the crime of wearing pants to work. She vainly believed the perfect woman had been made in her image: wealthy, attractive, straight, and white. Needless to say, a champion of women's rights and diversity she was not. Nate suspected Jack's younger sister was gay but too terrified, ashamed, or a combination of both, to come out to her parents for fear of being disowned.

"Tell your mother she needs to join the twenty-first century."

"She did say Kennedy was *exceptionally* beautiful."

Nate resisted the urge to roll his eyes as his friend's efforts to excuse his mother's remarks continued to fall flat. Nate changed the subject before he said something he'd later regret. "So, what do you have for me? I hope to hell Alberta's missing review is in there." He tipped his chin at the folder in front of Jack.

"Still working on that, but I just got word from Anthony in Legal. They're having a hard time getting the other side to the table. Neil plans to discuss it with you once he gets final word. I know you want to put this behind you as soon as feasibly possible, but that's becoming less likely by the day."

"Why the fuck not?" These were exactly the kind of lawsuits litigants wanted to settle. The lawyers usually urged them to settle. The only variable was the amount, and he hadn't made an offer yet. Their reluctance to come to the table didn't make sense.

"It sounds like the lead attorney wants to take it to court and let the jury decide. At least, that's what he hinted at."

Nate sat abruptly back in his chair. "Why the hell would he want to do that? We haven't gone through arbitration. We haven't made an offer. He's supposed to do what's best for his clients. How does he know taking it to court is for the best? And who the fuck is this guy anyway?" He was going to need to talk to Legal himself and find out what the hell was going on.

"Trevor Markham. He's some hotshot Black civil rights attorney. Word is he has his sights on a political career and is more interested in building name recognition than this case. The quicker it's settled, the faster the press coverage goes away. I say in the end, he'll probably agree to arbitration, but not until after he enjoys time in the limelight."

"What fucking limelight?"

"He's taking a page out of your book and plans to hold

a press conference once he can get more employees to join the suit. I heard he also plans to do the local TV news circuit with Alberta. So just as news coverage is fading, he'll be going out there to push the lawsuit back in the spotlight. The guy's fucking diabolical. He's got the instincts of an ad man and a politician."

"Have you met him?" Nate asked.

"No, but I've seen him. He's young—early thirties—and everyone who's met him says he's the best in his field and smooth as fuck. Women seem to adore him and men—"

Nate cut him off with an exasperated groan. "Don't tell me. The men want to be him, or some shit like that."

"No, actually, I was going to say, the men want to beat the shit out of him because he's a smug, self-serving prick."

Nate barked a laugh. "You sure *you* haven't met the guy?"

Jack grinned. "I'm paraphrasing. Those are Neil's words. But I'm looking into him myself. It's always good to know who we're up against."

Neil D'Orazio, head of the legal team, didn't mince words. If he said Markham was a prick, Nate would take him at his word.

"Well, if he's looking for a career in politics, he sounds like the right man for the job."

Wanted: smug, self-serving prick. The job description wrote itself.

"So what do you want to do?" Jack asked, his expression sobering.

"I've got to get my hands on Alberta's performance review and I'm going to talk to Neil about setting up a meeting with me and Markham. If he's as smart and ambitious as you say, I'm sure I can make him see reason." The longer this lawsuit dragged out, the worse it would be for the company.

Brow furrowed, Jack looked uneasy. "I don't know, Nate. You may want to let the lawyers handle that."

"Don't worry," he assured his friend. "I'm not going to speak with him alone. I'll make sure Neil is with me."

"Have you considered a scenario where the company is cleared by the investigation? What would you want to do then?"

It was a fair question, but no matter what he wanted to believe, the company did have both a gender and racial problem in management. The numbers didn't lie. He'd read the suit in its entirety and he had a hard time believing that *all* of the employees were exaggerating or making up the things they said occurred. Excuses of miscommunication and missing reviews didn't sit well with him. No, somewhere along the way in trying to make the company both diverse and inclusive, he'd fallen short of that goal, and he intended to fix it. Settling before the investigation was completed was a small price to pay.

"I'd like us to operate as if the outcome isn't going to be favorable to us. In the meanwhile, I'd also like to meet with Alberta one-on-one. Do you think Neil can make that happen?" Her case really stuck in his craw, and since Duncan Flynn was still on his honeymoon and hadn't returned repeated calls, talking directly with his former employee was his best bet.

"I don't think that's a good idea either," Jack said, shielding his eyes with his hand from the slice of sun that broke through the sky bridge above. "Let it go through the lawyers, or the next thing you know, you're being accused of intimidation or god knows what."

Shit. Nate steepled his fingers. Jack was probably right about that. He needed to let the lawyers do their job and earn the money he paid them—he had enough on his plate as it was. This afternoon he was meeting with senior management and HR. Because of the lawsuit, the company's promotion and advancement process was under the most intense scrutiny of its twelve-year existence, and he needed to find out why it didn't appear to be functioning as originally designed.

"Look, I understand this is hitting you hard and you want to fix everything now. But just remember the financials of the company are great, and on the whole, the employees are happy. This lawsuit is a bump in the road. It's all going to work out."

Nate gave his friend a wan smile. Jack was the consummate cheerleader. In high school and college, if he needed his spirits lifted, Jack had always been there, and almost never trying to be a prick about it. Fortunately, he was also one of the best, if not the best, chief technology officers in the business.

"You're right. And if I haven't told you this before, thanks for keeping the business running smoothly while I've been gone."

"Hey, it's nothing. I'm just doing my job."

Nate considered himself lucky to have him as his CTO but even luckier to have him as a friend.

Kennedy stood at the head of the conference room and took in the faces of the six contractors set to deploy to Fields Literary Agency the following day.

Before anyone was sent out to a client, they were brought in for a mandatory half-hour training session, where they learned what Token offered their contractors besides a paycheck. Jonathan had taken over teaching the class from her a year ago, but in the name of keeping herself familiar with the material, she tried to teach one every quarter. Today, her office manager was seated in the back, quietly observing, and there if she needed him.

"Okay, now that everyone is seated, let's do a quick roll call. I like to do this to make sure I get everyone's name right, so please let me know if I mispronounce yours."

She glanced down at the list of names in her hand. "Jane Tanaka, Annabella Cortez, Jamal White, Claudia George, Farid Kaur, and Andre Simpson."

After she called out each name, a corresponding hand went up. In the end, no one corrected her, which was great because names had been butchered in the past.

Kennedy then introduced herself and gave them the five-minute spiel about Token, explaining its mission statement and overarching goal.

She then spent the next fifteen minutes detailing all the benefits it offered its contractors, the most attractive being a guaranteed in-person interview at the client company for a permanent, full-time position for those actively looking for a job.

"Tomorrow you'll be reporting to Timothy Black, and—" Kennedy broke off when Andre, a thirty-four-year-old Black man, raised his hand.

"Is he white?" he asked.

"Uh, yes…" Interesting question. Usually, that was a given.

Andre pointed to Jamal, who sat in front of him. "So, Jamal White is Black and Timothy Black is white. Things could get confusing tomorrow."

Snickers and titters filled the room. Kennedy couldn't stop herself from joining in the laughter. There was a jokester in every group.

"I don't know how people will be able to tell us apart," Jamal added with a smirk, undoubtedly used to his last name being used as a punch line.

"You can always pencil a mole on your face. I heard that works," Annabella offered with a dimpled smile.

More laughing ensued.

It seemed as if the group would do well together tomorrow. As part of their duties, they would be participating in a photo shoot for the company brochure. The literary agency needed "candid" images of a diverse workforce—something they were working frantically to address. Where once upon a time, stock images would have done the trick, these days, companies chose to forgo their use. The risks of seeing the same images on another company's website or brochure were too high and opened them up to sharp criticism and unfavorable press.

Butting up against the half-hour finish time, Kennedy knew she needed to wrap things up. "Any other questions?" she asked, looking around.

Farid raised his hand. "How much diversity are they looking for? Like, should I wear a turban?" he asked in a distinctive New York accent.

Kennedy took in Farid's dark hair, which was cut close on the sides and back and longer at the top. "Do you normally wear one?" She highly doubted he did.

"No, but I could get one if that's the kind of diversity they're looking for."

"Then I suggest you do without one. I think you'll be perfectly fine the way you look now."

For many of the agency's recruits, this was more of an acting gig than a job. For others, this was a foot in the door. Kennedy knew for a fact that Claudia and Jamal hoped to land full-time jobs with the literary agency, and she'd made sure Timothy Black was aware of that. If her prior experience was any indication, their chances of being offered employment were high. They both possessed the right background for the positions the agency needed to fill.

When it came to Farid, it was clear theatrics were his bent. He'd give them all the diversity and culture their hearts desired. She loved his attitude.

"Excuse me, Kennedy, sorry to interrupt—"

Kennedy's gaze shot to where Mina Shah stood in the partially open door. Mina was the client coordinator and had been a part of the agency's first round of hires.

"—but something's come up." Mina's expression suggested a Category 3 hurricane was about to hit.

Senses on heightened alert, Kennedy quickly excused herself and hurried to the door. Jonathan joined her as she stepped out of the room. After he closed the door behind them, the three shuffled out of sight of the class.

"Ainsley Fields called from Fields Literary Agency," Mina said, her voice slightly breathless. "They just got a call from a reporter at the *Globe*. He's working on a story that accuses them of using stock images for a company brochure they put out six years ago. He's giving them twenty-four hours to respond and then the story's going live."

Jonathan groaned and shook his head. *"Oh shite."*

Well, that was that. There was no way the agency would be able to get away with *another* brochure full of fake employees. Not now and probably never again. Which meant the shoot tomorrow was off and no work for their six contractors.

Kennedy immediately began to plot out a damage-control strategy. "Well, it's better it happened now than after they put out the brochure that could lead back to us." Although, they did a pretty good job in covering the tracks that connected the freelance contractors to the agency.

"In that case, disaster narrowly averted." Jonathan hastily made a sign of the cross. He was agnostic.

"Tell that to Ainsley Fields," Mina said. "She's on the verge of a nervous breakdown."

Given Ainsley was looking to diversify her client list, the timing of the story couldn't have been worse. Not that there was ever a right time for a business to be discovered cooking their diversity books.

"I'll give her a call in a few. In the meantime, Jonathan, I need you to contact all our HBCU alumni groups and let them know we're looking for experienced literary professionals for upper- and middle-management positions."

Kennedy had advised Ainsley that diversity required a top-down and everywhere in between approach. It wasn't enough to simply bring on a few diverse faces as junior agents and clerical staff, and put out a company brochure that resembled an old Benetton ad. The publishing industry had changed since the former executive editor had hung out a shingle seventeen years ago. Ainsley had agreed but was dragging her heels when it came to the more senior positions and management.

Kennedy bet she'd be more amenable to her recommendations now.

"Got it. I'm on it, boss," Jonathan said with a brisk nod, and he made a beeline for his office.

Kennedy turned to Mina. "I need you to call Timothy Black and see if you can move up Claudia's and Jamal's interviews. The sooner we can get them in there, the better."

"I'll call him now," Mina said before hurrying off to do her bidding.

Squaring her shoulders, Kennedy returned to the conference room to give the contractors the news.

12

Minutes after dismissing her class, Kennedy, earbud in place, paced her office as she did her best to calm her panicked client. "Ainsley, listen to me. It'll be okay. I've got this. Leave the reporter to me."

"No, you don't understand. Dawn Robinson's manager called yesterday. Dawn is looking for *literary* representation and *I* made her short list. They want a meeting."

Wow! Okay. No wonder Ainsley was in a tizzy.

Last year, Dawn Robinson became the first Black person—man or woman—to take home an Oscar for best director. The win jettisoned her into the spotlight, and in a recent interview, the normally intensely private director revealed she was working on a memoir. Within days of her announcement, offers from publishing companies began flooding in. The bidding war for her book was shaping up to be one for the ages, and there was already talk of a movie deal. Needless to say, the forty-eight-year-old Oscar winner would be any literary agent's dream come true.

During another aimless trip from the door to the window, Kennedy came to an abrupt stop. She had an idea. If Hollywood was as small a world as everyone claimed, maybe Ainsley still had a chance at catching the biggest literary fish to come along all year. Or at least meeting with her.

"Take the meeting. I'll deal with the reporter and whatever press the story generates when it comes out. But you have to take the meeting no matter what."

"There won't be a meeting when she cancels," Ainsley stated mournfully, as if it were a foregone conclusion.

Kennedy might not be able to pull a rabbit out of a hat, but she did know a few people in the industry who had clout. "Well, my goal is to make sure she doesn't, and then the rest is up to you."

By the time Kennedy hung up the phone, Ainsley needed Tylenol instead of Valium and agreed to interview candidates for senior and management positions as soon as Jonathan could get them in the door. The diversity *top-down and everything in between* approach was in full swing.

Next on her to-do list was the reporter. Her conversation with him was cordial and intended to disarm. She gave him a spiel on how the use of stock images for marketing purposes was once common among businesses and colleges. Unfortunately, Fields Literary Agency got caught in the fuzzy transition between acceptable and frowned upon. In other words, unless he planned to take every other institution to task, this was a nonstory.

Expounding on that, she suggested perhaps the story would be better served as a compare-and-contrast piece. He could detail the changes society had undergone since the days when the use of stock images for that purpose used to be commonplace—a mere six years ago, in the case of the Fields brochure. *Who knows, your paper may have used them once too*, she offered guile-lessly. When he didn't dismiss the idea outright, Kennedy knew she'd given him something to think about, and she hoped he thought about it long and hard.

After finishing up with the reporter, Kennedy sought out her partner in business and crime. She found Aurora in her office at her computer, her hair done up in a sophisticated ponytail.

"Morning," Kennedy said as she took a seat in the guest chair and made herself comfortable.

Aurora tore her gaze from the monitor and stopped typing. "Hey, I heard what happened. You were on the phone when I came in, so Jonathan filled me in. All I can say is, we really dodged a bullet with that one."

Kennedy let out a dry laugh. "Don't I know it." The whole incident had begun to leave a bad taste in her mouth and she wondered, not for the first time, whether the carrot approach to attracting clients was the right way to go.

"So what now?"

"I say we pay everyone who was supposed to go tomorrow. Is that okay with you? I mean, it isn't their fault the whole thing went upside down and sideways."

"Absolutely," Aurora agreed, nodding.

"The reporter said he'll let us know twenty-four hours in advance before they run the story, so we'll have some time to get ahead of it." Kennedy now sincerely believed that no matter which story the paper ran, the literary agency would be fine. In the context of what was acceptable then and what was acceptable now, her argument was on solid ground.

"My dad's worked with Dawn Robinson, so if you need me to put in a word, I'd be more than happy to," Aurora offered before quickly covering her mouth as a yawn overtook her. Grinning sheepishly, she said, "I need to get more sleep."

Kennedy studied her friend. Her Spidey senses were tingling. Something was up. "All right, what's going on with you?"

Aurora stared at her, blue eyes wide and questioning. "What do you mean?"

"I'm talking about the fact that you're usually at your desk by eight every morning and in the last week or so you're coming in after nine. And now you tell me you haven't been sleeping. Are you seeing Jake again and not telling me?"

Six months ago, Jake, her ex-boyfriend, had issued Aurora an ultimatum: either they move in together—which entailed him moving into her multimillion-dollar brownstone—or he was gone. Since he'd said it while they were at said brownstone, Aurora had promptly retrieved his toothbrush and razor from the bathroom and kicked him out. At the time, they'd been going out three months.

Aurora's pretty face contorted in horror. "You *cannot* be serious. I wouldn't get back together with him if you paid me."

"Just checking." Kennedy was more than a little relieved. Jake was a straight-up gold-digging brat. His looks might pull a girl in, but his lack of ambition would send her running in the other direction clutching her wallet and ATM card. She didn't know how her friend put up with him for as long as she had. A guy could only leave his credit card at home so many times before he was washing dishes to settle the bill. Guaranteed, it would be the last time his trifling ass would "forget" it again.

"Then what's going on? Why haven't you been sleeping?"

Aurora's shoulders rose and fell on a sigh. "It's this thing with Nate, you know. I wish I could do more to help. Although I will say, the article out this morning is pretty positive. It makes a point to credit him for all the work the company does in underprivileged communities and gives him big props for the high school turnaround."

Seven years ago, Nate partnered with a high school in one of the most underfunded school districts in Brooklyn. He'd given millions to not only renovate the building inside and out, but funded a STEM program that had become the envy of public high schools in the five boroughs. In that time, the graduation rate went from 65 percent to a staggering 90 percent, 80 percent of which went on to college. And their college graduation gift from the company? A job offer. It was a win-win situation for the students, the company, and the high school.

"That's fantastic." Things were already working out on the PR front. He might not need her for much longer, as long as the case didn't go to trial.

Then why didn't the prospect fill her with joy? This was, after all, their goal. All that they'd hoped to accomplish. Falling for him again was not. And she had a feeling the likelihood of that happening was in direct correlation to the length of their charade.

Kennedy hastily pushed the discomforting thoughts aside. "What about you? You working on anything new? Sign any new clients?" They usually got together twice a week to catch each other up on their respective client lists.

"Funny you should ask. I just got a call that's probably better suited for you," Aurora said.

"Oh yeah, what's it about?"

Appearing more at ease, Aurora reclined in her tan leather chair. "Joseph Russo, the senior producer at WNLE, has been suspended for telling a Black female reporter that she won't be featured on air unless she changes her hair. He said his comments had nothing to do with her race."

"For the love of God," Kennedy exclaimed, exasperated.

"How hard is it for people to *not* say clearly racist and offensive things? I mean, seriously. Is that really asking too much?"

A long breath whistled past Aurora's lips. "Some habits are hard to break."

"Some habits should be smothered in their cradle at birth," Kennedy muttered darkly. "Honestly, it has to be one of two things. Either it's so second nature to them that they don't believe what they're saying is offensive, *or* they do and don't care." All her clients who ended up in a similar predicament swore up and down that it was the former, not the latter. Because of course.

True, her reward was the hefty fee the agency charged, but her satisfaction came when the company was then compelled—some might say forced—to diversify. Potato, po-tah-to, the results were the same.

"Viewers have threatened to boycott *Rise and Shine* if he isn't fired."

"Not surprising," Kennedy responded dryly. "This one isn't going to be easy. A woman's hair is her crowning glory. What was the hairstyle that triggered him?"

"The reporter, Alexis Montgomery, came to work with her hair in braids. He told her to go home and *fix it*."

Kennedy snorted a laugh and then couldn't stop laughing, tears filling her eyes. Once she finally caught her breath, she wheezed, "*Fix it?* Does he have any idea how long it takes to put those things in? She'd be lucky if it was a five-hour job."

"Honestly, white people," Aurora mocked, with an exaggerated roll of her eyes.

At that, they both erupted into gales of laughter, reminding Kennedy of their college days, when their smallest feats of hilarity could set them off. Like the time they convinced a bunch of drunk NYU students that they were fraternal twins, the only medical rarity of their kind in the country.

"So, when do I meet with this paragon of tolerance and inclusivity? And am I going to him or is he coming here?"

Aurora tapped her French-manicure-tipped finger twice on her desk. "He's coming here. They won't allow him in the offices while he's on suspension. I'm pretty sure he's available tomorrow, so just let me know what your schedule looks like and I'll slot him in. If not tomorrow, we can arrange it for later this week."

"No, I can see him tomorrow." Kennedy didn't have anything on her schedule that afternoon. She'd actually hoped to duck out early, but alas, that wasn't going to happen.

"By the way, how did your date with my brother go?" Aurora asked, as Kennedy turned to go. "I thought I'd get a call Sunday."

Kennedy deliberately made her tone light and breezy. "He picked up the tab and made sure I got home safely, so things went as well as they could." Nothing except ex-lovers having dinner, one intent on digging up the past, and stirring up everything else in the process.

"I doubt it'll make *Page Six* but we'll see how things go. Although, I have noticed a tone change in how they're covering the lawsuit since the picture of us together was published. And, as far as I know, there hasn't been another article insinuating that my appearance at the press conference was staged." Hail the almighty power of a nine-year-old photo with his arm around her. If only world peace could be achieved that easily.

"When are you going out again?"

Kennedy lifted her shoulder and let it drop. "I have no idea. We're playing it by ear."

The food had been delicious, the karaoke better than a few of the concerts she'd attended, and after the initial stumble, conversation between them had been surprisingly effortless. They'd stayed until ten before calling it a night. Nate hadn't had to wrestle her into his car to take her home. Her consent had been grudging, but she'd gone willingly. When they'd arrived at her apartment, she'd quickly exited his car, taking a good-night kiss off the table. The goodbyes were conducted with him behind the wheel, double-parked on her narrow street. When they'd see each other again wasn't discussed.

Aurora nodded. "Are we still hooking up with Sahara next weekend?"

"We're going out even if she has to bail," Kennedy assured her, before going back to her office.

These days, the singer-actress spent most of her time in LA. Whenever she was back in the city, they always made a point to get together, even if it was them grabbing a quick cup of joe at her favorite coffee shop.

At the ding of her cell phone, Kennedy hurriedly checked the new message.

Eager much?

Nate: Are you free for dinner this weekend?

Kennedy had no idea why she stood there grinning like an idiot, and why her stomach fluttered like a schoolgirl whose crush just invited her to the junior prom. She was a grown-ass woman who knew this thing with Nate wasn't real and would never lead to anything except perhaps another roll in the hay if she allowed herself to go there.

Taking a seat behind her desk, she texted him back, giggling to herself at her response.

Kennedy: On less than a week's notice? I think not!

She delighted at the inclusion of the exclamation mark. It conveyed just the right amount of faux indignation. Animated bubbles formed on her screen. She watched them avidly as she awaited his reply, only to be startled into almost dropping her phone when it vibrated in her hand.

"I have to give you a week's notice?" Nate lamented, before she could get out so much as a *hello, when we're doing this cutesy text messaging, you're not supposed to call.*

When it came to personal messaging etiquette, men's intuitive abilities were pretty dismal. They ranked a notch higher than understanding that when a woman said she was *fine*, she was exactly the opposite.

Kennedy made a sound of mock affront. "Who do I look like to you, last-minute Molly?"

"Seven days isn't exactly last-minute," he said, sharing the lightheartedness of her tone.

"I'm a working woman. My busy schedule means I require due notice."

"Due notice?" he asked, the *la-di-da* unspoken in his laugh. "You must be a hoot when it comes to spontaneity."

Kennedy made a face and stuck her tongue out at the phone. "There are a lot of other ways to be spontaneous."

"Oh yeah? Tell me."

For the rest of the day, Kennedy would marvel at how, with a mere drop in pitch, he could make those four words sound so dirty. She would also wonder why the low growliness of his voice always did it for her in *that way*. She literally had to treat her nipples like troops on the front line primed for battle and order them to stand down.

"Like surprise parties and marriage proposals." The second the words came out of her mouth, she wanted nothing more than to snatch them back.

"Been surprised by many birthday parties and marriage proposals, have you?"

Kennedy didn't know what to make of his tone, which on the surface sounded cavalier but carried a rough edge.

"Is that the yardstick you're measuring me by?" he continued more congenially.

"Of course not. I don't expect either from *you*. I was just giving examples of spontaneity that can easily fall within my week-notice rule." The rule she'd just made up and had now taken on a life of its own. That was what she got for her attempt at playful messaging.

"What can I do to get you to pare that down to something sooner?"

Eager to move the conversation along, Kennedy said, "How about for our next date, I make the arrangements. Dining out is great and everything, but there's a lot of other stuff we can do."

Lots of other stuff we can do?

What is wrong with you? You might try thinking before you speak.

Nate chuckled softly. "You're right about that. Okay, I'll leave the arrangements up to you and I'll send a car to pick you up. Just tell me the time, date, and attire."

Kennedy knew better than to argue with him about the car. The man was intransigent on the subject, as she'd discovered on their first date. She'd never dated someone of Nate's wealth. The closest she'd come was Aidan, who owned a lovely condominium in Astoria and drove last year's BMW Coupe but certainly didn't make *personal car service ready at his disposal* money. Nope, that was for the people who played in Nate's rarefied league.

"Good, then. I'll contact you with the details."

"And I'll be waiting. Have a good day, Kennedy."

Suddenly, she was overcome with a sense of uncertainty, and had to remind herself that *this*—what they were playing at—wasn't real.

"You too," she said softly.

After she ended the call, she stared at the phone, her mind swirling.

For something that was supposed to be for show, it sure was starting to feel a tad too real. She needed to slow things down to a crawl and create some healthy distance between them.

13

"You picked up," Sahara exclaimed, the smile in her voice unmistakable.

"What time is it where you are?" Kennedy asked, surprised by her friend's early morning call.

Phone pressed to her ear, she skirted two men in business suits stopped in the middle of the sidewalk carrying on a conversation. An unheard-of sight at seven-thirty in the morning in Manhattan. People had places to go, people to see, and work to get done. All of which applied to her at the moment.

"Way too early. But it'll be the last time I'll be up this early for a while. Today's the last day of filming and I'm due in the makeup chair at five-thirty sharp, so I have to make this quick. Instead of clubbing it on Saturday, how would you like to go to the launch party for the new couture line? Things have been so hectic, I forgot to tell you about it the last time we talked. And you know I want you and Aurora there. Please say you'll come. Pretty please."

Kennedy chortled. "You had me at 'new couture line.' We will be there in our evening best."

Sahara had told her about the line a year ago, when it was nothing but a long-held dream and rough sketches of princess gowns and elegant dresses. And now, a year later, the budding fashion mogul was about to realize that dream with a splashy launch party.

Kennedy dared someone to try and keep her away.

"I'll leave tickets for you at the door. Will six be enough?"

Kennedy did a quick count in her head. If she and Aurora brought dates, that would be four. But if six was Sahara's starting-off point, she would also ask Jonathan if he wanted to tag along, and of course he would bring Darrell.

"Six sounds good."

"Great. Gotta run now, sweets. My scene is up next. I'll see you Saturday." Lately, Sahara was doing more acting than singing, although the movie she was filming now allowed her to show off her vocal skills. After her last world tour, she'd wanted to stay put for a while and bought a beautiful mansion in the Hollywood Hills. There were bargains to be scooped up for a cool ten mil, something Kennedy would have to keep in mind the next time she went house hunting. Right.

She bade her friend goodbye and made her way up to the third floor. She quickly deposited her handbag in her office and then made a beeline for caffeine. The coffee was ancillary.

The agency's small break room contained the standard lunchroom fare, and a vending machine that included healthy snack options. If granola bars counted as healthy. Mina sat at one of the tables, mug in hand.

"Hey, Mina."

She regarded Kennedy, her expression strangely void of emotion. "It should be a crime to be that happy coming into work in the morning."

"The *Globe* isn't running the original story about Fields Literary Agency," Kennedy replied, smiling. "What's not to be happy about?"

After she'd gotten home last night, she'd received an email from the reporter that he was taking the story in the direction she'd suggested. When Kennedy called Ainsley with the news, the woman couldn't have been more grateful or relieved.

Mina took a careful sip of her coffee before answering. "Right now, there's a lot I could be unhappy about." Her expression turned downright sinister. "Did you know that if I killed my boyfriend in a crime of passion, I could get as little as eight years in jail? Which would you advise, state or federal prison?"

Kennedy halted in front of the sink, her eyebrows shooting up to her hairline. "That sounded awfully thought-out." Smothering a laugh, she opened the cupboard, grabbed her mug, and gave it a thorough rinse. "Please don't tell me we're going to have to get another client coordinator and I'm going to have to schedule monthly visits to some prison upstate. My weekends are full enough as is. And I don't think orange is your color. It would wash out that gorgeous complexion of yours."

Despite her narrowed glare, Kennedy could tell Mina's ire wasn't directed at her. "The bastard cheated on me." Her fingers tightened meaningfully around the handle of her mug. "In our apartment. In our *bed*." Moral outrage at the former and seething rage at the latter.

"In your bed?" Kennedy's voice rose to a squeak. That brought it to a whole new level of hurt, betrayal, and humiliation. "He could have at least had the decency to do it at her place or book a room."

Mina's brown eyes stormed. "He has *no* decency. He's a pig. And I wasted three years of my life I'll never be able to get back on that jerk." She gave her head a furious shake. "I'm not going to hear the end of it from my parents. They told me to stay away from those American boys."

"Aren't his parents from Pakistan too?" That was where her parents were from. Mina and her older brother were born and raised in Brooklyn.

"But he wasn't raised there. As my mother says, he's been *Americanized*," she said, mimicking her mother.

Kennedy had met Addy at the Christmas office party last year, and he couldn't be more "Americanized" than Mina herself. She didn't know what things were like in Pakistan, but when it came to her clothing, hairstyle—an adorable shoulder-length bob—and makeup, Mina was a New Yorker through and through.

"They can't actually believe that men *raised* in Pakistan don't cheat on their girlfriends or wives?" Kennedy retrieved milk from the refrigerator, checked the date to make sure it was still good before pouring some into her coffee.

Mina let out a disgruntled groan. "The man living with their daughter better not."

"Men are the same all over. It's all about finding the right one."

"Yeah, and now this weekend I'm going to have to tell them I'm not living in sin anymore. My mother was sure we were getting engaged this year." Tears filled her eyes as she whispered, "So did I."

Kennedy stopped what she was doing and hurried to the table. Putting her arms around Mina's shoulders, she gently smoothed her hair. "Oh, sweetheart, everything will work out. Addy's an idiot. He doesn't deserve you. But don't worry. One day you'll find someone who does."

Mina rested her head on Kennedy's stomach, her arms circling her slender waist. After a bit, she slowly pulled away.

"Men are pigs. As if I'd want another one of those," she sniffed, wiping her eyes. "I told him he has to give me money to buy a new bed, and to take the one he screwed his girlfriend on when he moves out."

"Good for you. Do you think he will?"

"No, but after I kicked him out last night, I transferred three thousand dollars from our joint account into mine. That should cover it. I left two hundred for his moving expenses." By the expression on Mina's face, that seemed to provide her with a measure of grim satisfaction.

With that kind of money, he'd be able to rent a U-Haul for a few hours and supply a couple of his friends with pizza and beer in exchange for the use of their strong backs and arms.

Pushing back the chair, Mina stood. "Anyway, enough of my depressing life. I sent you an email about Roger O'Brien. I was able to get in touch with the Simmonses. They heard about his problems and said they'd be happy to go on record about what a sweet child he was and how he'd always been kind to them."

"That's great. I'll let his coach know. The team will want to get someone out there to talk to them. Stage some sort of event with Roger and the Simmonses."

Zion had contacted her about their meetup at the sports bar. Said things went well. That they'd hit it off. Fans had taken pictures and posted them on social media. The majority of the feedback had been positive. A number of Black reporters appreciated that Roger was making an effort. Most important, the press wasn't talking about him anymore and calls to have him kicked out of the league had been reduced to a dull roar. Silence was success.

"And I'm already working on finding out all I can about your nine o'clock. Not much out there on social media, though."

"Whatever you find for now is fine. Hopefully, he'll give us more to work with after our meeting."

The next hour flew by, and before Kennedy knew it, Joseph Russo walked into her office. And plunged her into comb-over hell. She tried not to gawk at what must have been a painstaking arrangement. Single strands of hair were never meant to perform that much work.

Hairstyle aside, the news producer was physically impos-ing, his heavyset frame easily topping six feet. He was fifty if he was a day and moved as if he carried the weight of his newsroom on his meaty shoulders.

After polite greetings were quickly dispensed with, they sat and regarded each other like fellow gladiators readying for battle. Their goal was the same, but their method would in-evitably differ. Kennedy could guarantee that.

"Before you say anything, I want you to know that, de-spite what's being said about me, I have no racial animus to-ward anyone. And I'm not a sexist or a bigot or a misogynist or homophobic."

They did that a lot, her clients, coming out of the gate as if getting the first word in edgewise would give them the ad-vantage in the *I'm the least racist person you'll ever meet* competi-tion, and she was the presiding judge. And she didn't know if he'd just rattled off a list of his possible offenses or was simply being an ass. Neither was a good sign.

But Kennedy had a job to do, and hoped her smile conveyed that any fire that landed in his vicinity was the friendly vari-ety. "And now that we have that out of the way, Mr. Russo, I'm going to tell you one thing about me. I make it a rule never to judge someone based on what they say because peo-ple have a tendency to obfuscate or minimize their actions in these sorts of situations. I assess them by what they do. Our motto here is *Show Don't Tell*—that is, unless we're putting

out a carefully worded and properly scrutinized statement."
To that, she sent him a *wink and nudge* smile. "Now, why don't
you tell me what happened?"

For a moment he didn't say anything, simply stared at her,
mouth compressed into a straight line. Then he scrubbed his
hands over his face, making him appear more weary than
vexed.

"When I told Alex—Miss Montgomery—to fix her hair,
it had nothing to do with the style. It was the color. Parts of
it were green and pink. Not the whole head, mind you, just
the bottom half. Or maybe it was a third. I can't really remember anymore. But it was dyed those crazy colors. I can't
believe she expected me to let her on air looking like that."

He paused to inhale an agitated breath, before barreling on.
"She never said that when she filed the complaint, you know,
that she had it colored like that. And no matter how often I
told them, they didn't want to listen. Call me old-fashioned,
but I run a professional shop. I expect everyone to look and
dress appropriately for their job. I got a bunch of guys who
have tattoos and that's fine. They're usually covered and they
work behind the scenes. But hair the colors of the rainbow is
where I draw the line. Always have and always will. I don't
care what color skin you have."

And with that, Joseph Russo threw her a partial lifeline she
might be able to use to save his job. "For clarification purposes, does the station have a policy regarding hair color?"

His response came with a slow contemplative shake of his
head. "Not that I'm aware of. But you'd think these are things
you wouldn't have to tell grown adults. They're not a bunch of
clowns and they're not coming to work at a goddamn circus."

Such eloquence. Kennedy bit down on her bottom lip to tamp
down a smile. "So that's a no. Got it."

Strike one. The hair-color defense had just taken its first blow, but it was still a viable one. It certainly couldn't be considered racially discriminatory.

"All right, then. Is there any way you can prove what you're saying is true?"

"What do you mean? That she came to work with the different colors in her hair?"

"No, that you refused to put her on air because of the color and not her hairstyle."

Joseph Russo did nothing to hide his frustration, his mouth twisting. "How am I supposed to prove that? *I'm* telling you that's why I sent her home."

Kennedy wondered if he understood the deep existential meaning of *he said, she said*. It appeared she'd have to give him a crash course. "Which I understand, but not everyone is going to take you at your word. Some people will believe you're using it as an excuse to cover your true motive. You wouldn't, by any chance, have any other Black female employees with similar hairstyles?" She knew it was a stretch, but she had to try.

The senior producer threw up his hands in exasperation. "Oh, for Christ's sake, this whole thing is hogwash. *No*. Miss Montgomery is the only African American female on-air reporter at the station."

And then it happened: a strategically placed strand of hair became dislodged, revealing a patch of bald skin as it dangled in his face.

Neither of them spoke for several moments. Kennedy refused to breathe, fearing she was one tittering laugh away from losing her shit—and the account. Then he did the only thing he could under the dire circumstances. He swept the errant hair back in place.

Kennedy finally breathed. Crisis averted.

"The only one, huh," she mused aloud, picking up seamlessly where they'd left off. They might want to change that. But that was a conversation for another day and with the executive producers, who were usually in charge of staffing.

"What about your off-air employees or the office staff?"

"There's an admin assistant but her hair is fine," he muttered, looking decidedly uncomfortable.

"How so?"

"How so what?" he asked, perplexed.

"You said her hair was fine. What exactly did you mean by that?"

Tugging self-consciously on his right earlobe, he shifted in his seat. "The color."

"I didn't ask you about the color. I asked if there were any other Black females with a similar hairstyle as Miss Montgomery and you said the admin assistant's hair was fine. All I want to know is what you meant by that," she said patiently. Sometimes, if she gave them enough rope, they somehow managed to bind their hands behind their own backs.

"Her hair is smooth but sort of wavy."

So no braids for the lone female Black admin assistant. *Got it.* However, she was picking up some definite hair bias. Straightened hair was fine, but braids were not.

"Have you taken issue with any other employee's hair color before?" He'd given her something to go on, but it would be an uphill climb if the one and only time he'd ever raised the topic of inappropriate hair color was with Miss Montgomery. But they'd go with the hair-color defense if that was all they had.

It had nothing to do with hair discrimination—he's just a crotchety old curmudgeon, Your Honor, sounded about right.

His brow furrowed in concentration. "Actually, there was this kid about five years ago. He didn't work at the station long. Young, longish hair, and a couple tattoos on his arms, but, for the most part, he kept them covered. He came to work one day with the bottom part of his hair dyed blue or purple. I can't really remember which color. I'm pretty sure he was high that day too."

Promising. Kennedy picked up a pen and drew her notepad closer. "What did you do?"

"I told him the tattoos I could deal with but that the weird-color hair had to go."

"And what happened?"

"He quit right then and there and never came back. Said he was bored with the job anyway. Smart-ass." The latter he muttered under his breath.

"We'll need to get in touch with the young man to verify your version of the events."

"I've got no problem with that. Human Resources can get you the information. The kid couldn't have worked there more than a few months. I almost forgot about him."

That gave Kennedy pause enough to ask, "In general, how often do you think you've commented on your employees' hair color or hairstyles?" Given the circumstances, she would have thought the incident would have been foremost in his mind. It was, after all, the best defense he had that he hadn't broken New York State hair discrimination law.

Joseph Russo blinked owlishly. "I—I don't— I mean, I typically don't comment on things like that." After a beat, he added, "I may have complimented someone here and there. New hairstyle, a nice cut, that sort of thing. Nothing out of the ordinary."

"Have you ever complimented Miss Montgomery on her hair?"

"No, I don't believe so."

Oh, he knew. But what was becoming clear to her was that Joseph Russo had a thing with hair. He liked it presented a certain way. Neat and only in colors natural to humans.

"This may end up being a case where we can prove you didn't have any discriminatory intent in your objections to Miss Montgomery's hair, but the takeaway could be that you're too fixated on how and what your employees do with their hair, depending on what the employees who you've complimented have to say, if anything."

"What, so it's now a crime to compliment someone on their hair?"

Where had they stashed the machine that removed sticks from people's butts?

"What I'd suggest you do, once this is over and you have your job back, is keep those thoughts to yourself. You don't want anyone accusing you of favoritism, and that's what compliments of any kind tend to lead people to believe."

He opened his mouth to speak and then snapped it shut just as quickly, which was probably for the best. The less he said, the better things would eventually work out for him. He seemed to be straining against the restrictions his suspension placed on him, feeling helpless to say and do what he wanted. But that was because he knew that what he wanted to say wasn't in his best interest. Financially or career-wise.

"Here's what we need to do. First, we'll get in touch with the young man and get a statement from him regarding the circumstances around his departure from the station. And then we need to get a picture of Miss Montgomery's hair on the day of the incident. Right now, the picture going around social media isn't one with her hair dyed green and pink, and that's what's fueling the anger toward you. Once we have those two things, I'm positive the furor over this will die down and you'll be able to return to your job with little to no fanfare."

The strain of the last week was etched on his face, giving him a tired, beaten look. Or maybe that was the way he always looked. Really, who could tell?

"And maybe you could talk to her—Alexis," he said. "I think she'd listen to you and withdraw the complaint if she felt you didn't think what I said had anything to do with her race."

Reaching out to the plaintiff in situations like this sometimes backfired. Some women felt betrayed and believed she was siding with the enemy. But in the carrot-and-stick approach to diversity, she thought the carrot approach achieved better results. Faster.

"Right now, you have a lot working for you without me having to speak to Miss Montgomery. But if at any point I deem it necessary, I'll certainly reach out to her."

Mr. Russo nodded. "Thank you. I know you mean well, and I appreciate what you're doing for me. I sincerely do."

Kennedy could tell the words hadn't come easy but that he meant it. "It's all in a day's work," she said lightly.

14

Later that week, Kennedy informed Nate that they'd be spending their second official date with one hundred and fifty other people. Left up to him, he'd have opted for something more low-key, like a dinner, a play…and a late dessert, preferably at his place. The pair of messages he'd received dashed his hopes for an intimate party of two.

Kennedy: Ur in 4 a treat. On Sat we're going to a launch party for Sahara's new clothing line. And you won't need a car, Sahara is sending a limo! See you in front of your building at 8 sharp.

Kennedy: Oh, and in case it's not obvious, jacket & tie are NOT optional. 😊

Still, he'd taken solace in the fact they'd have some alone time during the ride. So, imagine his surprise when he'd climbed into the back of the limo to discover she already had company.

What his beautiful date had neglected to mention in her messages was that they'd be sharing a ride with her office manager, Jonathan, and his husband. *Isn't it great that Jonathan and Darrell are on the way? Now we can all arrive together,* she'd said brightly while sandwiched between the two men. In turn, he'd plastered a smile on his face and warmly greeted the couple as he watched his only chance to have her to himself for the evening go up in smoke.

The event was being held at a ballroom in the Ritz-Carlton near Central Park, and thankfully, the men excused themselves as soon as they'd all checked in at the door, announcing they were off to mingle with the stars. Guests at the event included several well-known actors, a few executives from the clothing manufacturer, and a sizable cohort from the music industry.

For the occasion, Nate had hauled out his navy blue Armani suit that had last seen action at the party he and his siblings had thrown to celebrate their parents' thirty-fifth wedding anniversary. Beside him stood Kennedy in a dark gold dress that exposed almost every inch of her slim, flawless back, the hem falling several tantalizing inches above her knees. Tonight her eyes appeared more gray than blue, and an abundance of dark hair spilled over her shoulders and down her back in shiny corkscrew curls. She was nothing short of stunning, as evidenced by the eyes that tracked their entrance.

"Now we just have to find the belle of the ball," Kennedy said, her gaze scouring the room for Sahara. "And watch out for Aurora. She should be here soon."

Nate closed his eyes as he prayed for strength. Wonderful. Although, he had suspected Aurora couldn't be far behind when he'd gotten into the limo and realized his date had been crashed, his place at Kennedy's side usurped—at least for the duration of the ride. Come to think of it, he was surprised they hadn't stopped by Aurora's brownstone to pick her up too in the evening's *the more the merrier* theme.

His irritation must have been plain as day on his face because Kennedy shot him a quelling look. "Don't look at me like that. She's Sahara's friend too. Did you honestly think she wouldn't be invited? Now, try not to be such a stick-in-the-mud. We're here to have a good time."

Clearly, they didn't share the same definition of a good time. After not having seen her all week, having her all to himself tonight was what he considered a good time. Short of that, this would have to do, because he was at the *take what he could get* stage of their arrangement. "It would have been nice if you'd mentioned this in your *text*." He couldn't keep the slight edge from seeping into his voice.

"There are over one hundred and fifty people here. What difference does it make if one of them happens to be your darling baby sister?" She huffed. "You're acting as if the two of you aren't close. You guys hang out more than any brother and sister I know."

"Yes, I love my sister and we get along great, but that doesn't mean I want her on my dates," he muttered.

In the midst of avidly perusing the room, Kennedy went motionless. Then she very slowly angled her head until her gaze met his, something almost questioning in her eyes. "Only this isn't a real date," she reminded him, unnecessarily.

Nate didn't say anything, simply returned her stare, one eyebrow raised.

Are you sure about that?

A hum of electricity vibrated in the air, and despite the din of a party in full swing, an intimate bubble of silence formed around them.

A moment later, a male voice behind them pierced that bubble with a warm and congenial, "Kennedy."

The pair turned in unison toward the intrusive presence. They'd been having a moment. Nate could already see their future dating life, a series of events in which men he didn't know were constantly calling out Kennedy's name, demanding her attention.

"Phil, it's so good to see you," Kennedy said, an affectionate smile wreathing her face. "Is Brenda with you?" she asked, taking a quick look around for his better half, as he lovingly referred to his wife.

Returning her smile, he replied, "Not tonight, but she asked me to send you her best and hopes to have you over for dinner again soon."

"That would be lovely. I'll be sure to give her a call," Kennedy said, and then turned to her date to perform the introductions. "Phil, this is Nate Vaughn, Aurora's brother. Nate, this is Phil Draper, a former client. He's the VP of Marketing at ECO Apparel, the company that manufactures and distributes Sahara's clothing line."

"Of course, Kurt Vaughn's boy. Wonderful to meet you," Phil enthused as the men shook hands. "As I've told your sister, I can't get enough of your father's work. I've seen every movie he's ever made. They don't make movies like they used to."

"I'll be sure to let him know he has a fan in you," Nate replied, smiling.

Phil turned and regarded her fondly. "Kennedy worked with us for six months and the place hasn't been the same since she left. We'd love to have her back. Maybe you can convince her."

Kennedy could feel herself blushing as warmth climbed from her chest to her face. "Oh, don't listen to Phil. I was the lucky one. ECO Apparel was our first client, and almost single-handedly helped launch the agency. And no one has sent more referrals our way than Phil himself. I owe him a lot." No one at ECO had been better to her than Phil, and she was proud to call him her friend.

"Always happy to help in whatever way I can," Phil said magnanimously.

He thought a lot of himself. She knew that. But he expressed it in a way she didn't find off-putting. The man had a heart of gold. Without his support, it would have taken twice as long or longer to *begin* to diversify ECO's workforce. The last time she'd stopped by the offices—six months ago—new and diverse faces were everywhere she looked. And it never got old, the satisfaction of knowing that Token had had a lot to do with the changes.

"I don't blame you for wanting her to come back," Nate said, his gaze drifting over her like a soft caress, intimate and warm. "Kennedy leaves an indelible mark wherever she goes."

Her heart practically skipped a beat as she swallowed hard and tore her gaze from Nate's. She needed a tamper-proof force field to resist his brand of magnetism, and the only thing she had was a little clutch purse.

"Well, it was lovely seeing you again, Kennedy. Make sure you give Brenda a call. We'd love to have you for dinner again, and you're more than welcome to bring a date." In the next breath, Phil shifted his attention to Nate and said, "Hope to see you again."

Kennedy bit back a smile. Phil couldn't have made his meaning more obvious if he'd come right out and asked Nate to join them for dinner.

"A man can only hope," Nate answered lightly, shooting her a look that made her acutely aware of the power of one of his barely there smiles and what it did to her insides.

Kennedy instinctively placed her palm on her lower stomach and then dropped it to her side when she realized what she was doing. With his return, it seemed the whole belly-whooshing thing was back for good. Let the roller-coaster rides begin again.

After Phil left them to mingle, Kennedy looked up at Nate and smiled. "That was nice. Isn't Phil great?" It was a rhetorical question, not one she'd expected to be met with silence.

Placing his hand on the small of her back, Nate silently guided her deeper into the room. He paused to snag two glasses of champagne from the tray of a passing bow tie–clad server.

Kennedy gracefully accepted the champagne flute from him and watched as he downed almost the entire contents of his. "What?" she pushed. "Don't tell me you didn't like Phil."

Nate made a *meh* face.

"You can't be serious."

His brow arched in response. *You wanna bet?*

"But you were so…" She struggled to find the right word. "Friendly," she concluded lamely.

"Come on, Kennedy. I wasn't raised in a barn. And it was only last week you gave me shit for not being nice enough to what's-his-name."

"Sam," she supplied.

"Yeah, what's-his-name."

Kennedy glared at him. "Very funny."

"I'm damned when I don't and then rebuked when I do." He shook his head and lamented on a heavy sigh, "Kennedy Mitchell, you are one hard woman to please."

"Enough with the jokes. I want to know why you don't like him. He couldn't have been nicer to you. He even waxed poetic about your dad's movies." Kennedy took a sip of her champagne. Phil was a sweetheart.

"Well, in that case, he's a saint."

"Okay, now you're lying."

"Of course I'm lying. It seems that's the only way to end this interrogation."

"Then just tell me the truth." Now it was imperative she know. Her character judgment was at stake.

"I grew up with men like him and my gut tells me he's as authentic as a three-dollar bill." Nate finished the rest of his champagne in one long swallow.

"Your gut?" Kennedy scoffed. "Ever think your gut could be off?"

"It hasn't steered me wrong yet," he stated smugly.

"Well, it's wrong when it comes to Phil. He's the—"

The second she caught sight of Aidan beyond Nate's broad shoulders, everything stopped, foremost her ability to speak. It was like hitting a brick wall. Or getting hit by a speeding train.

Her thoughts scrambled. *What the hell is Aidan doing here?*

She must have looked like someone in a horror movie, because Nate immediately shot a look behind him. Then he turned back to her and muttered under his breath, "Don't tell me—another ex-boyfriend?"

Kennedy could only nod as she did her best to stop panic from overwhelming her. There wasn't much she could do about the fear and dread. They seemed content to accept a shotgun role in the unfolding events.

"It's okay. I've got you." Nate caught her around the waist and pulled her tight to his side as Aidan closed the last bit of distance between them. "Everything is going to be fine. You're with me now," he whispered in her ear.

Didn't he get it? That *was* the problem.

15

"Hi, Aidan. This is a surprise." No lies detected there. "I had no idea you'd be here." Kennedy wished it didn't sound as if she was having problems dislodging a boulder-sized obstruction from her throat. She took a gulp of her champagne.

Sahara. It had to be. It could only be her.

It was funny, but except for a faint tinge of sadness, seeing him again didn't fill her with the bittersweet longing she thought it might, considering she hadn't wanted to break up.

"I can see that," Aidan remarked coolly as he looked pointedly at Nate, who now held on to her like a toddler clutching his favorite toy.

That was okay—she'd heard the bottom ribs were basically for show. And who really needed to breathe? She couldn't think of a bodily function more highly overrated.

With her ex and current date acting like two cowboys facing off at a showdown at dawn, it was clear introductions were long overdue. Smiling, Kennedy performed the thankless duty. "Nate, this is Aidan Anderson. Aidan, this is Nate Vaughn, Aurora's brother."

Curt nods of acknowledgment and cool stares were the extent of the men's responses. Kennedy tried to ease out of Nate's hold, but his arm remained firm around her waist, not allowing an inch between them. It was funny because when they'd been sleeping together, he hadn't come across as the possessive type.

"I didn't realize you and Aurora's brother were—so friendly," Aidan said in a low, growly voice, his meaning unmistakable. "As a matter of fact, I got the impression you barely knew him."

Nate's arm contracted around her waist. Aidan had hit a nerve. He recovered quickly, exclaiming in mock disbelief, "Barely know me? Are you kidding? Nothing could be further from the truth." He then flashed her an adoring smile. "No, Kennedy and I go *way* back."

Oh dear lord, she was in for it now.

"Now that we've established how well I know Kennedy, how do you know her? I'm usually good with names, but I don't remember her ever mentioning yours," Nate said, casually slipping the metaphorical knife between her ex's ribs.

Aidan's eyebrow rose, his gaze briefly meeting hers. "Then you can't have been around much the last two years. She's my girlfriend." Given the sharpness of his tone, one would expect he possessed fangs instead of incisors.

"Ex-girlfriend," she was quick to correct. "Aidan and I are not—not together anymore."

Kennedy silently fumed at how two intelligent grown-ass men resorted to snark and innuendo at the slightest provocation. Had neither of them ever heard the saying *never let them see you sweat*? She didn't find their passive aggression remotely appealing and resented the fact that neither appeared to care about the position they were putting her in. She didn't wear discomfort well and it didn't go with her outfit.

To prevent the situation from deteriorating—someone had to be the adult in the room—Kennedy sought to reduce the rising tension. "Nate has been away. A lot. In France. He only recently got back." Good lord, she sounded like an automaton, her words stiff and disjointed.

"Yes, and now I'm back, and as you can imagine, Kennedy and I have a lot of catching up to do."

Nate's tone may have been cool, but his statement possessed the heat of a flamethrower's blast. Aidan's eyes narrowed. Nate's arm contracted around her again, practically plastering her to his side. Kennedy worried that if she didn't hurry and get away from him, he'd transform into an alpha dog and pee a circle around her.

Aidan's expression darkened as he turned his attention back to Kennedy. "Don't forget to tell him all about me, then."

Nate made a sound in his throat, and she sensed this had just been turned into a penis-measuring contest, and as every woman knew, no man could stand to lose that.

"Kennedy, may I have a word with you…*alone*?" Aidan said, the sentence ostensibly a question.

Dear lord, why? She was here with Nate. She'd moved on. Why couldn't Aidan just let it go and move on too? What was the point of dragging this out?

But what choice did she have? The last thing she wanted was a scene, and right now, Aidan was more than capable of embroiling her in one. Kennedy looked at Nate. "I'll be right back. Why don't you get us something to nibble on in the meantime?" she said, praying he wouldn't give her a hard time. Having to deal with Aidan was stressful enough.

Nate's jaw worked as if he were grinding his teeth. It took a few moments, while he faced off in a staring contest with her ex, but eventually his hold on her loosened enough for her to smoothly extricate herself and regain complete autonomy of movement. She held her near-empty glass tight in her hand.

"I'll be back," Nate said, his words sounding more like an ominous warning. But if she'd expected him to saunter off quietly into that good night, she could kiss that dream good-bye. Because he was who he was, he had to get the last word. Or in this case, a kiss, which he planted lightly on her lips.

Someone growled, and for a moment she didn't know if it was her or Aidan.

It wasn't her.

Nate was gone before she could impale his foot with her stiletto. The kiss itself, however, had been potent; the jolt it sent through her stirred up too many warring emotions. The euphoric high of coming together versus the precipitous fall back to reality of going their separate ways.

Damn. Why after all this time was it the same?

"If this is some sort of joke, I don't find it funny," Aidan growled the second Nate was out of earshot. "You can't honestly expect me to believe you're dating *that guy.*" He spit the latter as if it were an expletive.

Kennedy's back went up, suddenly unaccountably protective of Nate. "Whether I am or not is none of your business." Then, attempting to bring the temperature of the situation down, she tagged on a gentle reminder. "We aren't together anymore."

Aidan gave her a pointed look and then shot a glance to the side, the equivalent of rolling his eyes. "Do you want to know how many dates I've been on since you turned down my proposal?"

At this point, she didn't care to know.

"Nate is a good friend and he's going through some things right now," she said, annoyed at herself for offering an explanation. But she was willing to do and say anything to keep the peace. She took after the *let's not air our personal business out in public* side of the family. Her sister, Cheryl, was a whole different story.

"Right, the poor rich white guy is being sued because his company was caught screwing over people like us. Yeah, I read all about it," he sneered. "Then, suddenly, you're his biggest champion. Don't you get it, Ken? He's using you. And you're letting him."

That got her back up again. And her chin, which rose perceptibly. "You don't know anything about my relationship with Nate."

Skepticism and disdain didn't combine for a pleasant sound. Aidan snickered. "What relationship? Last month you were *my* girlfriend. He's playing you for a fool, Kennedy. Why can't you get that through your head? That's what white guys like him do to beautiful Black girls like you. They'll use you, then toss you aside. Open your eyes."

It was like facing the onslaught of a storm and being pummeled by one gust of wind after another, each individual raindrop like a pin piercing her flesh. She'd never seen this side of Aidan before. How many times had he told her how beautiful she was? That any man would be lucky to be with her. But clearly, he hadn't meant *any* man, and certainly not a man like Nate; white, wealthy, handsome, and pedigreed. To men of Nate's ilk, she served only one purpose. Beyond that, they'd have no use for her.

Within her, a meteoric rise of anger swiftly crowded out the pain of his hateful words. Now *she* was seething but did her best to contain it—although the urge to throw her drink in his face was strong. Shooting a quick glance around to make sure no one stood within hearing distance, she leaned toward

him and whispered, "He was my first. That's the kind of relationship we have."

Aidan's head jerked back slightly, his eyes widening in the
surprise he couldn't hide. Just as quickly, he narrowed his
gaze at her, his lip curled in contempt. "Decided to set your
sights higher, huh? Well, the joke's on you, Ken, because he'll
never marry you."

Kennedy breathed deeply through her nose, her throat tight,
and her heart simultaneously aching and breaking. Shattered
expectations had that effect. "You know what, Aidan? Jealousy and spite isn't a good look on *you*. Now, if you'll excuse
me, I have to get back to my date. Have a lovely evening."

"See you on your way down," he managed to get in before
she turned and walked away.

Kennedy had no idea where she was going, and tears began to
encroach on her waterproof mascara. God willing, it wouldn't
be put to the test.

"*Whoa!* Where're you going? I got us some hors d'oeuvres."
Holding a plate in his hand, Nate stepped in front of her, block-
ing her path to nowhere.

"Hey, what's wrong?" he asked softly, concern knitting
his brow.

"Nothing." She finished off the rest of her champagne
and then plucked a bite-sized flaky pastry from the plate and
popped it in her mouth. As she chewed, she discovered inside
were cheese and spinach. She took another one.

Nate looked directly into her eyes, his gaze unwavering.
"I know you a lot better than you think I do. You're upset.
What did he say to you?"

It was the ominous hardening of his tone that flipped a
switch in her, and she found the perfect person to vent all her
frustrations on. The *right* person, because he was the cause of
it. "What did *he* say to upset me?" she practically hissed. "It

wasn't enough that I had no idea he was going to be here to-night, but if I'm upset, it's because all you did was make a bad situation worse."

Nate appeared genuinely surprised at the force of the anger directed at him. "What are you talking about? I was only try-ing to help you. And he was the one who started in on me with—"

"Kennedy!"

This time her name was uttered in a familiar feminine squeal of joy, saving Nate from the verbal neck-wringing she was about to give him. She wanted to tell him not to breathe easy too soon. This was simply a pause in their conversation, not a cessation.

Kennedy quickly slapped a smile on her face when she spot-ted Sahara approaching as quickly as her high heels and form-fitting dress would permit.

"There you are," her friend exclaimed, flashing a beaute-ous smile as she shimmied over to Kennedy's side. "Was I ever glad to see you when I came in." Embracing Kennedy tightly, she pressed a light kiss to her cheek. "You look gorgeous. That dress on you… *Guurrrl*, you're killing it."

Kennedy couldn't have been happier to see her. "Look who's talking," she said, gesturing at the singer's sleeveless royal blue dress, the bodice a daring combination of chiffon with royal blue boning, and a skin-toned underlay, giving the illusion of translucency.

It was the sort of dress you'd see on the red carpet. Made to be seen, not touched. For show and not convenience. But it looked great on her, displaying a prominent amount of cleav-age and a whole lot of leg.

"Oh, this old thing?" Sahara said coyly, eyelashes fluttering dramatically. "I found this up-and-coming designer in New York—her name's April Rose, she's Black, she used to model, is insanely talented, and she's going to be *huge*. You may have heard of her husband, Troy Ridgefield?"

Kennedy shook her head. "Nope."

"Troy Ridgefield?" she coaxed. "He plays for the Giants." At Kennedy's blank stare, she flicked her wrist dismissively and continued. "Never mind, then. Just take my word for it—you're going to love her when you two finally meet. She was supposed to be here tonight, but her son is running a fever, so… Anyway, I told her I wanted something like the scrumptious emerald green Vera Wang dress Zendaya wore to the Emmys a few years ago, and she came up with this." The singer made a sweeping ta-da gesture with her hands.

"*Insanely talented* is right," Kennedy said approvingly. "She did a great job in giving it a similar look, while not copying it outright."

"Which is what I love about her. She has a trademark style all her own," Sahara enthused. Then her gaze shifted to Nate, who stood behind Kennedy like a sentinel.

Kennedy was quick with the introductions. "Oh, Sahara, this is Nate Vaughn, Aurora's brother."

Nate smiled and extended his other hand. "Nice to meet you."

"The computer genius!" Sahara gushed before brushing his hand aside and throwing her arms around his neck. "Any gorgeous brother of Aurora's is a friend of mine," she said, flirting shamelessly.

After a quick hug, Nate placed his hand on Kennedy's lower back, the imprint of each finger searing her bare skin like a branding iron. Sahara followed the proprietary movement, her eyes going wide at the sight.

Her gaze shot to Kennedy's. *You and Aurora's brother? When did this happen and why didn't you tell me?*

She and Sahara had fallen into a habit of touching base with each other once a month. Her famous friend's schedule was crazy busy on a good day. Kennedy had planned to tell her about her breakup with Aidan the next time they spoke, but everything going on with Nate kept pushing all thoughts of her ex to the back of her mind. And her relationship with Nate wasn't something she wanted to explain to Sahara over the phone, much less via text. That kind of conversation required in-person, eye-to-eye contact, and a modicum of privacy.

Kennedy ignored the question in Sahara's eyes, replying innocuously, "Nate agreed to be my date tonight."

Unlike their encounter with Aidan, Nate knew to make himself scarce without being told. Smoothly plucking the empty glass from her hand, he said, "Why don't I get you another drink?"

Sahara turned and followed his retreating form before turning back to her. "Aurora has a *very* fine-looking brother. Why am I only learning about this now?"

"He's all right," Kennedy replied in the understatement of the year.

Grabbing Kennedy by the hand, she pulled her into an alcove several feet away. "Wait—so you're not with Aidan anymore?"

"No, we broke up, but—"

"Oh my god! I wish you'd told me," Sahara interrupted. "When he showed up without an invitation, I assumed he was with you."

Kennedy was stunned. She hadn't taken her ex as the party-crashing type. "He asked me to marry him and I said no."

"Damn," Sahara softly exclaimed, her eyes flaring wide. "Did he see you with…?"

Heaving a sigh, Kennedy nodded.

"Ah, now it makes sense. I thought it was weird when he

told me he had to go, since he just got here not even thirty minutes ago."

Aidan had left. She breathed a sigh of relief.

"I saw a side of him I'd never seen before."

Sahara grimaced. "I can imagine." Then a small smile lifted the corner of her mouth. "Girl, you got all these men trying to lock you down. Do you know none of my exes have ever proposed?"

"That's because you break up with them before they can. And didn't you say you begin all your relationships with the *I'm working on my career, and I won't be ready to get married for eons and eons* speech?"

Sahara pouted prettily. "Oh, come on. If you really loved and wanted to marry someone, would you let that stop you?"

"Did you want any of them to propose?"

"No, but that's not the point."

Kennedy laughed. "I wouldn't worry about it. I have a feeling the man you *want* to ask *will* ask."

"Well, I certainly haven't met him yet," Sahara said with feeling. She'd just come out of a yearlong relationship with an up-and-coming singer, and discovered too late that he hoped to use her as a stepping stone. And like most people, Sahara hated being used. Claimed it made her "ragey."

"You will," Kennedy assured her. Beauty, talent, and riches beyond most people's wildest dreams weren't a bad starting-off point when it came to looking for a husband.

Sahara's expression turned playful. "So, a computer guy, hmm?" she asked, raising perfectly manicured eyebrows.

"He's here as a friend." Even to her own ears the words sounded hollow.

Sahara snorted in disbelief. "Friend, my ass. The man practically had his hand on your ass. The only friends who act that way are friends with benefits," she teased with a suggestive swivel of her hips. "Is that the kind of friends you're talking about?"

"First of all, his hand was not on my ass," Kennedy insisted, her voice fierce and low. Close to it, maybe even grazing it a little, but not actually *on* it. "And there are no benefits." And God willing, there wouldn't be.

"Let's see how long that lasts," Sahara said with another snort. "I know men, and that man was looking at you like a man who wants to…be more than friends."

"Don't I have a say in the matter?"

"You didn't seem to mind his hand on your ass." Without giving her a chance to register her protest, Sahara forged on. "Funny, I never figured you for a blonde."

"Aurora is blonde. Her brother is not."

"Okay, light brown or whatever. You know what I mean."

Kennedy knew exactly what she meant. A white guy. Except for Nate, she'd never dated one before, and she hadn't told Sahara about him.

Sahara peered out into the room and spotted him weaving his way through the crowd toward them. She murmured appreciatively, "But if you're going to spread your wings, you definitely want to fly his way. He looks like he's got the goods."

Kennedy's face grew warm. "*Oh stop.* It's not what you think." It was close enough to what she was thinking.

Sahara gave her the look. "How about you quit lying? You know you want his hands on a lot more places than your gorgeous ass," she said with a knowing, impish smile.

There was no talking to her when she was in this mood.

When Nate reached them, he merely smiled and handed her another glass of champagne.

"Okay, now that your man's back, let me run along. Duty calls. We'll catch up later. And don't you dare leave without coming to see me first." Sahara departed with a swish of her skirts and more than a glimpse of a long, slim thigh.

A smile spread slowly across Nate's face. *"Your man?"* he said, cocking an eyebrow. Her date seemed to be enjoying himself way too much for her liking.

"Ha ha, very funny," Kennedy said, rolling her eyes. "That's her idea of a joke."

His glass was midway to his mouth when he paused and asked, "Don't you think her *joke* has a ring of truth to it?" He drank half the contents in one swallow, and the sight of his throat working was a surprisingly erotic one.

Oh shit, she was in trouble. The evening had just started and she was so tipsy that Nate swallowing was turning her on—*on less than two glasses of champagne!* Either she'd turned into a lightweight overnight or this man was making her crazy. He'd managed to spark a light under her libido that she didn't know needed a spark. But if he thought flirting would make her forget the way he'd behaved earlier, he had another think coming.

"Don't think you're off the hook. I'm still mad at you," she huffed.

His blue eyes widened a fraction. "Come again?"

There would be no coming once, much less again. At least, not with her.

"Aidan," she said through clenched teeth.

"You don't have to worry about him. He's gone."

"You know that's not what I meant. I'm talking about that performance you put on for him."

And then, because the timing gods obviously had her in their crosshairs tonight, they were interrupted *again*, proving these kinds of events were not conducive to private, meaningful conversations. This time their interruption arrived in the form of Aurora accompanied by her date, the lieutenant governor's pretty nineteen-year-old daughter.

Kennedy did her best to hide her surprise. Aurora hadn't mentioned that Brittany Faulkner was her plus-one. Kennedy also hadn't realized the two were that close. But then again, it made sense, considering the girl's father had recently called trying to finagle a backstage pass to Sahara's upcoming concert. To the teen, her favorite star's glitzy launch party was probably ten times better. It certainly appeared that way by the gleeful look on her face.

When it was time to sit down to eat and for the fashion show to begin, Jonathan and Darrell joined them at their assigned table, thrilled to have met two of their favorite singers.

Nate, still not out of the doghouse, picked up the gorgeous Desert Queen gift bag from her chair and handed it to her. There were identical gift bags on the chairs at every table. Kennedy graciously accepted hers and peeked inside to find an assortment of perfumes, colognes, a box of Godiva chocolate, a smartwatch, and a Desert Queen five-hundred-dollar gift card.

How lovely. Her mother and sister would love the perfume and the smartwatch, and she'd give the cologne to her father and brothers. The chocolate and the gift card were hers. Closing the bag, she placed it on the floor beside her.

Nate pulled the chair out for her. As she sat, he brought his mouth close to her ear and whispered, "I'm sorry."

Startled, Kennedy watched as he took the seat beside her. While everyone else was *oohing* and *aahing* over their gift-bag goodies, she leaned over and whispered, "Why did you have to take the bait? I expected you to be the bigger man."

When she saw he appeared to be struggling to prevent a smile from making an appearance, she could have kicked herself. It was a poor choice of words, but of course he'd take it like that.

"You're not suffering from a broken heart," she clarified. Although, after the things Aidan had said to her, she didn't think he was either.

The only way to describe the look Nate gave her was piercing emotion simmering just under the surface. "Then what am I suffering from?"

"I didn't say you were suffering from anything."

Nate watched her for a beat, his expression shuttered. "What did he say to upset you?"

The table had quieted and Kennedy noticed Aurora giving her the *is everything all right?* look. In response, she flashed her a reassuring smile.

"Nothing. Nothing that matters." Aurora would say Aidan had been hurt and was lashing out. Her sister would say someone should slap him upside his head.

Nate's mouth tightened a fraction. "Okay, how about this. I want to talk to you alone tonight. Just us. Can we stop by my apartment before I take you home?"

Kennedy stared at him, not knowing quite what to say. "Talk about what?"

"How we're going to handle your ex-boyfriends in the future. It's clear we'll be tripping over them every time we go out." He said it all with a straight face. Then his mouth eased into a smile. "Plus, I have a French press at home, and I know how you love your caramel macchiato frappes."

Her heart shouldn't palpitate at those words, but it did. She couldn't believe that, after all these years, he remembered.

"I have a French press at home too."

He raised an eyebrow. "But I bet you're out of caramel."

Kennedy bit back a gasp. Either he was a master psychic, or he'd recently broken into her apartment.

Nate let out a laugh. "I was right, wasn't I?"

"I'm checking my surveillance video when I get home to-night," she joked.

"As in, when I take you home after we stop by for a drink at my place?" he asked, his tone one part hopeful and two parts persuasive.

Damn, the man knew how to wear a woman down. "All right, one drink," Kennedy relented. Later she would blame it on her obvious state of inebriation (she had to be drunk—what else could explain why she would agree to be alone with him in his apartment?) and that thing he'd done to her libido when she'd realized the column of his throat was just as sexy as his abs.

Seriously, though, one caramel macchiato frappe wouldn't hurt, would it?

16

What on earth was I thinking?

Kennedy could only marvel at the sheer depths of her stupidity. Agreeing to go to Nate's apartment alone wasn't just a bad idea, it rivaled the decision hapless college students made in those cheesy horror movies to go into the woods at night instead of toward the running car. Or was she getting that mixed up with an insurance commercial? Whichever, they were one and the same when it came to truly stupid decisions.

Why hadn't she taken her butt straight home tonight?

"You know we could have had this conversation in the limo," she remarked as he turned on the lights in the hall.

Nate's two-story penthouse apartment was equally as luxurious as his sister's place but double the size.

"So you said in the car," he replied, his voice dry. "But that wasn't our agreement. Anyway, I think we'll be more comfortable here." He gestured toward the living room that looked like something out of a lifestyle magazine. "I don't think you've been to my place before." His gaze turned speculative. "Unless Aurora brought you here while I was gone?"

Kennedy shook her head and looked around. Aurora's description of the place more than lived up to her expectations. Strangely, however, it had a single-family-home feel to it if you didn't look out any of the windows, of which there were too many for her to count in the initial sweep of her gaze. The woodwork was a carpenter's dream, the staircase leading to the second floor like nothing she'd ever seen before in anything classified as an apartment.

"So it's empty while you're in France?" Kennedy stepped out of her heels with a contented moan. And just like that, his height advantage increased by three inches. The sandals might look great on, but they were definitely not made for walking. Or standing too long either.

"Someone comes in twice a month to dust. And unless you tell me otherwise, my sister picks up the mail once a week."

"Every Saturday by noon, come hell or high water," Kennedy confirmed. She fell in step beside him as they entered the two-story living room that had skyscrapers for windows.

Nate motioned to the two oversized couches surrounding a beautiful stone fireplace. "Make yourself comfortable. Do you want whipped cream with your sugar-and-caffeine monstrosity?"

Kennedy smiled in amusement as she padded across the wood floors and a plush area rug to the couch opposite a giant flat-screen television mounted on the wall. "No, that would be sugar overload." The caffeine would do her good for her ride home. Nothing like falling asleep and having the driver shake her awake when they arrived at her apartment. "Oh, and just because I'm teetotaling it right now, it doesn't mean you have to. Feel free to have a real drink."

On his way to the kitchen, Nate turned back to her once

he reached the island and shrugged out of his jacket. "Are you trying to get me drunk?" he teased.

"Very funny," she muttered, rolling her eyes.

The striptease didn't stop at his jacket. He proceeded to take off his tie, and then unbutton the first two buttons of his pristine white shirt. Kennedy thought she was handling herself just fine until he removed his cuff links and rolled up his sleeves, exposing a pair of sexy-as-sin forearms. That was when the apartment became unbearably hot and her mouth went dry, making it almost impossible to swallow.

"...for dessert?"

She blinked rapidly, his voice penetrating the momentary short-circuiting of her brain. "I'm sorry—what?" she asked, dragging her gaze up from his tanned forearms.

Nate chuckled softly as if aware she'd been ogling him. "I asked if you'd like a slice of carrot cake or ice cream for dessert. I noticed you didn't touch yours at dinner."

"That's because I was saving those delicious empty calories for this."

Pull yourself together, she sternly admonished herself. *You will not let this turn into a booty call.*

But the devil on her other shoulder demanded to have a say. *Oh, who the hell do you think you're fooling? You're at his apartment, aren't you? If you thought all you were going to do was talk, I have a bridge in Brooklyn in sore need of repair to sell you. C'mon, now. Be the twenty-first-century woman that you are and own your sex drive. You have physical needs like everybody else, and Nate is sending out signals brighter than the one Gotham City uses whenever there's a misbehaving penguin on the loose.*

Tearing her gaze from him completely, Kennedy shushed both voices in her head. There would be no sex tonight. They'd do what they came to do, and then she'd go home to her own bed.

Her big, lonely bed.

"Okay, let's have that talk now." It was best she initiated and steered the conversation. "First off, we've only run into one of my ex-boyfriends. Sam was a blind date."

Nate shot a look at her over his shoulder. "You in a rush? Do you have somewhere else to be tonight?" he asked, amusement in his voice.

"I figured a man of your vast accomplishments would be able to multitask," she replied smartly, twisting around to place her feet on the couch and reclining against one of the overstuffed cushions. *Much better.*

"You didn't answer my question. Do you have somewhere else to be tonight?" he reiterated, making clear he was going to be a dog with a bone about it.

Kennedy snorted softly. "Where would I go at eleven-thirty at night dressed like this?"

Nate stood with his back to her. There was a momentary pause to whatever he was doing, and then all she heard was the clink of a utensil against ceramic. Seconds later, he was striding toward her carrying a saucer and a white ceramic mug.

"I'm sure there are lots of places where you'd be welcomed dressed like that." His voice was low and suggestive.

Kennedy felt the heat of his gaze as it made a thorough tour of her body, from the tips of her pink-painted toes to her blazing-hot face. Clasping the handle of the cup tightly in her hand, she took a tentative sip. The drink was hot and so was she. It didn't make for a comfortable combination. And of course, Nate was a whole different kind of hot.

He remained there, at the couch, standing over her, watching her, his eyes giving off a heat of their own. She'd seen that look before. He'd been getting ready to peel her out of her clothes.

Kennedy took another sip, her gaze meeting his in question. *Would you please sit down already?*

"I'll take your cup when you're ready. So you won't have to move," he added, his gaze drifting over her bare legs stretched out on the couch.

"Oh. Okay. Thank you," she said once she realized she'd have to get up if she wanted to place her mug and saucer on the coffee table, which was several feet away. She took one more drink before readily surrendering both to him and watched him set them down.

Stretched out as she was, Kennedy thought Nate would take a seat on the adjacent couch. She was wrong. She'd swear he owned the place—and her—the way he casually lifted her legs, sat down, and then placed them on his lap.

Kennedy could only stare at him, surprised and hopelessly turned on at the same time. She immediately attempted to place her feet on the floor, but Nate gently grasped her legs. "It's okay. I don't mind," he murmured as his thumb began making sensuous forays of her ankle.

Heat bloomed at every point of contact and beyond. She stared at him, literally holding her breath because, at this point, breathing was impossible.

"What are you doing?" she practically squeaked.

"I'm making myself comfortable without disturbing you."

Without disturbing her? It was as if the man shoveled shit for a living, he was so adept at it.

"Well, you may be comfortable, but I'm not." She was hot, and other formerly dry parts of her were not anymore.

Okay, now say it like you mean it. Your *lady doth protest too much* act won't hold sway with this audience.

"Relax." If he intended to come across as calming or soothing, he missed it by a long shot but hit smoldering right on the mark. "We're not going to do anything you don't want. We're just here to talk."

Not going to do anything you don't want?

Good lord, was that supposed to make her feel better when her panties were about to combust into a raging inferno?

"I meant what I said earlier. I'm sorry about what happened with what's-his-name. I should never have taken the bait. You dumped him and he saw you with me, so of course he was upset." One hand now rested on her bare shin and the other cupped the heel of her foot, his finger lightly stroking the soft flesh of the arch. "Now tell me what he said to upset you."

He couldn't seriously expect her to carry on a conversation like this. She'd never been so tense in her life. But short of removing her legs from his lap—which she was not inclined to do at the moment because it had been a while since she'd played with this kind of fire—what other choice did she have but to bite her lip, clench her thighs, and suffer the torture like any woman of free will was wont to do when an attractive man held her feet captive?

You can at least talk a good game.

"What do you think he said? He warned me about men like you."

Nate didn't appear at all surprised by her answer. "And what kind of man is that?"

"The kind who would use a girl like me," she replied, remembering the sting of Aidan's words.

Other than the slight tightening of his jaw, Nate's expression remained unchanged as his palm lightly cupped the ball of her foot. "And what kind of girl are you?"

"I'm just a pretty face you'll use and toss aside," she stated blithely. As if the words hadn't shaken her confidence and hurt her pride.

Nate's eyes flashed with anger. "Screw what I just said. I

should have kicked his ass when I had the chance. I knew I shouldn't have left you alone with him."

"No, I'm glad I talked to him. At least I know what he *really* thinks of me." She couldn't bring herself to tell him how race had factored into it, but she sensed he knew.

"I want you to listen to me very carefully," he said, trapping and holding her gaze with his. "Don't let anyone convince you that you're just a pretty face. You're much, *much* more than that, and if you don't know it, I'd be happy to tell you until there isn't an ounce of doubt left in your mind."

Kennedy blinked at him as her stomach did that whooshing, dipping thing. She didn't know what to say. No one had ever said that to her, and certainly not with such heartfelt sincerity. At least, no male who wasn't related to her by blood.

"I don't need you to do that. I know I'm more than a pretty face." Her job had always been to convince other people of that, which was too often easier said than done.

Okay, he really, *really* needed to stop touching her. She would stop him if not for the fact that it felt *so* good and she was embarrassingly weak, something she'd pay for later when she couldn't look herself in the mirror.

Oh, give it a rest. It's your feet, an inner voice chided.

It's my feet that I just discovered is one of my erogenous zones, thank you very much.

Having put the naysayer properly in her place, Kennedy continued, "Look, I probably made too big a deal about what happened with Aidan. He started it by needling you, and you gave as good as you got. It isn't as if you were jealous or anything like that."

Why did the latter sound as if she was asking a question and not stating an unequivocal fact?

The smallest of smiles ghosted his lips. "We know that, do we?" he murmured, quietly holding her gaze. Then he shifted his attention to the foot he held cupped in his palm. "You have such pretty feet. Pretty toes." He paused, his eyes heavy-lidded when they met hers again, and he whispered in a throaty voice, "Pretty all over."

Kennedy stared at him, eyes wide on a swift intake of breath. "Are you flirting with me again?"

On a scale of one to ten of stupid questions, that came in at a solid eleven. He'd left flirting behind five minutes ago. He was deep in *seduce her off her feet* mode, and currently halfway there.

In response, he pressed gently but firmly into the arch of her foot, startling a whimper from her throat.

"Tense?" Nate asked innocently. He slid his hand ever so slowly up her leg, his palm traversing her ankle, calf, until it hit her knee, where he briefly halted.

Tense? Turned on? Who could tell the difference anymore? "It has been a long night," she said, doing her level best to stave off the choppy breathlessness creeping into her voice. "And either you're trying to get me in bed or..."

"Or what?" he prompted, his fingers drawing circles on her knee, setting off sparks of pleasure.

Kennedy swallowed with difficulty. "That's when you're supposed to cut me off and tell me I'm mistaken and that you're not trying to seduce me," she admitted. Even if he didn't mean it, he should have said it so she wasn't the only one keeping up the pretense that *this*—his hands on her and her doing nothing to stop him—wasn't happening between them when it most definitely was.

That smile again, and it landed where it had the first time he'd turned it on her: right between her legs. He peered at her from beneath a thick veil of dark blond lashes. "If I were, how am I doing so far?"

"As if I'm going to tell you." It was good she still had a sense of humor about it.

As if to make a point—and torture her into willing submission—his hand resumed its journey, this time up her thigh, momentarily skirting the hem of her dress.

Kennedy instinctively clamped her legs together—tight—trapping his hand between them. For a second, neither of them moved, as if both had been startled by the action. The sight of his hand between her legs was both intimate and scorching hot.

When he turned his hand sideways, she involuntarily performed a few seconds of Kegel exercises. His desire-roughened voice indicated she wasn't the only one affected. "Just say the word if you want me to stop."

And Kennedy knew she could take the monstrous bastard at his word. How dare he put the onus on her. Yet how diabolically clever of him.

"What word?" she whispered.

Nate laughed then, the sound a throaty rumble. "*Stop*...but you have to say it in French."

"How do I say *stop* in French?" she asked, ever conscious of her legs relaxing and drifting apart and his hand moving under her dress. The long length of her legs afforded her an additional second or two before it reached its destination, if what was under her now-damp thong was his ultimate goal.

"*Arrête,*" he purred, never once removing his gaze from hers.

The low, sexy cadence of his voice, the touch of his hands, and the expression on his face—those slumberous blue eyes—all did a number on her. It was like she was whisked back in time to that day at her and Aurora's apartment.

With Aurora in California with her high school boyfriend before she moved to New York permanently, Nate had come by the apartment to make sure she was settling in okay. They'd met the year before when Aurora had invited her out to New York for the summer. After an hour of small talk and flirting, he'd made his move and she'd been with him every step of the way.

"How do you say *don't stop*?"

Why don't you cut to the chase and tell him to fuck you?

His eyes flared as his hand contracted against her slim upper thigh. *"N'arrête pas,"* he growled.

Where she found the fortitude to play coy, she had no idea, but she did. "What about *kiss me*?"

His eyes darkened and dropped to her lips. *"Embrasse-moi."*

To an English-only-speaking person, his French sounded sexy good. In the future, she'd demand he speak it to her more often. Especially on occasions like this.

Kennedy knew she wasn't so much playing with fire as she was tossing igniter fluid on it. "What about *do me*?" she whisper-laughed, husky and taunting.

Nate made an inarticulate sound in his throat, but she got his meaning all too well. And it was the last thing she heard before his mouth was on hers and she was flat on her back.

Kennedy let out a startled moan that ended in satisfaction as she willingly gave herself up to longing, pleasure, and lust. She hadn't felt like this in a long time. She wouldn't go as far as to say Nate had spoiled her for other men, but he'd done something that made the taste of him on her tongue and weight of him on her, over her, between her legs, an experience she'd never forgotten and had wanted to repeat over and over again.

"God, you feel good," he mumbled against her lips, kissing the corners, and then her chin and the slope of her neck.

Ditto. Kennedy plowed her fingers through his hair and palmed the back of his head. She didn't know if that was to keep his mouth close or for her own support. Her mind was a dizzying mix of emotions, of wants and needs. She needed his mouth back on hers, and on her breasts, her stomach, and between her thighs. On all the needy parts clamoring for his attention.

Taking matters into her own hands, panting, she urged his mouth back to hers, welcoming the thrust and parry of his tongue, the kiss as ardent and ravenous as she could ever wish for.

A riptide of sensation engulfed her, every erogenous zone in her body under siege and overwhelmed. And they were both still fully clothed.

It had been a long time, but she wasn't sure she was mentally or physically prepared for how her body would react without a stitch between them.

She didn't have to wait long to find out. With a mumbled, "Bed," Kennedy was soon off the couch and in his arms in a move so deft and smooth, one would have thought it was choreographed. With his mouth still on hers, he carried her up the stairs to his bedroom. There he placed her on the mattress, only then breaking the kiss, something he appeared reluctant to do, if the way his mouth lingered on her neck and collarbone was anything to go by.

When he finally lifted his head and stood at the side of the bed, Kennedy cast a look around the spacious room, vaguely noting the king-sized bed and the navy blue comforter beneath her.

"If you don't want to go any further, this would be a good time to tell me," Nate said, his erection prominent against the fly of his pants.

A smile crept across her face. "If you're going to talk, you can explain to me why you're still dressed."

Her words seemed to act as the starting gunshot of a race as to how quickly he could get them naked. If there was a record to be broken, he appeared determined to shatter it. His shirt came off first. His dress pants and briefs, pooled at his feet, soon followed. When he started in on hers, he made it clear he didn't need or want her help, because what started as a show of quick efficiency slowed significantly when it came to removing the matching bra-and-thong set.

Kennedy couldn't keep her eyes off his body, the thrum of desire at her core growing stronger with each new rush of moisture. He looked the same as she remembered him but different. He'd filled out from the twenty-three-year-old who'd relieved her of her virginity and shown her how unbelievably pleasurable sex could be when had with the right person. Broader in the shoulders, more muscled throughout, his body beautifully proportioned and firm.

Reaching out, she ran her palms down his rippled chest and abs. In the same moment, he pushed the flimsy cups of her bra aside, exposing her breasts.

Gaze riveted, he drew in a breath. "God, you're beautiful." His voice was hoarse.

Kennedy let out a whimper. "So are you."

He swiftly covered her nipple with his mouth and had her gasping. She didn't remember much beyond that. The way he touched her, the way he kissed her, had her desperately moaning and panting beneath him. She closed her eyes at the intensity of what he made her feel, eagerly parting her legs and tilting her hips as he sheathed his erection and entered her.

She cried out, a breathless sound of pleasure that ricocheted off the walls and elicited an "oh fuck" from him that sounded as if it were expelled through gritted teeth.

"Fuck, that feels good," he groaned as he pulled out and drove into her once again, his hands pinning hers above her head on the mattress.

Her legs circled his hips. She wanted him closer. And closer still.

He laved her other nipple, her inner walls clamping down hard on his cock. Nate released a string of curses, his breathing quickly becoming labored.

As he drove into her, his pace hard and unrelenting, her body raced headlong toward a climax she sensed—no, knew—would level her.

"Open your eyes," he rasped, his mouth next to her ear.

Kennedy heard him but couldn't make sense of his words and responded by arching her hips in tandem to the downward plunge of his.

"Kennedy, open your eyes." Though still choppy and breathless, there was no mistaking the firmness of his tone.

"I can't," she gasped. She wanted to touch him, but her hands were still secured by his.

Nate slowed his thrusts. "Yes, you can. C'mon, baby. Open those pretty eyes of yours."

How could she when her lids felt as if they weighed one hundred pounds?

"Open your eyes, beautiful, or I'll stop," he said, his tone more playful than threatening, but he slowed his thrusts even more.

Kennedy let out a moan of dismay but did as he demanded, her mouth pushed out in a pout. She opened her eyes to find Nate's blue ones slitted and positively devouring her.

"Good. I want to look into them when you come."

That grumbled remark alone would have been enough to set her off, but added to that was, with her acquiescence, he resumed the pace of his thrusts, sending her body hurtling into a paroxysm of pleasure. Nate followed seconds later, his grip on her hands tightening as his body shuddered in completion.

Boneless and sated, Kennedy felt more alive than she'd been in a long time, her skin flushed and damp from all their delicious exertions. She'd read somewhere that orgasms had a restorative effect. Hers had been earth-shattering, so the benefits had to be exponentially greater.

Nothing beats sex like this.

It took another minute for their breathing to even out, and Kennedy barely moved when Nate pulled out of her and rolled onto his back. Seconds later, he got out of bed, and she couldn't take her eyes off his firm, tight ass as he walked, in all his naked glory, to the bathroom to take care of business.

He was back before she could miss him. This time she was able to admire the front view, which was just as impressive as the back. Gaze hooded and without saying a word, he slid in beside her and snuggled her into his arms, spooning against her.

"Give me fifteen minutes and we'll do it again," he grumbled into the tousled dampness of her hair.

The hangover she had from fantastic sex caused a lethargy that made it almost impossible for her to lift her head off the pillow of his arm. She purred contentedly.

Her lethargy was all but forgotten fifteen minutes later. Just as he'd promised.

17

"Working hard or hardly working?"

Nate lifted his gaze to find Jack framed in the doorway. Smiling lazily—nothing like great sex to start the week off right—he sat back in his chair and gestured at his friend. "This is what I get for having an open-door policy. It encourages the riffraff to drop by anytime for specious reasons."

"*Specious?*" Jack asked with a grin as he sauntered in. "When have I ever needed a good reason to stop by your office? But I would argue that shooting the shit is good reason enough. And who the hell are you calling *riffraff*? My car costs more than most people make in a year."

Nate snorted. "I wouldn't brag about spending that kind of money on a depreciating asset." Last summer, Jack had dropped almost two hundred grand on a Porsche 911 Turbo. He swore his friend would marry the damn thing if he could. After over a year, it still had that "new" car smell.

"Look who's talking. How much did you spend on your mansion in the sky?" Jack smirked.

"A lot. And I'll sell it for a lot more," Nate cheerfully shot back.

"Yeah, but can it go from zero to 199 miles per hour in 2.6 seconds?"

Nate shook his head, chuckling. "What's up?"

Jack peered down at him, his stance wide. "Nothing yet. What'd you do this weekend? I called you Saturday. Thought you might want to hit the new club near Madison Square Park. A bunch of us went."

"I went to a launch party."

"Oh yeah? With the woman from the press conference? Aurora's friend?" he asked, his expression intrigued.

"Yeah. Aurora was there too."

"I thought you hated that shit."

Nate shrugged. "Kennedy asked me to go."

For a beat Jack simply stared at him, his gaze assessing. "You must really like her. Kennedy."

"Yeah, what's not to like?"

Beautiful. *Check.*

Smart. *Check.*

Kind and caring. *Check.*

Body. *Smoking.*

Sex. *Hot.*

So hot. He hadn't wanted her to leave when she'd stretched out naked on his bed and told him she had to go home. It had been two in the afternoon the following day. They'd spent the morning in bed, their hunger for each other indefatigable. An entire day in bed with her wouldn't have been enough. Sadly, he hadn't gotten that, and had reluctantly driven her back to her apartment late that afternoon. But this time he'd left her limp and dewy-eyed at her door after a searing goodbye kiss. Things were definitely looking up.

"Not much. She sure isn't afraid to speak her mind. But I got the impression you and her were for show. You know, because of the lawsuit. I mean, you just got back, and the day after the press conference—" Jack snapped his finger "—*bam!* You're going out, and you did say she was doing you a favor."

"She was. But it's more than that now."

"Obviously. You sleeping with her?"

Nate narrowed his eyes at him. "What's with the third degree?"

Who he dated, the women he slept with, had never been a secret between them, but whatever was going on between him and Kennedy was...theirs. He didn't want to open it up to critical scrutiny, and those were the vibes Jack was putting out. The operative word being *critical*.

"Hey, you know me. I'm good with whatever you want. I'm curious, that's all." When his cell phone began to ring, he paused and silenced it. "So when am I going to get an introduction?"

"I thought you met her." Nate had seen him standing next to her during the press conference.

"She said she was a friend of your family. I sure as shit didn't know you were going to start seeing her."

"What does that matter?"

"What, you don't want to introduce her to me?" Jack sounded irked.

Nate tried to remember when his friend had ever been this interested in one of his girlfriends. Oh, he remembered now. Never. "Okay, spit it out. If you have something to say, just say it."

"I'm just looking out for you. Looking out for the company."

"What does the company have to do with Kennedy?"

Jack met his gaze. "Trevor Markham."

"Who? The lawyer? What about him?" Nate wished he'd hurry up and get to the point.

"I told you I was looking into him since he seems to be the sticking point when it comes to arbitration. Just wanted to know what I could find out about him. What makes him tick and so on…and that's when I discovered his connection to your—to Kennedy."

Nate shook his head because none of what his friend was saying made sense. "What do you mean his connection to Kennedy?"

Jack absently scratched the back of his neck. "From what I was able to find out, it looks like they dated. I'm not sure how long, but it was before he started working for Goldberg & Johnson."

So Kennedy once dated the lawyer who was currently suing his company. No big deal. He was sure it happened all the time.

"And you think this is important why?" Nate asked.

Jack straightened to his full height, his hand dropping to his side. "You can't be serious."

"I am. She has no idea which firm is handling the case, much less the individual lawyers working on it." In truth, Nate didn't know shit. They'd never talked about it, but if he had to put money on it, he'd swear Kennedy didn't know, because if she had, she'd have said something to him.

"She runs a PR agency with your sister. Do you honestly think she doesn't know? After the show she put on at your press conference?" Jack scoffed.

Nate was trying hard to remain calm, but his friend was beginning to test his patience. "What exactly are you accusing her of, Jack?"

"I'm not accusing her of anything. All I'm saying is the guy is pushing his team to take this to court and you want to settle. He wants a jury to decide without knowing how much money's on the table. My question is why. Why doesn't he want to at least hear what you're willing to offer?"

"And you think Kennedy has something to do with that? That she put some fucking bug in his ear? That she's scheming behind my back to help a guy she used to date? Is that what you're suggesting?"

Nate knew his friend had real trust issues when it came to women, stemming from his ex-fiancée, but this, what he was insinuating now, was bullshit. If nothing else, Kennedy was as loyal a friend as Aurora ever had, and she wouldn't do this to him.

"All I'm saying is it doesn't look good for you or the company, *and* I don't want you to get hurt. Sue me for caring about one of my oldest friends and the best boss I've ever had. And tell me you wouldn't do the same thing if the situation was reversed."

What would he do if the situation was reversed? Nate asked himself.

Of course you'd tell him, if for no other reason than he had a right to know. And if there's nothing to it, all is well. Nothing to see here, move along. The end.

"Okay, I get it. And now that you've proved your loyalty, you can tell me whether you've heard back from Duncan Flynn," Nate said, quickly changing the subject. He didn't want to talk to him about Kennedy, the woman he was sleeping with. The woman he was falling for, again.

"My, don't you look bright-eyed this morning. Are you getting laid by Mr. Tech Billionaire?"

Besides Aurora, only Jonathan had the temerity to speak to her like that.

In the midst of hanging up her linen jacket on the coat stand near her desk, Kennedy turned with a dramatic huff and treated him to her fiercest mock glare. "Mr. Tech Billionaire? Really, Jonathan?" she asked with a supercilious arch of her brow. "I'd prefer if you referred to him by his given name."

Julie, the agency's contract lawyer, popped up behind him, the top of her head reaching his shoulder. "Did I hear something about someone getting laid? Who're we talking about?"

"Jonathan."

"Boss Lady."

At the simultaneous answers, Julie's gaze ping-ponged between the two before coming to rest on Kennedy.

"Right, except we know he's getting laid," Julie said, jerking her head at Jonathan.

"Now now now," Jonathan tsked. "Assuming and knowing are two different things. I'm a professional, and I don't discuss my love life at work."

Kennedy's eyes met Julie's, and they instantly burst out laughing.

"Then I must have heard about your third anniversary trip to Hawaii and the romantic wedding suite you stayed in from someone else." Julie's brown eyes were sparkling.

"I'm not denying I told you, but it was during happy hour, which comes with entirely different rules. And I thought what was said during happy hours can only be mentioned during happy hours," he mock admonished.

"Does that mean my favorite boss is getting laid?" Julie asked, circling back to her original question.

Kennedy responded by pressing her lips together.

Amusement lit Julie's eyes. "Good for you. It isn't good to stay off that horse too long."

Jonathan guffawed and Kennedy laughed despite herself.

Julie was really something else. Initially, she'd presented herself as a buttoned-up professional; no cursing, no idle chit-chat, no vulgarity, and no caffeine. The latter Kennedy considered a crime against humanity. She'd been working for the agency almost a year when Kennedy accidentally knocked over her purse. A makeup case, a tampon, and a pregnancy test tumbled out—a great way to break the ice, by the way. Kennedy hadn't known if congratulations were in order. That was when Julie confided to her that she and her surgeon husband had been trying to get pregnant for the last three years with no success.

But she'd been good about it. At thirty-two, she claimed she wasn't going to start officially panicking for another two years, since the fertility specialist had told them there was nothing wrong with either of them. They'd been told it could be stress, which was why Julie had left her high-stress position at a top law firm and taken a position as their part-time contract lawyer.

"How about instead of worrying over whether I'm getting laid—which, by the way, is no one's business but mine—Jonathan can tell me why I have a phone call appointment with the chairman of the board of Hanson's in a half hour and I'm only finding out about it now."

Hanson & Co. was the most exclusive chain of luxury jewelry stores in the world. Retaining them as a client would be an incredible coup and would do a lot to add to their credentials. But she'd have appreciated more than thirty minutes to prepare.

"He said it was urgent. He also said you came highly recommended by Phil Draper over at ECO Apparel." Jonathan sent her a wink. "Word's really getting around."

"All right, since I'm sure I got my answer, I'll leave you

two to talk work," Julie said, and bade them a goodbye with a teasing smile.

Kennedy sat down, blew a lock of hair from her eyes, and turned on her miniature desk fan. "Okay, then. What is going on with Hanson's?" she asked, angling the fan toward her. The cool air felt wonderful on her overheated face.

Jonathan sent her a look. "Buckle in. It's going to be a wild ride."

18

A lot had changed in ten years, but some things stayed the same. Some things might never change—at least, not in her lifetime. Speaking with Elliott Bellamy, Hanson's chairman of the board, keenly reminded her of that. Certain attitudes were entrenched, so thoroughly ingrained in the DNA of the country it was hard to imagine life any other way. People like Margaret Hanson-Gertz would never change.

Which led her to Nate.

They'd had sex. Now what? Where did they go from here? Would this be another fling? Did she want anything more? What exactly was *he* looking for?

He'll never marry you.

Aidan's words now haunted her.

Nate was the only white guy she'd ever gone out with or had sex with. And it wasn't as if she hadn't had plenty of other opportunities. But when push came to shove, she'd chosen to keep her distance. At the time, she'd told herself the relationship would be a road to nowhere—a dead-ender—so why bother. Whether that would end up being the case or not, she didn't know, but she did know that her relationships with Black men had ended much the same way. And there was some irony in that her most serious relationships to date had ended in proposals of marriage, and she'd been the one who'd walked away.

Her actions were a mass of contradictions. She'd always thought of herself as someone who wouldn't allow herself to be limited by her gender or race, and that included romantic relationships. And as a relatively young, attractive female, that should mean the world was her oyster. After all, her first sexual experience had been Nate.

But maybe that was the crux of the matter.

He'd been her first and it hadn't worked out the way she wanted. Not that back then she'd been looking for a long-term commitment, but it would have been nice if it had lasted longer than four weeks. It would have been nice if it hadn't been so easy for him to slip back into the *best friend's older brother* role.

Kennedy wouldn't say he'd broken her heart, but it had been plenty sore after things ended between them.

Getting involved with him now would be even more complicated. Which brought her full circle; where did they go from here? She was currently screwing her fake boyfriend and the sex was *fabulous*. Nate had shown her how much better it could be with time and experience. And frankly, she didn't want to give that up. She wanted more.

After a brief gut check, Trepidatious Kennedy asked, *But what happens if you fall head over heels this time?*

Fly-by-the-seat-of-her-pants Kennedy was equally quick to respond. *For the love of God, Kennedy, stop overthinking this and just go with the flow. You want him and he wants you. Get naked and have lots of sex for as long as it lasts. Who knows, maybe that's all you'll ever want from him?*

Trepidatious Kennedy snorted at that. The one thing that hadn't changed between them—once they both let down their guard—was the red-hot chemistry, which was undeniable. If she'd thought he knew which of her buttons to hit before, he was even better at it now. What this man could do with his hands, lips, tongue, and—

The ding of her cell phone yanked her from her lustful thoughts. She picked it up off her desk.

Nate: Busy tonight? We need to talk.

We need to talk? What happened to, I had a fantastic time this weekend. The sex was 😏. When can I see you again?

Kennedy: Is something wrong?

Nate: Can't talk now. On my way to a meeting. After work at my place? I'll send a car.

Kennedy tried not to let her thoughts run away with her, but what was going on? What did they need to talk about— besides how this weekend had been a game changer—and why was he being short with her? She fired off a response.

Kennedy: If something's wrong, tell me now. That way I can prepare myself.

Nate: Nothing major. Gotta run. The car will be there at 6.

Who was he kidding? *We need to talk* in no way equated to *nothing major.*

She had a good mind to tell him she wasn't free tonight, but that would be petty, and she was saving the petty shit for if or when they passed the three-month mark. But it was cruel of him to send that kind of cryptic message when she still had another six hours to get through. Practically a lifetime.

He had her mind zigzagging in a dozen different directions. She assumed they were exclusive, but they hadn't actually talked about it since their fake dating moved to real sexing. One could conceivably say they'd done what they set out to do in garnering positive coverage of him. What if he wanted to propose something different? *Or*, what if sex with her was just an itch he'd needed to scratch, and now that he'd scratched it—many times—he wanted out of their arrangement? It would certainly be an easy way for him to kill two birds with one…big dick.

Chillax! Stop thinking about it or you'll just drive yourself crazy. He wants to see you tonight at his place and he's sending a car. Does that sound like someone who doesn't want to see you again?

Kennedy did as her inner voice demanded: she took a deep breath and chillaxed.

"Have any room in your busy schedule for me?" Aurora's query, accompanied by a light tap on her open door, was the distraction she desperately needed right now.

Then Kennedy got a good look at her and blinked. Her best friend looked extra something today. The sleeveless white-and-red polka-dot dress she wore could only be described as flirty, and the hip-hugging skirt revealed several inches of tanned bare thigh.

"Don't you look…gorgeous. Is that new?" she asked, flitting her hand at the dress.

"I bought it Saturday. You like?" Aurora twirled around and sent the tulip skirt fluttering around her thighs.

"It's beautiful and looks great on you. But—and I ask this with no judgment—what happened? This isn't…you," Kennedy finished weakly.

Aurora preferred tailored blouses and slacks, and pencil skirts to dresses, and as far back as Kennedy could remember, her friend was averse to thigh-revealing clothes in workplace settings—with good reason.

"I know, right?" Aurora said, grinning. "But I don't have any client meetings today and it's supposed to be hotter than Hades out, and I thought, what the hell."

Kennedy laughed. "I'm sure no one's going to complain. And the hair, is that also a new office look?" At work, Aurora usually wore her long straight locks in a loose chignon or an elegant ponytail. She complained it got in the way too much. Today, she wore it loose.

Aurora gave her head a flirty shake, sending her blond hair swaying and curls bouncing. "The hair went with the dress."

"Are you sure there's something you're not telling me?" Kennedy asked, studying her closely.

"Can't I show off my new dress without it raising your suspicions?" her friend teased. "Now, on the good-news front, Sahara came through. Brittany Faulkner got two backstage passes to her concert."

"That's wonderful. You're better than a fairy godmother."

"She's such a sweet kid. It breaks my heart that she's had to grow up without a mother, but she's lucky she has such a great dad. Adam's done a fantastic job with her."

"Adam has, has he?" Kennedy inquired, her brow raised in speculation. "And how would we know this?"

Aurora made a face. "Oh stop. She's a great kid and he's been raising her on his own since she was five. Give the man *some* credit. He's earned it."

"All right, fine. He or some overworked nanny and a cadre of babysitters did a good job of raising her," Kennedy joked.

"You're terrible," Aurora scolded playfully. "*Anyhoo.* What about you? How did things go with my brother? He seemed a little tense at the party."

Kennedy stared at her best friend and debated what to do next. What to say. It took her only seconds to reach a decision, and then she motioned for her to close the door.

"Okay," Aurora said with a strained laugh as she turned and pushed the door shut before plopping her shapely ass on the guest chair. "Let me take a wild stab in the dark. You're sleeping with him."

"What?" Kennedy sputtered. Aurora's matter-of-fact tone surprised her more than the *nail on the head* accuracy of her statement.

"That is what you're going to tell me, right? That you're sleeping with Nate?"

Eyes wide, Kennedy could only gape at her. "You know?" What, had he called his sister the second she'd left his apartment?

"Kennie, I've known since freshman year."

Kennedy's jaw dropped then. She'd known from the *beginning*, not just since their latest romp in the hay.

"*Oh. My. God.* I can't believe you've known about it this whole time," she said, her voice little more than a strangled breath of air.

"Oh, don't worry," Aurora said with a dismissive flutter of her fingers. "It wasn't anything *you* did or said. It was Nate, and he fessed up when I confronted him."

Making Nate an egregiously weak link. She filed that nugget of knowledge in the back of her mind.

"Don't you have anything to say about it?" Kennedy couldn't understand her friend's reaction. She'd braced herself for something other than calm acceptance.

"What *can* I say?" Aurora gave a negligent shrug. "You're both adults. Although, I should be mad at you. And hurt. I get that he's my brother and it makes things awkward, but you're my best friend. We're supposed to tell each other these things. I'd tell *you* if I slept with one of your brothers. And it's not like the thought never entered my mind. Cam and Jay are *hot*."

She and her sister had once joked that it was a mandatory phase all their girlfriends went through: crush hard on the Mitchell brothers and then move on with your life.

"How could I tell you after you told me what happened after Nate broke up with your friend?"

Aurora's gaze softened. "Ken, you're the sister I never had. We may occasionally bicker, but nothing is ever going to come between us. And that includes my brother."

Smiling, Kennedy blew her a kiss, and Aurora caught it. They giggled.

"Okay, now I have a question," Kennedy said, clearing her throat. "You said Nate gave us away. What did he do to make you suspicious?" At first, she wasn't going to ask. However, curiosity got the best of her—as it usually did.

"It was when Spencer asked me to spend August with him in California before classes started. Nate was the one who encouraged me to go. That's when I got a feeling he was going to try something. Especially when he promised to keep an eye on you." Aurora snorted a laugh. "Keep an eye on you, my foot. More like keep his—"

"Aurora," Kennedy exclaimed, cutting her off amid a furious bout of blushing.

Aurora laughed. "Anyway, when I came back, and you didn't say anything, I figured nothing happened. Then Nate started acting weird—weirder than he had been before—and I came right out and asked him. He denied it, of course, but I know when he's lying, and I just kept after him until he finally told me the truth. He asked me not to say anything to you, so I didn't. I figured if you wanted me to know, you'd tell me yourself." She shot a pointed look at her watch. "And look, it only took eleven or so years."

Kennedy made a face. "Very funny."

"Hey, don't think I'm not still holding a grudge about that," Aurora said, half teasing before her expression became thoughtful. "What's most important is it didn't ruin things between us. I mean, there were the times the tension between you two was off the friggin' charts, but other than that, I'd say things have been pretty chill."

Yeah, right. They clearly had different definitions of *pretty chill*. Dealing with Nate after…everything had been the polar opposite of *chill*.

"And don't worry. You played it off much better than Nate. You did a good job at acting as if you guys hadn't slept together, while he couldn't seem to stop himself from acting like a jilted lover."

Jilted lover, really? Because if his indifference to her had been an act, he deserved an Oscar.

"You may want to give yourself a pat on the back too, because you're a pretty good actress with all your *Don't worry— Nate likes you*," Kennedy said, mimicking her friend's frequent refrain.

"That wasn't a lie," Aurora exclaimed, feigning innocence. *Who, little ole me?*

"No, but that means you knew full well why I balked whenever you invited me to go out with you guys."

"Like I said, I didn't want things to change between us. You're my best friend and he's my brother, and those are two things in my life that will never change. Whether anything is going on between you two or not, I want—no, I *need*—you guys to get along. You're both going to be in my wedding and you're going to be godmother and honorary aunt to my kids. Who knows, you may even be their aunt by marriage too." She casually tossed in that stick of dynamite at the end.

Kennedy completely ignored the resulting blast intended to tease a reaction from her, suggestive eyebrow waggling and all. No one was talking marriage and happily-ever-afters. She'd taken a pass the last two times they'd been offered to her. Right now, she and Nate were simply enjoying each other. A whole lot.

"All right, then. I promise that no matter what happens, it won't change a thing between us. Happy?"

Aurora smiled. "Now, I'm not trying to jinx things, but I have a really good feeling about you two. I saw the way he was with you at the party. Nate likes you a lot. I can tell."

He also liked Junior's cheesecake and the view of Central Park from his bedroom window a lot too, so it was good to keep things in perspective. She, on the other hand, was getting perilously close to liking him a little too much for the current trajectory of their relationship. The last thing she wanted to do was get ahead of the curve or overshoot the landing.

"Speaking of this weekend, what happened to you on Sunday? You said you were going to call," Kennedy reminded her. Not that it was a big deal. After a night and morning in Nate's bed—she could tell sex with him could quickly become an addiction—she hadn't minded going home to take some time to herself and regroup. She'd then spent the rest of the day resisting the urge to invite Nate over to watch Netflix and chill, where there'd be lots and lots of chilling.

Aurora began picking at her skirt, something she did when she was nervous. Or guilty. Or flat-out lying. "I know. I'm sorry. It turned out to be a big cleaning day. The fridge, the oven, the floors. I cleaned everything and now the place is immaculate."

Kennedy studied her, replying slowly. "No worries. Just curious."

"Anyway, I'll let you get back to work," Aurora said, her smile overly bright as she quickly departed.

"You called?" Kennedy queried with a raised eyebrow when Nate opened his apartment door to her.

"It was a request, not a demand."

"Right," she said, smirking as she walked past him, only to be hauled unceremoniously into his arms.

"Don't I even get a kiss?" he murmured, his breath warm and minty on her cheek.

Kennedy pretended to ponder the question before turning puckered lips up at him. But Nate wasn't having any of that, plowing his hand into her hair and taking her mouth in a *make you forget what day it is* kiss, employing his lips, tongue, and teeth in a manner that had her nipples standing at attention and started a familiar thrum between her thighs by the time he finally broke it off.

"Much better," he said, smiling down at her. "You look beautiful, by the way."

Aroused and breathless from his kiss, Kennedy could only nod. She'd come straight from the office and thought she looked fairly conservative in her tailored skirt and blouse. He, on the other hand, had on worn blue jeans and a striped T-shirt, his size eleven feet bare. She found the look incredibly hot.

Nate paused beside her while she removed her heels, and then followed her to the living room. "Does the kiss mean this isn't going to be one of those talks?" she asked, her tone light.

He grimaced. "Yeah, sorry about that. That's how I get when I'm running late for a meeting and stressed out at the same time. Sit down. Can I get you a drink?" He headed toward the kitchen.

Kennedy let out a snort of amusement as she settled onto the couch. "Are you serious? After the day I had, I came here fully expecting to be fed."

He treated her to a Cheshire cat smile and a wink. "Don't worry. Dinner is on its way."

"I hope it's something good, because I'm starved." The Hanson & Co. *emergency* call had been the highlight/lowlight of her day. Talk about mission impossible. Margaret Hanson-Gertz would be lucky if she emerged from her ordeal with only her reputation in ruins and her stores being picketed for a month. It was a near certainty the board would vote her out as CEO and president, which had been Kennedy's recommendation.

The woman needed to step down.

Like yesterday.

"So tell me about the emergency you had at work today."

Kennedy watched as he deftly opened a bottle of wine. "You know Hanson's on Park Avenue, right?"

"My mom says it makes Tiffany look like a thrift shop."

A slight exaggeration, but she got his point. The place was ridiculously expensive and only serviced an *elite* clientele.

"Well, last night, they refused to allow Vanessa Scott into the store and..." Kennedy's voice trailed off with a sigh. The resulting scandal spoke for itself.

Two glasses of wine in hand, Nate handed her one before joining her. "Vanessa Scott?" He let out a low whistle. "So your new client just insulted the richest Black woman in America. Looks like somebody's about to lose their job or the company is going to lose a shitload of customers. I don't need to flip a coin to know which one they're going to pick."

"I wish it were that simple," Kennedy said. "Apparently,

the employee in question came forward with an email sent by Margaret Hanson-Gertz, the CEO, saying—and I'm paraphrasing now—that certain minorities were not welcome in their stores because most can't afford the merchandise. Exceptions were of course made for celebrities, but Vanessa Scott was dressed in jeans and wearing little makeup, so no one in the store recognized her. When they wouldn't let her in, her cousin pulled out her cell phone and started recording. It only took one hour for the video to go viral."

Nate placed his wineglass on the end table at his side, and then carefully pulled her into his arms, as though he'd been doing it his whole life. "What did you tell her?"

"Not her. I spoke to the chairman of the board. I told him she needed to step down for the good of the company."

Pushing her hair aside, he nibbled her ear. "What about her? What does she think should happen?"

Kennedy let out a hum of pleasure. The man was deliciously distracting. "It doesn't matter. Saving the company's reputation is what really matters, and it'll go on better without her at the helm."

"Then she has to go." His warm breath bathed her ear and cheek, sending tendrils of lust through her.

Burrowing closer to him, Kennedy took a sip of her wine. "Okay, so now I told you about my day, why was it imperative you see me tonight?"

"First, I wanted to see you tonight regardless," he said, playing with long, curly strands of her hair. "Second, I wanted to ask you about your relationship with Trevor Markham."

Kennedy immediately went stiff in his arms. Why was he asking her about someone she'd dated over two years ago? And by dated, that was it. They hadn't even slept together and had parted on friendly terms. Hell, she'd helped get him his job at Goldberg & Johnson. They'd kept in loose contact, but she hadn't heard from him since last year, when they'd exchanged Christmas cards.

Slowly, she wriggled her way out of his arms, and placed her wine on the coffee table before turning her narrowed gaze on him.

"What do you mean my *relationship* with Trevor? How did you find out we even know each other?" Kennedy prided herself on how calm she sounded. Nate was lucky she wasn't one of those women who jumped to swift and erroneous conclusions. Lucky that she was adult enough to listen to what he had to say before jumping down his throat.

"Because Trevor Markham is the lead attorney representing the employees in the lawsuit against my company."

19

"What!" Kennedy exclaimed, her eyes round.

And that was all the answer he needed. She didn't have a clue. The tension in his shoulders eased.

"You can't be serious." Despite her words—as if spoken to herself—her expression conveyed the opposite.

He arched an eyebrow at her. "What do you think the chances are of me joking about your ex-boyfriend being the lead attorney suing my company? How many laughs do you think I'd hope to get out of that?"

"You know I didn't mean it that way," she said, wrinkling her nose. "And he was never my boyfriend."

Then what was he?

"Although, when I think about it, it makes sense," Kennedy continued. "Goldberg & Johnson have been trying to rehabilitate their reputation since what went down after they won the Landal lawsuit."

"Catch me up. What happened with the Landal lawsuit?" Nate asked.

"Two years after the verdict, internal documents revealed how the retail company had been cheating their workers out of overtime. That's when the law firm decided to take on pro-worker cases and diversify their legal team. They brought Trevor on because his specialty is civil rights. He may be young, but he's one of the best out there."

"If you're trying to make me feel better, you're going to need to work on your pitch," he said in a voice drier than the Sahara.

"But you have nothing to worry about. Unlike too many companies, you *want* to do the right thing," she stated confidently.

If nothing else, her faith in him was gratifying and, in this instance, fully justified. He was going to make this right if it was the last thing he did. Reaching out, he pulled her back into his arms, settling her against his chest.

"Okay, so now tell me about Trevor. What's the deal with you two?"

Kennedy snorted softly. "There is no deal. I told you he was never my boyfriend. But if what you really want to know is whether we had a sexual relationship…" She paused, purposely keeping him in suspense. "Not that it's any of your business, but no, we did not. We went on a few dates before I started going out with Aidan. And as unbelievable as it may seem, despite his Regé-Jean Page chiseled jaw and manly bone structure, the sparks simply weren't there. For me, I'm pretty sure it all boiled down to the lack of British accent. The face without the accent just isn't the same," she said, giggling impishly by the time she finished waxing poetic about the guy's looks.

Maybe there hadn't been any sparks for *her*, but he was sure they'd blazed like an inferno for Markham. Which sane available straight man wouldn't be attracted to her?

Slowly, he slid his hand from her waist to the side of her breast. At his touch, her breath hitched. "Exactly how many British guys have you dated?"

"None. But if I'm going to, I wouldn't want to settle for an imitation."

Nate was too busy enjoying the slight weight of her breast in his palm, and the way her nipple pebbled at the repeated swipe of his finger, to make sense of what she was saying.

"Can I ask you a question?" Her breathing was now audible as she gripped his wrist.

Covering her entire breast with his palm, he replied, "Ask me anything."

She made a sound between a whimper and a moan. "Are—are you going to feed me before or after we have sex?"

Nate chuckled and dipped his head to press a series of kisses down the length of her neck. He breathed her in. Her scent was intoxicating and her taste even better. Dear god, the things he wanted to do to her. "What are you hungry for more?" he whispered between kisses.

She took his hand and guided it between her legs. He let out a primitive growl and took over from there, immediately cupping her warmth.

"Does that answer your question?" she panted as she turned around in his arms, hooking her arms around his neck and offering up her mouth.

The ring of his cell phone served as a momentary interruption. He ignored it, crushing her parted lips beneath his. Everything got hot fast. The kiss. The blood coursing through his veins. And hard. His erection strained against the fly of his jeans.

"They're not going to stop calling until you answer,"

Kennedy said, her breathing shallow as she reluctantly ended the kiss.

What? It was only then Nate realized his phone was still ringing. That whoever was calling hadn't given up.

"Nate, it might be someone from work. Something to do with the lawsuit," she prompted.

It was a good thing at least one of them was still lucid.

Dragging his body from the soft warmth of hers wasn't an easy feat. The phone had stopped ringing but started again as he reached the island in the kitchen.

Still hot and distractingly bothered, Kennedy drew in a breath and levered herself to a sitting position, slowly emerging from a sexual fog.

Whew! The man knew how to kiss and played a serious game of foreplay. But then, he'd been dealt a pretty nice hand. Incredibly talented hands. And lips and tongue.

She then ran her fingers through her hair, a mess of dark tangled curls, which reminded her that it had been about a month since she'd worn it straight. She'd make sure to take care of that soon.

"This better be important," Nate said, speaking to the poor soul on the other end of the phone. That person would never know what they'd interrupted.

"Hold on. Let me check." Looking at her, he mouthed, *I'll be right back*, before he exited the kitchen and disappeared down the hall toward his office.

Kennedy would bet her beloved iPad that *I'll be right back* translated into more than fifteen minutes. Fine, just as long as he knew that when he came back, he'd simply have to get her hot and bothered all over again. No hardship there.

She took a big gulp of her wine before hoisting herself off the couch. When she was at his place, she never seemed to have a lot of time to really look around, inspect things. Her gaze halted on the shelves of books surrounding his *ginormous* TV.

Back when they'd first hooked up, his pleasure reading had strictly been books by authors like James Patterson, Stephen King, and John Grisham. These days she had no idea what he liked, which was how she found herself studying his collection of trade and hardcover books.

More James Patterson and a few books by Vince Flynn. Her eyebrows rose at the sight of *Team of Rivals* by Doris Kearns Goodwin. The book next to it had those same eyebrows practically meeting her hairline: *How to Be an Antiracist* by Ibram X. Kendi.

For a moment Kennedy stood there, unable to do anything but stare at the lightly creased spine. Then she ran the tip of her finger down it in a state of dazed wonderment. Once the shock wore off sufficiently, she snatched the book off the shelf and whipped it open.

Nate bought this? Had he actually read it? That question was answered soon enough once she began flipping through the pages, revealing comments in his handwriting along the margins. A lump formed in her throat and tears stung the backs of her eyes. Why she was getting this emotional about a book couldn't be put into words. It was as if he'd opened a secret part of himself to her, allowing her inside.

"Reading anything interesting?" he asked from across the room as he made his way toward her, his expression full of lascivious intent.

Countdown to hot and bothered had begun, and she was more than ready for the sequel.

"Have you been reading behind my back?" she asked coyly, batting her eyelashes and turning the book so he could see the cover.

His eyes lit in quiet amusement. "Just some light reading to pass the time on the plane."

She carefully placed the book back on the shelf, dragged her tongue slowly across her upper lip, and gave him her full attention. "You have no idea how sexy I find you right now. How much I want to fuck you senseless."

Kennedy Amelia Mitchell, did those words just come out of your mouth? It's like I don't know you anymore. The Aunt Pauline part of her preferred to clutch rosary beads instead of pearls, as it offered a better chance of not burning in hell.

You're not a practicing Catholic, and fucking is a beautiful thing.

Nate didn't give her a chance to take a word of it back, his blue eyes blazing as he hauled her to him, his mouth capturing hers in a bone-melting kiss.

Devouring.

Positively ravenous.

While relieving her of every stitch of clothing, he growled, "Wait until you see the James Baldwin books I have in my office."

Just when she thought he couldn't turn her on any more, he managed to kick his desirability up another notch. The man was proving to be an irresistible combination of good looks, intelligence, with such a strength of moral character, humanity, and compassion, it was hard to believe he was real. He literally took her breath away. As in, she was having a hard time catching her breath, his large hands caressing her all over.

"Here, the sofa, or the bed?" His voice was husky as he laid out their options, his hand kneading her ass and dipping between to tease her moist center.

"Whichever will get you inside me the fastest," she replied breathlessly, a cry of pleasure bubbling up inside her.

Pushing her hair aside, he nipped her neck with his teeth before soothing the spot with his tongue. "Okay, hold on," he rasped, kneeing her legs wider apart. "I'm going to take you like this."

Kennedy was panting so hard, so consumed by his taste and touch, the sound of the condom wrapper being torn open didn't fully register until he thrust into her and she could feel every inch of him as he sank deep.

Tightening his grip on her hips, he went motionless as if savoring the initial moments of being inside her. She involuntarily clamped down on his erection, squeezing him tight, prompting a low and tortured groan from his throat.

Kennedy undulated her hips and clawed at his back, her sense of gravity lost in the whirlwind that encompassed them. He pulled out and slammed into her again, wrenching a sobbing cry from her. Her arms circled his neck as she sank her teeth into the taut flesh of his shoulder.

"*Fuucck.*" Everything he was feeling seemed to be encapsulated in the solitary uttered word. Then the chase was on, as he pounded them both to blissful completion.

Minutes later, when the vestiges of an explosive orgasm still held her body in thrall, she sagged and would have crumpled to the floor if he hadn't scooped her into his arms.

Smiling dreamily up at him, she brushed his hair off his sweat-damp forehead. "That was good," she murmured.

Nate chuckled and dropped a hard kiss on her swollen lips. "After I feed you, not only am I going to show you that collection of James Baldwin books I promised, but I'll add in a couple from Jane Elliott if you're good."

Kennedy giggled and snuggled into the crook of his neck. "Looks like you're angling for a blow job tonight."

To that, Nate threw back his head and guffawed. After his laughter subsided, he lifted her chin with his finger and stared deep into her eyes. "I would like that very much."

He kissed her again and she smiled against his lips.

She didn't know for sure if she was falling in love—at this point, she wasn't even sure she'd *ever* been in love—with this man, but she could safely say she'd officially crossed the line of liking him a lot to liking him too much. Way too much.

"Oh good, you're here. Mrs. Hanson-Gertz is here to see you. She doesn't have an appointment, but she said she'd wait, so I put her in the small conference room," Mina announced the minute Kennedy walked into the office the following morning.

What a lovely way to start off her day. From Nate's strong arms to a personal visit from the dragon queen herself.

"I don't think people are allowed to say no to her. For such a tiny woman, she's pretty scary. She sure scares the crap out of me." Mina's expression was deadly earnest.

Kennedy snorted a laugh. "I guess I won't be able to say I wasn't warned." She studied her young employee. "How are you doing? Are things getting better?"

Mina hadn't taken the breakup with her ex-boyfriend well, but she didn't talk about killing him anymore. Progress. But more than once Kennedy had caught her coming out of the ladies' room, eyes red-rimmed and complexion mottled by the effects of tears. Addy had officially moved out two weeks ago, and today was the first day Mina looked close to her normal, cheerful self.

"Things aren't getting better—they're actually pretty good. I have a new roommate as of yesterday. Her name is Jazmine. She's Iranian and Black and knows all the good places to go in the city and says I'm going to go out with her and have fun if it kills her—or me," she concluded with a laugh.

"That's great." After everything she'd been through with her cheating ex, Mina deserved to be happy. She deserved to have fun.

"We went shopping yesterday and she picked this out. What do you think?" she asked, standing to show off a cute pair of sage-green three-quarter pants and a white petal-sleeve blouse. Mina had been trying to lose twenty pounds since Kennedy hired her and was self-conscious about wearing anything that revealed too much of her figure.

"You look great. Green is the perfect color on you and the slim cut makes your legs look long." As far as Kennedy was concerned, she didn't need to lose a pound.

"Thanks," Mina said, her face flushed with pleasure. "Going forward, I'm going to treat myself to a new outfit every time I get paid."

"Good for you. You deserve it. By the way, where's Jonathan?" Kennedy asked, glancing over her shoulder at his dark, empty office. He was usually the first one in.

"Doctor's appointment. He won't be in until eleven."

Duh. How could she forget—he'd only reminded her before he left the office yesterday. Kennedy blamed her memory lapse on her orgasm hangover, which couldn't be cured with aspirin or caffeine, but didn't come with the headache and cotton mouth brought on by alcohol.

"Okay," Kennedy said, letting out a deep breath and squaring her shoulders. "Let me get this over with."

Mina saw her off with an encouraging thumbs-up.

Margaret Hanson-Gertz was exactly how Kennedy pictured her. The photo she'd pulled up of her on Google had to be at least ten to fifteen years out of date. The face that greeted her when she stepped into the conference room was more lined, the crow's-feet around her hazel eyes deeper. The shots of gray running through her dyed blond hair were barely discernible to the naked eye.

At seventy-three, she was a handsome woman in the way Adam Driver was a sex symbol. Maybe not at first or second glance, but the longer a person looked, the arrangement of her individual features grew more pleasing when observed together. She wore a cream pantsuit that fit her petite figure in a way that screamed its custom-made origins.

"Mrs. Hanson-Gertz, this is an unexpected surprise." Kennedy greeted her politely.

"Is it really a surprise? After your recommendation to my board, I thought you'd be expecting me," she said in a voice that sounded as if she'd recently given up cigarettes after decades of chain-smoking two packs a day.

Oh wonderful. It was going to be one of *those* conversations. Kennedy had naively hoped the woman would want to do what was best for the company. Clearly not.

"What can I do for you?" Kennedy asked calmly, ignoring her sharp tone and the question.

Irritated, the jewelry heiress thumped her veined, age-spotted hand on the table and replied, "You had no right to advise my board to fire me."

Having watched more than her fair share of period dramas, the heiress reminded Kennedy of a haughty nineteenth-century British aristocrat who made it their job to belittle "the help" to the point of enragement.

"I'm sorry, Mrs. Hanson-Gertz, but under the circumstances, it was the right thing to do."

"What circumstances?" Her voice rose imperiously. "Whatever it is you were told, I did not write that email. In your line of work, I would think you'd want to hear the whole story."

One day, Kennedy would love it if the first thing out of a client's mouth was them taking responsibility for whatever mess they'd gotten themselves into. *It's all my fault. I take full responsibility.* However, it looked like she'd have to wait for hell to freeze over for that to happen, and until then, *this* was what she'd be dealing with. A litany of denials upon excuses upon denials.

"I did hear the whole story and I've viewed all the evidence. And as I told Mr. Bellamy yesterday, whether you wrote that email or not is immaterial. It was sent from your email address and your signature was at the bottom. If that was done in error, the mistake should have been corrected three years ago, not now." The woman was trying to close the stable doors long after the horse had been let out. Long enough for the horse to have been impregnated and given birth several times over.

"You didn't hear from me," she said crossly.

Good lord, the woman was a piece of work.

"I may begin to sound like a broken record, but as I told Mr. Bellamy, the only thing I can do is to try and salvage the company's reputation, not yours. The email is too damaging, and your employees have established, to everyone's satisfaction, that they were following orders. Now, as I said, the sooner you issue Ms. Scott a public and personal apology, the sooner the press will lose interest."

Vanessa Scott had already issued a statement of her own. Not only had she vowed never to step foot in any of their stores again, she was also returning the three-hundred-thousand-dollar diamond bracelet she'd purchased from their store in England the week before.

"This is my company. They are going to vote me out of the company my grandfather started at the turn of the last century." She was all self-righteous indignation with her gratingly strident tone.

Kennedy took her job of being the voice of reason seriously. "I understand how you must feel, Mrs. Hanson-Gertz—"

"With all due respect, Miss Mitchell," she snapped, "I doubt very much that you do. You can't possibly understand what it's like to watch your life's work being taken from you."

Haughty must be second nature to her, as she lapsed into it effortlessly. Haughty was also a surefire way to get Kennedy's back up. "While this agency hasn't been open quite as long as Hanson's, nor does it come close to its considerable net worth, I do understand hard work and, more than that, I understand what it's like to start with nothing." She made a pointed reference to the Hanson heiress being handed a thriving multimillion-dollar business upon her father's death more than twenty years ago.

Mrs. Hanson-Gertz cast a dubious look around the room, no doubt comparing it unfavorably to the offices and conference rooms she was accustomed to. But her smile, doggedly stiff and polite, never once wavered. She'd been at this a long time and was used to playing the game.

"Managing a half-billion-dollar company that spans several continents and countries isn't quite the same as running a business...less involved."

Kennedy kept a tight rein on her derision. The woman was a caricature of a caricature, a jeweler mogul version of Cruella de Vil come to life.

"Well, I can only imagine what that's like. But as I said before, there is nothing I can do to extricate you from this quagmire you've gotten yourself into."

The older woman studied her through narrowed eyes. "I don't want to hear any nonsense about quagmires," she said, sucking her teeth. "I was told you're the best at what you do, but what is clear to me is that you don't want to help me."

Such damning praise. Kennedy would take it.

"Whoever told you that was right. I am the best at what I do. But what I'm not is a miracle worker, and that's what you would require. Now, I'm not sure whether you're a snob, a bigot, or a racist, or all the above, but at this point, it doesn't matter. Your current position as CEO of Hanson's is untenable and is already having an adverse effect on the company.

The last time I checked, your stock was down fifteen percent. If you resign today, you can turn it around, and with that I'm sure the calls for boycotts will cease. No customer wants to run the gauntlet of protesters to shop at your stores."

Since the incident, protesters had arrived with signs in hand to picket the Park Avenue store. There were also protests going on at their London and Paris stores, successfully keeping customers away.

Mrs. Hanson-Gertz pursed her lips, causing deep lines to snake from her lips like tributaries. "Just because I bring my old-fashioned values to my business, it doesn't make me a bigot or a racist."

Kennedy noticed she didn't deny being a snob. But then again, being a snob didn't make someone a social pariah.

"If by old-fashioned you mean posting a figurative *wealthy whites only* sign on the doors of your stores in the form of store employees, I don't agree with you. Which is *your* problem. Those days are over, despite efforts to resurrect them." Kennedy kept her voice free of censure and malice, simply letting her words do the unpleasant but necessary work of dressing down a racist.

Mrs. Hanson-Gertz remained stone-faced as she rose from the chair and huffed, "Well, this was a waste of time."

Kennedy quickly followed suit, towering over the older woman. "I wouldn't call our meeting time wasted." Although, she could think of a dozen other things she could be doing right now and a hundred she'd rather be doing, like running the New York City Marathon in ninety-degree heat. Neither she nor her hair could survive that.

"I don't imagine you would," the older woman replied, the insult hardly veiled.

The Hanson employees owed her for helping to remove the detestable woman from her position.

You're welcome. No need to hold a parade in my honor.

Before Kennedy could blink, Mrs. Hanson-Gertz was at the door, clearly eager to leave.

"Mrs. Hanson," she called before the heiress breached the threshold. "Can I ask you a question?"

After a beat, the woman reluctantly inclined her head in a nod and a disdainful sniff.

"Would I have been allowed into any of your stores?"

Mrs. Hanson-Gertz visibly stiffened in obvious affront. But a moment later, she ran a critical gaze over Kennedy, taking in her formfitting dress, her eyes lingering absently on the bell sleeves. Then she looked Kennedy square in the eye. "I honestly don't know," she intoned, obnoxiously overbearing to the end.

Kennedy couldn't fault her for her honesty. "Which I believe proves my point. That it's time for you to step down. And I think you have too much pride to allow the board to fire you."

"We'll see about that." And with those words, she was gone.

Kennedy could only count her blessings that she dealt with more Roger O'Briens than she did Margaret Hanson-Gertzes. And she hoped it stayed that way.

20

Less than ten hours after the wretched woman marched herself out of Token's doors, Hanson & Co. released a statement that Margaret Hanson-Gertz would immediately be stepping down as CEO and president.

The news hit social media while Kennedy, Aurora, Sahara, and April—the performer's twenty-eight-year-old designer—were enjoying appetizers and their first round of cocktails. The women were the sole occupants of the VIP section in a small club Sahara liked to frequent. Its intimacy, celebrity-indifferent clientele, and staff discretion made it the perfect venue for their girls' night out.

By their second round of drinks, conversation had moved on from whether Mrs. Hanson-Gertz was experiencing karma or her just deserts, to the rights and wrongs of nepotism. Sahara's cousin was looking for a job. Unfortunately, he wasn't qualified for much, so if she hired him, she would be taking a chance.

"Personally, I don't think there's anything wrong with nepotism *per se*. And it's not as if everyone else doesn't do it," April said, as someone whose sister's modeling career helped pave the way to her own.

"I'm not saying your sister being a model wasn't helpful, but you would have gotten representation without her," Sahara insisted, eliciting sounds of agreement all around.

The biracial, green-eyed beauty was smart as well as ambitious. She'd started her design company after graduating with a master of fine arts degree in fashion design. Last year, business had grown enough for her to hire another designer. With her new contract with Sahara and ECO Apparel, she planned to hire another.

Aurora popped a glazed meatball into her mouth, instantly moaning her appreciation as she chewed.

"It sounds like you're going to need to book a room for you and your meat*balls*," Kennedy joked.

Laughter and giggling ensued, a refreshing change from their previous conversation.

Having a famous friend did have its perks. She could hang out with a bunch of women, comfy in overstuffed chairs while listening to music at a volume that didn't impede conversation. The best was being able to enjoy herself without random men deciding she would be the lucky recipient of their unwanted attention for the night. It was amazing what a difference it made to be able to have a relaxing evening out with just the girls.

"Are you dating anyone?" April asked, directing the question to Aurora. "All that moaning means you're not getting *it* enough or you're getting *it* too much. Which one is it?"

The question caused Aurora to nearly choke on the crab-stuffed mushroom she'd just put in her mouth.

Kennedy reached over and patted her on the back. "I don't

know how to perform the Heimlich maneuver, so please don't get that thing stuck in your throat."

Aurora grabbed an untouched glass of water and swallowed a mouthful before she was able to speak. "I think it went down the wrong pipe," she croaked, tears filling her eyes. Turning her gaze to April, she said, "Warn a girl when you're about to ask her if she's having non-self-induced orgasms."

The entire table erupted into peals of laughter.

Sahara clucked her tongue in mock sympathy. "I'm sorry, doll. You should have said something to me. But no worries— I know just the man who can take care of that. And before you go getting the wrong idea, let me first say that there was nothing going on between me and Grant on the set. He was the perfect British gentleman, but I did hear things. Very good things. Loves giving as much as he loves receiving, which isn't always the case. A lot of guys can be selfish that way."

"Not my husband," April said, blessing them with a smile of the sexually satisfied.

Or Nate. But Kennedy judiciously kept that to herself, his sister being right there and all.

Aurora cast her gaze heavenward. "That'll be a hard pass from me. I'm never getting romantically involved with any-one remotely connected to Hollywood."

"Who said anything about romance?" April snorted. "Sex for sex's sake alone isn't a bad thing."

"Says the only happily married mother at the table," Sahara teased.

April laughed, her eyes sparkling. "Says the woman who sexed it up with her husband *before* we started dating. I know of what I speak."

And Kennedy could certainly understand why. She'd Googled him after the launch party, and the wide receiver was hot with a capital *H*.

"What's the point of boxing yourself in?" Sahara asked, dipping a golden-fried coconut shrimp in the cocktail sauce. "What if your soul mate turns out to be someone famous? What if it's Grant? Would you kick him to the curb just because of what he does for a living?"

Aurora gave an exaggerated eye roll. "First, let's get something straight. Grant Musgrove is *not* my soul mate. Second, *not* having sex with a man I don't know and who has women constantly throwing themselves at him isn't exactly a hardship. And for me, it's not about looks and money. Being attractive is great and everything, but I need a man I can relate to. We have to have stuff in common. And let's face it—in Hollywood, good-looking people are a dime a dozen, present company excluded. You, my dear, are one in a million," Aurora said, blowing the singer a kiss.

Sahara gave Aurora the side-eye. "Is that an Aaliyah reference?"

"Sweetie, you got to let it go. If Aaliyah looked like a troll, I'd understand how that would be offensive. But she was gorgeous. Take it as a compliment," April soothed.

"How can I take it as a compliment when people think that's the only reason I made it in the business? Do you know that ass Cyrus called me Baby Girl in an interview last week, and I've never wanted to smack someone so hard in my life."

Kennedy laughed, imagining the one-hundred-and-twenty-five–pound actress up against the music producer, who was almost double her size. She would pay for front-row tickets to see that. Sahara would destroy him.

"Right, but that's just human nature," Aurora said. "People love drawing comparisons. How many times have we heard that some new artist is the next whoever? At one time, wasn't Mariah Carey supposed to be the next Whitney Houston?"

"*Hell-o,*" Sahara sang out, raising her hand. "Guess whose

mother loved Whitney Houston so much she named her only daughter after her?"

"And what a disappointment you turned out to be, becoming a famous singer, an Oscar-nominated actress, and creating your own clothing line instead of following after your namesake," Kennedy lamented, tongue in cheek.

Sahara smiled and fondly groused, "You are so extra."

"I don't know how you manage it all," April said. "Just keeping up with my son every day is a full-time job. I'm getting ready to switch him from half-day care to full days. No more of this take-your-son-to-work stuff when his dad is on the road."

Mention of her three-year-old son had Aurora demanding pictures. Ever the proud, doting mother, April immediately obliged. While her phone was being passed around to *oohs* and *aahs* over her adorable kid, Kennedy's own phone dinged. She discreetly checked it, expecting to see a message from Nate, but to her surprise, it was from Julie.

Julie: No baby. Got my period today. Taking tomorrow off. Going to bed now. 'Night.

Kennedy immediately shot back a reply.

Kennedy: Oh honey, I'm so sorry. 😔 It'll happen when you least expect it. 🤞 Never lose hope. 🖤

"Is something wrong?" Aurora asked, watching her as April tucked her phone back in her handbag.

Now Kennedy had everyone's attention, Sahara and April also wearing similar expressions of concern.

"One of our employees has been trying to get pregnant for over two years. Today, she told me she was going to buy a test on her way home because she was two weeks late." Kennedy sighed. "She texted to let me know she just got her period, so of course, she's absolutely crushed."

"Oh, poor thing," Aurora whispered, her voice full of emotion. "I know how much she and Kwan want kids."

"Wow." April's eyes filled with compassion. "I got pregnant with our son almost as soon as we started trying. Sometimes I forget it's not the same for everyone and that I'm one of the lucky ones."

"You have no idea *how* lucky." There was unexpected vehemence to Sahara's words. She then added more solemnly, "That could be me, what's happening to her."

Alarmed, Kennedy froze midsip, slowly lowering her glass of brown cow to the table. "What do you mean?" she asked, her voice hushed. "You don't know if you'll be able to have kids?"

"Oh my god, what's wrong?" Aurora asked, stricken.

Sahara held up her hands to calm their escalating concerns. "No, I didn't mean it to come out like that. I have endometriosis, which is a condition involving the uterus lining that might make it difficult for me to get pregnant. The longer I wait, the worse it could get. But don't worry," she said as their faces fell. "I have a backup plan. I had my eggs frozen four years ago, so if I run into problems, I can always do IVF."

Kennedy breathed a sigh of relief. "My aunt has endometriosis too. She had five kids in six years, all in her twenties. She said the pain during her period is unreal. Like bring-you-to-your-knees kind of pain."

"She's not kidding. When I was in my teens, sometimes it was so bad, I had to miss school. After all I've gone through, labor might not be that bad."

Sahara's remark elicited a derisive snort from her designer. "That may be taking things a little too far. I was in labor for twenty-three hours. You want to talk about pain. Oh my god, I squeezed Troy's hand so tight, he swears I cut off his circulation. Labor is no joke."

"Well, it's good you have options." Kennedy was impressed with her maturity and foresight. From what Kennedy knew about egg retrieval, it was like going through the IVF process, which was no walk in the park.

"I'm just glad I don't have to rush the process. I'd really like to have my acting career fully established before I take time off for a husband and kids, you know?"

"Of course," Aurora said sympathetically.

"And you're well on your way," Kennedy said. "You're known as much for your acting as your music these days." And that was the God's honest truth. Sahara's acting career was on fire. Casting directors loved her because she was gorgeous and had a versatile look, directors loved that she was a natural and eager to learn, and her costars loved that she was easy to get along with on and off the set.

"I hope so. What about you?" Sahara directed her question to Kennedy. "How are things going with the hunky Mr. Vaughn?"

"Mr. Vaughn?" April asked, looking at Aurora. "Any relation, by chance?"

"Oh, that's right, you don't know. Kennedy is going out with Aurora's brother. The one who owns the tech company." Sahara quickly caught her designer up on the goings-on. They then turned their gazes to Aurora.

"Why are you looking at me?" Aurora appeared mildly amused by the expectant expressions on their faces. "I have no problem with it. I received assurances that no matter what happens between them, Ken and I will always be friends, and since my parents would be royally pissed if I disowned their son, I'm pretty much stuck."

"Is that the best you could do? Couldn't you find another young, good-looking billionaire to date who wasn't related to your best friend?" April was all smiles and tongue-in-cheek humor.

"Yeah, but why keep looking if you've already found *The One*, right, Ken?" Sahara sent her a wink.

"No one said anything about anyone being *The One*." He definitely felt like *The One* in bed, if that counted for anything. "We're dating and having fun. That's it," she said, deliberately downplaying the relationship. No need to raise expectations or get their hopes up. Whatever happened would happen, all in good time.

"Right, but you know what they say," Sahara said with a smirk.

Kennedy almost hated to ask, but it wasn't as if she had a choice. "Actually, I don't. What do *they* say?"

"That it's all fun and games until it's not."

Sahara may not have meant it as a warning, but Kennedy would have been better served if she'd taken it as one.

"Okay, tonight, no dining out, takeout, Uber Eats, or anything like that. Tonight, yours truly is going to cook for you." Kennedy turned and beamed a smile at Nate as she closed the door to his industrial-sized refrigerator.

She considered herself a fairly good cook but didn't usually have a gourmet kitchen to showcase her talents in, except when she cooked at Aurora's, which wasn't often. The sheer counter space alone was making her giddy.

Smirking, Nate leaned against the counter, looking deliciously casual in low-hanging blue sweats and a graphic tee. "Oh, you can cook? Why haven't I ever seen evidence of that?"

Her finger encountered only smooth muscled abs when she laughed and poked him. Thwarted, Kennedy wrinkled her nose. "Because you weren't worthy of it before. Not even sure you've proved yourself worthy of it now. You're lucky I'm giving you the benefit of the doubt."

In response, he abruptly tugged her into his arms and kissed her soundly on the lips. But what started as teasing turned hot within seconds. Because that was how it was with them. Their compatibility in bed was like nothing she'd ever experienced before, and the sex seemed to get better the more they engaged. Since her night out with the girls three weeks ago, she'd spent every weekend at his apartment and at least one day during the week. Things were going so well, she was giving serious thought to getting another Waterpik to leave there.

Hey, a girl is allowed to splurge every now and then.

Before things got out of control—she'd learned from experience how easily that could happen—Kennedy pressed firmly on his shoulders, reluctantly ending the kiss. "How am I going to cook if you keep doing that?" Her breathing wasn't quite steady.

"I'm just following directions." He stared pointedly at a pair of red lips and the KISS THE COOK emblazoned on the front of the apron she wore over a red T-shirt and black yoga pants.

Emitting a murmured sound that was both amusement and desire, Kennedy palmed his cheek that sported a sexy five-o'clock shadow. "I promise, we'll get back to this after dinner."

Nate's blue eyes smoldered, his voice dropping a suggestive octave. "Dessert?"

"Have I ever sent you to bed without?"

"It's in bed that you give it to me."

Kennedy laughingly shooed him away. "Out. I can't concentrate when you're this close." Although, it was less a lack of concentration than it was he couldn't seem to be within touching distance without needing to have his hands all over her. She didn't exactly have a problem with it, but there were times when she had to get something done that didn't require her hands being on him in return.

When he refused to budge, Kennedy threw up her hands. "If you insist on hovering, do it over there." She pointed to a row of stools on the other side of the large granite island.

"Okay, I'll be good," he promised and then squeezed her left butt cheek, eliciting a surprised yelp from her and a light whack on his arm. Chuckling, Nate reluctantly did as instructed and moved his fine self out of arm's reach.

"So whatcha feeding me?" he asked, watching as she began seasoning the chicken.

"Chicken curry and roti."

Nate licked his lips. "I like curry with chicken, but you're going to have to tell me what roti is."

"Think of it as a fluffier, flaky version of a flour tortilla." Kennedy had been getting this question almost her entire life and had learned that comparison was easiest to understand and came closest to the truth.

Nate was a world traveler. She figured he'd be up for trying something new, even though she considered roti fairly run-of-the-mill when it came to West Indian cuisine. It was the spicy chicken curry that made the meal.

"Sounds good. Which one are you making first?"

"I'm only making the curry. The roti is pretty time-consuming, so I buy it at a Guyanese restaurant in Brooklyn that makes it even better than my mom. And if you ever tell her I said that, you'll never see me naked again," she warned, pausing to point the shaker of salt at him.

Her lover's gaze became hooded as he slowly perused every part of her body visible to him, leaving a trail of heat in its wake. "Then I didn't hear a word you just said."

While they shared a conspiratorial smile that promised tangled sheets and entwined naked bodies in the not-so-distant future, the temperature in the room started to climb. But if they left the kitchen to get out of the heat, they'd be heading straight to the bedroom where it would be even hotter.

The ringing of the doorbell brought Kennedy back to earth with a start. Tearing his gaze from her, Nate reached for his phone. The doorman called or sent a message via the building app to let him know when someone was on their way up.

"Is it Ror?" she asked.

"I didn't get a message, but it has to be someone I know." Placing the phone back on the counter, he slid off the stool and made his way to the front door.

Kennedy kept her ears perked as she grabbed several spoons from the drawer. If not Aurora, then who? Not that he didn't have friends here; she knew he did. But in all the time they'd been spending together, he rarely mentioned anyone outside of work. No one visited when she was here, and as far as she could tell, no one did when she wasn't.

Curiosity and not nosiness had her edging closer to the front entrance—as close as she could get without leaving the kitchen. She heard the door open and nothing else. Were they whispering? Did Nate not want his visitor to know she was here?

Soon she heard the murmur of male voices, alleviating a bit of her apprehension. It wasn't a woman. Not an old girlfriend who heard he was back in town. But even if it were, it shouldn't be a big deal. Because of course Nate had women in his past, just as she had men in her past. As quietly as possible, Kennedy scampered back to finish seasoning the chicken.

"Yeah, but it's time I got an official introduction," was the only thing she heard right before Nate and his male visitor came into view.

She instantly recognized Constellation's CTO. His hair was shorter, and in blue jeans and a dark green Henley, he looked younger than when she'd met him at the press conference two months ago. But that usually happened when you took people out of their workplace setting—five years of stress instantly melted away.

"Look who stopped by," Nate announced upon his return, his friend a step behind him. "Kennedy, you remember Jack, don't you?"

Kennedy hastily wiped her hands on a dish towel before offering it to Jack with a teasing smile. "How could I forget the person who egged me on at your press conference, and urged me to defend you?" One thing had become clear over the last few months: the men weren't as close as they had been growing up and in college. Nate never talked about him—at least, not to her.

"It's lovely seeing you again," Jack said, studying her, his handshake perhaps a beat or two on the long side.

"What do you mean he egged you on to defend me?" Nate may have posed the question to her, but he was looking at his friend.

"When the reporter said that stuff about the lack of diversity in your personal relationships, Jack encouraged me to defend your honor, in a manner of speaking." She didn't include that Jack had hightailed it out of there soon after.

Nate arched a brow. "Really? I don't remember you telling me that."

"Somebody needed to defend you, and since Kennedy was already on a roll…" Jack shrugged, unabashed. "Besides, how would it have looked if I'd added my two cents? As far as the reporter was concerned, I was part of the problem."

Kennedy preferred not to think back on the event that resulted in their *arrangement*. Although, as silver linings went, as it was a big part of the reason she and Nate were now together, they'd achieved a pretty good one. And now with settlement rumors being bandied about, Kennedy was convinced the company's reputation would soon be on the rehabilitation fast track, and six months from now, Nate's halo would be fully restored above his saintly head.

"For all intents and purposes," Jack continued, looking directly at her, "I think things worked out well. The lawsuit brought Nate back home, so you can't say it's all been bad. And now that the two of you are a couple, even that has faded from the news. The stock has fully rebounded from its five percent drop, and from what I can see, the company's reputation is on the mend."

"Don't go claiming victory just yet. We're not entirely in the clear," Nate cautioned.

"Ah, come on. I think you can both claim *some* victory." Jack's gaze made a general sweep of the kitchen and the family room beyond. The next statement he directed at Kennedy. "I'd say you're doing well for yourself. The way the situation with the presser was resolved was a master class in crisis management. And that kind of exposure can only be good for your agency."

"The agency does well enough on its own. If anything, that kind of exposure makes attracting new business harder, not easier," Nate said, taking exception to the wrong part of his friend's remark.

I'd say you're doing well for yourself? Kennedy was still stinging from the oh-so-clever dig. How the hell had Nate missed it? Jack hadn't meant it as a compliment. Not a word of it. And he was making his disapproval of her known in clear but subtle ways. For those paying attention.

Kennedy sprinkled paprika on the chicken. Well, this sucked. Her boyfriends' friends usually liked her. Some a tad too much. But then, all her ex-boyfriends didn't have net worths in the millions, much less billions, and they didn't have Nate's background. In too many ways to count, Nate occupied a plane of his own.

The man was out of her league.

And then, like a daily absolution, a voice inside her shouted, *Stop it! You're no better than anyone, and no one is better than you.* Kennedy didn't know where she'd first heard it, but it had sounded like words to live by.

"Has business been down?" Jack pointedly asked her.

Kennedy hated to prove his point, but she couldn't bring herself to lie. "Uh, no."

Jack had the decency to not look smug.

When a beat of silence passed, it seemed incumbent on Kennedy to fill it, so she did what any good hostess would. "Would you like to join us for dinner? We're having curry chicken and I'm making more than enough."

To her gracious invitation, Jack smiled and shook his head. "No, I'm good. I already ate. I'm here with news about the lawsuit. Thought I'd deliver it in person."

"I hope it's good news," Kennedy said, relieved he didn't intend to stay long.

"It's the best that we could hope for right about now," Jack replied.

"That's great. What have you got? Are we getting any closer to getting them to agree to arbitration?" Nate asked, a spark of hope in his eyes.

"Maybe we should—should discuss it somewhere else and let Kennedy get back to cooking," Jack said, clearly reluctant to discuss the matter in front of her.

Kennedy forced a smile. "Of course. Nate, why don't you go to your office?"

Nate sent his friend a shuttered look. "Yeah, sure. This way."

"She's a sweetheart. Leave it to you to get the whole package," Jack said once they were inside the office.

"Isn't that what everyone wants, the whole package?" Nate

asked, making his tone light. There was something about his friend's comment he found unsettling. Something he couldn't quite put his finger on.

Jack looked around as if he had never been in the room before. He had a number of times. "Yeah, but we don't always get what we want."

True. Nate couldn't deny that.

Parking himself on the edge of his desk, Nate casually asked, "If she's so great, why couldn't you say whatever you have to in front of her? Better yet, why didn't you just call? I know damn well you didn't happen to be in the neighborhood." Jack lived on the other side of the city with a more happening nightlife.

"Are you saying I'm not welcome here anymore?" Jack shot a glance out the window, taking in the sight of Central Park, which was one of the biggest selling points when Nate bought the place.

"Cut the crap," Nate muttered. "I'm just saying, you could've called. I told you I was spending tonight with Kennedy."

Jack shifted his gaze to the books on the oak shelves lining the back wall. "When *don't* you spend your nights with her?" He looked over his shoulder at Nate. "And if I hadn't shown up uninvited, when were you going to introduce us? It's like you're hiding her away or something."

"I'm not fucking *hiding* her away. We go out," Nate shot back, trying not to read too much into his friend's choice of words.

"You two go out *alone*." Jack returned his attention to the shelves, his gaze idly skimming the books.

Damn. What the fuck is his problem?

"You'll have to forgive me for wanting to spend time *alone* with my girlfriend. You said it yourself—she's the whole package."

Seriously, what the actual fuck was going on with his friend?

"Impressive reading material you have these days," Jack remarked, turning back to him with a smile on his face that bordered on cynical.

Nate grunted a humorless laugh. "Yeah, well, I don't base my selection on the desire to impress."

"Do you know that since you came back from France, we haven't gotten together once? I call you to go out and you're always busy. The only time I see you is at the office, and the only thing we talk about is work and the lawsuit. I thought we were friends."

Aww shit. Sighing, Nate ran a hand through his hair. "We are. We are. But you know how it is when you start dating someone."

"No, how is it?" Jack asked wryly. "I haven't dated anyone seriously in a while, so I'm kinda rusty when it comes to blowing off my friends."

This coming from the same guy who'd had to check with his ex-fiancée if he wanted to take a leak.

"You're such an ass. Just tell me when we can put the damn lawsuit behind us."

"I don't have a specific answer to *that* question, *but* Neil says Markham's finally willing to talk settlement. So, I'd say within a month."

At one time Nate thought those words would make him happy, but today the only thing rushing through him was relief.

"Let's just hope he doesn't change his mind. People like Markham—men with political aspirations—have a habit of playing both sides against the middle to further their personal agendas," Jack warned.

"No, if he's ready to talk settlement, they're ready to settle." Nate knew how this went. The only variable now was the amount. "What about the classes? Do we have a final tally? Has everyone taken them?"

It had been six weeks since he'd given the first edict to all his managers. Every employee in the building would have to attend their annual sexual discrimination and diversity training class within sixty days. No one was exempt, and that included all of senior management.

"There's a couple of stragglers who've been out on leave, but everyone else has taken them."

Nate gave a grunt of approval. "What about HR and the résumé workshop? How did they do with that?"

Jack grimaced and ruefully acknowledged, "That one didn't go so well. We may need to use the screening service."

Nate had had a feeling that recruiting using the screening service would produce more equitable results. "You know that was Kennedy's idea, right? She told me it would remove some subconscious biases most people don't realize they have. Even the most well-meaning of us."

"I thought it had something to do with her. Her instincts are good."

"She's damn good at what she does," Nate stated proudly. "I was thinking of hiring the agency to design a few of our classes."

Jack crossed his arms. "You don't think that might be a conflict of interest? You are, after all, sleeping with the woman."

Nate dismissed his concern. "It isn't as if she would be working for me. The agency would be dealing directly with HR. It's contract work. Once it's finished and handed over, that's it," he said, swiping his palms together.

"I'm just saying, you may want to think twice before you go mixing business with pleasure."

"What the hell are you talking about? Your brother-in-law works at the North Carolina office and your cousin worked here for three years until he moved to Texas. Please tell me what I'm missing."

A flicker of annoyance appeared on Jack's face. "Dude, you're comparing apples to oranges. It isn't as if my brother-in-law and cousin weren't qualified for the positions. They were, or I wouldn't have recommended them. And the chances that my relationship with them goes south and causes problems for the company are slim to none. On the other hand, hiring the person you're fu—sleeping with—" he shook his head "—is asking for trouble."

Asking for trouble?

"Are you saying that nepotism where you're concerned is fine but contracting my girlfriend for a job is a bridge too far?" Seriously, fuck that.

"As long as the person is qualified, I don't see anything wrong with a little nepotism. Family businesses are built on it."

"I didn't say I had a problem with nepotism. What I'm having a problem with is the pushback I'm getting from you about hiring an agency that is *more than qualified* to do the work the company needs done."

Jack blew out a long breath. "Just think it over is all I'm saying. The woman you start dating isn't the same woman you break up with. It's the same thing they say about marriage and divorce."

"Cynical much?" Who said anything about breaking up with her? And he wasn't *just* fucking her. He was in lo—

Whoa. Nate pulled back sharply before completing the thought. He then addressed his friend more gruffly than he intended. "Boy, Kaitlin really did a number on you."

Jack remained silent, not denying it.

Even after he found out his ex cheated on him, he hadn't

called off the wedding. Who did? Kaitlin, two weeks before they were supposed to walk down the aisle together. And if that wasn't enough, his father started dating a woman almost half his age not even a month after their divorce papers were filed. Jack had to hear about it every time he visited his mother, who now used him as her personal sounding board.

Women sucked. Marriage sucked. Relationships with the opposite sex sucked. That was the place Jack was coming from.

Nate didn't envy him. And for that reason alone, he cut him some slack. "Think of me hiring the agency as an act of nepotism since Aurora's an equal partner."

Jack studied him before holding his hands up in surrender and conceding with a tight smile. "Hey, your company, your call."

"Good. I'm glad that's one thing we can agree on."

21

Breaking News: Massive cyberattack hits Fortune 500's top companies.

Kennedy received the first notification on her phone on Friday at four o'clock in the afternoon. She instinctively reached out to their IT administrator. Token was about as far from a Fortune 500 company as one could get, but it never hurt to check and make sure their system was in the clear.

"I knew you'd call. I'm on my way," Keith said as soon as he picked up. Not a half minute later he was in her office. Keith Smith, a heavyset, fifty-three-year-old Black father of six, had been one of their first hires and was worth every penny they paid the experienced IT professional.

"I guess you heard," he said as he approached her desk. "It's all over the news and social media, but you don't have to worry—we're good. Our system is airtight. Payroll is good and so is the client database."

"Have they said which companies were hit? Is it a ransom attack?" Kennedy asked as she scoured the article on her monitor for names.

Keith came behind her desk and peered over her shoulder. "I don't think it's a ransom attack. A reporter tweeted there's been an email dump. They're going through it now."

Kennedy looked up at him, eyes wide. "Oh crap. That might actually be worse than a ransom attack. I hope everyone kept their emails G-rated."

Keith harrumphed. "I wouldn't count on it."

"You'd think after the Sony debacle people would learn."

"If people learned from history, the world wouldn't be in the shape it's in."

Kennedy couldn't argue with that. Humans were the stubbornest species in existence, and just as past hacks hadn't stopped people from sending inappropriate emails, this one would likely find the same. The only question was the amount and scope of the damage it would do.

"Okay, well, as long as we're good, I guess I can breathe easy." But her mind had already leaped to Nate and Constellation. As one of the top tech companies in the world, one would think their security rivaled whatever held the nuclear codes.

"Oh, and in case you're wondering, I called a former employee who works over at Constellation, and it doesn't look like they've been hit. Or at least, it doesn't look like anyone was able to get through. But she'll let me know more when she does. She thinks there could have been an attempt."

Keith used to manage the IT department at a small software development company in northern New Jersey until it was bought by a software giant in California, which was where his job went. Several of his former employees had subsequently attained positions at Constellation.

"That's a relief." Nate had enough on his plate in having to deal with the lawsuit. Not that there was ever a good time to have to deal with a hack. Hacks were notoriously a bad thing.

When her cell phone started to ring, Keith quickly excused himself, saying, "I'll let you get that. I'll keep a lookout to see if any of our former or current clients were hit and let you know."

Nodding absently, Kennedy answered her lover's call. "Speak of the devil and he shall appear—or in your case, call. I was just talking to Keith about your company."

Nate chuckled. "Wondering if we were part of the hack, huh? Not a chance. We have the best security in the business. What about you? Sounds like things are good."

Kennedy turned and gazed at the gray overcast sky that promised a dreary day of rain and umbrella-crowded sidewalks. A tepid rainfall spattered raindrops against the window. "That's the beauty of operating under the radar. Most people don't know we exist, which is exactly the way we like it."

"If you want, I can have someone on my security team check out whatever safeguards you guys have in place," Nate offered.

That emotion filling her chest was gratitude, not the L word. She'd resisted putting a name to it, simply telling herself that she was most definitely *in lust* with him. The sex was fantastic. The best she'd ever had. That he was also easy to talk to, considerate, and he loved that she was ambitious didn't mean he was *The One* for her. It didn't mean she was in *L.O.V.E.* with him. Real love required they make it beyond the honeymoon stage of their relationship.

Love is easy when things are going right. It's when things are not that love either withers and dies or deepens and strengthens to survive the storm.

Her parents' love had deepened and strengthened over their thirty-five years of marriage because, her mother swore, they lived by those words.

"Let me check with Keith and see what he thinks." She trusted him implicitly when it came to this stuff. They wouldn't have hired him otherwise. And as sweet as Nate's offer was, no way was she going to step on Keith's toes by bringing in someone to look over his work without asking him first.

"Yeah, of course, whatever's good with him."

"About tonight—"

"Would you mind—"

At their simultaneous utterances, they both fell instantly silent.

"You go first," Nate said. "What about tonight?"

"No, no, you go," Kennedy insisted. "Would I mind what?"

Nate took his time responding, and then when he did, his voice was flat. "Jack wanted to go out tonight. He says I've been blowing him off since I came back."

"Then go," she urged. "Honestly, I don't mind. We can do something tomorrow." Kennedy knew this wasn't coming out of nowhere. She sensed something like this coming after Jack showed up at Nate's place last week. She wasn't sure whether Jack's dislike of her was the general variety kind, or if he specifically disliked her for Nate; all she knew was that it was there. It was there in the way he'd looked at her and some of the bothersome comments he'd made.

The lawsuit brought Nate back home, so you can't say it's all been bad.

She'd had to bite her tongue at that remark.

Let's just hope he doesn't change his mind. People like Markham—

*men with political aspirations—have a habit of playing both sides
against the middle to further their personal agendas.*

When she'd accidentally on purpose overheard him say *that*
was when she'd realized who'd told Nate about her and Trevor.

She'd debated whether to say anything to Nate after his
friend left but had decided against it. What good would it do?
Nate would tell her she was being too sensitive and blowing
things out of proportion. After all, the men had been friends
since high school, and Jack was the trusted chief technology
officer of his company. She wasn't about to test the bonds of
their friendship against whatever was going on between her
and Nate. It was too new and fragile.

"Are you sure? Because, to tell you the truth, I'd rather
spend the evening with you."

Kennedy smiled. "Lately, you've been spending every evening with me. One night apart won't hurt us." Yes, it would.
She'd gotten used to frequent and earth-shattering orgasms.

"Hold on a second. Who said anything about us spending tonight apart? I was hoping we could meet at your place
after. For dessert," he said, his voice dipping seductively low.

"I think you can get by without *dessert* for one night," Kennedy stated, all bravado with her empty words. In truth, without him beside her, she'd probably be twisting and turning in
her bed all night. "Plus, I'm going to use this time to catch up
with my girlfriends. Jack isn't the only one feeling neglected."
It had been at least two weeks since she and Aurora had hung
out, and Sahara was back in town, making it the perfect time
for a girls' night out.

A grumbled sound of denial emerged from his throat. "You,
of all people, should know how much I need my dessert. I
can't go without it. And most nights I have at least two serv-
ings, and another in the morning."

Kennedy's face suffused with heat just thinking about how

thoroughly they always indulged. Up against walls and book-shelves, on the kitchen counter, and on the rug in front of the fireplace, there wasn't a room in his apartment they hadn't thoroughly debauched. "What if I said I'd make it up to you?" she teased, her tone husky.

"Then don't make any plans for Saturday that require clothes."

Kennedy gave a throaty laugh. "So you plan to keep me naked all day?" She would have laughingly dismissed it if the idea wasn't such a turn-on. She had no doubt that he'd do it, and since he'd be supplying the orgasms, she was fully on board.

"Do you blame me? I mean, have you seen *you* naked?"

Kennedy bit her bottom lip. She'd seen *him* naked and that was reason enough.

A movement at her door drew her attention to Mina, who stood on the threshold, a frantic look on her face.

Oh shit. "Listen, Nate. I've got to go. I'll call you later. Have fun tonight," she said and hastily got off the phone.

"We have a problem," Mina stated, giving voice to her expression.

"Who is it?" Kennedy steeled herself as a half dozen possibilities ran through her head.

"Roger's personal email was part of the hack, and apparently, there's more to the original video than what the public saw, and none of it's good."

Kennedy froze, air escaping her lips in a rush. Her shoulders slumped as she covered her face with her hands. "Oh crap." After a moment, she peeked at Mina from between her fingers. "How not good is it?"

Mina made the *yikes* emoji face. "I sent you a link to the video. It's already gone viral. I'm sure you'll be getting a call from his management any minute now."

"Okay, thanks for the heads-up," Kennedy said. Turning to her computer, she tapped her finger on the keyboard, opened the email in question, and watched.

She watched it two more times after that.

Okay, then. She closed the browser.

After his injurious *and* injudicious use of the N-word, her lovely client had gone on to make his displeasure known at the attempts being made to change the names of sports teams derogatory to Native Americans. Shockingly enough, he didn't find the names offensive. Kennedy was sure Cecelia's Cherokee ancestors had something to say about that.

Hell, *Kennedy* had something to say about that.

The video had only gotten better when his friend Weston had started them down the road leading straight to #MeToo hell. His opinion of what should be considered sexual harassment and assault should have him locked in #MeToo prison until he learned the meaning of consent. That the word *no* didn't mean *try and change my mind.* Roger's noncommittal grunts probably saved him from a life in hiding, but his friend wouldn't be spared the pitchforks coming for him. But then again, there was the matter of guilt by association, so Roger's relative silence on the subject didn't necessarily put him in the clear.

But Roger's most egregious crime came with his enlightened commentary on all the recent protests and marches: civil rights, police brutality, women's rights, transgender rights, gay rights, voting rights, abortion rights, et cetera, et cetera. To that, he'd said, *Jesus Christ, people need to lighten the fuck up. Go live somewhere else if they don't like it here.*

Kennedy inhaled deeply through her nose. She felt a migraine coming on, and she'd never had one in her life.

Roger was well and truly fucked.

Her office phone rang then, and the caller ID indicated it was exactly who she'd expected to call, the team's head of PR.

Kennedy spent the next fifteen minutes agreeing with Louis, that yes, the hack was reprehensible. But it didn't matter now that his comments were public. He would be judged by them, and not favorably. Even the people who privately agreed with him, none of them would stick their necks on the chopping block to defend him.

Since Roger was already working with the diversity outreach program, and his former neighbors had already lent their support the first time around, there wasn't much else she could do for him. Truth be told, there wasn't much she *wanted* to do for him. The idiot had managed to cast his insult net wider than before. At this rate, he was going to send his poor mother into witness protection. From shame.

She'd barely hung up with Louis when her cell phone rang. Kennedy looked down at her screen to see it was the now *twice*-disgraced hockey player himself.

Snatching it up, she practically stabbed at the screen. "You lied to me," she said, her tone flat and anger threading her voice.

"No, no, no. I swear I didn't lie to you." He sounded panicked. And as well he should.

"I asked you if there was anything else—"

"And there wasn't anything else. This was from the same day, and I didn't even realize the fu—the video uploaded to the cloud automatically. I thought it was deleted everywhere."

"But you knew you said those things when we talked."

"Oh, come on, Kennedy. Did you expect me to tell you? I was ashamed enough as it was. And I knew if I told you, you'd—" He broke off and emitted a heavy sigh.

"I'd what?" she snapped, her patience with him already threadbare and that little bit was quickly fraying.

"That you'd look at me different. That you might not want to help me. I didn't want you to think I was some bigoted dipshit."

Suddenly weary, Kennedy closed her eyes and slowly shook her head. Bone-deep tired of it all. "Are you a bigoted dipshit?"

"I'm beginning to think so," he admitted grimly. "I didn't know what the fuck I was talking about. Obviously. Working with the kids at the program is showing me that. You want to talk about toughness and resilience?" he huffed. "Most of those kids have more at their age than I will in my whole life."

"That's because they *have* to. They aren't given a choice. They either toughen up or the world around them will eat them alive."

"Yeah, but they shouldn't have to."

"No, they shouldn't, but this is life, and life isn't always fair. Actually, life is usually never fair."

Roger snorted. "I guess that means I'm going to get what's coming to me. No more hockey, no more endorsements. There's no coming back from this, is there? Everyone hates me now. My mother was at a march last week. She said she can't believe I'm her son."

As livid as she had been when she'd heard the video, Kennedy found it impossible to hold on to her anger. That kind of toxicity had a habit of eating a person alive, and in her line of work, she couldn't afford to allow it safe harbor. Especially now she realized she was more disappointed than anything else. She liked Roger. She'd believed in him. In his innate goodness. Did that make her a putz? A bad judge of character? She sure hoped not. Because, despite everything, she believed he was being sincere now.

"Maybe the endorsements are gone for good, but I think if

you go out there and talk to the public like you're talking to me, there's a good chance your hockey career can survive this."

"So tell them the truth is what you're saying." He sounded as if he'd rather claim his body had been taken over by an alien. Truth as a strategy might not be up to the heavy lift of resurrecting a reputation currently on life support.

"At this point, it's all you have."

It was almost eight when Kennedy left the office. The entire media ecosystem was on a sugar high. The nonstop coverage of the hacking story was coming at breakneck speed. Prime-time anchors were back behind their desks—no doubt for all-nighters—in the name of special reporting for the extended coverage. One would think a passenger plane had disappeared over the Atlantic Ocean.

She called Aurora for the third time in as many hours, hoping she would pick up this time. But once again, the call went straight to voice mail. After Kennedy hung up—this time without leaving a message—she debated what to do next. Nate was out with Jack, and she didn't want to bother him. But she couldn't go home until she got in touch with her friend. She hadn't seen Aurora since she'd ducked out of the office at two that afternoon, announcing she had an appointment with a client downtown and from there would be going straight home. The meeting should have ended hours ago.

Then why isn't she answering her phone?

It was the lack of answers to that question that had Kennedy fretting. To calm her fears, she took an Uber to her friend's brownstone, which was a short fifteen-minute ride.

Standing at the front door, Kennedy rang the bell and waited. The curtains were drawn, so she couldn't see in. When she couldn't hear anyone moving around, she fished the spare key Aurora had given her out of her handbag and let herself in.

"Anyone home?" she called into the darkened entryway. "Ror?" She closed and locked the door behind her, before turning on the light and venturing down the hall into the open space between the living room and the kitchen.

The faint sound of movement in the direction of the bedrooms piqued her ears. "Ror, is that you?"

More silence.

Shit, what if someone else was there—robbing the place? Clutching her handbag tightly in front of her, Kennedy glanced around. She needed a weapon just in case. Her gaze caught sight of the butcher block of knives.

A loud thud drew a startled scream from her throat. Her flight instinct warred with the one telling her to grab one of the knives and fight. Preferably, the one with the biggest and sharpest blade and sturdiest handle.

Before she could do either, one of the bedroom doors opened and light flooded the hallway. Aurora, clad in a short hot-pink robe, emerged breathless and disheveled. Seriously, her hair was a tangled blond wreck.

Relief nearly sent Kennedy to the floor in a faint. "You're home. I've been calling you for hours and it kept going straight to voice mail. I came by to check and make sure you're okay." She gestured toward the door. "I rang the doorbell and no one answered, so I let myself in."

Aurora had yet to say a word, her blue eyes luminescent and heightened color in her cheeks. She had a death grip on the front of her robe as she held it closed, the sash dangling at her sides.

"Ror, what's going on?" Kennedy shot a look behind her and realization finally dawned. "Oh my god, I interrupted something, didn't I?" Pointing at her friend's closed bedroom door, she exclaimed in a hushed whisper, "Oh my god, you're seeing someone. Who is it?"

At having established that her friend was safe and sound, perhaps another friend would have tiptoed quietly away. After all, a girl did need her privacy. But that wasn't their friendship. Had the situation been reversed, you wouldn't have been able to drag Aurora out of there without demanding to know the identity of the mystery man. Keeping the identity of a lover a secret was only condoned when it was your friend's brother. And Kennedy knew with a 99 percent certainty that neither of her brothers was behind the bedroom door.

Guiltily, Aurora followed the direction of her gaze, shooting a quick look over her shoulder. "He's not— We're not— We were just— It's not what—" Her response sputtered along before dying like a defunct car engine.

Kennedy decided to put her out of the misery that reduced her friend to marginal coherency, calling out to whoever was hiding in her room. "You may as well come out because I'm not leaving until you do. I'm Aurora's best friend, so we're bound to meet sooner or later. As we're both already here, now works."

The answer to her summons came at the opening of the bedroom door and a man slowly emerging into the lit hall.

Kennedy's lips parted on a gasp. *Well, knock me over with a feather.*

"Lieutenant Governor," she whispered by way of acknowledgment rather than greeting.

She hadn't met him in person, but she'd seen him on TV a bunch of times. She'd certainly never seen him like this, his shirt three-quarters buttoned and untucked from a slightly wrinkled pair of tan slacks, his feet bare, and his hair appearing finger combed.

Memories started running through her mind like clips from a movie: the new spring in Aurora's step, the flirtier way she'd been dressing lately, and how close she'd recently gotten to Adam Faulkner's daughter. It all made sense now.

She's screwing the guy.

His gaze flicked to Aurora before meeting Kennedy's, his expression guarded. "I know how this looks."

"It looks like you're sleeping with my friend. Does that about cover it, or is there more?"

"Ken, we aren't doing anything wrong," Aurora interjected. "We're both consenting adults."

"Ror, he's a former client. A *paying* client," she stressed. "And he's the *lieutenant-fricking-governor!*" The former should have made him off-limits, and the latter, kryptonite. Getting involved with a politician was like allowing yourself to be tied to a railroad track. It was just a matter of time until you got run over.

Adam Faulkner sighed and ran his fingers through his hair, which was thick, dark brown, and, surprisingly, without a hint of gray. He probably colored it, the vain bastard. "Believe me, I'm well aware of that," he muttered.

And yet he still chose to sleep with her, selfish bastard.

Aurora swiftly closed the small distance between them and ran her hand up and down his arm. A gesture so familiar and lover-like, it caused Kennedy's heart to ache, because she knew he was the train that was going to run her best friend over.

"You're not a client now, and that's what's most important," Aurora soothed, staring lovingly up into his eyes. Then she turned and addressed Kennedy. "I know what I'm doing."

Kennedy got it. She did. She completely understood how her friend could fall for a man like him. He was very attractive, not *that* old—she'd learned that forty-one became less old once you were on the precipice of thirty—and kept himself in shape enough to be featured on the cover of *Men's Fitness* last year. He was the whole political package, good looks, intelligence, pragmatism, empathy, and an abundance of charm, which was how he'd won his last election by over twenty points.

But he was a widower with a nineteen-year-old daughter. And *he was a politician*! That alone should have been enough to send Aurora running for the exits and then the hills…in Switzerland. How could she swear off celebrities and become involved with a man in politics, a necessary evil (although some would strenuously disagree on the *necessary* part) but as dirty and seedy a business as there ever was?

"I should get going," he said, giving Aurora's hand a squeeze.

"Come on. I'll see you out," her friend said softly, sending a pointed *we'll discuss your unwanted interference into my love life when we're alone* look at Kennedy.

Kennedy prepared herself for the coming confrontation. Although, after the day she was having, the last thing she wanted was to fight with her best friend, especially because of a man.

It didn't take long for the lovers to say their goodbyes. Robe now tightly belted around her slender waist, Aurora crossed her arms over her chest as they stood facing each other. "I know what you're going to say, but you'll be wasting your breath. I'm in love with him. I didn't mean for it to happen, but it did. And he's not a client anymore. I wouldn't have slept with him if he were."

Kennedy let out a mirthless laugh. She hated playing the heavy, but someone had to. "Oh, come on, Ror. You've been falling for the man probably since you first met him. Isn't that why you're so chummy with his daughter? Just because you two only recently started having sex doesn't mean a whole lot of emotional boundaries hadn't already been crossed." She should have suspected something was up when Aurora brought Brittany to the launch party. That should have been the tip-off.

Running her palm over her tangled hair, Aurora briefly

averted her gaze. She knew. She knew becoming involved with Adam Faulkner was a disaster waiting to happen. "Ken, what am I supposed to do?" Her eyes implored. "I'm in love with him and that's not something you can just turn off."

With one step, Kennedy pulled her into her arms. "Oh, sweetie, I know. If only our hearts didn't have minds of their own, our love lives would be ten times easier to manage, and relationships would be a walk in the park."

Aurora returned her embrace. "Under different circumstances, I really think you'd like him. More than that, I think you two would really get along. He's the kind of man you've always admired. He has all those qualities."

Gripping Aurora by the shoulders, Kennedy gently set her back and looked her in the eye. "Ror, he's in *politics*. You refuse to date anyone connected to anything celebrity related, yet here you are with the highest-profile politician in New York, who was cleared of bribery charges a year ago."

"Exactly." Aurora nodded fervently in agreement. "Which only goes to prove my point. Do you think that I would put myself in this situation on purpose? Don't you think I tried my hardest to run from it? Ken, you know me. The last thing I wanted was to fall in love with Adam. You have no idea how hard I fought it."

Taking in Aurora's pained expression, Kennedy was overcome with compassion. Actually, she did have an idea. How many years had she fought her feelings for Nate? Too many. And where had it gotten her in the end? She was in deeper than she'd ever been.

"Does he love you?"

The vulnerability in Aurora's big blue eyes as her shoulders rose and fell in a helpless shrug tore at Kennedy's heart. "I don't know. He hasn't said the words, but I know he cares about me a lot."

"Do you want a future with him?" *Would you be happy being a politician's wife?*

Another shrug. "I don't know. It's too soon to tell, but I want to see where it goes."

Kennedy wasn't fooled by her friend's sudden flash of sang-froid. They were the same age, on the cusp of three decades' worth of living. Nowhere close to old but not twenty-one either. She couldn't see Aurora taking a wait-and-see approach with a man she'd rearranged her professional ethics to be with. The man she now professed to love. Of course she wanted a future with him. That she wouldn't come right out and admit it spoke volumes. Her friend was in over her head. Just how far was the question.

"What does *he* want?"

The question elicited a soft blush, and a starry-eyed smile stole over Aurora's face. "Me. He wants me."

Kennedy gave her another hug and tried to ignore the sinking feeling in the pit of her stomach.

22

Nate felt like a teenager with his first crush. The out-of-control feeling was humbling after so many years of having to control his emotions around Kennedy. Now he didn't have to, but it wasn't the freeing experience he'd thought it would be. It made him vulnerable. It had him doing things like showing up at her apartment at eleven o'clock at night because he couldn't bear the thought of going home tonight without seeing her. He believed the technical term for it was *pussy whipped*.

She'd already buzzed him in and was therefore aware he was on his way up. At his light tap, the door swung open immediately. He must have caught her getting ready for bed, because she was rubbing something on her face.

"Now that you've caught me putting on my moisturizer, all the mystery is lost, so you may as well come in," she said with an impish smile.

Nate entered and closed the door behind him.

"Hey, cat got your tongue?"

That was when Nate realized he'd been staring. "Your hair. It's straight," he announced, stating the obvious.

"It's black magic," Kennedy said with a dramatic toss of her hair as she gestured from the top of her head down her sides in a classic Vanna White move, her fingers fluttering. "What do you think?"

Nate pulled her into his arms and crushed her mouth under his. Her lips instantly parted, and their tongues tangled, taking the kiss deeper. She smelled good, felt good, and tasted like heaven. He pulled back to say, "Black magic, huh? Well, I'm going to perform some white magic on you." He smirked, sifting his fingers through the shiny dark strands that fell almost halfway down her back. He hadn't realized it was that long without the curls.

Kennedy sputtered a laugh. "White magic, huh?" She then coyly asked, "Is it the kind where you use a wand?"

Nate's eyes darkened with promise. "Yes, and my wand will give you as many orgasms as you can handle," he said huskily, kissing her again, this time longer, deeper.

When they finally came up for air, Kennedy pressed her palms against his chest and said breathily, "Ah, that white magic. I think I'm addicted to it and your—" she cast a pointed look down at his crotch "—magic wand."

Nate's wand instantly hardened, ready to start producing those orgasms he'd promised.

"Okay, now are you going to tell me what you're doing here? I thought you were out with Jack."

"We did go out. But I was in the neighborhood and decided to stop by."

She gave a throaty laugh. "You just happened to be in the neighborhood, huh? Doing what?"

"Looking for you. Missing you," he said huskily as he slid his hand down her back and cupped her perfect ass. There was nothing he wanted more right now than to kiss every delicious inch of her. To feel her long, slim legs wrapped around his hips and feel her tightening around him.

"Ah, so you came for a booty call," she said, her voice sultry and low.

"I haven't come yet, but I intend to make us both come." He was deadly sincere about that. And that was when he heard it, the strains of music coming from her bedroom.

He peered down at her, his mouth tipped up at the corners. "Listening to music, were you? It's almost as if you were expecting me."

"Or someone," came Kennedy's saucy response.

"Someone like who?" Nate scoffed dismissively. He knew she was teasing, but that didn't stop a part of him from wanting to declare her off-limits to all other men as long as he drew breath. "I'm the only man allowed in your bed."

"You're the only man I'm permitting in my bed." Although she didn't voice it aloud, the *for now* hung over him like approaching storm clouds. "See the difference?"

"Then why are we still standing here?" he asked, as he ushered her through the dimly lit apartment to her bedroom. In the last several weeks, he'd been over a few times. He usually waited in the living room while she finished dressing, but she'd given him a tour of the place during his first visit. It was small and comfortable, and distinctly feminine. The place reminded him of her.

In her bedroom, he made quick work of ridding himself of his jeans and sports shirt. Thankfully, Kennedy was wearing just an oversized T-shirt and panties. He made quick work of that too, and within a minute, he had her on the bed and under him.

After the frenzy of movement, he stilled and stared deep

into her eyes. "I couldn't go home without seeing you first. I've also discovered I don't like to sleep without you beside me."

"Me too," she whispered, sifting her fingers through his hair.

The music, which had been relegated to background noise, suddenly took center stage in his mind as it changed from something soft and dreamy to something more upbeat; the singer's voice, a deep bass, was singularly unique.

Distracted, he paused and listened to the words. At the end of the first chorus, a huge smile crawled across his face. "Is this for me?" he asked softly, staring into her smiling eyes.

Kennedy chortled—the sound a mixture of amusement and desire—as she hit him playfully on the shoulder. "How could it be? I had no idea you were coming over tonight."

As the song continued to play, Nate lowered his head and kissed the corner of her mouth. "But you like it, don't you? Because it's the way you feel about me."

"Would you stop." Her shoulders began to shake with laughter.

"Admit it, everything in that song applies to me. I am your first. Your last. Your everything." From her kiss-swollen lips, his mouth trailed down to her collarbone and to her breast, taking the nipple into his mouth.

Admit it, you're mine.

Kennedy gasped as she clutched the back of his head, keeping his mouth right there while "You're the First, the Last, My Everything" by Barry White continued to play on the speaker on her night table.

"Admit it," he coaxed, batting at her nipple with his tongue.

Kennedy moaned, finding it difficult to concentrate on his words. "Yes, you were my first. You know that."

Nate nipped lightly on her breast, making it clear he wasn't satisfied with her answer. "And the rest."

Kennedy battled her way through a haze of desire and lust to turn the tables on him by asking, "What about you? Am I your last and your *everything*?"

Nate froze. He slowly raised his head and searched her face. "Do you want to be?"

She'd meant it as a joke—sort of—but the look in his eyes and the tone of his voice were anything but.

Everything inside her screamed, *Yes. Yes, that's exactly what I want*, but she decided to play it safe, not yet willing to expose her heart to the sometimes harsh elements of complete transparency, replying instead, "What I want is for you to make love to me."

Perhaps he sensed the cause of her hesitancy, because he didn't insist she answer—he simply parted her legs and drove into her, pinning her beneath him with a single hard thrust.

Kennedy felt him everywhere, her body welcoming and reveling in his possession. She bit her lip, trying to muffle a cry of pleasure, but the sound emerged broken from her throat.

"Don't hold back. I want to hear you," he rasped, his thrusts quickening as he set a relentless pace.

Her peak came too soon, the explosion taking her by surprise. That was what he did to her. Her orgasms now had hair-trigger tendencies. She never knew exactly what would set them off, and she had no control over them seconds before they did. Nate, on the other hand, got off on her absolute lack of control, praising her, telling her how good it felt to be inside her, and how beautiful she was.

She hung on, her hands on his butt as he raced to his own completion. His body went stiff after the final thrust, his face contorted in bliss, his neck strained and taut.

Looking up at him, Kennedy faced the truth head-on. He

was who she wanted for good, bad, and until death did they part. As the song said, her first, her last, her everything.

"I need you closer." Satiation laced the deep rumble of his voice, the weight of his body still covering hers as the cool air turned them into sticky human magnets.

Kennedy smiled drowsily. "I think we're as close as physically possible." She referred to the fact that he was still inside her.

"No, I'm talking about you living in the city. Have you ever thought about it?" Peering down at her, his gaze half-mast, he didn't appear in a rush to go anywhere.

Kennedy huffed a laugh. "Asks the man who has billions at his disposal. I've also thought about rocketing into space—" a bit of hyperbole, but it appeared that was what all the tech billionaires were doing these days "—but when does one find the time for a quick trip with all my prior engagements?" she teasingly mocked.

His gaze drifted down to her breasts. He slowly licked his bottom lip, that look back in his eyes. Then his gaze shot back up to hers. "What would you say to me buying you a place?"

A startled laugh broke from her throat. "You can't say things like that to me when you're still inside me," she protested, as if he'd broken one of the golden rules of intimacy they'd agreed to abide by.

His mouth quirked up at the corner. "Fair enough." Within seconds, her warm and slightly sticky human blanket was gone. His disappearance into the bathroom was followed by the flush of the toilet and then the sound of running water. Her queen-sized bed dipped slightly upon his return to her side, where he immediately tugged her into his arms, chest to breasts, face-to-face.

"Or you could move in with me," he said in another stunning offer.

"What?" Her voice rose perceptibly. The second his question sank in, her mind instinctively rejected it. Yes, she wanted a future with him and all that, but it was too soon for them to move in together. Way too soon. They hadn't been together three months, and six was the bare minimum a couple needed to be together before broaching the subject.

"Don't tell me—you think it's too soon?"

"And you don't?" came her instant retort.

Nate dismissed the question with a quick shake of his head. "I knew that's what you'd say if I asked, which is why you getting a place in the city would suit us both. You'd be closer to your office, and you wouldn't have to rent anymore, and I'd have you closer to me. It's a win-win situation." He gently brushed her hair over her shoulder.

"Honestly, Nate, I appreciate the offer, but you can't just *buy* me an apartment in New York City. You have to see that, right?" This was the craziest conversation she'd ever had with a man.

"Why not?" he asked, as if he didn't understand the power of his billions. "I guess that's where you and I differ, because I don't see the problem. It would be a gift."

Kennedy stared at him, flummoxed. Was this how rich people operated? "Nate, you're not talking about an expensive handbag or a nice piece of jewelry. You're talking about real estate in one of the most expensive cities in the country. It's one thing for you to pay when we go out, but buying me an apartment that's so above my financial means I'd need a rocket launcher to see it…is bonkers."

More than anything, her pride wouldn't allow her to accept such a— What would it be called? Because "gift" seemed wholly inadequate. She didn't want him for his money and didn't want him to see her as someone who couldn't give herself the things she wanted.

Nate stroked her cheek with the tips of his fingers. "Rocket launcher, huh? That can be arranged," he said with a smile. "Okay, forget I offered. We'll do it your way until you're ready for the next step."

Kennedy blinked at the swiftness of the withdrawal of his offer. It was almost as if he'd been testing her and putting her on notice at the same time.

Until you're ready for the next step.

Which meant he was ready and simply waiting for her.

Monday came too soon, and at eight-thirty in the morning, it was already slow-walking its way through the week. If only she could have remained in her and Nate's bubble a little longer. From her place on Saturday, they moved to his on Sunday, lazing the day away having sex and watching Netflix. They had food delivered because neither had wanted to step a foot outside their cocoon of bliss. Although discussion of her moving in with him or him buying her an apartment hadn't been broached again, she couldn't stop thinking about it.

Logically, Kennedy had always known Nate was rich. Like, really rich. But it had taken his offer to make her realize the enormity of his wealth and fully illuminate that chasm-wide difference between them. She was with a man who could give her the moon—or a rocket launcher, if she asked—without it putting a dent in his bank account. And he wanted to be with *her*. Wanted to *live* with her. It was mind-blowing and heady at the same time.

Despite her telling him it was too soon for her to move in with him, she wanted to, and knew in her heart that day would come. What scared the crap out of her was navigating the power dynamics of such a move without her pride getting in the way. She'd pulled her weight in all her relationships, and she was determined that her relationship with Nate wouldn't be any different.

Dragging her mind back to the present, she noted that one of the emails sitting unread in her company email account had been sent on Saturday. Kennedy sighed. How many times did she have to tell Mina not to work during the weekend? Time off was important for people's mental health.

"Morning," Mina announced from Kennedy's office door. Clad in a flowy midcalf-length blue dress, she looked as if she'd happily embraced the new her.

"Good morning, Mina. I was just reading the email you sent on *Saturday*," she said, her tone chiding.

Mina laughingly held up her arms as if warding off an attack to the face. "I forgot to send it before I left on Friday, so I wasn't working during the weekend. I wanted to make sure you saw it as soon as you got in."

"I guess that's okay, then," Kennedy muttered, suppressing a smile. She quickly read the email, growing more and more perplexed with every word. Her gaze lifted to meet Mina's. "Are you saying the young man Joseph Russo claimed would back up his story can't be found or doesn't exist?"

"Their HR department has no record of anyone fitting his description having ever worked at the station. No one," she replied with a shrug.

"And no pictures of Miss Montgomery with her hair dyed any of those wei—unconventional colors?"

Mina shook her head. "Not one. I checked her social media, professional and private. Her hair is brown in all of them. Usually straight, but in some of the most recent ones, she has her hair in braids."

Dammit. When it rained it really did pour. "Okay, thanks for letting me know. I'm going to have to take this up with

Mr. Russo myself." Kennedy wasn't looking forward to the call even a little bit.

She was still trying to make sense of things when her cell phone vibrated on her desk and Aurora's picture lit up the screen. A call from her at this time usually meant she was either running late or had an off-site client appointment that morning and would be in later. Kennedy answered, only to have her chipper "Hey, what's up?" be greeted with silence, and then an audible, tearful sniff.

Her heart plunged straight down to her toes. "Ror, what's wrong? What happened?" she asked, her voice urgent.

The pause that followed lasted long enough for the alarm that initially beset her to turn to full-blown panic. "Ror!" she practically yelled into the phone.

"He doesn't want to see me anymore," came Aurora's hoarse, tear-laden whisper.

Oh shit. Inhaling deeply, Kennedy bowed her head and stared sightlessly at the light wood-grained surface of her desk. She'd been afraid this would happen. Had been dreading it like a reunion of Marky Mark with his Funky Bunch.

"Oh, honey, I'm sorry." While she meant every word of it, she was convinced that this was for the best. Hopefully, somewhere down the road, Aurora would realize it too.

Another tearful sniff. "I don't know why I let myself believe I would be different. That he'd stick around for even a little while after the sex." Then her heartbroken friend began to sob in earnest. "I really thought he cared about me, but at the first sign of trouble, he bailed."

And she, Kennedy Amelia Mitchell, had been that sign of trouble. It had been her catching them together that set the wheels of his breakup in motion.

"Damn, I'm sorry, Ror. It's all my fault. I should have never—"

"No!" Aurora exclaimed, her voice surprisingly firm and adamant. "It's not your fault. We were going to be discovered at some point, and better you than the tabloids or a member of the other party. No, the truth is Adam doesn't think being involved with me will be beneficial to his political career, and that matters more to him than I do."

Kennedy's heart pinched. The matter-of-factness of her friend's tone did more to lay bare her pain than conceal it.

"Any man who would choose a career in *politics*—" she spat out the word as if it were an expletive "—over you doesn't deserve you."

"No, he doesn't, but I still want him, Ken. I love him," Aurora said, ending in a hiccupy sob.

Kennedy hated doing this over the phone. She wished she could be there for her friend. That she could hug her tight and tell her everything was going to be all right. Unfortunately, the phone, despite all its technological marvels and conveniences, would have to do.

"Sweetie, I know you do. But in time, things will get better. They always do. There are a million and one men out there who would give their eyetooth to be with you, and half a million who will love you and treat you the way you deserve."

Aurora let out a watery snort. "Maybe a dozen or two, but definitely not half a million."

That her friend could find even the tiniest bit of humor in it was a good sign. "Why don't you take a few days off, and I'll come over after work and bring dinner? Whatever you want, your wish is my command."

Another sniffle. "I love you, Ken."

"I love you too, Ror. Now, I want you to go and relax. I don't want you thinking about work, and for goodness' sake, don't read the tabloids. This hacking scandal is getting worse by the day, and you don't need that in your life right now.

That is, unless it'll make you feel better to watch a few of the mighty get knocked off their pedestals. Because, in that case, have at it."

"I think I'm going to go back to sleep." She sounded drained.

"Okay, sweetie, you do that. Call me if you need anything."

Kennedy didn't even have time to take a breath after they'd hung up when Jonathan was at her door. His expression said everything.

She groaned. "Oh god, what now? Don't tell me there's another video of Roger out there." She'd kill him!

Jonathan entered without saying a word and took a seat in his regular chair. "I'm glad you're sitting down and that I am too, because what I'm about to tell you isn't going to be easy."

Sometimes, Kennedy conceded, their office manager could be a tad dramatic. He'd watched every season of *Keeping Up with the Kardashians*. "Whatever it is, just say it." Monday was already off to a rollicking start—might as well pile on the sunshine.

"ECO Apparel was hacked."

Her jaw went slack. "No!"

Jonathan nodded. "Oh yes, and it gets worse."

Oh crap. She almost didn't want to know, but the expression on his face said she couldn't keep the bad news at bay, and willful ignorance wasn't an option.

"What's worse than getting hacked?"

"What's in some of the emails."

"Did Phil call? How bad is it? Are they looking for damage control?" Kennedy would always have a soft spot for the company. That was where she'd gotten her start. The reason Token existed—in its current form. And the number of clients Phil had sent her way couldn't be overstated. Helping them in their time of need was the least she could do.

Jonathan, appearing uneasy, briefly averted his gaze. "There is an email chain about you."

It took several moments for Kennedy to digest that. "Derogatory?" she asked, already knowing the answer, but she needed to be sure.

He responded with a curt, decisive nod.

"How bad?"

"Do you want to read the email chain for yourself?"

In other words, he didn't want to read it to her or spoon-feed her the paraphrased version. Which meant it was bad.

Jonathan began typing on his cell phone. Moments later, her own pinged. She clicked on the link and the image of an email filled the screen. Taking a deep breath, she began to read.

Sahara-Kennedy Mitchell ???
Phillip Draper <phillip.draper@ecoapparel.com>
Tuesday, June 6, 2020

To: Sam Weber
She's got some fucking nerve. But what are we going to do, the bitch has us over a barrel and she knows it. If she goes, she's taking Sahara with her. We have no choice but to give her what she wants. But make goddamn sure you make her work for every fucking penny.
Phil

Pain shot through her like shrapnel from an explosion. A punch in the gut would have been kinder. Her shocked gaze flew to Jonathan, who looked equal parts sympathetic and blazing mad.

Kennedy had been prepared for some sort of racist or sexist bullshit—what else would be newsworthy? Never in a million years had she thought it would be coming from Phil, whom, up until ten seconds ago, she'd considered a friend. She'd had dinner over at his house, for goodness' sake. He'd recommended her services to his friends and business associates. She'd thought he genuinely liked her.

Well, it was definitely time to put that fairy tale to rest for good. Stiffening her spine, she forced herself to read on.

Re: Sahara-Kennedy Mitchell ???
Sam Weber <samuel.weber@ecoapparel.com>
Tuesday, June 6, 2020

To: Phillip Draper
On her back. LOL. That's all they do anyway, eat, sleep, fuck, and push out a kid every year so they can get on the public dime. This would be a step up for her.

She'd always thought Sam was an ass. At least she'd been right about that.

Re: Re: Sahara-Kennedy Mitchell ???
Phillip Draper <phillip.draper@ecoapparel.com>
Tuesday, June 6, 2020

To: Sam Weber
As far as I know, she doesn't have any kids, so a fucking unicorn. But she's hot. I'd do her. I see a shit-ton of late nights in her future. She can be my first. LOL.
Phil

When she thought Phil had already reached rock bottom, he performed a Houdini maneuver and sank even lower. How had she not seen this side of him, astute judge of character that she was?

Re: Re: Re: Sahara-Kennedy Mitchell ???
Sam Weber <samuel.weber@ecoapparel.com>
Tuesday, June 6, 2020

To: Phillip Draper
Then sign me up for a threesome with her and the blonde. I
won't tell your wife if you don't tell mine. ;)

Kennedy wanted to throw up. The men were vile and re-
ducing Aurora to "the blonde" was reprehensible. Setting her
phone down, she raised her eyes to Jonathan. "I have a feeling
they won't be calling me to help fix this one."

Jonathan growled, baring his teeth. "Bastards. Racist, sexist bastards."

Kennedy rolled her shoulders before reclining in her chair.
She'd never been one of those *massages are the ultimate de-stressor*
people, but her neck, shoulders, and back wouldn't say no to
one right about now.

"I shouldn't be surprised. I'm sure this stuff happens every
day. But you know what they say—what you don't know won't
hurt you. Ignorance is bliss. That's never been my philosophy. I hate being kept in the dark about things like this. My
dad always said it's better to know your enemies. Well, now
I know." She wasn't going to lie—this one hurt.

"What are you going to do? A reporter just called asking for
a comment, and they're going to keep calling—and digging—
until we provide them with a statement."

Like sharks smelling blood, the media had already begun
to circle. She, of all people, knew how this worked. But she
was usually on the other end of reputation-damaging scan-
dals, not personally embroiled in them. She needed time to
think. Time to formulate a plan, because this kind of exposure wasn't simply personally unwanted and intrusive. It wasn't

good for the agency. Certainly not the part of the business that required anonymity for their clients.

"I'll come up with something. Give me a few hours. In the meantime, tell the staff not to talk to the press. And if a client calls with concerns, send them through to me."

The day, which had just started, now stretched out like a prison sentence.

23

If what is contained in the emails attributed to Phillip Draper and Samuel Weber from ECO Apparel is authentic, I can only convey my disappointment at the language and sentiment expressed in the emails. That kind of appalling and unprofessional conduct cannot be tolerated if we ever expect to have full equality not only in the workplace but in all aspects of society. The Token agency, which was founded to encourage and facilitate a more diverse and inclusive workplace, no longer does business with ECO Apparel.

Kennedy Mitchell

Kennedy reread the statement, and once she was satisfied it properly conveyed her feelings—without the inclusion of a single use of the word *motherfucker*—she emailed it to Julie to check over. Although it wasn't a legal document, it never hurt to have a lawyer read it over before sending it out into the world.

Sahara commenced what would be a torrent of calls, practically shrieking furiously into the phone the moment Kennedy picked up.

"I'm going to bury them if it's the last thing I do. Girl, they are so done. Because either they go or I'm gone. I don't care what I have to do to get out of the contract, I'll do it." Her friend then went on to use every derogatory word in the book she could think of to describe them. Surprisingly, the list was more expansive than one would think.

At the end of her tirade, Sahara did an emotional one-hundred-and-eighty-degree pivot and inquired sympathetically, "So how are you doing?"

"Apart from the tire marks from the truck that ran me over, I'm doing all right," Kennedy replied wryly.

"I know a couple guys who'll rough them up for free. They'd do anything for a good cause, and if this isn't one, one doesn't exist."

Kennedy gave a dry laugh. Her friend played a convincing mafioso. *Not.* "A friend willing to commit a felony for me. I'm truly blessed."

"If not your friends, then who? We women have to stick together, especially us Black women. Let's face it—if that's what Phil and Sam said about you, can you imagine the shit they've been saying about *me* behind my back?"

Sahara had a good point. Celebrity or not, the fact that a young Black woman was calling the shots regarding what was then a potential multimillion-dollar deal probably hadn't sat well with them. They may not have expressed their true feelings via email, but she bet they'd communicated them.

"If they did, they were smart enough not to memorialize it. After all this time, you'd think people would learn that noth-

ing in the *tech* stratosphere is ever really deleted or private."
Sighing, she grabbed her stress ball from her desk and began
to squeeze. "And imagine, I did everything I could to help
them win their contract with you."

"How could you possibly have known?"

"The total lack of Black employees should have tipped me
off," Kennedy replied wryly.

Sahara harrumphed. "They were *not* alone. Dozens of companies were exactly like them. Plenty still are. You know that.
But because of you, the company's, what, ten times more diverse."

"That was because of you, not me. They wouldn't have
done any of it on my insistence alone."

"All right, all right, then I say we call it a draw. We did it
together." There was an amused smile in her friend's voice.

"It's your clothing lines that are now half of their annual
revenue. They literally can't afford to lose your business."
Which put Sahara in the driver's seat. If she wanted the men
gone, there wasn't a doubt in her mind—the men were going,
going, gone. It was simply a matter of time.

"And don't think I'm not loving this right now. Which re-
minds me—I have a call from Donald Edwards to return. You
gotta know he's straight-up panicking right now."

Kennedy could only imagine. Donald Edwards, ECO Apparel's
CEO, must be beside himself. Value of their stock had more than
doubled since the debut of Sahara's clothing line. Anything that
jeopardized the company's bottom line would be treated like the
five-alarm fire it was.

After promising Sahara that she'd call if she needed anything, even if it was just to vent, Kennedy hung up.

Then, as if a family newsletter about the incident had gone
out that morning, like the opening of a spigot, the calls began
to pour in. Her mother—who spoke while her father made

noises of support in the background—was more the hovering, concerned mother hen than outraged, *they will rue the day
they were born* parent.

"My poor baby. Do you need me to fly up there?"

"No, Mom, that's okay. I'm fine."

"What would be wrong with you having a couple children by now? you're almost thirty, not fifteen. Why don't you
come home for a bit? Take some time off work. Your father
agrees with me."

"It's okay, Mom. And tell Dad I'm fine. I really don't want
you guys to worry."

Her parents meant well.

While her mother continued through a litany of things sure
to help Kennedy through the ordeal—offering to next-day
deliver her a container of pholourie, because wasn't food the
answer to most problems?—her sister called.

Where their mother had covered the concerned parent,
Cheryl had the outraged part down pat. The severing of a
certain male body part required for procreation came up during the heated, mostly one-sided conversation. Making that
another woman in her life willing to commit felonies for her.
Her sister had always been protective of her, but this violent
streak in her was new. Kennedy had never felt more loved.

Her brothers were all brimstone, fire, and fury. So *much*
righteous bristling masculine fury. They didn't need to hire a
hit man, as they were more than willing to do the wet work
themselves. Cam and Jay could be scary intimidating when
they adopted their *do not fuck with my sisters* persona.

The phone calls didn't stop with her immediate family.
Current and former clients, friends from college, and even a
long-lost friend from back home in Raleigh—Kennedy didn't
ask how she'd gotten her cell phone number—called to lend
their support and express their outrage.

By the time Nate called at minutes after noon, enough time had passed that the world didn't feel as though she was still suffering the effects of the bomb blast that was Jonathan's news.

"Hi." He sounded grim but oddly subdued, and she had never been happier to hear his voice.

"Hi. I was going to call but the phone won't stop ringing."

"He's a fucking asshole. I knew there was a reason I hated the guy." He tactfully avoided saying *I told you so.*

"It looks like you were a better judge of character where he was concerned," she conceded. Although, it wasn't as if Nate didn't have his own troubling blind spots. But that was a matter for another time, one they'd have to deal with eventually. Front and center now was the issue of the emails and navigating her—and the agency's—way through the gauntlet of unwanted publicity.

"I've met enough men like him in my life," Nate stated in an uncomplimentary tone. There was some seething in there too.

"I wish reporters would stop calling," she lamented. For the most part, Jonathan was handling those.

"Yeah, well, one just called me. He wanted to know what I thought about my girlfriend being the subject of such *disparaging emails.* Then he asked if I knew exactly what services your agency provided to ECO Apparel."

That was exactly the kind of attention she'd desperately hoped to avoid. Unfortunately, given the nature of the media these days, questions like this were inevitable. The hunt was officially on.

"What did you say?"

"I told him I had no comment. Partly because, at the time, I had no idea what emails he was talking about. Google took care of that," he said drolly. "After I read them, I saw red for so long, I thought I was going blind. Then I just wanted to beat the shit out of them."

Kennedy's heart swelled. Not a felony, but close enough. It was the thought that mattered, and he must have understood that he wouldn't be any good to her in jail.

Her office phone started ringing at the same time Jonathan bellowed from outside. "It's Clive Macintosh from Delany and Associates. He's looking for assurances."

"Listen, Nate, I've got to take this call. I'll call you later."

"I'll pick you up after work," he said in a tone that brooked no refusal, and she wasn't in the frame of mind to offer one. If she made it through the day, she wanted nothing more than to end it in his arms.

With the exception of the clients who contacted her after the bomb dropped, Kennedy preemptively contacted the remaining. Better they hear the news from her than an enterprising reporter in search of a story within a scandal. That was, if they hadn't been made aware of it already, since news traveled fast, bad news even faster, but salacious news was by far and away the fastest, touching one hundred times the people in one-tenth the time.

The businesses she'd personally dealt with didn't appear too concerned about their exposure—the agency having produced tangible work product for them in the form of training classes and inclusivity and diversity plans, as well as professional referrals. It was wealthy and celebrity clients, like Roger O'Brien who were worried about their names surfacing in connection with the agency. They'd been guaranteed anonymity and expected nothing less, despite the most sophisticated cyber hack and invasive email leak the country had ever experienced. Thank God her agency hadn't been caught up in the dragnet. Some other smaller businesses hadn't been as fortunate.

To date, the casualties of the email leak included four CEOs, two VPs, and a dozen managers, all of whom had been forced to step down. The reasons ran the gamut from inappropriate office relationships to insider trading and every negative "ism" known to mankind. So far it was crickets from ECO, but a text message from Sahara an hour ago informed her a company statement was forthcoming.

When Kennedy had read that, she'd rolled her eyes. *I can hardly wait.* Truthfully, she didn't want an apology, which would be performative gibberish anyway. A flimsy Band-Aid slapped on a gushing wound, when a doctor, anesthesia, and stitches were required. She'd more likely believe words blurted in a drunken stupor than those uttered under the bright light of sobriety and media scrutiny. People tended to say what they meant when their guards were down. Phil and Sam—and all the others—had been caught with their pants down around their ankles.

In the midst of a chaotic day—the phone would not stop ringing—Aurora called. She'd woken up at one in the afternoon to find her Twitter timeline filled with links to articles and videos covering every lurid detail of the disgusting email conversation. One of four cable news stations was covering the fallout wall-to-wall. It had taken Kennedy fifteen minutes to convince Aurora that she had it all under control and not to come in. For now. And with her friend's approval, she finally issued the statement she'd written earlier. Hopefully, with that out, reporters would stop pestering Jonathan.

Just when Kennedy thought she'd be able to leave the wretchedness of the day behind her, her office phone rang. Not a call transferred to her by Jonathan or Mina, but someone who had her direct line. Apart from her clients, not many people did. And her family and friends called her on her cell phone.

Crossing the office to her desk, she reluctantly answered.

One more and then she was leaving. The car would be there in ten minutes, and she hated having the poor guy wait.

"Hello, Kennedy Mitchell speaking."

"Hi, Miss Mitchell, this is Jeremy Friedman from *Times Square Chronicle*. If you don't mind, I have a few questions to ask regarding your time at Columbia."

"I'm sorry—what?" *My time at Columbia?* His question threw her off so much, she didn't have enough wits about her to issue her standard *no comment* comment and hang up.

"I'm sorry," he said in an amiable voice. "Let me explain. Everyone wants to know more about the woman at the center of the emails and I've been calling around trying to fill in your background. I'm sure our readers will be interested in your journey from—" he paused "—North Carolina to Columbia to owning your own PR agency. I just got off the phone with a source at the university and I was told that you were a scholarship recipient, but I'm having problems pinpointing the source of the scholarship. It appears to have come from an anonymous donor and the university refuses to reveal their name."

Kennedy sat down hard in her guest chair, bewilderment morphing into embarrassment and then seesawing back. How did he know she'd been a scholarship recipient and why did that matter? And an anonymous donor? That made no sense.

"I'm sorry, but I have no idea what you're talking about. And I can assure you, my life is not that interesting." So what if she'd attended a top university on scholarship? She and thousands of others. It was nothing to be ashamed of. That said, what was he hoping to find?

"Are you kidding? You're the subject of some pretty horrible comments. Everyone wants to put a face to a name, and you have a great story. I think readers will love the small-town girl from North Carolina moving to the big city, excelling in college, and eventually opening her own business. It's a real pull-yourself-up-by-the-bootstraps story, and readers love them."

The sad thing about the reporter's pitch was that he thought it was a compliment.

"Mr. Friedman, I hate to burst your bubble, but Raleigh isn't exactly a small town. Second, both my parents are college educated and I grew up in a middle-class home. As you've also discovered, I was fortunate to have the grades to get into an excellent university and studied like hell to be able to graduate in the top five percent of my class. I don't believe that fits the customary *up by the bootstraps* story." Sure, life wasn't fair, and as a Black person, she'd lived it firsthand. But she'd realized early on that she was more fortunate than most, and she refused to be depicted as a character of woe. More people than she cared to admit had it a lot worse.

As if sensing he'd well and truly put his foot in it, Mr. Friedman cleared his throat—an uncomfortable scratchy sound—and said, "All success stories are inspiring. As for the matter of the anonymous donor—"

"There was no anonymous donor," Kennedy stated firmly, cutting him off. "Whoever gave you that information was mistaken. The scholarship for gifted students I received was offered by the university."

"*Through* the university," the reporter corrected. "The funding, however, came from an anonymous donor, and that's the part of the story I find intriguing. And since it sounds as if you're only finding out about it now, wouldn't you like to know who helped fund your education? I know I would, if it were me."

"I'm sorry, Mr. Friedman, but I really have to go. Goodbye."

Kennedy hung up before he could say another word, and

then picked up her cell phone and purse before locking up the empty office. The car Nate had sent was waiting when she emerged from the building. She flashed the driver a tight-lipped smile when he opened the door for her. Inside the dark gray interior, she thought a lot about what the reporter had claimed, sounding supremely confident in his facts.

Anonymous donor, though? That couldn't be right. Whoever his source was inside the university had to be mistaken.

Yet the more she thought about it, the more she questioned what she'd always believed to be the truth. Her recollection of the days she sat filling out application after application, both for college and financial aid, was mostly a blur of mental exhaustion and frustration. There'd been so many of them. Most she'd been able to fill out online, but some she'd had to complete by hand and return via snail mail. Kennedy had welcomed any and all help and had been grateful to Aurora for finding the scholarship. She hadn't thought twice about having missed it herself. At the time, she'd qualified for two small grants but would need a lot more tuition assistance in order to be able to afford a university like Columbia.

Three weeks after she'd applied, she received notification that she'd gotten the scholarship, which would pay roughly 85 percent of her tuition and housing costs. She would never forget the overwhelming sense of relief she'd felt in knowing she'd be able to put herself through school. She would have to take out a loan, but it wouldn't be an amount that would bankrupt her after she finished. Her parents were already in debt paying off the student loans they'd taken out to help her older brother and sister. She refused to add her educational burden to their already full financial plate and had been determined to do it on her own.

And she had.

At least, she thought she had.

★ ★ ★

Dinner was ready. Nate had made it himself, and done a good job of it, if he could say so himself. His abilities in the kitchen weren't exceptional, but he could read and follow simple instructions and hadn't attempted anything beyond his mediocre cooking skills. The baked salmon in a seasoned, brown sugar, oil, and soy sauce was an easy layup. Baked potatoes and sautéed vegetables were another can't-miss. Now all he needed was his girlfriend to arrive and she could taste with her tongue what else he brought to the table in their relationship.

Just as he was placing the food in the warmer, his phone pinged with a message from his driver, letting him know he'd just dropped Kennedy off in front of his building. It was touches like that that made the service stand out from its competitors.

Nate expected a knock on the door in the time it took her to take the elevator up to the top floor. But the minutes came and went until ten had passed. Worried, he opened the door, intending to stick his head out before calling her to find out what was taking her so long. Startled, he reflexively jerked back at the sight of her standing at his doorstep, head down, arms at her sides.

"Hey, what are you doing out there? I thought you'd gotten lost."

Then she lifted her gaze to his and he knew something was wrong.

"Hey, what's wrong?" He gently tugged her inside and closed the door. He hoped to hell it wasn't another fucking email full of racist stereotypes and sexist garbage. Seriously, the whole thing was enough to make him lose his shit.

"Wrong? I'm not sure," she replied, her voice flat.

"Something must be if I don't even get a kiss," he said, trying to coax something from her. Anything.

Kennedy stared at him, her eyes unblinking and her expression opaque. "If I ask you something, do you promise to be honest with me?"

Oh shit. That was like asking him if he'd rather die in the electric chair or by firing squad.

"Yes, of course. But why don't we sit down first?" He had a feeling he was going to need the support.

"No, I'm good right here."

He sent a pointed look at her heels and dove-gray pantsuit. The first thing she usually did when she got to his apartment straight from work was kick off her shoes and change into something comfortable. She kept a few pairs of yoga pants and T-shirts in a spare drawer in his bedroom.

Something was definitely wrong and getting worse by the second. He'd never dealt with Kennedy when she was like this. Cold. Unyielding. Emotionless. What the hell was going on?

"Did you pay for me to go to Columbia?" Her voice was calm, her tone measured.

Frozen in place from shock, Nate didn't blink or breathe. Of all the things he might have expected her to ask, her question hadn't even registered on his radar.

Are you seeing someone else? Did you marry someone when you were in France? Did you get someone pregnant? He'd been prepared for something along those lines, to which the answer would have been a resounding no. Easy stuff.

This wasn't going to be easy.

"You shouldn't have to think about it. It's either yes or no," she prompted coolly. "Although, judging by your reaction, I think I know the answer."

Nate swallowed hard. "Yes. I did."

She gave a sharp nod. "I thought so."

"How did you find out? Who told you?" He'd been promised that no one would ever be *able* to discover the source of the funds, much less trace it back to him. His identity had been thoroughly masked, they'd assured him a number of times over the years. So much for fucking anonymity. Heads were going to roll for this breach.

"A reporter called. He mentioned the scholarship and asked if I knew who the anonymous donor was. His source at the university apparently wasn't privy to the information. I guess he thought who better to ask than the lucky recipient herself and thought his readers would love an *up by the bootstraps story* starring yours truly." She dipped low in a mock curtsy. "And can you imagine his glee when he discovered I didn't even know there was a donor, anonymous or otherwise? And that my college education had been funded by a wealthy donor who chose not to have his generosity known. And so the plot thickens." She shivered dramatically, her eyes ice-cold. "Wouldn't this make a great feel-good story for a news feature? Bringing together the lucky *hard-luck* scholarship recipient with her anonymous donor so I can thank you in person? The public would eat it up."

Nate winced. "You know it's not like that."

"Then tell me what's it like, Nate. Tell me why you would go behind my back and do something like this. What is it? Do you have a white-knight complex? Or was it guilt?"

She froze him off when he tried to touch her, this time moving beyond his reach. He wisely withdrew his hand at the risk of sending her bolting.

"Kennedy, when you and Aurora were accepted at Columbia, I wanted to give you both what you wanted, and I did what I needed to do to make that happen."

"Oh, don't give me that. You were giving me what *you* wanted. Do you know how I know? Because you knew that if you simply offered me the money, I would have said no. So instead, you devised this phony scholarship for the *academically gifted*. You needed me to believe that I'd earned it on my own, when the only criterion was that I was your sister's best friend who couldn't afford an Ivy League school education. Let's face it—you felt sorry for me."

"You were academically gifted," Nate rebutted forcefully. "And I didn't feel sorry for you. I wanted to help you get what you deserved."

"Who said I deserved it, Nate, you?"

At the slight catch in her voice, he instinctively reached out to her, only to stop himself when she automatically took another step back, her entire posture screaming *stay away*.

"I was just trying to help." Nate had never felt so utterly helpless in his life. More than a little disconcerted, he ran a weary hand through his hair and gazed at her, his eyes imploring. "Look, I'm sorry I went behind your back. And you're right—I knew you wouldn't let me just give you the money or pay for it outright, which is why I didn't cover everything. I thought it might make you suspicious. But I never wanted to hurt you or make you feel bad about yourself or your abilities. My money may have helped fund your education, but you were the one who did the work. You're the one who got the grades and graduated at the top of your class."

What he was going through now? *This* was why he'd abandoned the idea of buying her a place in the city after receiving her pushback. A lot of women would have accepted the offer the second it was issued. Not Kennedy, though. She was simply too proud to accept a gift that extravagant. And as frustrating as that could sometimes be, he fucking adored that about her.

Kennedy stared at him, slowly shaking her head. "How can I expect you to know how I feel? You can't. And I guess that's the crux of the matter. I don't want or need a white knight to save me. And believe me, a few Black ones have tried." She briefly averted her gaze and swallowed before continuing. "You have no idea how proud I was of what I was able to accomplish. I didn't ask my parents for a dime and managed to earn an undergraduate *and* master's degree *on my own*. And all that time it was you carrying me on your shoulders. Making everything I have now possible."

"No, you earned it," Nate insisted, panic rising inside him like a tide. He was losing her. He could feel her slipping away in a vortex of doubt, despair, and anger.

Suddenly, she narrowed her eyes at him, her expression turning fierce. "Jack knows, doesn't he? That's why he made all those snide comments about how well I'd done for myself."

Nate was taken aback by the vehemence in her voice. "What are you talking about? Jack doesn't know anything about this. I didn't tell anyone what I was doing. And when did he ever make snide comments to you?" he asked, feeling a tiny stab of annoyance. So now she was going to find another reason to cry foul. Find something else to blame him for by casting Jack as the enemy, when, ironically, it was the asshole she'd trusted who had been the one talking shit about her behind her back.

Chin jutted, she said, "I wasn't imagining things, Nate. Maybe you didn't pick up on his attitude, but I did."

Man, she was on a tear and not letting things like facts get in her way.

"Please don't do that." His irritation came through in the terseness of his tone.

"Do what?"

"This tit-for-tat shit. Just because I was right about your asshole of an ex-client, don't go looking for things to accuse Jack of."

"*Looking* for things? Are you kidding me?" she asked, her voice rising in disbelief. "You're so blinded by your friendship with him you refuse to see what's right in front of your face. He was belittling me and you didn't do or say anything to defend me."

"You're mad at me. I get it. But to accuse me of sitting by while my friend insults you really shows how highly you must think of me." He couldn't deny that it hurt.

With a frustrated huff, Kennedy furiously flicked her hair over her shoulder. "See, this is why I didn't say anything when it happened. I was afraid this was the way you'd react, and lo and behold, I was right."

"Dammit, Kennedy, not everyone is out to get you. Stop looking for enemies in every corner." The second the words were out of his mouth, he knew he'd crossed a line. "I'm sorry. I didn't mean it like that."

Kennedy stood motionless, the air around them palpably thick with tension. This was probably what it felt like in the seconds leading up to the explosion of a bomb. But when she spoke, her voice was eerily calm and very much in control. "I will when you pull your head out of the sand and see that one of the reasons your company is being sued has been standing right in front of you the whole time. Unfortunately—or fortunately, I guess, depending on your circumstances—I don't have the luxury of turning a blind eye to injustices simply because the perpetrator is a friend."

It took a second for Nate to grasp what she was saying. What she'd just accused him of, and the roiling implications. The woman was deadly, managing to gut him without drawing actual blood. But that didn't make it hurt any less.

Mute and somewhat shell-shocked, Nate watched as she turned and jerkily opened the door.

"I'm leaving. And don't worry. I'll find my own way home." The words sailed over her shoulder as she exited his apartment.

Moving to the doorway, Nate stared at her retreating form as she disappeared from view with only one thought in his mind. *What the hell just happened?*

24

Kennedy's life was imploding in such magnificent fashion, it came as no surprise to her the next day when a client wanted to put a *pause* on their contracts, requesting they push out the start date of their services. Another called to say they wouldn't be requiring the five people they'd previously requested. They hadn't offered an explanation, but she knew why. Right now, her agency was toxic when it came to those services, and who could blame them for staying away? Whether they intended to use *any* of Token's services in the future was up in the air. Kennedy had her doubts.

So not only had she and Aurora been maligned, but what she feared was coming to pass. The resulting attention was costing the agency business. And the day had only begun.

Normally, she wouldn't be working on three hours' sleep, but these weren't normal times. She'd come home from Nate's last night utterly spent, nearly numb. Too upset to cry and too angry to call and rail to her sister, her stalwart sounding board, she'd spent most of the early morning lying in bed staring at the ceiling, a multitude of thoughts going through her mind.

Knowing what Nate did changed things; she just didn't know exactly how. She owed him, but she didn't know what. What she did know was she hated being in anyone's debt, and that included the man she was in love with. Especially him.

Had Aurora known Nate was behind the scholarship? That was the other question that haunted her. Kennedy didn't want to think so. But how could she not have known? She'd been the one who "found" it and urged her to apply. And one of the things friends didn't do was secretly help their billionaire brother pay for your Ivy League education and keep it from you. With her best friend still nursing a broken heart, Kennedy wasn't eager to confront her about it. Thankfully, she had time, since Aurora wasn't expected back to work until tomorrow.

Or so Kennedy thought, up until the moment her friend walked into the break room while she was pouring herself a second cup of coffee. It was nine o'clock.

Actually, *tiptoed in* more accurately described the way Aurora approached, her blue eyes wary.

Clearing her throat, she stated softly, "I spoke to Nate."

That, Kennedy had surmised the second she saw her face.

"I didn't know at the beginning, Ken. Nate told me he heard about the scholarship from someone who worked at Columbia, and that you immediately came to mind. He said you met all the criteria." Aurora took a step closer, bringing them within a foot of each other. "I was so excited, I didn't think there was anything odd about it. It was his alma mater. I figured he had the inside track on things like that. And then when you got it, the only thing that mattered to me was that we'd be going to school together, and I'd be rooming with my best friend."

Aurora began fidgeting, rubbing her palms up and down her outer thighs.

Lifting the cup to her mouth, Kennedy blew lightly on the hot liquid. "So when did you know?"

"When we applied for the master's program," her friend said before pausing when Julie walked past the open door. As soon as the sound of clicking heels faded down the hallway, she continued. "This time, when Nate said he'd heard about another scholarship that would cover it, I finally wised up. It was just a little too coincidental to be believable a second time. When I pressed him on it, and kept pressing, he finally told me the truth. I wanted to tell you, Ken, but he begged me not to. He said if I did, you'd refuse it. And the thing is, I knew he was right, so I kept my mouth shut."

Kennedy took a sip of the coffee. She should have stopped by Starbucks and gotten a caramel macchiato Frappuccino, but she hadn't been in the mood—or had the patience—to wait in a line this morning.

"I'm sorry, Ken," Aurora said, managing to look both miserable and contrite. "Are you mad at me? I couldn't stand it if this ruined our friendship."

"I was at first, and I was going to call you last night when I got home, but I couldn't handle the thought of another argument. Then this morning I realized that no matter what or when you knew, I can't in good conscience hold you responsible for something your brother did. Plus, he's your brother, so of course when he asked you not to tell me, what choice did you have?" Kennedy shrugged. "He's your brother. He's blood."

"Yes, but you're the closest thing to a sister I've ever had, and I love you like one, and I don't want to lose you."

Kennedy's heart immediately softened. Aurora didn't apologize fairly, making it impossible to stay mad at her for long.

"Damn you. I love you too," she grumbled, suppressing a smile. "I'm not saying you're out of the woods yet, just that I understand the position he put you in."

A hundred-watt smile lit Aurora's face. She waited a beat before inquiring tentatively, "What about Nate? Will you be able to forgive him?"

Kennedy's lips tightened. "I don't know. I'm sure I will… eventually. But where we go from there, I don't know," she said, sighing. "What about you? How are you doing? I thought we agreed you were going to take a couple days off."

A shadow of pain flashed across Aurora's face. "Sitting at home alone only makes it worse. And anyway, Justine Ingram called. She's concerned I may not be able to represent her the way I should because of the crap in the email. It took me a bit to convince her the scandal hasn't affected my competency or commitment. I also promised to keep the lowest of low profiles and work strictly behind the scenes. She finally agreed to that."

Kennedy vacillated between relief and frustration. It wasn't fair. None of it was. Not to her and certainly not to Aurora. Then why were they paying the price for what Phil and Sam had done?

Earth to Kennedy. Life isn't fair. Never ever forget that.

After informing Aurora about the casualties the agency had suffered just that morning, she said, "At this point, I'll be happy if we're able to keep your accounts. The diversity and inclusivity part of the business is taking a hit, and lord knows how long it will continue. I'm being told the attention on me in particular is too much of a distraction."

"If we lose a few clients, we lose a few clients. We'll be fine," Aurora said with the confidence of a woman whose financial status had always been and would always be secure. She wouldn't let the agency fail because she could afford not to. She had money in reserve, and her brother was Zuckerberg rich. Kennedy, on the other hand…

"If I'm going to be detrimental to the agency, I'll walk away. I refuse to drag you down with me."

"I'm not even trying to hear that," her friend stated adamantly, shaking her head. "We started this together—hell, it was *your* genius that came up with it—and that's the way it'll end, which won't be for a very long time."

Kennedy didn't want to argue with her, so she wisely kept her thoughts to herself. But in the end, she'd do what she had to. She already owed Nate too much.

Nate. Her heart squeezed just thinking about him.

Turning, she set her half-filled cup down on the counter behind her. And it wasn't just about the scholarship. The way he'd reacted when she'd brought up Jack had landed like the proverbial gut punch, and she was still reeling from the pain of it.

Stop looking for enemies in every corner.

But it had been the wake-up call she'd needed. She might not know a lot of things, but she sure as hell knew when she was being condescended to.

"How well do you know Jack?" Kennedy asked.

Aurora looked at her curiously, clearly surprised by the question. "Jack Walters?"

"Yes."

"I've known Jack since grade school. He's a sweetheart, which is amazing, considering his parents."

Wonderful. Saint Jack strikes again.

"Why're you asking? Don't you like him?"

Instead of sidestepping the question, Kennedy decided to be honest. "Actually, I don't think *he* particularly likes *me*. At least, not for Nate."

Aurora's brows gathered above the bridge of her nose.

"Really? What did he say? Because that doesn't sound like Jack."

"You know what? Never mind. I'm probably being too sensitive."

She was *not* being too sensitive, but she didn't want to have this fight again. Apparently, the guy walked on water to every member of the Vaughn family, and budging him off his pedestal wasn't a task she wanted to take on.

"About Nate," Aurora said, bringing the subject back to her beloved older brother. "He means well and I know he really cares about you."

Unfortunately, sometimes meaning well wasn't good enough. After all, the road to hell was often paved with good intentions. At least, that was what someone who must know hell better than her had once said.

"Um, Kennedy."

Kennedy turned to find Jonathan hovering in the open door. "Joseph Russo is returning your call."

She huffed in annoyance. It was about time. For a while there, she'd thought he'd ghosted her. In her experience, people in his situation were eager to clear their name and would have called her back the same day she called.

"We'll talk later," Kennedy said, lightly touching Aurora's arm before hurrying to her office.

Once there, she sat down and snatched up her phone. "Good morning, Mr. Russo. It was nice of you to return my call." She wondered if he picked up on the sarcasm in her voice.

"I hope you called with good news," he said, as if he had no idea what she could be calling him about.

"Sorry to disappoint you, but it's quite the opposite. In speaking with your HR department, there's no trace of the young man you told me about, and no one we spoke to remembers anyone like him. Also, Ms. Montgomery denies she colored her hair, and we can't find anyone or anything like a picture to prove otherwise."

Kennedy expected him to reassert his claims and perhaps offer an explanation. Give her *something* more to work with. What she got was lengthening silence. It went on so long, she was compelled to ask, "Mr. Russo, did you hear what I said?" Did he have hearing problems they hadn't told her about? They'd met in person the last time, which would have made it easier to read her lips.

"Yes, I heard you. You can't find the young man or a picture of Miss Montgomery with her hair dyed." He paused before asking, his tone objectively mild-mannered, "Isn't it your job to do whatever needs to be done to make my story fit what I told you?"

Of all the things she'd been asked to do in her professional career, this one took the cake. So much so she ran the question over in her mind several times, isolating every word to make sure she wasn't mistaking their meaning or context.

"Are you saying you made him up? That Alexis Montgomery didn't have her hair dyed when she came to work that day?" Her voice was hushed, her tone appalled.

"I'm fighting to get my job back and you're being paid to help me. Hire whoever you need to back up my story. Do that thing they do with photos to color Miss Montgomery's hair." No denials, no nothing. He sounded as if he were making a logical request.

Dazed, Kennedy shook her head. The man was off his rocker if he thought this would work. "Th-that's impossible. She'd be able to prove you're lying."

"Oh, come on. I'm sure you've done this kind of thing before," he openly scoffed.

She had, but not like this. Never to impugn an innocent

victim's integrity. What he was asking was libelous, which was a crime.

Good lord, we do have standards.

Although, perhaps they weren't high enough, if he thought her capable of this.

"It would be her word against mine."

The gall of the man.

"No, Mr. Russo, it would be your word against hers and a number of other people who could back up her story. And do you truly believe the station will allow you to make up an employee out of whole cloth without someone coming forward to dispute the person ever worked there or, if he did, would be able to disprove he came to work with his hair dyed as you said?"

Joseph Russo made a gruff sound in his throat. "What if I told you that I have someone who is willing to say she came to work that day with her hair dyed?"

"I'd say you're barking up the wrong tree. And if you do that, I'll be forced to tell the public what we found. I am not going to be a party to this. My primary goal is to help diversify the workplace, not help men like you escape the consequences of your actions," she stated indignantly but with a self-righteousness that was starting to ring a tad hollow.

"Funny, I was told you did exactly that," he replied, a hint of derision in his tone.

Flinching, Kennedy felt more than a prick of conscience. It was a stab by a knife with a sharp, unforgiving blade. "If that's the reason the station hired me, they were misinformed, and I'll be more than happy to let them know."

Fifteen minutes later, she did just that, severing the contract under the never-before-utilized morality clause. After she hung up the phone, she stared sightlessly ahead, her mind in turmoil, before burying her face in her hands.

★ ★ ★

Hours after Kennedy left his apartment, Nate had called her. When she didn't answer, he'd left a voice mail. When she didn't return his call, he'd texted her. Several times. She'd eventually responded via text and asked him to give her time, the request terse and simply worded. He'd reluctantly agreed, and in the following days he couldn't get what she'd said out of his mind. He'd lost sleep over it.

Her accusations about Jack ate away at him. The idea that his friend had anything to do with the lawsuit was laughable. He wasn't like that. He'd been with Nate every step of the way when it came to the programs and the diversity goals he'd set for the company. He'd been one of its staunchest supporters.

But Nate couldn't dismiss Kennedy's feelings. And he cringed every time he thought about accusing her of seeing enemies in every corner. She was the furthest thing from being oversensitive. That wasn't her. In all the years he'd known her, she'd accepted her lot in life with a smile and a steely determination to change the status quo. To make things better for the underdog and the underrepresented, and she'd set out to do it without the billions he had at his disposal. Though some might question her methods, what they couldn't question were her results. She was changing the demographic makeup of companies in New York City one company at a time.

What if he was wrong and she was right? Had his friendship with Jack blinded him to what was right in front of his face? Was the company being sued because of something in his leadership? A culture he'd contributed to? As much as trusting his gut usually served Nate well, the grievances expressed in the lawsuit had occurred over the course of years, not weeks or months. Which meant somewhere along the line, he'd either dropped the ball or taken his eye off it. Contrary to widespread belief within the industry, his instincts weren't infallible.

Picking up his phone, he called the one person he hoped could help him get to the bottom of things once and for all.

A smiling and tanned Duncan Flynn arrived five minutes later. Marriage appeared to be treating him well. He looked younger and trimmer than the last time Nate saw him.

"Welcome back, Nate. It's been a while," Duncan said with genuine warmth.

"Hi, Duncan. Thanks for making time for me." Nate motioned for him to take a seat.

"*Pfft!* I always have time for the guy who signs my checks," his employee joked, reclining comfortably in the high-backed chair.

Nate offered a tight smile. "I wanted to talk to you about Alberta. I know you told Jack you didn't promise her the project manager position during her last review, but that seems to be contradicted by the copy that's turned up." He treated Duncan to a level stare and prayed his gamble would pay off. This was literally all he could come up with to prove or disprove his hunch.

His project director's eyes flashed with alarm as his entire demeanor underwent a dramatic change. He sat up straight, one hand white knuckling the arm of the chair, proof that Nate had hit a nerve.

"And before you say anything, think very hard about how you want this to go. Your job is on the line, so don't lie to me."

Duncan opened his mouth several times before sound finally emerged. "Jack told me there was a misunderstanding about the position, and he decided not to fill it. Next thing I know, Regina informs me I need to interview Brent for another position. After I went over the job description, I told her it was the same as the project manager position, and she told me to take it up with Jack. When I spoke to him, he said the old position had been revised to reflect a certification requirement, something Alberta didn't have but Brent did. I thought that was the end of it, until I heard about the lawsuit. When I got the message, I called Jack and asked him how he wanted me to handle it, and he told me that since I hadn't offered Alberta the position we ended up filling, her claim could never be substantiated, and I had nothing to worry about."

"You're talking technicalities and you know it. You promised her that position and then you hired someone else for it."

"Nate, you have to understand the position I was in. Jack's my boss. I was following his orders. He promised something else would come along for Alberta and I took him at his word. The company has been expanding like crazy. Positions are constantly opening up..." he said, his voice trailing off.

Nate stared at him and sighed heavily.

Fuck!

He knew who he needed to speak to next.

"Hey, you got a sec?" Nate asked, sticking his head in Jack's office hours later. The guy had spared no expense when he'd decorated it, installing a ten-by-three-foot putting green to give it the pampered executive touch he swore clients loved. The appearance of success was every bit as important as success itself. That was his friend's philosophy.

"It's your lucky day. I've got ten," Jack said, smiling broadly.

Nate grabbed a golf club from the rack mounted on the wall and sauntered over to pick up the ball sitting next to the hole. "Can I ask you a question?"

"Shoot. I'm all ears." Jack pushed to his feet and strode over to stand at the opposite end of the green as Nate positioned the ball and lined up his shot.

He wasn't a golfer but needed something to do with his

hands that didn't include using his friend's face as a punching bag. "When you told Kennedy she'd done well for herself, what did you mean?" he asked in a deceptively neutral voice.

Jack's shoulders rose and fell in a shrug. "Exactly that. She's doing well with the agency. Most people will never be able to start their own business, much less make a success out of it."

Nate shot his friend a quick look before giving the golf ball a hard tap. After traveling a straight line for a couple feet, it began to veer right, rolling to a stop inches from the hole.

"You always did suck at golf."

Ignoring the friendly insult, Nate casually remarked, "You'll never guess who I spoke with today."

"Who?"

"Jacob Spencer."

Jack's eyes widened a fraction as a certain wariness entered his gaze. "Seriously? Wow. It's been a while. How's he doing?"

"He's doing great. Did you know he's back in New York, working for a start-up? Says he misses it here, though." Nate walked over to the ball and sank the inch-and-a-half putt with a light tap.

"Yeah. He was a great CFO. Too bad he had to leave," Jack said.

Nate glanced at him as he set up his next shot. "I also spoke to Carol Morton—you know, our old human resources director."

Now Jack eyed him, brow furrowed. "Are you thinking of asking them to come back?" Then he gave a strained laugh. "Because their old positions are filled."

"Since I wasn't here when they left, I figured they were long overdue for an exit interview." At his second attempt, Nate hit a hole in one, if such a thing existed in office, putting green golf.

"They both had exit interviews."

Idly rubbing the smooth head of the club, Nate steadily regarded him. "Yeah, but not with me."

Jack's wariness turned to discomfort as he shifted on his feet. "Okay, so what did they say? It has to be something or you wouldn't be here."

Eyes narrowed at his friend, Nate straightened to his full height. "They said you forced them out. You undermined Jacob with his direct reports and staff, and you hired Will, who basically took over Carol's duties and elbowed her out. They said they saw the writing on the wall and left before they were officially shoved out."

They had been the only two Black executives in the company before he'd left for France, and within a year, they were both gone. After talking to Duncan, Nate knew it couldn't have been a coincidence and it became imperative he speak to them. It had taken him two hours to track them down and get their side of the story. Something he should have done when he'd initially been told about their departure. After all, he'd interviewed and handpicked them for the positions himself.

"Wait." Jack held up his hand, his expression one of mild shock and genuine surprise. "Are you insinuating what I think you are?" Before Nate could answer, he continued. "Because remember, I'm the guy who helped you with the exchange program. Me," he exclaimed, stabbing his index finger against his chest. "No matter what they're saying now, I didn't force them out. They left on their own."

"Then I guess it was just a coincidence that Allan's the son of your mother's divorce lawyer and Will's brother just happens to own the gym you invested in six years ago?"

When Nate had interviewed Allan Randall to replace Jacob as CFO, Jack hadn't said anything about the connection. And as for Will Mathers, their current human resources director, Nate had had nothing to do with his hiring. He'd been in

France, and as far as he was concerned, the company was in capable hands. But the connections were easy to find if you were looking for them, and he'd spent the past hour doing exactly that.

"What exactly are you accusing me of? Come on. Spit it out."

It had been a long time since Nate had seen his friend like this, his face flushed and eyes sparking angrily.

Good, because he was angry too.

"Not only did you force them out, you did the same to Alberta."

"You don't know what you're talking about. No one promised Alberta shit. Her problem was that she wasn't qualified for the job she wanted. Acted like it was owed to her. But instead of being grateful for the job she had, she starts spewing garbage, hires a lawyer, and sues the company."

"So she should be grateful? Why? Because she came out of the STEM program and was hired here straight out of college?" It was all starting to fall into place, the way his soon-to-be ex-CTO's mind worked.

"Dude, she's making north of ninety grand and she owes that to this company. To you."

Nate's vision was starting to go red and he felt his head exploding. "She owes me nothing—you got that? Not a goddamn thing. She's here because of her own hard work. And let's get another thing straight. She *was* qualified for the senior project manager position, until *you* changed the job title and added a certification requirement. A requirement, I might add, that Brent Houseman was given the chance to obtain at the company's expense before he was promoted to the position."

That was the other thing Nate had learned: Jack had been behind all of it. It had been done under his direction and with his explicit approval.

"I don't know what you're talking about. I told you, she wasn't promised a promotion—"

"Don't lie to me." Nate smacked the club hard against the floor, punctuating his anger. "I spoke to Duncan. I know you're lying. Now all I want to know is why. Why did you work overtime to make sure Alberta didn't get the promotion she was promised? The position she deserved."

Irritation flashed in Jack's eyes and his voice cooled ten degrees, his entire posture taking on a defensive crouch. "Who said she deserved it? Because she's a woman and a minority? Do you know how many other college graduates just like her aren't making close to what she makes? Some who won't make that much in their lifetime?"

"What are you saying—she should be grateful for what she has and not strive for more? Because that's what you fucking did? Because that's what I did? Because that's what most white men in this industry do? Goddamn you, Jack, for being so much like your fucking parents. I thought you were better than that, but it's obvious you had me fooled."

"Oh, give me a fucking break. Just because I didn't think she deserved a promotion doesn't mean there's a white robe and hood hiding in my closet." Now his friend was all scorn, going for the obvious stereotype because it was easy to ridicule the card-carrying racists.

"Not only are you a racist, but you're a sexist too." Everything Kennedy had said about him was true. "Which I can't have in the CTO of my company. You're fired."

Jack glared at him. Then, with a dark, humorless laugh, he shook his head and treated him to a disdainful look. "It's Kennedy, isn't it? This is where this is coming from. What, she convince you I'm the big racist boogeyman?"

"Keep her name out of your mouth," Nate warned, his tone ominously flat.

Jack's expression hardened. "What happened? She find out she was an affirmative-action admission at Columbia?"

"Fuck you." Nate had never come closer to laying his former friend flat on his back. Instead, he tightened his hand around the head of the club until his knuckles turned white.

A coldness entered Jack's eyes. "I'm the best fucking CTO you'll ever have. Have fun trying to replace me." His friend had always thought a lot of himself.

"I'll try not to put too much of my back in it," Nate said dryly. Financially, his ex-friend would be fine. The company stock he owned would be more than enough to make sure his annual country-club dues were paid for life.

"I'd think very hard about this if I were you. There's no coming back from this. Once I walk out that door, I'm gone," Jack said in final warning.

Rounding the putting green, Nate returned the golf club to the rack. "I wish *you'd* thought about that when you started playing God, picking winners and losers without a fucking thought of the damage you were doing to the company and everyone involved." Alberta, Jacob, and Carol might just be the tip of the iceberg. Who knew where else and how many times he'd tipped the scales. "Now you have thirty minutes to pack your things and leave."

How long had this been going on? He'd have to take over the investigation now to make sure they got to the truth.

"Damn, Kennedy really has you by the balls," Jack sneered.

Nate exited the office without responding and immediately called the head of IT to tell him to disable Jack's security credentials for all the systems ASAP. Then he called his head of security to ask him to escort his ex-friend out of the building in twenty-nine minutes.

He and Jack were done.

25

They'd been hacked.

Kennedy didn't know whether to laugh or roll her eyes. She did both.

When a response finally came, after a mind-boggling fifty-two hours, that had been the explanation from Phillip Draper and Samuel Weber. As for the company itself, the day before ECO Apparel had put out a statement that said it was investigating the authenticity of the emails. They didn't want to act rashly and all of that *blah, blah, blah*.

When it came to business, the agency hadn't acquired one single client since the leaked emails became public and her—and now her face—a household name. A curiosity. While most of the attention remained focused on the two men, the number of calls from local media for an interview with her hadn't ceased.

Kennedy blamed that on the way ECO Apparel was handling the situation. What they should have done was immediately issue an apology. An abject apology. Not so much for her but for the sake of the company. Second, they should have announced that both men would be placed on unpaid leave during the investigation—which shouldn't take more than twenty-four hours. Once the emails were authenticated, the men should have been fired. They'd quickly fade from the spotlight and so would she. And maybe then business would resume as normal. Instead, she remained on tenterhooks, wondering if the agency would survive the scrutiny.

Should it survive?

Her conversation with Joseph Russo was like the shifting of tectonic plates and she was still reeling from the ongoing aftershocks. What he'd asked her to do was far more egregious than the things she did for her clients. At least, that was what she tried to convince herself, but the more she thought about the differences, the more blurred the lines became. Although one was illegal and the other was not, the variegated shadows of gray between the two didn't cast her methods in a good light.

Once upon a time, she'd told herself the ends justified the means. That, technically, she wasn't doing anything wrong and no one was getting hurt. And while that might still be the truth in a narrow vision and scope, what effect was it having on society as a whole? Why not let the companies take their lumps and learn from their mistakes the hard way, instead of her coming in and cushioning the fall? But more than anything, she didn't want Token to be seen the way the likes of Joseph Russo saw it. As an agency so bereft of morals it would knowingly take the side of a liar and help manufacture evidence against an innocent victim—and a Black woman at that. It was the exact opposite of their mission statement and goal.

Maybe a pause in business wouldn't be a bad thing. It would give her time to think things over and decide the best way forward. This was something she'd have to discuss with Aurora, but her gut was telling her it was time to make some changes in the kind of services the agency offered.

And as if that wasn't weighing enough on her mind, Nate was never far from her thoughts. She was still smarting from the scholarship revelation and couldn't quite pinpoint why it was hitting her so hard. Why it felt more like a betrayal than what most people would see as a gesture of lottery-winning proportions.

Legs stretched out on her couch, Kennedy opened the social media app on her phone. She'd been following the #HackVillains hashtag, otherwise known as *You About to Lose Your Job*. Her story hit the national news, only to be quickly supplanted by the email of a top sports agent whose client— an NFL player—had recently come out as gay. The use of the F word had been shocking enough, but when the agent had blamed his public disclosure on the growing permissiveness of society, he'd all but guaranteed that not only would his remarks elicit a swift and furious backlash, he wouldn't have a job by the morning. He was fired by the agency within hours of the first report.

Then she saw it, the breaking news headline as big and bold as ever.

ECO APPAREL DISMISSES EXECUTIVES OVER EMAIL LEAK—SAHARA: "MY FRIEND DIDN'T DESERVE THIS."

Kennedy's heart thumped and her breath suspended. Sahara? What did she say?
After hitting several paywalls, she finally found an article without one containing her friend's full response to the firings.

Kennedy is a dear friend and she didn't deserve this. No one deserves to be talked about like that. What's even more upsetting is that I know these men. I worked with them, and I had no idea they held these kinds of views. Kennedy worked with them, and I witnessed their interactions, and she was always a consummate professional. She's incredibly smart, and to quote an earlier statement from someone who knows her better than I do, she's as beautiful on the inside as she is on the outside. She didn't ask for any of this. Speaking as her friend, I'm asking the media to please respect her privacy at this time.

Pressing a palm to her chest, Kennedy did her utmost to stave off the tears—she hadn't yet removed her mascara and eyeliner, and didn't know whether they would hold up under a drizzle of tears, much less a storm—as she was overcome by emotions. She blinked rapidly and gave a tearless sniff. When she'd first met Sahara, she'd immediately picked up on her overall goodness and decency. In the years that followed, Kennedy was able to experience her unflinching loyalty firsthand.

Not wasting another second, Kennedy picked up the phone and called her. As soon as she answered, Kennedy spoke to her from the heart. "You. Are. A. Doll. What did I do to deserve you as my friend?"

"You must have won the friend lottery."

"Well, if I don't say this often enough, I want you to know how much I love and adore you."

"Aww," Sahara crooned. "I love and adore you too, sweets. Now you're going to make me cry."

Kennedy gave a hiccuping laugh. After days of her stomach being twisted in a knot, she felt it loosening. "Don't you dare cry or you'll turn me into a spigot."

"*Spigot?* Is that the thesaurus word of the day?" her friend teased.

Kennedy laughed. "How to prove you know me without saying you know me." Her love of words—she was a big reader, after all—wasn't a secret to all those who knew her.

"Seriously, that man of yours is something else. Makes me think my type meter is broken. Maybe I need someone like him, you know, someone who worships the ground I walk on. Shouldn't you be showing him your appreciation right now?" she teased with a suggestive *waggling of the brow* tone to her voice.

Wait! What? "Are you talking about Nate?"

Sahara huffed in amusement. "How many men do you have? Unless you're sexing it up with another tech hottie, and let's face it—another one doesn't exist. Of course I mean Nate." She paused. "You have seen his statement, haven't you?"

A breath of air rushed past her lips. "No. I didn't know he put one out."

At her dazed admission, her friend chortled. "Who did you think I was talking about when I said I was quoting an earlier statement?"

Sahara was ten steps ahead of her. Kennedy scrambled from the couch to grab her laptop from the desk in the corner of the kitchen. Placing it on the counter, she typed in his name, and an article posted an hour ago popped up first on the search results.

Her breathless "I found it" could only be attributed to anticipation and nerves.

"I was going to send you the link but never mind," Sahara replied.

A quick tap on the link and the article came up. Her eyes zoomed straight to the block of text.

In the eleven years I've known Kennedy Mitchell, she's always believed in the goodness and decency of people. Whether her faith was misguided or not is yet to be determined. However, my faith in her is unequivocal. She is talented, ambitious, intelligent, and as beautiful on the inside as she is on the outside. The men who maligned her aren't fit to kiss the ground she walks on. And that's as much oxygen as I'm going to waste on them.

I prided myself with creating a diverse and inclusive workforce, and I thought I had the numbers to back it up. It wasn't until my company was sued that I realized numbers aren't the only things that matter. No matter how diverse a company is, if it's not equal in opportunities for growth and advancement, the problems stemming from racism and sexism will continue to persist. I'm grateful to Kennedy for helping me see that. Her dedication to equality and fair play makes her the best at what she does. The perspective she brings to her work is invaluable, and I can't thank her enough for helping me with my blind spots.

On a more personal note, Kennedy is an incredible woman, and if you're lucky enough to have someone like her in your life, don't squander it. I certainly don't plan to.

Kennedy's breath quickened, her heart thudding loud in her ears. Everything he'd said about her... The things he'd admitted about himself. She didn't know what to say.

"You still there?" Sahara asked, breaking the silence that had gone on for several long seconds.

"I'm here," Kennedy whispered, her hand not quite steady as she held the phone to her ear.

"See! What did I tell you? Your man means business. He wants the whole world to know how he feels about you. I want the kind of man who would do that for me," Sahara said, her tone half teasing, half wistful. "It's instant foreplay."

Kennedy let out a shaky laugh, her thoughts churning as she

returned to the living room and sank down onto the couch. "What blind spots is he talking about?" she mused. It had to be about Jack. His was the only name she'd mentioned in that context during their argument.

"You mean you don't know?"

The question had Kennedy squirming in place. "I haven't talked to him in a few days," she replied in a small voice. Then she told Sahara about the scholarship, Jack, and the resulting fight.

"If you want my opinion, his friend sounds like a jerk, and hopefully, Nate has figured that out. Now, about the scholarship... I don't know, sweets. I can't work up too much outrage over that." She then hastened to add, "Not that I don't understand why you're upset about the way he did it, but why were you okay with taking the money from some faceless entity but it's a problem now that you know it was from him?"

That question had plagued Kennedy the last two days. She tried to convince herself it was the underhandedness of it, but she quickly realized that wasn't the crux of it. "I thought I'd earned it on my own."

"Who said you didn't earn it? How many scholarships did you apply for that you didn't receive because an applicant had connections with the powers that be? You told me you also applied to a few other Ivy League colleges and didn't get in. Why not? You had the grades and the test scores. Maybe a legacy student got the slot that should have rightfully gone to you. Did you ever think of that? And I highly doubt Nate would have paid for you to go to a school like Columbia if your grades and test scores didn't warrant it. When you have billions, as generous as it is to write a check for a good cause, that's the easiest part."

"I get all that, but—"

"Sweetie, I hope you'll take what I say next in the spirit

it's given, from someone who knows. Your boy had money. He saw you needed it. He filled that need and didn't tell you because he knew you'd refuse it—and he was right. Listen, I understand you feel in his debt and you understandably hate that. But it's not about the money, honey. For him, that was an act of love."

Hugging her knees to her chest, Kennedy stared at her fire-engine-red toenails. "I don't know. Maybe I'd feel different if we weren't sleeping together. It isn't as if our relationship isn't lopsided enough."

"What do you mean lopsided?"

She absently flicked a clump of hair that came dislodged from her ponytail over her shoulder. It was more wavy than straight, days after the blowout. "You know what I mean. He's got it all. He's worth billions. His parents are part of the whole Hollywood crowd. And he's *gorgeous*. He could probably have any woman he wanted even without all the money and glam. Sometimes I feel I'm hitting way above my weight class."

There was no feeling like not feeling good enough. It was soul destroying.

"And he's white, right?"

"Yeah, there's that too," she replied gloomily. Another brick in the wall between them.

Sahara released an audible sigh. "You have to know you're a catch, right? You're all the things he said in his statement, and on top of that, you're one of the kindest, most compassionate people I know. *And* you're pretty funny too. But I understand how you feel. I'm living a life I could only ever dream of, but there are always doubts. Am I good enough? Will they like me? What if my film or album bombs? What if after all of this, I never get married and have the family I always wanted? I think about all that stuff. Everyone does, Ken. And probably Black women more than anyone. But it's normal. You're not alone. At the end of the day, though, *he* would be the luckiest man in the world to have you, and judging by his statement, I think he knows it too."

Kennedy gave a self-deprecating laugh. "I've been telling myself that a lot, and then I discover he basically paid my way through college. And not just any college—an Ivy League one." Which put her in his debt. A debt she'd never be able to repay.

"Take it from me—no one becomes successful on their own. It's literally impossible. Intelligence, talent, ambition, and hard work only gets you so far. Whether it's being born into wealth or being lucky enough to be born with a voice and a face that can sell millions of records, behind every successful person there are usually a host of people *and* the right opportunities that helped pave the way. You did all the hard work, so give yourself a break. You don't have to be superwoman all the time."

Kennedy huffed a laugh. "I wish." If that were true, Joseph Russo wouldn't have thought her capable of something as reprehensible as throwing a Black female reporter under the bus. The complete antithesis of what she was trying to do with her agency.

"Look, I'm not trying to take anything away from your man, but he was born on third base. If he wants to pay it forward, let him. You don't owe him anything, which is why his name wasn't attached to the scholarship."

How could she not owe him anything when he'd put her through college? That was no insignificant thing. It had everything to do with where she was in her life right now and where she'd end up. She had to come up with something to level the playing field. But first, she had to talk to Nate. See him and touch him. If there was one thing she knew, they were far from over.

"Hey," Sahara said, her voice penetrating Kennedy's thoughts. "Everything is going to work out. With Phil and Sam out of the picture, things will calm down and get back to normal. And if you need me to run interference with the press, just say the word. You know me—I have a knack for distraction. Now, go find that hunky man of yours and put him out of his misery. Have yourself some of that good, wall-banging makeup sex and thank me in the morning."

Kennedy smiled. Her friend did have a way with words. "How about I just thank you now in case I'm too busy in the morning?"

"When the time comes, promise to name your little angel after me," Sahara said, amusing herself to no end.

Teasing or not, normally Kennedy would have told her friend not to get ahead of herself. Today, in the midst of a pandemic of disasters, she found herself laughing along.

If Nate had known when he'd promised to give Kennedy space that after three days he'd be going out of his mind missing her, he would have insisted on a time limit.

Checking the time every hour didn't help; it just made the day longer. Work kept him relatively busy during the day. Markham had finally agreed on a settlement amount, and four of the company's former employees would be getting their old jobs back—with a nice raise. Jack was gone and Nate was on the hunt for a new CTO, and he was implementing significant changes to human resources personnel and their entire recruiting and in-house promotion process. The face of management at the company had to change, and that wasn't going to happen if they continued to do the same thing that had landed them in trouble in the first place.

Nate checked his phone again. Nothing. What he needed was to get out of his head and his bloody apartment. Take a

walk. Get some fresh air. Maybe take a drive across the Brooklyn Bridge and grab a bite to eat at Junior's. He could go for
a slice of strawberry cheesecake.

Mind made up, he grabbed his keys and headed for the
door. Sometime during his half-hour trip, he took a turn that
bypassed his intended destination and somehow ended up at
Kennedy's. Five minutes later, he rounded the corner to her
apartment to find her turning the key in the lock of her door.

"Going somewhere?" he asked.

Kennedy gave a startled yelp as her head swiveled in his direction and her hand jumped to her throat.

His heart received the same jolt it had when he'd first laid
eyes on her. God, she was beautiful. And for some reason she
looked younger. It took a moment to pinpoint what was different about her today. She wasn't wearing makeup, or if she
was, not much of it.

"You scared the hell out of me. What are you doing here?"
she asked, her hand dropping to her side.

He slowly approached, stopping when they were only inches
apart. "Answer my question first."

She visibly swallowed. "I was on my way to see you."

"I was hoping you would say that," Nate said, breathing a
little easier.

Gently brushing her hand aside, which was gripping the
key still in the lock, he unlocked the door and led her inside.

"I guess I'm not going anywhere after all," Kennedy said,
as she turned on the lights in the tiny hallway, toed off her
sneakers, and made her way to the living room.

Nate followed closely behind and had to rein in the compul-
sion to touch her. It was too soon, he told himself. He needed
to proceed with caution. For all he knew, the reason she'd
been going to see him was to break up with him for good.

Although, that wasn't what he was picking up from her. Something in her eyes told him their days apart had been just as hard on her as they had been on him. Added to that, she'd been about to head into the city in a pair of leggings and sneakers, with her hair in a messy ponytail. Very uncharacteristic of her. It was as if it'd been a spur-of-the-moment decision and she'd been in a rush and threw on whatever was close at hand.

He drew in a breath and followed her down onto the sofa as she settled in among the cushions, her gray-blue eyes intent on his. "Before you say anything," he began, "first let me say I'm sorry. I was wrong. I was wrong about a lot of things. I shouldn't have done what I did with the scholarship, and I shouldn't have asked Aurora to keep it from you when she found out. And I was wrong about Jack and you were right. You were right when you said I had blind spots where he was concerned."

Reaching out, he cupped her smooth cheek in his palm. "I'm sorry I dismissed your feelings about him. I'm sorry for saying that shit about you looking for enemies in every corner. You were seeing what I refused to see. It was an arrogant and condescending thing to say. I hope you can find it—"

"*Shh,*" she said, her voice soft. "It's okay. I understand. He's your friend and you've known him a long—"

"No, none of that matters," he said, cutting her off. "*You* matter to me. Kennedy, you've got to know I'm head over heels in love with you."

At that, her lips parted and her eyes became glassy. "I love you too. I'm crazy in love with you and I've never felt like this about anyone before in my life."

"Thank God for that," he said against her mouth as he kissed her. Then he quickly pulled back, the sweet taste of her still on his lips. They needed to talk, and if he started kissing her now, he wouldn't be able to stop, and he didn't want to make love to her without clearing the air between them.

Nate inhaled a deep breath. "Let's get through this first. Now, about Jack. He and I have been friends for a long time, but it's obvious there are things about him I didn't know. Or maybe I didn't want to know." Hindsight being 20/20, he was sure there had been signs. But he'd been too busy building and expanding, too concerned with the big picture to pay close enough attention to many of the details. He'd forgotten that companies like his needed constant vigilance if they wanted to keep the advantage diversity gave them.

"Or maybe," she offered gently, "he was careful to keep that side of himself from you. Have you ever thought of that? Remember, he knows who *you* are. You're Mr. Equity and Equality for All. If there was anyone he'd do his best to hide it from, it's you."

God, he loved her.

Nate stole another kiss, her heart-shaped lips plush and pliant against his. He pulled back again. "Well, he's gone. I let him go. He'd been lying to me, and if it weren't for you, God only knows how long it would have taken me to figure it out."

"Not long. People like him eventually out themselves. Now, are you going to ask me why I was coming to see you?" Kennedy asked, smoothing her hands over his shoulder as she sat pressed against his side, practically in his lap. Forget the sex for a moment—she'd also missed the sound of his voice, the ocean breeze scent of him, and simply having him within reach, being able to touch him.

He peered down at her, brow arched. "Do I want to know?"

"I wanted to explain about the scholarship. Why I reacted the way I did."

Nate covered her hand and held it still against his chest. "You don't have to explain. I understand—"

"No, I do," she insisted, planting a kiss on his jaw. "Hear me out."

His arm tightened around her waist.

"In all my relationships, I've always seen myself as an equal. Even if the guy made more money than me, I was fine with it because we were still on the same plane. In the same league, so to speak. People wouldn't look at us and think, *Why would he settle for her when he can do better?*"

Nate stiffened against her, his chest stilling beneath her palm. She knew he was about to interrupt and tell her she was being irrational. "Please, let me finish," she urged softly. With those words, she felt his body lose some of its rigidity. "Then you came along. Twice. Once when I had no sexual experience to speak of. And I fell for you hard. Not in a married, happily-ever-after way, though. I was too young for that, and you *were* my first. But I did hope it would last longer than a month," she stated with a dry laugh.

"You couldn't have wanted it more than me," he said, his tone equally dry.

"But you were probably right to end it when you did. I needed to concentrate on school and you had your company."

He tipped her chin with his finger and stared deep into her eyes. "Even if I wasn't growing my company, you were too young for what I would have wanted."

Kennedy's whole body shivered at the huskiness in his voice and meaningfulness of his tone. She cleared her throat. "But this time—" She broke off, in search of the right words. "This time I decided to just go with it. See how far it went. But I knew I had to accept everything that came with. Your wealth, your looks—"

"You like my looks?" he asked with a look of feigned surprise.

"—your parents being who they are," she continued, as if he hadn't facetiously interrupted for an ego stroke. Vain, *vain* man. "And because we're an interracial couple, we'd get the stares and the double looks. I knew it all came with the territory and I was willing to accept that."

"If they stare at us, it's because you're so beautiful," Nate whispered, briefly kissing her on the lips, no doubt in an act of repentance for his vanity.

"Okay, whatever," she said with a small smile. "But you know what I mean. That's our reality. And then I found out about the scholarship, and what I considered my biggest accomplishment—putting myself through college—wasn't even mine anymore. It was yours. A degree from an Ivy League school opened doors for me that would otherwise have been closed. It was the foundation of everything else—my jobs, the agency, everything. I owed you so much and it made the gap between us wider, and I hated that."

Sighing heavily, Nate briefly closed his eyes, his expression pained. Gently touching her cheek with the pad of his thumb, he said, "The last thing I ever wanted was to make you feel as if you're somehow indebted to me. You're not. That's not why I did it. And everything you've achieved, from your degrees to the agency, is because of your intelligence and hard work. I didn't do that. You did."

Kennedy worried her bottom lip with her teeth as she looked into his eyes. "I knew that in a logical sense, but it was hard to change how I felt. Of all the people in my life, I *needed* you to see me as your equal, and the scholarship made me feel like a charity case. Like your personal cause. And that's the last thing I wanted to be to you."

"Sweetheart, you're more than just my equal. You're the love of my life."

You're the love of my life.

Kennedy shivered as tears pricked the backs of her eyes. She'd *never* tire of hearing him say those words to her.

"Do you want to know what used to scare the hell out of me?" Nate asked, his expression solemn.

"Without question," Kennedy replied. The more she learned about him, the more she wanted to know.

"I was afraid that one day you'd decide you wanted a nice quiet life with someone like your ex. A life where no one stared at you because you're with me and all the other shit that can go with us being together. I was afraid one day you'd throw in the towel and decide *I* wasn't worth the aggravation."

Wow! She never would've imagined he'd harbored those kinds of fears. But then again, she'd subconsciously placed him in the driver's seat of their relationship. He, on the other hand, had seen them as co-drivers, both equally capable of driving it off the road or stopping and getting out. Of course, she preferred the version where they drove off into the sunset together.

As she looked into his blue eyes, suddenly he appeared more vulnerable, making her fiercely protective of him. "Nathaniel Vaughn, you are worth *every* aggravation."

His expression softened. "That's exactly how I feel about you. I looked at the scholarship as a gift. Maybe it's because I've been given so much in my life, but I think it's natural to want to do the same for others, especially the people I care about. And if there's one thing I'm one hundred percent certain of, it's that if our positions were reversed, you'd do the same. You'd use your money and all your advantages to help others. You've always had that equal justice warrior streak in you. It's what you're doing right now with the agency."

Kennedy's heart swelled. She wanted desperately to believe she was doing good, but after what had just happened with Joseph Russo, she wanted to do better. Vowed she would do better.

"When I was talking to Sahara about this earlier, she said you were born on third base, and I—"

Nate interrupted with a barked laugh. "I'm surprised she didn't say *first and goal*. Didn't she perform in the Super Bowl halftime show a few years back?"

"No, she sang the national anthem," Kennedy corrected. "And she didn't mean it in a negative way."

"I know exactly how she meant it." He smiled, indicating he took no exception to the remark.

"So in keeping with the baseball analogy, I changed it a bit. You see, in my scenario, you're born on third base, but on your next time up at bat, you hit a home run."

Chuckling softly, he kissed her on the forehead as his hand slid up her waist, coming to rest right below her breast. "I think you're giving me a little too much credit. I'm only thirty-four and I have a lot more to do in life—things that have nothing to do with what's in my bank account or how much my company is worth."

"Things like what?"

"Oh, I don't know, like a wife and a couple kids. I've been told I'd make a wonderful husband and father," he stated with the same humility it must take for a man to declare himself the handsomest in the world.

Suppressing a smile, she arched a brow. "Oh really? Who told you that?" Women who wanted to be said wife and bear him said children, no doubt.

"My mom," he replied, his expression deadpan.

Kennedy erupted in a fit of giggles, and soon he was laughing along with her.

After the laughter subsided, his expression sobered. "You know, if the whole scholarship business still bothers you, I think I've come up with a solution."

Kennedy blinked twice in quick succession. She thought

they'd moved on from that. And what could possibly resolve a debt north of two hundred grand?

"What do you mean? What solution?"

"You can pay me back."

"Pay you back?" she squeaked. Okay, that took an unexpected turn. She certainly hadn't seen it coming.

"You said you didn't want my money and I'm trying to fix it. So if paying me back would do that, that's what I want." This time she didn't miss the amused twinkle in his eyes.

Beast. He was playing with her.

"But I wouldn't have gone to Columbia without the scholarship because I wouldn't have been able to afford it," she reasoned, playing along for shits and giggles.

"I'm sure you can afford it now you have your own business," he murmured, stroking her hip and his other hand encompassing her breast over her shirt.

Kennedy's breath hitched as her nipples pebbled beneath his questing fingers, pleasure swamping her. "I guess I could if I were paying it on my back. But then, what would be the point? You're already getting that for free," she said in a breathy, uneven voice.

"And I love my freebies," he said, his voice dark and low as he eased her back and grasped the hem of her shirt. In one swift motion, she was half reclined on the sofa in her cranberry demi-cup bra and yoga pants.

Dragging his smoldering gaze up from her pert breasts to her face, he said, "Will you please do something for me?"

Anything. Kennedy nodded. She wanted out of the rest of her clothes and Nate out of his. It had been a long four days, and the deleterious effects of sex deprivation were coming to a head.

Yes, all the puns intended.

"Say you accept it as a gift and then we'll never talk about it again."

Pushing up on her knees, she began unbuttoning his shirt. "No, I don't want it to be barred from all future conversations. We should be able to talk about it." She paused after the second button, braced her hands on his shoulders, and kissed him sweetly on the lips. "Thank you."

Nate gave her a slow and seductive smile. "The pleasure was all mine."

"There's a chance that when this is all over, we may not have a business," she warned lightly, resuming the unbuttoning of his shirt. "Which means your girlfriend may be unemployed." She didn't intend to change direction completely, but their service of supplying companies with diverse employees for show had run its course. Hopefully, they'd be able to make up the financial loss elsewhere.

"I'm not going to think about the worst happening. But even if you don't have the agency, you'll still have me, Kennedy. For as long as you want."

Brushing her hands away, he assumed the task of unbuttoning and removing his shirt.

His chest bared to her lustful gaze, she eagerly ran her hands over the taut muscles lightly covered by hair. He inhaled sharply. Lifting her eyes to his, she said huskily, "That could be a while."

"Take all the time you want. I'm not going anywhere," he said, his voice dropping to a throaty grumble. And then he removed the rest of their clothes and took his time bringing her pleasure throughout the night and into the wee hours of the morning.

EPILOGUE

One year later

"Do you want to stay through the karaoke?" Kennedy asked, looking across the table at her boyfriend.

They'd been together over a year, and she'd moved in with him six months ago. Truthfully, it hadn't been that big an upheaval in her life. She spent most of the time there anyway. In the months before the move, she'd barely seen her apartment, usually only going there to get more clothes and collect her mail.

"Isn't that why we came?"

"I thought you liked the food," she said.

"Yeah, that too."

Narrowing her gaze, Kennedy eyed him. He'd been acting funny all day. Something was going on, but she didn't think it had anything to do with work.

Constellation was doing better than ever, having recently secured a large government contract. Employee morale was high and senior management was the most diversified it had ever been. After months of interviews, Nate had hired Taylor Young to replace Jack, making her the youngest Black female CTO of a Fortune 500 company at thirty-one. Kennedy thought she was a brilliant find and the two got along like a house on fire. He'd also managed to convince Carol Morton to come back but this time as the VP of Human Resources.

Token itself had undergone significant changes after days' worth of discussions between her and Aurora. They'd decided to discontinue the service that provided fake employees or friends. Now the agency worked with colleges—mostly HBCUs—and professional alma mater groups to provide fully vetted, professional job candidates, who were predominantly diverse. And added to their classes and services, they now consulted with companies by helping them diversify well *before* a crisis point was reached. That part of the business was doing better than she and Aurora could ever have dreamed. They were thinking about opening another office on the West Coast.

The lights in the room dimmed and a spotlight lit up the stage, where a curvaceous middle-aged Black woman in a spandex-looking purple dress stepped up to the microphone and began belting out "I Will Survive," a karaoke staple, giving it a soulful Aretha Franklin touch.

"Great voice," Nate murmured, as the crowd clapped and cheered at the end of the song.

"I wish I could sing like that. One of these days, I'm going to bring Sahara. Can you imagine everyone's reaction if she went up there and sang one of her songs?" Kennedy said, returning her attention to Nate, only to find him pushing his chair back and rising to his feet. Dressed all in black—her man rocked a turtleneck like nobody's business—and still sporting a gorgeous tan from their trip to Hawaii, he'd had heads turning the moment they'd arrived. Scratch that—he had heads turning everywhere they went.

She stared at him, her hands halting midclap.

"Wish me luck." With that, he winked at her and sauntered to the stage, mounting it in two easy steps.

Kennedy followed his progress, her brain trying to catch up with what her eyes were seeing.

What on earth is he doing?

He pulled the cordless microphone from its stand, a sly smile on his face as he gazed out into the crowd at her.

Her fight-or-flight instinct kicked in then. *Oh my god! I have to stop him.* She had to *save* him.

Then the music started to play and, in the midst of getting ready to rush the stage to save the love of her life from making the biggest mistake of his, she sat her ass back down.

Kennedy was shook.

The too familiar beat of "You're the First, the Last, My Everything" filled the room. And her lover began to sing, rendering her stock-still and speechless. Her eyes were as wide as they could go and her heart had long since leaped from her chest.

Mind blown, she wondered how it was possible that she'd known this man for over a decade, lived with him for as long as she had, and had no idea he could sing? That he was actually a damn good singer?

How had she not known this?

Nate's was a low baritone, not Barry White's slumberous bass, but he somehow made it work for the song. An appreciative whistle pierced the air, followed by a scattering of cheers.

He had yet to take his eyes off her as he crooned, "You're my sun, my moon, my guiding star."

Overcome with feelings so strong, she found it hard to contain them, Kennedy sat with her heart in her throat as she watched him gyrate in time to the music. They'd gone dancing a bunch of times, so his rhythmic abilities were well-known to her, but the way he was moving to the music blew her away.

Honestly, every time she thought it was impossible to love him more, he somehow managed to prove her wrong.

His riveting performance drew a lot of hooting and hollering and enthusiastic applause. Kennedy was up on her feet to greet him when he returned to their table.

Without saying a word, he enveloped her in his arms and kissed her.

"You're trembling," he murmured, his breath warm against her lips.

Kennedy gave a shaky laugh. "You were *so* good. I didn't know you could sing like that."

"Come on. Let's go home," Nate said, chuckling softly.

Kennedy collected her handbag and Nate drained the rest of his drink. After dropping a sizable tip on the table, he captured her hand in his and led her out of the main room.

"How long did you have this planned?" she asked, peering up at him as they walked hand in hand toward the front doors. It didn't make sense, but she felt a little starstruck. And horny as hell. She wanted to get him alone *so* bad. Oh, the things she wanted to do to—

"Kennedy?"

The sound of her name was jarring, the voice vaguely familiar. Her head snapped to the front, and heading directly toward her was Malcolm Coombs, her ex-boyfriend from what felt like eons ago. He was also the first man to propose to her.

Nate's hand tightened around hers, a sign his possessive instincts had kicked in. "Another ex, I take it?" he muttered under his breath, sounding like the proverbial long-suffering boyfriend.

"Yes. Now, be nice," she whispered, as Malcolm's long strides swiftly closed the distance between them.

Except for a few grays on his closely cropped head and a little more meat on his frame, he looked the same. He looked good.

"Malcolm, I can't believe it's you. It's been years." How did she greet the man whose heart she'd been told she broke eight years ago when she was with the man she was in love and living with?

"It's been *too* long," he replied with an amiable smile, his gaze flicking to Nate and taking in their clasped hands.

Kennedy delicately cleared her throat. "Malcolm, this is my boyfriend, Nate. Nate, Malcolm's an old friend."

The men exchanged polite nods.

Returning his attention to her, Malcolm asked, "How are you? It looks like things are going well."

She glanced at Nate and smiled. "Things are wonderful. How are things with you?"

"I'm doing great. Married five years now," he said, holding up his left hand to display a thick platinum wedding band. "As a matter of fact, there she is now," he announced, turning his attention to a pretty Asian woman approaching from the direction of the ladies' restroom.

Everything seemed to get easier then, the conversation lighter. By the time they parted, the initial awkwardness was long gone. Malcolm's wife had been friendly, proudly showing Kennedy pictures of their four-year-old son.

"That was nice," Kennedy commented once she and Nate emerged from the lounge into the lit city streets.

Nate huffed, tightening his arm around her waist and pressing her closer to his side. "It's bad enough your hockey player is dating your twin. Now I'm being forced to make small talk with every ex-boyfriend who ever proposed to you."

"She isn't my twin," Kennedy denied for the third time since Nate had seen a picture of the couple on the front of *People* magazine. Although, she had to admit there was a strong resemblance, but the woman was hardly her twin. Her eyes were hazel and her hair was a little shorter.

"Ah, come on," Nate scoffed. "He couldn't have you, so he got a woman who looks like you."

He wasn't the only one who thought that. Aurora, Sahara, Jonathan, Julie, and Mina thought so too. The couple were the talk of the hockey world, many claiming it proved Roger's innocence. How could he be a racist if he was dating a Black woman? And formerly shunned by every major brand, he'd managed to rehabilitate his reputation enough to sign a lucrative endorsement deal with a cologne company. Romantic that she was, she hoped he wasn't using the woman, and if he was, Kennedy hoped she was in on it.

"Are you saying you find her attractive?"

"I'm saying she looks like you, so of course she's beautiful. Lucky for me, I have the genuine article."

Kennedy smiled. The man was obviously biased and she loved him dearly.

"Now come on. That's our ride," he said, pointing his chin toward the—limo—waiting at the curb in front of them.

Kennedy stopped abruptly and stared at him. "That's for us?"

"I thought I'd treat us to something roomier tonight," Nate replied, urging her toward the black stretch limo.

Roomier for what? Did he think she was going to have sex with him in the back of a limo? Silly man.

After helping her inside their luxurious ride, Nate joined her, and soon they were on their way. While she took in the cream interior, leather seating, and expansive bar, he moved to the sound system.

"This is nice," she said, smoothing her hand over the leather seat. "But wouldn't you rather do it in the comfort of our bed?"

Her question elicited a hearty laugh. "You think that's what this is all about?" he asked.

She took another look around. "What did you expect I would—" Kennedy broke off when her gaze swung back to him...because in his hand was a black velvet box, and nestled inside was a solitary diamond ring.

"Yes!" she said, excitedly preempting his proposal.

"Would you let me propose first?" Nate lovingly chided. "I want it to be something I can tell our kids."

At his words, Kennedy immediately fell mute, on the verge of happy tears for the second time that night.

"Kennedy, I meant what I said in there. You are my first love, my last love, my everything. Will you marry me?"

Tears spilled down her cheeks as she cupped his gorgeous face in her palms. "You're mine too." She kissed his lips. "And yes, I'll marry you whenever and wherever you want."

Raising her left hand, he carefully slid the ring on her finger. "I'm going to hold you to that." She only had a second to admire the way it looked on her hand before he crushed her mouth beneath his.

She was going to marry the love of her life. Third time had indeed been the charm.

★ ★ ★ ★ ★

Discussion Guide

1. With the title *Token*, what did you think the book would be about? Did it meet your expectations? Were there any surprises?

2. What was your reaction when Kennedy found out why she was sent to meet with the CEO of ECO Apparel?

3. When Kennedy accepted money to help ECO Apparel win Sahara's business, was that ethical? Why or why not?

4. How would you describe the work that Token does?

5. What are some examples of how diversity, racism, and equity are addressed in the story?

6. Should Nate have known about the discrimination going on in his company?

7. What are ways wealth and equity are addressed in the story and in character motivations? For example:

   O *What significance, if any, does Nate's background of wealth and fame, and early business success, have on his relationship with Kennedy?*

O *Kennedy comes from a working-class, part-immigrant family and believes in paying her own way. What did you think when she resisted Nate's offer to buy her an apartment and when she felt betrayed and angry that Nate had paid for her education without telling her?*

O *Was Nate being underhanded? Generous? Patronizing? Insensitive?*

O *Was Kennedy ungrateful? Scared? Proud?*

8. Is *Token* a rom-com? Is the story romantic? Were there any memorable funny moments? What are some deeper elements to the story, if any?

9. Who were your favorite secondary characters and why?

*Read on for a special sneak peek at the next book
by Beverley Kendall.*

"So when's the wedding? I'm going to need to block out the time on my calendar at least six months in advance," Sahara teasingly informed her friend, who was one of the few exceptions to her *don't interrupt me when my office door is closed* rules. When Kennedy called, she was available.

"Were you not listening to me?" Kennedy laughed. "He asked me to move in with him, not get married."

"Sweets, he asked you to move in with him *last year*. What's new is that you finally agreed. Plus, you were practically living with him anyway. You're only making it official by letting USPS and your landlord know the deal. What *I'm* talking about is the wedding. And don't even pretend it's not happening or that it's going to be some time in the distant future."

Not only did Sahara know this, she felt it deep in her bones. Her friend had found the love of her life and was giddy with it—all the time. As well she should be. Nate was one of the good ones. It also didn't hurt that he was fine as hell *and* rich with a capital *B*, as in *billionaire*.

"You need to cool your heels," Kennedy said, a smile obvious in her voice. "We're taking it one step at a time. Right now, we're *living in sin*, and if the sinning continues to go as well as it has been, *then* we can talk marriage."

Stretched out on the couch of her home office in Hollywood Hills, Sahara absently glanced down at the Dorothy Dandridge biopic script open on her lap. "Oh, don't give me that. You know damn well you're marrying this one. Just don't make him wait too long."

Kennedy made a sound that was a mixture of amusement and exasperation. "What do you mean wait too long? We've only been dating six months. We have lots of time to think about marriage."

Sahara snorted a laugh. "You've got to be kidding. That's the length of three of my relationships." Dating in Hollywood was a crapshoot, and so far, she was a horrible gambler.

"Speaking of relationships, how are things going with Jay-Tee?"

A light knock on her office door sounded before she could answer.

"Hold on for a sec, Ken," Sahara whispered, her finger lightly touching the AirPod in her right ear. "Come in," she called out to her assistant, the only other person in the house with her.

Tiffany poked her head in. "I know you said not to put any calls through for the rest of the day, but a Dr. Mills from Special Blessings called for you. He asked that you call him back the first chance you get." After a pregnant beat, she added, "I wasn't going to interrupt you, but it sounded important, so I thought I should tell you before I head out for the day. Just in case, you know, you wanted to call him back. Before the end of the day. He said he'd be in the office until six."

Sahara instinctively glanced down at her cell phone. It was five now.

She hadn't seen or heard from Dr. Mills in five years. She'd had no reason to. So why was he calling her now?

"No, you did the right thing in telling me. Thank you, Tiffany. I'll see you tomorrow. Have a good night."

"Good night," her assistant said, smiling shyly before closing the door.

"Shit. Shit."

"Hey, what's wrong?"

Sahara started at Kennedy's voice. She'd forgotten she was still on the phone. Shaken, she swallowed hard. "Do you remember me telling you that I froze my eggs because of my endometriosis?"

"Yes, of course, I remember."

"Well, the doctor at the clinic where my eggs are stored called. He needs to talk to me."

"What do you think he wants?"

"I don't know. I think something must have happened to my eggs. Something like they destroyed them." Sahara took a deep breath in an attempt to calm herself.

"You can't know that for sure. It could be something else. Anything else." Kennedy sounded more like she was trying to convince herself of that—that there was some benign reason behind the call.

"What else can it be? It's the only reason he would call. It's the only thing that makes sense. Which means I'm going to have to go through IVF all over again." Her stomach turned just thinking about it. The injections. The misery of being pumped full of hormones for weeks on end.

She closed her eyes and prayed for strength. *Please, God, don't make me have to go through that again.*

"Listen, I'm going to call him back now. I'll talk to you later."

"Call me and let me know, okay?"

"Yeah, I will. 'Bye."

"'Bye."

Sahara quickly found the number of the clinic in her contacts and was put through to Dr. Mills as if he'd been waiting for her call.

Not good.

"Ms. Richardson, thank you for calling. I know how busy you are, so I appreciate the prompt response." After a nerve-racking pause, he said, "This isn't the sort of thing I wanted to have to tell you over the phone, but it couldn't wait."

Oh god. Oh god. I'm right. My eggs are gone.

Would you calm down? Things could be worse. Think of all those women who don't even have this as an option. It's not the end of the world.

Inhaling a deep breath, she exhaled slowly and braced herself for the words that would confirm what she already knew to be true.

"I don't know how to tell you this—"

Just say it and get it over with. Say it so I can start making plans.

Although, she had no idea when she'd be able to carve out the time to go through the treatment again. Four weeks from now, she'd be on a tour junket promoting her next movie—a coveted theatrical release in a sea of streaming movie releases. And after that, she'd be in England filming her first period piece. She didn't have time for this.

"—but there has been a mix-up at the clinic and DNA testing has confirmed that you are the biological mother of a baby born via a surrogate to a married couple." He took a moment to clear his throat. "And the husband is the biological father."

Find out what happens next! Coming winter 2024!